ROUGH DIAMOND

THE ERICA JEWELL SERIES - BOOK 1

KATHRYN LEDSON

PILYARA PRESS

ISBN: 978-1-925827-11-8
Cover Art by Kellie Dennis at Book Cover By Design

Pilyara Press
Melbourne

For Paul and Gloria

CHAPTER 1

So I'm standing at my front gate and I'm soaked and it's been the worst day in history. Everything's gone wrong since I got out of bed. The milk was off. I put a finger through my brand-new tights and I don't even have fingernails. I left my umbrella at home knowing full well a storm was coming and now I can't find my keys and the rain's stinging my face.

I booted the gate open and stumbled through it, wondering why I'd forgotten to lock it. My old veranda gave no shelter from the horizontal rain. I dumped my bag on the ground and squatted over it, gazing into the abyss, hoping for a glimpse of silver, cursing the broken light and my stupid boss and the late, crowded, smelly train. 'And,' I shouted at my bag, 'that stupid goddamn police barricade!'

Thunder crashed and I jumped. I whipped my head around to yell at the black sky, but something caught my eye. Something snug and dry by the front door. My stupid yellow umbrella! I swiped at it, launching it into the night, and watched it land with a splat in the middle of my courtyard garden. But the sunny yellow seemed so wrong in this new, strange scene. Which contained a human shape. Lying on its side. Facing me.

Lightning lit the walled space. The guy looked pretty much dead.

· · ·

I SQUATTED ON THE DOORMAT, gaping at the dead guy's dark form.

He lifted his head and said in a hoarse whisper, 'No police. Please.'

'Not dead,' I whispered back.

Fitful flashes of light froze the scene. He squinted at me through the rain. I stood slowly and glanced at the gate, which suddenly seemed a long way away. I let out my held breath in a long, slow trickle, and edged toward the gate.

'*Please,*' he groaned.

I dashed for the gate, wrenched it open and ran through. I stood in the gutter between parked cars, watching the gate swing shut, peering back through the wrought iron rails at my sprawled bag. *No. This is not happening.* Rain pounded my head. I gulped breaths and shaded my eyes, looking over the roofs of parked cars at the blurred flashing lights at the end of my street. I looked back at the gate, breathed in – *should've gone to the pub* – breathed out.

The lights from the police barricade flashed at the edge of my vision. In my mind I heard the man's plea. Could see the pain in his eyes. Hear sirens. One more glance down the street and I sucked in a great, deep breath as some invisible force pushed my feet forward, through the gate and up the path to my handbag. I picked it up, hugging it to my chest, and turned slowly to look at the man. He was watching me. I shuffled closer. His face was ghostly white under long straggly black hair and a beard. Dirt streaked his face. I leaned in, staring at him in the erratic light as he squinted back at me. Not dirt. Blood. Watery blood seeped from his head and joined a black river that flowed from his body, across the pale pavers and into my geraniums.

'Shit!' I groped for my phone. 'I'll get help!'

'*No!*' he gasped, his hand stretching toward me and I stepped back. 'No doctors. No police. Please!' The man's fingers held a small white card. I stared at it. His hand started to shake and his breath came in quick puffs. I reached out slowly and took the card. He groaned and rolled onto his back, his head flopping to one side.

'Are you all right?' No response. I poked him. The storm was retreating; rain stopping as abruptly as it had started an hour earlier. A dark puddle formed under the man. I tilted the card toward a street light. Through bloody fingerprints I could just make out a mobile phone number, embossed in gold. No other details, just the number.

No doctors, no police. I found my phone and pressed 000, squatting by the man. I looked at the phone and back at the card, my thumb hovering over the green button. The man's hand closed suddenly around my wrist. I jumped and tried to pull away but he was strong. In the weak light, his dark eyes held mine for a long moment.

'I can't just let you die,' I whispered.

He shut his eyes and his head rocked from side to side. 'Don't call police. National importance ...'

I could barely hear him. I leaned closer.

'Death is better. Trust me, please, *Erica.*'

CHAPTER 2

I paced my yard, chewing my thumbnail until it bled. I'd
pushed some towels under the man and covered him with
a blanket, and now every passing minute was like an hour.

A police helicopter hovered nearby. I felt calm, panicky, calm,
panicky. When I was calm, I was happy about the dark shadows in my
courtyard. When I panicked, I wanted to run out to the street and
wave at the nearest cop.

The man drifted in and out of consciousness, muttering. I was
bending over him, trying to hear what he was saying, when a car horn
blasted and the gate crashed open, a torrent of extremely bad
language barging through it. Lucy.

My friend stopped, stared at the injured stranger, and then me.
'Jesus, Erica, what the hell?'

I wrung my hands. What to say? Lucy is a nurse – an excellent one,
according to her – and she'd arrived within fifteen minutes of my call,
dragged away from the pub not knowing what the emergency was.

'Who the hell is this?' She thrust a finger at the man.

'I don't know.'

'What's he doing *here*?' She waved her arm.

'I don't know!'

The man groaned and his head rolled around. Lucy lowered her voice. 'Why haven't you called the police? All you have to do is step onto the street and yell.'

'Um ...'

'Well?'

'He asked me not to.'

Her mouth dropped open. 'And you don't think he might have something to do with the seriously intense police activity around here?'

Standing there, shivering in my garden, I couldn't think of a single sensible response. 'He knows my name,' I spluttered. I wanted to be right about him. I *really* wanted it. I just didn't know why.

She pointed at my letterbox. 'He read your mail.'

'And he said "death is better". I think he meant better than calling the police.'

Lucy shook her head and bent over the man. 'That's because he's a friggin' criminal.' She slapped his face.

'Lucy!'

She slapped him again. 'Hey!'

The man groaned. Lucy picked up the hose and turned it on him.

'Stop, Luce!'

He opened his eyes, angry.

She demanded, 'Why shouldn't I get the police?'

He closed his eyes again, head flopping to the side.

'Luce, please, let's just get him inside.' I gripped her arm and shook it, forcing her to look at me. '*Please*, Lucy.'

'Why?' Her mouth hung open.

'I don't know!' Tears rolled down my cheeks and I swiped at them, cursing my own pathetic-ness.

Lucy's glare forced me back a step and she searched my face for signs of insanity. Her mouth snapped shut and she poked the man. He squinted at her.

'We're going to take you inside,' she said. 'Can you stand?'

He nodded once.

I unlocked the front door and pushed it open. We stood either side of him.

'Not the shoulder,' he growled.

Lucy slipped a hand under the man's lower back and held his elbow with the other. She told me to do the same on the other side and we linked hands under him. As we helped push him up and on to his feet, he screamed under his breath and staggered back, legs buckling.

Lucy said, 'Hold him!'

We led him inside, bouncing off the walls of the long passageway to the spare bedroom. We all fell backward onto the bed and he stifled a scream, then passed out. A circle of red grew under him. Lucy sent me for more towels and packed them under his shoulder.

She turned her cold glare on me. 'Why the hell are we helping this guy?'

The equally cold glare of the bare light bulb didn't help my thought processes. My mouth opened and closed like a fish and my eyes flashed back and forth between the dying man and my best friend. 'Ah ...'

Watching my confusion, Lucy's eyes softened. My Rottweiler friend has a mushy heart. Way, way deep down. 'Okay, honey,' she said, 'let's take a look at your stranger.'

I helped roll the man onto his side and Lucy sat next to him. 'He's feverish,' she said and sent me for some scissors, which she used to cut away his jumper and T-shirt. I found a torch, which I aimed shakily at his injuries. He was hurt in other places too; cuts and grazes all over his back, like he'd walked through a sheet of glass. I watched Lucy as she inspected his head wound and a nasty looking shoulder wound. She re-packed the towels and stood, staring down at him for a long moment. Then those angry eyes were on me again.

'What is it?' I said.

'That's a *bullet* wound in his shoulder, and the bullet's still in there!'

'Oh,' I said, faintly.

CHAPTER 3

'Erica, I'm calling the police if you can't give me a good reason not to.' Lucy sat at my dining table. I pulled a cask of red wine out of my pantry and went to fill two glasses.

She made a face. 'Haven't you got something better than that?'

'Well, I have, but I was saving it for a special occasion.'

'Honey, if this isn't special, I don't know what is. Bring out the good stuff, please!'

I produced a bottle of my ex-husband's expensive red, poured two glasses and sat opposite Lucy.

She took a sip and nodded her approval. 'Now, tell me what you know.'

So I did.

'Let me get this straight,' she said. 'You trusted him because he was bleeding from a bullet wound in your front garden and didn't want you to call the police?'

'Ah ... yes.'

'Jesus, Erica.'

'I know, but there's more to it.'

'I should hope so.'

'He said it was of national importance.'

'National?'

'Yes. And remember, he knows my name. He said, "Trust me, Erica."'

'Yeah, right. "Trust me, I've just broken out of jail."' She waved a dismissive hand. 'He read your mail.'

'I don't think so, Luce.' I handed Lucy the blood-smeared business card with the gold-embossed number. 'He gave me this and told me to call the number and say what's happened.'

'And did you?'

'Not yet.'

We stared at each other for a long time.

'I think you should make the call,' she said.

I looked for my phone, then had a thought. I found the remote control instead, aiming it at the television. 'Let's see if there's anything about the police in my street.'

'Good plan.'

We sat on my sofa and I flicked to the news channel. There was something about stolen fertiliser. A truckload of it.

'What's the big deal about someone stealing fertiliser?' I said.

'You can make bombs from it.'

'Oh, right. Scary.'

And then a live cross to Richmond – a fuss of television reporters in front of my local Chinese restaurant.

'Shit,' said Lucy. 'That's just down the road.'

I realised I'd been holding my breath. 'They weren't there when I walked past before. It must have just happened.'

'... repeating that there has been a shooting at a Richmond flat earlier this evening ...' The reporter looked grim as she pointed to the broken window of a flat above a shop in my street, '... involving the federal police. Arrests have been made and one man is thought to be on the run, possibly injured ...'

'So,' said Lucy, 'you're harbouring a criminal. How do you feel about that?'

I chewed my nail. 'Maybe we should call the police.'

'Uh-huh. Now you're talking.'

The man called out from the spare room.

I glanced at Lucy. 'I'll just see if he's all right. And then I'll call the police. I promise.'

'Whatever.' She waved her hand and turned back to the television.

I stood at the spare bedroom door. A shaft of light from the passageway cut across the bed, but the man's face was in shadow. He hadn't moved. We'd removed his T-shirt so he was bare-chested. As my eyes adjusted to the dimness, I could see that he was watching me.

He whispered something. I couldn't hear him, so I shuffled closer. 'What did you say?'

He tried to sit up but collapsed back on the bed with a deep groan. 'Don't call the police. Please.'

He shivered and I flicked on the heater. 'I'll get you a blanket.'

The blanket I'd covered him with outside was now wet and bloody on my bathroom floor; I ran up the passage to get another from my bedroom. When I came back, Lucy was standing there, hands on hips.

'What the hell are you doing?'

I pushed past her and lay the blanket gently over the man.

'Erica.' Lucy stood at the door. She beckoned me. Follow Lucy or stay with the bullet man? I didn't know which was scarier.

'Okay.' I sighed. 'Coming.'

'Wait,' said the man, his voice hoarse. 'On the news, before, what were they saying?'

'There was a shooting down the road,' I said. 'Someone's on the run. Is that you?'

'Yes. But I mean the other thing. The fertiliser.'

'Oh,' I said and glanced at Lucy. Her expression changed from murderous to one of surprise. 'Um. A truckload of fertiliser was stolen.'

He sucked in a breath. 'Have you called that number I gave you?'

'No, I —'

'Please. Please just do it.'

'Okay,' I said, slowly, and then with considerable resolve, 'I will.'

· · ·

I DIALLED the number on the card but hung up before it answered.

'Do I say who I am or do I just make an anonymous call? What should I do?' I said.

'What should you do?' said Lucy. 'You should call the police.'

I gave her a look.

She sighed. 'Anonymous. We don't know what this is about yet.'

I squared my shoulders and dialled. The phone answered immediately. A man's voice said, brusquely, 'Yes?'

His abruptness made me nervous and I hesitated. What was I expecting? Dial one for bullet wounds? I said, 'A man is hurt and he gave me a card with this number.' Silence. 'He's been shot.'

'Who is the man?' said the voice.

'I don't know. He's in my house.'

'Have you contacted the police?'

'No.' Then, bravely, sticking my chin out, 'Not yet.'

'What is the address?'

I glanced at Lucy. She watched me, frowning.

'Where are you holding the man?' he pressed.

I gave him my address, cringing while Lucy stood in front of me, waving her hands, shaking her head, mouthing, *No! No! No!*

'Care for him,' said the phone man. 'Do not, under any circumstances, call the authorities. And do not call me again unless he dies. I'll contact you.' He hung up.

I told Lucy what he said.

'Unless he *dies*? Who the hell are these people? You gave him your address, for God's sake!'

I waited while she paced around, ranting, flapping her arms.

'Luce, there was something about the phone guy. Something familiar.'

'Familiar?' she huffed. 'What, like someone you know?'

'I'm not sure.' I knew the voice. Who?

'Well, whoever Mr Hotshot is, what does he expect us to do if this bloke drops dead in your house?' She strode across the room to the French doors, peered out at the black sky, snatched the drapes closed and whirled to face me. 'Huh?'

'I don't know, but he said he'll call me.'

'When? And in the meantime, we just wait around, at his beck and call?'

'I really feel we should help this man, Luce.' Actually, I'd already made a decision about that, but I needed to tread carefully with my friend, because, well, I was scared and I needed her.

'Erica, you are out of your mind! And you've got to stop letting people boss you around!'

I watched my tiny blonde friend stomp around the living room, bossing me around.

'Also,' I said, 'remember that he said national importance.'

'And you believe him.'

'Yes.' I nodded solemnly. 'I do.'

Lucy continued with the why-are-we-friends-again? glower. She crossed her arms. 'This wouldn't have happened if you'd come to the pub tonight.'

Lucy had called me at work this morning and before I could even say hello, she'd said, 'Come to the pub tonight or I'll never speak to you again!' This was harsh, even for Lucy. But my resolve is strong. A resolve gained through finely honed skills in denial, cheapskateness, and an overwhelming desire to not be forced into happiness.

'I can't afford to go out.'

'You *can* afford it. You just refuse to spend money on anything but your stupid mortgage.'

'I'm trying to pay off my debts. You know that.'

'Hon, you'll be eighty and still paying off your debts. You need to start enjoying life again!'

The man groaned. We looked toward the bedroom and waited, but he was silent. Lucy paced up and down, then gave me a quick, fierce hug.

'Okay, you silly cow. Get me some more clean towels, hot water, a shitload of pain killers and some whiskey.' She pulled out her mobile phone.

I ran around, doing as asked. When I returned, Lucy was on her way out the front door. 'I'll be back in half an hour,' she said.

I didn't know where Lucy was going or what she was doing but I waited at the dining table in stillness and silence. At one point, I tiptoed to the man's room. He still hadn't moved. I squinted into the darkness. Was he looking at me? In my mind we were staring at each other, but I couldn't be sure. The thought of it gave me the creeps and I backed away.

Lucy arrived soon after with a bag full of stuff.

'What have you got?' I said.

'I could tell you but then I'd have to kill you.' She held up her hand. 'It's just better if you don't know.'

Lucy barged into the spare room, snapping on the light. The man's eyes were closed.

She said, without looking at me, 'I'm impressed about the heater.'

I knew she was referring to the fact that I was spending money on heating, which I wouldn't normally do. I made a face at the back of her head.

The man's long black hair was splayed out on the bed, and his face looked a little less pale.

'Unconscious,' I whispered.

'Actually, I think he's just asleep,' she said in a normal voice. He snored softly and suddenly. Lucy jerked the blanket off him, but he still didn't move.

I crept closer. 'Did you notice that his chest hair is fair?'

'Nice chest,' she said.

'That's hardly important.'

I watched her inspect his arms and torso. 'Nice everything, actually,' she said as she reached for the button on his jeans.

'Lucy!'

'I'm just getting him out of these wet clothes. Give me a hand.'

I eyed her suspiciously, then helped her gently tug the jeans off, noting with relief that he was wearing undies. Very sexy trunks, in fact, with a distinctive D&G logo. His eyes flickered open and he muttered something. I stepped back. Lucy didn't move.

She said, 'Have you got something he can wear?'

I ran to my bedroom and rifled around in the wardrobe, finding some old track pants and a pullover of my ex-husband's. I trotted back to the spare room.

'Here. They're Danny's.' I handed them over, ignoring the raised eyebrows.

I leaned over the man and whispered, 'I think his hair and beard are dyed black.'

We looked at each other and shrugged. The man muttered again. We leaned closer to hear what he was saying, but nothing made sense.

Lucy said, 'He's speaking another language.' She looked at me. 'Arabic?'

'Why are that bastard's clothes still in your house? Two years after he dumped you for some bimbo?'

'Eighteen months.'

'Well?'

'Ask me something else.'

'Why won't you call the police?'

'Third time lucky?' I sighed. 'Luce, not now. About Danny, I mean. Okay?'

She huffed.

'So,' I said, diverting the conversation, 'can you remove a bullet?'

She was thoughtful for a minute, sitting across from me at the dining table. 'I'm not sure.'

'Will you have to cut it out?' I tried not to sound too enthusiastic. I watched all the reality medical programs – between my fingers – alternately fascinated and horrified by the operating-room scenes.

'Maybe. I'll need tweezers.' She looked around the room as though bullet-removing tweezers might be lurking somewhere. 'And I'll have to do it soon,' she mused.

'I've only got eyebrow tweezers.'

Lucy rolled her eyes. 'I've *got* surgical tweezers.'

I sat with the phone man's business card in my hand, running my thumb lightly over the embossed number. 'It doesn't fit,' I said.

'What doesn't fit?'

'Well, the guy's dressed in bargain-basement clothes, but his underwear and this card are expensive. The gold embossing is real.' I chewed on a stale biscuit and sipped my wine, intrigued and even a bit excited. 'Why do you think he speaks Arabic?'

Lucy frowned. 'I don't want to think about that.'

'Why?'

'Because I'm afraid of what that might mean.'

'You mean you think he might be a terrorist?'

'Don't say that!'

'Oh, sorry! Are you racist and you don't like Arabs?'

'Erica, you know exactly what I'm thinking. The man has been shot, and he's maybe speaking Arabic, and he looks like you-know-who.'

'Jesus?'

'No!' She lowered her voice and leaned in. 'Osama whatsy.'

'You think I've got Osama bin Laden in my spare room? Even though he's dead?'

She scowled.

'And he's got fair chest hair,' I said and the scowl changed to a glare. 'And he knows my name.' Lacerating glares. I was having fun. 'Luce, for some strange reason I can see your logic, but remember, we've spoken to this man. In English.'

'And?'

'His accent was Aussie. True blue.'

Lucy and I set up some lights in the spare room and it was lit like an operating theatre. To complete the picture, Lucy scrubbed up in my bathroom and I helped her into some surgical gloves and a white gown that she'd pulled out of the mysterious bag.

I started to feel very nervous. 'You don't want me in there, do you?'

'Don't be ridiculous.' She marched through the spare bedroom door and elbowed it shut behind her.

I blew out my breath and looked around. There was plenty to do while Lucy was operating. I started with the blood on the floor and walls in the passageway, scrubbing and cleaning probably more than was necessary, then I changed out of my now dry but bloody work clothes. My hair was a big frizzy ball.

I crept by the spare room and listened at the door. There was no screaming so I assumed Lucy had anaesthetic.

My mobile rang suddenly and I nearly wet my pants. I ran to find it – for some reason needing to shut it up – and saw that it was Rosalind, my boss. On a Friday night. Typical. Probably couldn't find her stapler. I ignored the call, and the beep a minute later that said I had a voice message.

There was a knock on my front door. I froze, holding my breath. The knocking continued. I crept to the door and peered through the peep hole. As my eye adjusted to the darkness, two silhouettes appeared against the distant flashing sky. Cops! I kept my breathing shallow and inaudible, but my heartbeat was like the crash of drums. They kept knocking. I waited. They finally turned and left. I counted slowly to fifty before trotting out to the gate and looking through it. Cops gone. I locked the gate and checked my courtyard for blood. It was too dark to see if it was still there, but I picked up the hose and blasted the pavers anyway.

As I walked back into the house, Lucy emerged from the man's room, pulling off her cap and gloves, frowning at my hair. 'Who was at the door?'

'Police.'

She gasped, glancing at the floor and walls. 'What did you say?'

'I didn't open the door.'

'God help us if we get caught. Prison green is *so* not my colour,' she said. 'Hold out your hand.'

I did as I was told and she dropped a surprisingly heavy, bloody, mushroom-shaped bullet onto my palm. I swooned enough for Lucy to need to catch me.

'I knew it. Another patient. Come on, honey. Let's sit you down.'

She walked me to the dining table and pushed me onto a chair, shoving my head down between my knees. She came back a few seconds later with a glass of water.

'So, it went well?' I asked feebly, sitting cautiously upright and sipping the water.

Lucy shrugged, pulling off the blood-smeared gown, which she screwed into a ball and threw into a corner. 'As best as I could do, under the circumstances.' She sat heavily. 'But I did a pretty good job, I think. I should've been a surgeon but I couldn't bear the thought of all that study.' She looked off into the distance for a moment or two, and shrugged again. 'Oh, well. Sweetie, where's that delicious shiraz?'

IN THE MIDDLE of the night, I was jerked out of sleep by a very loud mobile phone. I fumbled in the dark, climbing clumsily over Lucy and causing her to wake up squealing and flailing. Lucy's elbow corked my ribs and I yelped; she found the light switch and I snatched up my phone. We exchanged dirty looks as I hit the answer button.

'Hello?' I croaked, glancing at the clock – 3am.

The voice said, 'Is the injured man still with you?'

I looked wide-eyed at Lucy, pointing at the phone. 'Yes.' My heart pounded.

'Presumably alive?'

'Yes, well, last time I looked.'

He gave me a street name in South Yarra. 'There's a small park. Bring him in one hour then call this number.' He hung up.

I told Lucy.

'Did he apologise for waking you?'

'Of course not.'

'Arrogant pig.'

Lucy's Volvo was parked in the lane at the back of my house and we helped the man into it. I'd told him that we'd heard from the business card guy and that we were moving him, and he almost leaped off the bed. As we loaded him into the car, Lucy said, loudly, 'Careful of his stitches. I don't want him bleeding all over my upholstery.'

The man lay silently on the back seat as we headed for an out-of-the-way part of South Yarra. We found the tiny park, which faced a row of small terrace houses with high fences. Lots of big old trees and bushes. There was no one about. Of course not. It was 3.55 on Saturday morning. What maniacs would be out at this time unless they were coming home from a party or involved in some sort of criminal activity? I pulled out my mobile and dialled the golden number. No greeting, just the voice saying, 'Park near the bench seat.'

This told me he wasn't watching us, because we were already parked in front of it. I looked around. There were three cars nearby that looked empty, plus a Pee Wee Pies catering van.

'We're already parked near the bench.'

'There should be a newspaper on it.'

'There is.'

'Is anyone around?'

I looked again. 'No.'

'Put the man on the seat and cover him with newspaper.'

'So he looks like a homeless person?' I said but he'd hung up. I told Lucy what he'd said and waited once again while she cursed him to hell and back.

We helped the man to the bench and covered him with newspaper.

Lucy said, 'I'm glad it's not windy.'

'Yep. Good that it's not windy.'

'What would we have done if it was windy and the newspaper blew away? What would Mr Bigwig expect us to do then? Huh?'

'It's probably not worth worrying about because it's not actually windy.'

'Well, the arrogance of this phone man!' she said, loudly.

'Ssh! Hopefully we won't have to refer to him ever again. Let's get out of here.'

But I stood for a moment looking down at the man, who was lying still with his eyes closed. 'Well, all the best. Hope you get better.' His head rolled away and he didn't respond.

'Erica!' Lucy called from the car. I climbed in and we drove away.

I watched over my shoulder until the man was out of sight. I had a strange sense of foreboding.

'Let's go back,' I said. 'I want to see what happens.'

'Damn good idea.'

So much for the foreboding. A woman's innate desire to sticky-beak beats fear of death every time. Lucy drove a little further and parked. We jogged back down the street and found a safe spot to watch through some overhanging bushes. We waited about five minutes. The man didn't move, but a breeze picked up and some of the papers blew off him.

'I knew it,' Lucy scoffed.

I grabbed her hand. 'Look!'

We watched the Pee Wee Pies van pull away from the kerb and drive slowly up the street. It stopped at the park bench. I held my breath as two men got out of the van, walked quickly to the back, opened the doors, picked up the man and put him inside. They got back in the van and drove off. Toward us.

'Crap.'

'Just stroll with me up the road,' said Lucy. 'Let's admire the roses in this garden.' She quickly assumed the strolling and admiring role. I fell in step beside her as the van cruised slowly past. We didn't look at it, but I felt eyes burning into the back of my head.

I said, 'Do you think they saw us?'

'Oh, I don't know,' she said calmly. 'Lots of people stroll around admiring roses at four in the morning.' She faced me. 'Of course they saw us!'

My phone rang and I pulled it out of my pocket. 'It's him.'

'Are you going to answer it?' said Lucy, but I already had.

'Hello?'

'Please forget what you've seen today,' said the phone man. 'This is very important. You'll be remunerated for your trouble and I'll assume this will also buy your silence. You have done a great service.'

'What great service?' But, as usual, he'd hung up.

I told Lucy and waited for her indignant response, but she just nodded thoughtfully. 'What remuneration do you think he means?'

'Dunno. Enough to replace my spare bed, I hope.'

We got back into Lucy's Volvo, now without a purpose, and drove to my place in silence. We went back to bed, dozing until about 8am, then we sat with coffee at my kitchen bench, gazing at the wall oven.

'I'm starving,' I said suddenly, which I realised too late was the wrong thing to say to Lucy on a Saturday morning.

CHAPTER 5

Of course Lucy wanted to go to the South Melbourne Market for dim sims and of course I didn't because it was something Danny and I used to do together. And that made it even more tempting for Luce because it was 'good therapy'. A bit like the way spider-phobes need to sit in a room full of spiders until they're desensitised. I didn't agree, but found myself in her car being driven to South Melbourne anyway.

The Saturday morning queue at the dim sim shop was shorter than usual – it extended only to the corner without crossing the road and blocking traffic. I ordered for both of us. 'Two steamed and two fried, thanks.' We plastered soy sauce all over the best dims sims in the world and tucked into them, strolling up the street, checking out the market stalls.

But the joy didn't last long because I heard shouting behind us and, along with every other person in the neighbourhood, looked to see what the commotion was about. Across the road, outside the corner pub, four people argued loudly. Two dark men, a blonde woman, and, surprise, surprise, my ex-husband, Danny Malleta.

'I knew it! Lucy!'

'This is good,' she said. 'Now, we should go say hello.'

'No way!'

'I've got a few things to say to him myself.'

I walked quickly away and she followed.

'What do you think all that shouting's about?' she said, watching over her shoulder.

I didn't want to know what it was about, and the scene brought back some unpleasant memories of supposedly pleasant weekend outings interrupted by angry, scary people looking for money owed to them by my husband.

'Money, most likely, and I don't want to know. Been there, done that.'

As we walked away, I noticed a Pee Wee Pies van cruise slowly down the street. Now, I know that happens. One day you don't even know Pee Wee Pies has vans cruising around the streets, then you see it once, and suddenly they're everywhere. But I couldn't help wondering if it was the same van as last night, and if they were following me. I couldn't say anything to Lucy, who was still trying to watch the scene with Danny. She'd be shitty, thinking I'd caused trouble for us.

'Let's get out of here before he spots us,' I said, looking once more through the crowd for him. I'd only seen Danny a couple of times since he'd walked out of my life and into the (crappy old) sports car of his (blonde bimbo) girlfriend. Mostly I'd seen him from a distance and he always looked good. But I was over him. It's true! In fact, I was over the entire notion that men and women could coexist and still be happy.

AFTER THE MARKET and a mooch around the shops, checking over my shoulder for Danny and/or Pee Wee Pies vans, Lucy dropped me home. I checked my mobile phone. I'd been ignoring it all morning, knowing it was Rosalind calling, and now I was ready to face her. Actually, I'm never ready to face her, especially on the weekend, but it's my job and I do quite like it. Rosalind and I work for Dega Oil, one of Australia's biggest companies. Rosalind is director, media and investor relations and I'm media relations officer.

She picked up straight away. 'Erica, what on *earth* have you been doing?'

'Sorry I missed your calls. What's up?'

'What's *up*? Haven't you seen the news?'

'News?'

'The stolen fertiliser!'

'Yes ... Oh! That was *ours*?'

'Really, Erica, sometimes I wonder if you care about your work at all.'

I do care about my work, but I don't care for Rosalind a great deal, and it hadn't occurred to me that the stolen fertiliser was a truckload of BIG fertiliser. I was still getting used to it – Dega Oil had bought the company just the week before and besides, I'd had a few other things on my mind.

'Do you want me to come to the office?' I said.

'Well, for the life of me I can't get hold of John either.'

She was talking about John Degraves, CEO of Dega Oil. I scratched at the back of my neck, which was suddenly prickling.

Rosalind continued, 'I thought we'd meet at the office, talk about how best to tackle it, but there's no point if I can't reach JD.' Rosalind looks after all public matters for the company. I usually draft up the media releases, which she then checks and passes on to JD for his approval. If he likes it, she takes the credit. If he's not happy, she tells him I wrote it.

'Okay, well, I'll keep my phone with me,' I said. 'Let me know if you need me.'

'Please watch the news, Erica, and start thinking about responding to the media. They're saying this could mean a national disaster. If terrorists have it. You know.'

Jesus, no, I didn't know. We don't have terrorists in Australia. In Melbourne. Do we?

· · ·

BY 6PM I'D decided I wasn't going to hear from Rosalind again that day. I watched the news and felt the horror that the rest of the country was no doubt feeling. A whole truckload of fertiliser – the nasty stuff that's got bomb-making ingredients in it – had been nabbed on the Hume Highway on Friday night. And what hadn't been announced the night before was that the driver of the truck was actually found shot dead on the side of the road. Execution style, they said. Which left little doubt in everyone's mind about *why* it was stolen. Clearly not an opportunistic farmer.

Suddenly John Degraves appeared on screen with the managing director of BIG Fertilisers and the prime minister, speaking to a room full of reporters, assuring them and the rest of the population that all available police and armed services personnel were on the job to hunt down the worst kind of criminal this country has potentially ever known.

I stared at John Degraves on the television, listening to his familiar voice. The hair on the back of my neck stood to attention again, and now I knew why.

JD was phone guy.

THE NEXT MORNING I checked my phone as soon as I woke up. Nothing more from Rosalind. I lay in bed, thinking. There was a lot to think about: terrorists, Danny, fertiliser, media releases, John Degraves, Rosalind, the man in my spare room. Surely I was wrong. What could JD have to do with the bleeding guy? I went into the spare room to see what needed to be done. General dusting and vacuuming. Removal of peeling paint. The hole in the floor patched. Light fitting for the bare bulb. Window coverings. And, I thought, a nice piece of art for the wall. Lucy and I had hauled the bloody mattress out to my carport, so I also needed a new one of those. I sighed and went to make toast.

Standing there at the kitchen bench, eating toast and sipping tea, feeling suddenly lonely, I gazed across the living room through the timber French doors and focused on the garden. Well, not so much a garden as a bunch of weeds that fringe a tiny paved terrace with more weeds sprouting through the cracks. I'd pretty much neglected the garden since Danny left.

Something inside caught my eye. It was a black cockroach scuttling into a hole in the crumbling mortar of the bare brick wall of my living room. Ew. And then I was annoyed. Annoyed that I'd been forced to look at that wall, which separates my house from its twin, next door. But it's pretty hard to avoid as it runs the length of my entire house and is like a dark, looming presence in my otherwise light, orderly world. I found a can of cockroach killer in the cupboard under the sink and drowned the traitorous brick, then waited, watching the hole to see if the intruder would stagger out so I could stomp on it. But I should've known better. I mean, I should have known better than to stand there staring at that brick wall, especially with Danny already on my mind.

Rewind eighteen months to a sunny Friday afternoon in April. I've come home early from work, having faked a headache. I actually have a hairdressing appointment, not a headache, but Danny has clearly forgotten about our friends' wedding because as I walk in the front door he's heading out of it, looking shocked to see me. He has a suitcase in one hand and a smaller bag in the other and he stammers something about a note in the kitchen. I watch him run through the gate, not bothering to close it, and jump into the passenger side of a car I've never seen before. I shuffle down the long passage to the kitchen and pluck a blu-tacked note off the brick wall. It says that Danny is leaving me, and that he'll come back some time for the rest of his stuff. So I stare at that brick wall, and think about one day getting it plastered over. And painted a nice light colour. Getting the whole place painted in fact. The other walls are an awful 1980s peach colour. Yes, I think to myself, I'll get my house painted.

Danny never did come back for his stuff and I never did plaster my walls or paint my house. I stood there with my toast, forcing myself to think about renovating instead of grieving, and, happily, this made me think about Steve. Which in turn made me think about how handy it was to have a builder friend with lots of handyman knowledge and tools. And a trailer. Which brought me back to the issue at hand.

I called Steve and asked him if he could help me get rid of a mattress that was inappropriately stained. He didn't ask questions and he didn't hesitate.

'No worries. Actually, I'll come now if you want. I'm waiting for that mongrel concreter to show up.'

'Thanks, buddy. I'll put the kettle on.'

As kids, Steve and I had been next-door neighbours. We were in nappies together – there are embarrassing photos to prove it – and good friends ever since. Not only that, Steve had recently started dating Lucy. This was something I wasn't totally happy about, mainly because I was terrified they'd break up one day and I'd have to choose. There was no way I could do that.

Steve blasted his horn at the back of my house fifteen minutes later. I ran outside and struggled with the rusty old roller door; it suddenly shot up and I was face to face with my enormous grinning friend: six feet four, surfy blonde, tanned and fit was Steve.

'You really should get an automatic door,' he said.

'Well, I haven't heard that one before.' I punched his arm.

'So, where's this ... oh.' His smile disappeared when he spotted the mattress.

'Probably best if you don't ask. I promise I didn't murder anyone.' I'd wondered if Lucy had said anything to Steve about her night at my place, but the look on his face suggested not.

'No worries.'

I struggled with one end of the mattress and Steve snatched up the other like it was a bit of fluff. We loaded it onto the trailer, blood side down.

'How will you explain this at the tip?' I said.

'I won't be taking it to the tip.'

'Where, then?'

'Probably best if you don't ask.' He gave me a wink and a grin.

'Touché. Kettle's boiled.'

We sat among the weeds on my back patio, drinking coffee,

admiring the view of the trailer and stained mattress. 'What are you concreting on a Sunday?' I said.

'Carport for Michelle.'

'Hope she's paying you.'

He shrugged. 'I don't mind. I get to see the kids.'

'Lucy working?' I said.

'Yeah.'

Steve often made an excuse to go visit his kids, much to Lucy's annoyance. Lucy and Michelle hadn't been in the same room since Lucy and Steve started dating. I wouldn't mind being a fly on the wall when it finally happens.

CHAPTER 6

On Monday morning I was at work early and headed straight for the kitchen to arm myself with caffeine before facing Rosalind. Marcus was there, regaling some of the girls with hilarious stories of his weekend. Marcus is my favourite work buddy. He's the main reason I can cope with Rosalind because he always manages to turn my misery into laughter. Marcus is her personal assistant, but for some reason Rosalind thinks the entire media and investor relations department is her personal assistant.

Marcus and I walked together to our respective desks, next to each other but separated by a partition. As we approached I saw John Degraves standing at Rosalind's office door. Marcus rushed ahead and I stopped, my expression probably a frozen mix of laughter, surprise and anticipation.

JD said goodbye to my boss, turned and walked toward me. 'Good morning, er ...'

'Erica.'

'Ah yes, Erica.' He held eye contact for a long moment then continued on his way.

I called Lucy, whispering into the phone. 'I think the phone guy is John Degraves.'

'What? The big boss at your work?'

'Yep.'

'You're joking! How do you know?'

'The voice. I'm sure it's him. And he looked at me ... funny.'

'What kind of funny?'

'Dunno. Like he knew that I knew or something. He pretended he couldn't remember my name.'

'Arrogant pig.'

My phone was beeping. Rosalind was trying to call me. From her office. Which was three metres from my desk.

'Gotta go,' I said to Luce and hung up, picking up Rosalind's call.

'Morning, Rosalind.'

'Marcus hasn't brought my coffee yet,' she said.

'Um, I don't think he's here.' I stood and peered over the partition and was greeted by a paper clip aimed at my nose. I ducked back down.

I chatted further with Rosalind about her needs: coffee, her lunch appointment and where was her dry cleaning? Paper clips bounced off my head and finally, a whole box showered down all over me and the only way to cover up my laughter was to have a coughing fit and hang up.

I picked up a handful of clips and hurled them back at Marcus. He held up his hands in mock horror, surrendering, calling a truce. For now.

Usually I try to be as quiet as possible when I'm at my desk, thinking that if Rosalind can't hear me, she might forget I exist. It doesn't seem to work though. She called me again, this time without the phone: 'EriCAR!'

I stuck my head through her office door. 'Yes, Rosalind?'

Without looking up, she said, 'Have you got my coffee yet or do I have to die of thirst?'

I was thinking that I shouldn't be getting her coffee, or even that Marcus shouldn't be getting her coffee. That maybe she should get her own. I got her coffee and tried to deliver it without being noticed. She sat there, head down, writing furiously.

'Don't leave,' she said.

I stared at the top of her head. I suspected Rosalind Rogers was really a drag queen. Her immaculate black hair looks like you could pluck it off her head in one big lump.

'Sit, sit,' she said, waving at the chair opposite, not looking at me.

'I'll just grab a pad and pen,' I said, but she shook her head – the hair didn't move – and waved at the chair again.

'You won't need it. I want to talk about the fertiliser.'

I sat. 'Anything new?'

She looked at me and I jumped.

'We need to be prepared,' she said. 'The public is outraged. The prime minister is very worried. And I don't need this extra work or stress!'

'Do you want me to draft up something for the media?'

'Yes, but in conjunction with BIG's PR people. John wants to make a joint statement. We want to give the public a sense that everyone's working hard to find the fertiliser. Not just the police.'

'Do they, um, think it was terrorists?'

'Of course,' she said, waving me away. She was already looking back at the paper on her desk. 'And send Marcus in.'

I DECIDED to skip my usual Monday dinner at my parents' to work on the stolen fertiliser business. But I was tired. I'd spent all day fielding calls from the media. Dega's stand on the matter was that we were putting all available resources into 'helping the police with their enquiries'. I'd called BIG's office in Sydney and introduced myself to Susan, the PR manager, who didn't seem to think Dega should be getting involved at all. She was all honey voiced, but there were hidden prickles. Her sarcasm was honeyed too, which made it even worse, as she said what a *shame* it was that Dega had bought BIG Fertilisers and some was stolen the very next week. How *annoying* for us, she'd said. Eventually we managed to get our stories straight. She agreed to let me draft the joint release but for her approval. I said that was fine, knowing that ultimate approval would come from Rosalind and JD. When we hung up, I poked my tongue at the phone.

By the time I walked through my front gate it was already after 7pm. I couldn't help glancing at the space where I'd found the bullet-wound man. Happily, there was no one there, but as I opened my front door I noticed a bag had been pushed behind the large pot plant next to the door. My first thought was how someone got through my locked gate to leave something there. I picked up the bag and opened it. The crappy old clothes I'd given the bleeding guy, laundered and returned. Well, I thought, these people have nice manners. There was also a plain white envelope in the bag. I opened it and found a fat wad of one-hundred-dollar notes.

It was only Monday night but I already needed another weekend. I needed time to think. There were too many things to think about, now including what to do with ten thousand dollars.

My home phone rang. Out of habit I let it go, expecting either someone looking for my ex or someone calling from India about changing my electricity provider. Instead, a man's weak but deep voice said to my answering machine, 'I know you're there, Erica. Pick up the phone.'

Bullet-wound guy! I hesitated for one-hundredth of a second before snatching up the phone. 'I'm here,' I said quietly, my heart thumping.

'I hope you found the bag at your door.'

'I did. Thank you.'

'And the envelope.'

'Yes.'

'I need you to do something for me. It's important.'

I thought briefly how annoyed Lucy would be that he hadn't said 'please' or 'how are you?', and how she'd respond. So I said, in my snippiest voice, 'Well, I think I've done enough!' But I couldn't help wondering how he was.

'You have, but you'd be doing a great service if you could help once more.'

'More great service! What's the great service? And I don't really see
how this benefits me.'

'Ten thousand dollars.'

'Yes, well, there is that.'

'So, will you help?'

I COULDN'T BELIEVE I was skulking down my street at night, dressed
like a homeless person. Bullet-wound guy said he'd thrown something
in the rubbish bin near my local Chinese restaurant, and he needed
me to get it before the next morning when the rubbish was collected.
He told me to take a heavy-duty bag to carry the thing.

I'd asked why he couldn't send someone else and he hadn't seemed
to know what to say for a moment, but then he'd said, 'It needs to be
someone I can trust.' And I thought that was nice.

I'd also asked what I was looking for and he'd said, 'You'll know
when you find it. Don't attract attention.'

He also told me how to dress and how to behave, and to wait until
late when the street would be quiet. I had to admit that it was a bit
exciting – undercover work and all that.

I reached the bin. A few people strolled by, so I loitered, taking my
time. A couple came out of the restaurant and the guy flicked a dollar
coin at me. The money clattered to the ground and I picked it up,
shrugged and put it in my pocket. There was a quiet moment on the
street and I stuck my face in the bin, and reeled back. It stunk. Of
course it stunk! I held my breath and reached right into the mess
inside. I hadn't thought about what else I might find in there. I
grabbed something gooey and made a face. A passer-by mirrored my
expression and walked more quickly. I probed about some more.
There was something hard and cold. I grabbed it and pulled. It was
heavy and it was caught on something. I yanked hard and pulled it
right out of the bin into the bright light of the restaurant's window.

My hand was wrapped around the long barrel of a gun. I gasped
and hid it quickly under Danny's old coat, looking around to see if
anyone was watching. No one on the street, and no one left in the

restaurant except a busy waiter cleaning up. I let my breath out slowly, carefully put the gun in the bag, and walked quickly home.

I stood under the shower, scrubbing the bin's filth off my hands and arms. Through the glass screen I could see the weapon sitting on my vanity, its darkness offensive against the white of the room. I dried myself and approached it warily. I'd never seen one up close before. I didn't realise they were so big and heavy.

Bullet-wound guy had said he'd be in touch. I guess he wanted his gun. Probably covered in his fingerprints. And mine. I picked it up, rubbed it with a towel, carried it to the laundry hamper in my bedroom and dropped it in. I covered it with a pile of dirty washing.

'You could've told me what it was!

'Would you have done the job if I had?'

'Of course! Maybe.' Probably not. It was the next morning. Gun guy had called me too early, waking me up, pissing me off. 'Besides, I could've shot myself.'

'It's not loaded.' He sounded stronger. 'Hide it well. I'll retrieve it when I can.'

'You sound better.' In fact, his voice was strong and deep, his accent distinctly Australian but with a hint of something else, I thought.

'I'll be in touch,' he said, and hung up and I sat there for an hour staring out my bedroom window.

I wondered when he'd be in touch. I didn't like not knowing. I would have liked him to say, 'I'll be in touch on Thursday at three o'clock,' or 'I'll come by tomorrow at six,' and do so, and go on his merry way. What I want in life makes a very short list: no debt, no surprises and definitely no men. Except the ones at work and the mechanic and the ones who get the spiders out of your car. I work normal corporate hours and on Mondays I go to my parents' for dinner. On cheap Tuesday I like to see a movie with a friend, although I can't remember doing that yet this year and it's now October. Wednesday is my being-sensible-at-home night, when I pay bills and deal with paperwork. The rest of my week is open but I'm usually at home in front of the TV.

Safe. Predictable. Cheap.

But right now, still in my pyjamas when I should be getting ready for work, and with a strange man's gun in my dirty laundry, and having missed dinner with my parents the night before, and with no interest in the television or seeing a cheap movie, I had the very definite feeling that things were about to change.

CHAPTER 7

The next day I called Lucy and brought her up to date, including the good news about the cash, but not the gun retrieval episode. I wasn't completely suicidal.

She said, 'Do you think we should accept the money?'

'I can't see why not. We earned it.'

'Hon,' she said, 'I'd really like to know more about these people. What if it's blood money?'

'What's blood money?'

'I don't know. I heard it in a movie once.'

She waited while I googled 'blood money'. There were a couple of options. One said that it was money paid for a contract killing, and the other said it was money paid to the next of kin of a murder victim as a fine. I was relieved. We hadn't killed anyone, and we weren't next of kin of a murder victim.

'It's not blood money, Luce. I think we can accept it.'

'Let's shop on Saturday. Bridge Road.'

'I'll meet you at ten.'

Lucy and I met for pre-shopping coffee that Saturday morning. I slipped her an envelope containing five thousand dollars, and her eyes lit up when she saw it.

'Where do you want to go first? Freedom or shoes?' Lucy has a thing for shoes and I have a thing for housey stuff – Freedom Furniture being my favourite store – but I hadn't yet broken the news that I had no intention of spending a cent of my five grand. I'd already put it all against my loans because I didn't trust myself not to blow the lot.

'Luce, this money is going against my debt, and there's nothing you can say to change that, but,' I added quickly, 'I'll help you shop.' I held up a hand in a just-let-me-speak gesture. 'I'll love that just as much as spending on myself.' I smiled broadly and she glowered.

'Sweetie,' she said, 'you need things in your house. You have bare light bulbs. You have chipped wine glasses. Your towels are wrecked. You *will* shop today.'

'No, I won't.'

'Yes, you will.'

'I won't.'

'You will.'

'No.'

'Yes.'

We sat back in our chairs, arms crossed. She hit me with the lowest of blows. 'I won't be your friend.'

I gaped at her. 'That's really childish.'

'Call it tough love.'

I re-thought my strategy. 'All right. I tell you what. Today we'll shop for you, and we can shop for me next week.'

Her eyes narrowed as she inspected me, looking for tricks and lies. I set my expression to innocent.

'Okay,' she said. 'Next Saturday.'

I nodded once, pleased. 'Next Saturday.'

By the following Saturday, the missing fertiliser business had all but disappeared from the newspapers. It hadn't been found, the police were all over it, apparently, and everyone thought about it a little bit less. And I was back to more routine stuff at work. I hadn't seen John Degraves again and decided that my theory was off the mark. I mean, why would JD be associating with a man with a gun and a bullet wound? And so secretly.

The gun was still in my laundry hamper. I'd tried to forget about it by avoiding doing any laundry, and I tried to forget about the bullet-wound man but it wasn't easy. I was running out of clean clothes, and the guy intrigued me.

I walked around the corner to my favourite breakfast café with an hour to kill before I met Lucy. I was still trying to think of a way out of shopping. I was reading the morning paper, eating scrambled eggs, when a man sat opposite me and said, 'Can I buy you a coffee?'

I blinked at the man, and glanced around the store. 'Do I know you?'

'Yes.' He smiled. Lots of perfect white teeth. 'I probably look a bit different to when you last saw me. I believe it was on a park bench.'

'Oh. OH!' I could feel a dozen or so pairs of eyes on me and I blushed. Gun guy's gaze didn't move from my face and he didn't blush. Coffee arrived in front of him.

He looked up at the waitress, still smiling. 'Thanks.' She lingered and seemed to be swooning.

Gun guy was wearing a baseball cap and didn't look like Osama whatsy at all. In fact, he looked like he belonged on the cover of *Gorgeous Hunk* magazine, and I don't mean the Middle Eastern edition either. The cap shaded his face but I could see that those dark eyes were now ice blue, and they were inspecting me with an intense, unblinking gaze that made me feel like he knew what colour undies I was wearing.

I leaned forward and whispered, 'You look nothing like the half-dead guy in my spare room.' What had been stringy black hair was now dark blonde locks that curled out from under his cap, and the straggly beard had transformed into a fashionable stubble.

'Yeah, well, half-dead is one of my disguises,' he said with a look of slight irritation.

'You were in disguise?'

'Yes.'

'Why?' I asked loudly. 'Why were you in disguise? Why did you have a bullet wound? Who were the guys in the Pee Wee Van? What —'

He reached across and pressed a finger to my lips, and spoke very softly. 'It's important you don't speak about those things in public.' I nodded and he withdrew his hand. 'Finish your breakfast,' he said, 'and we'll go to your place.' He downed his espresso.

I pushed my plate away, suddenly not hungry, and tried to think of something clever and brave to say to disguise my fear. 'I'm a bit scared.'

'Of what?'

'You.'

'Why?'

'Why?' I asked, incredulous. 'Why wouldn't I be?'

'Fair enough. But there's no need. I'm just a guy. A good guy, actually.' He stood and flung a fifty-dollar note on the table. 'Let's go.'

I stared at the money. 'I need to pay for my meal.'

'I just did.'

We walked together out of the café. I couldn't help noticing that people looked at him, both men and women. He was much taller than I remembered, although before he was pretty much bent over in pain. Bullet-wound man took my hand. I flinched and tried to pull away, but he held my hand firmly and said, 'Relax. Smile. Chat to me.'

I didn't relax or smile or chat, but I shuffled next to him up the street, my hand stiff in his.

'Are you married?' he said.

'None of your business!'

'That's better. Chatting.'

'I'm not chatting.'

'Smile.'

I thought I might cry.

When we reached my house, he took my keys and opened the gate, and my front door. He followed me in and shut the door behind us.

He asked, 'Where is it?'

I stood with my back to the wall. 'I'm scared of you.'

'There's no need. Where is it?'

We were in front of my bedroom door, and I pointed to the basket in the corner. 'In there, in the laundry hamper.'

I stayed by the door while he upended the basket on my bed. All my dirty laundry. I was now way more embarrassed than afraid. He pulled his gun out of the pile and was about to shove it down the back of his jeans when there was a loud knocking at my front door. Gun guy and I looked at each other. There was more banging and 'Police! Open up!' shouted from the other side of it.

Gun guy whispered, 'Open the door in ten seconds.' He was stuffing the gun and dirty laundry back into the hamper. He pushed past me and trotted silently down the passageway to the living room.

'Just a minute,' I called out, counting in my head to ten. I thought I might in fact vomit in ten seconds.

A man shouted back, 'Open the door *now!*'

Shaking and sweating, I stepped up to the front door, counting under my breath, *eight, nine, ten.* I opened it and two men in plain clothes – one young and one older – pushed past me, holding up ID badges.

The older guy stopped and explained, 'We have a warrant for the arrest of this man. We believe he just entered the house with you.'

The scratchy photograph was of a man walking out of a building wearing a baseball cap. I knew the man. It was my ex-husband.

CHAPTER 8

The senior cop ran down the passageway to where I heard shouting. I ran after him. Bullet-wound man was facedown on the floor in my living room, the young cop in the process of handcuffing him.

'This is not who you're after!' I blurted.

Everyone ignored me. I looked frantically at the scene and around the room. A newspaper was open on my dining table. Gun guy had been reading it when the cops burst in.

The young cop was reading him his rights. They stood gun guy up and he winced, caught my eye and winked. His cap had fallen off his head and I could see why he was wearing it. The gash on his head had left a nasty looking scar and the hair around it hadn't grown back yet.

I shouted, 'This is not my ex-husband!'

Everyone looked at me.

The older cop said, 'Ma'am, is this man not Danny Malleta? Your husband?'

'*Ex*-husband actually and no, he's not! What the hell is this all about?'

The young cop fished around in gun guy's pocket. He pulled out a wallet, opened and examined it. He handed it to the senior cop, who

40

looked from the licence photo to gun guy to the grainy photo of my ex. 'She's right. This is a different man. This man is Jack Jones.'

Jack Jones.

'Of course I'm right! I think I know my husband! Ex-husband ...'

The young cop was un-cuffing Jack Jones, who still hadn't spoken. Senior cop gave him back his wallet and he pocketed it. The young cop picked up the cap and said, indicating the wound on Jack Jones's head, 'What happened to you?'

'Motor accident. Nothing too serious.' Jack Jones suddenly had a British accent. Clipped. He placed the cap on his head.

The senior cop said, 'We're very sorry for this intrusion and misunderstanding.'

Jack Jones held up his hands. 'It's understandable.'

Senior cop turned to me. 'We have reason to believe your ex-husband was involved in an embezzlement at the company he works for.'

'That'd be right,' I muttered.

'Do you know his current whereabouts?'

'Last I knew he was living in an apartment at Docklands. We've been separated eighteen months.'

'This is the last address he gave his place of employment.' The cop glanced around the room, indicating my house. 'The people at his workplace are under the impression you have reunited and —'

Jack British-bullet-wound-gun-guy Jones interrupted. 'No, she's with me. Obviously.'

Obviously.

The cops looked from Jack Jones to me, and at each other. Jack Jones was watching me. The young cop looked doubtful, apologised again, and we all walked to the front door. Senior cop handed me a card. 'If Danny Malleta gets in touch with you, please contact me directly.'

I looked at the card. It said: *Bill Lucas, Senior Detective.* 'Okay. Sure.'

Bill Lucas and the young cop left. I followed them out, locked my front gate, and went back inside. Jack Jones was in the kitchen, stripping off his T-shirt.

'What are you doing?' I said, stepping back.

'Bleeding.' He turned his back to show me. The cop had been rough with him – blood oozed from the bullet wound bandaging.

I ran to the bathroom and found the medical stuff from two weeks earlier, and came back with a small bowl of warm water, disinfectant, a sponge and a clean towel.

'I don't think it should still be bleeding,' I said.

'I'm not very good at lying around, nursing injuries.'

He was sitting, leaning across my dining table, and blood was trickling down his back into his cupped hand. I pressed the towel into his hand and gently pulled the bandaging away from the wound.

'How does it look?' he said.

I checked out his smooth, muscled back and broad shoulders. 'Nice.' Actually, *very* nice.

'The wound looks ... nice?'

'Oh.' Whoops. 'Um, the other cuts are healing well. How did you get them?'

'Jumping through a window. I should have opened it first.'

I smiled at his joke; he seemed vulnerable now, which made me feel less so. I carefully sponged the wound. 'Does it hurt?'

'What do you think?'

I mopped the trickling blood. 'It doesn't look too bad, actually. Did you have surgery?'

'No. Your friend did a good enough job. Or so I thought,' he muttered.

'Oh, shit!' I looked at my watch. 'I'm meant to meet Lucy in ten minutes.'

Then I remembered the events of the past ten minutes. I stepped back and stood in front of him, hands on hips. 'Did you know that was about to happen? The police?'

'How could I? Amazing timing, don't you think?'

'You were pretty cool with those cops.'

'State police,' he said. 'I knew they weren't after me.'

'So, why did you hold my hand if you didn't think you were being watched?'

'To look normal. I'm often being watched. Besides, I thought you might like it.' He smiled.

'I didn't!' I walked around the kitchen bench and rinsed the sponge under the tap. 'What happened to your English accent, by the way?'

'I don't need it now.'

'Why did you need it before?'

He took a breath. 'You'd better sit down, Erica. I want to explain some things to you.'

CHAPTER 9

I called Lucy and told her I had to cancel, and finished re-dressing Jack Jones's wound. Lucy wasn't happy, assuming I was trying to get out of shopping, but I said the gossip later would be worth it. Jack Jones gave me strict instructions to tell her nothing more, that it was 'top secret', so I told her it was about Danny. That would be good enough goss for Luce.

I made instant coffee while Mr Jones flicked through the newspaper from two weeks earlier. I sat opposite him at my dining table. 'So, is your name really Jack Jones?'

'As far as you're concerned, it is.' He frowned at the coffee.

'Why are you covered in cuts and bullet wounds, Jack Jones?'

'There's only one bullet wound, Erica Jewell.'

'How do you know my name?'

'There's not much about you I don't know.'

'How? Why? Who are you?' I demanded.

He sighed and said, 'If you'll let me get a word in, I'll tell you.'

'Pee Wee Pies is a business that fronts a much larger organisation.'

'But Pee Wee Pies are wonderful! I love Pee Wee Pies. My whole family loves Pee Wee Pies!' I panicked that Pee Wee Pies might not be real.

'Don't worry about Pee Wee Pies,' he said, a bit gruffly, and continued. 'Two years ago, a very wealthy man you and I both know —'

'John Degraves?'

'Yes.'

'I knew it.'

'Degraves contacted me and a number of other, let's say, experts on armed conflict about a private, on-going assignment with a new organisation he was planning to establish ...'

I was wide-eyed and riveted. It was better than a Robert Ludlum novel. Jack Jones told me all about the secret, illegal organisation he worked for, which was established by billionaire John Degraves, who didn't think the government was doing enough to protect the country from a serious terrorist attack.

'And he's right,' said Jack. 'The government's *not* doing enough.' He watched me for a long moment, presumably to make sure I was listening. I was, but I may have looked slightly dubious, because he spun the two-week-old newspaper around so I could read the headline. THREE TONS FERTILISER STOLEN. FEARS OF MAJOR TERRORIST STRIKE.

'I'm aware of that. But the police will get them. Won't they?'

'That's pretty naive, Erica.' I didn't know what to say to that so I said nothing. 'My role is to infiltrate local terrorist groups and disable them.'

I studied Jack Jones. His gaze didn't leave mine.

'I don't believe you,' I said.

He shrugged and sat back in his chair, and checked his watch.

'So ... what's it called, this secret organisation. Control? Kaos?'

Unappreciative of my feeble attempt at humour to hide my fear, he said, 'We just call it *the Team.*'

'The Team,' I muttered and looked around my sunny, friendly living room. '*Local* terrorist groups?'

He nodded once.

'What's his role? John Degraves?'

'To pay me and my team a lot of money.'

'You're a mercenary?'

He frowned slightly. 'It's not *about* the money, Erica. We provide an important service to the community.'

I'd never thought of 'community service' in this way before. Jack continued with the details about how the organisation behind Pee Wee Pies had formed to fight terrorism, and I felt suddenly annoyed that Jack Jones was somehow responsible for the terrorists being in Melbourne.

I said tartly, 'Who shot you that night?'

'Feds. They raided my party.'

'What party?'

More sighs. 'Erica, the night you found me in your garden, I'd just left a six-month undercover assignment working with a local terrorist group —'

'Wait a minute. When you say *local*, are you talking about Richmond? As in, my neighbourhood?'

He nodded. 'It had taken me that long to be trusted and accepted by them, and invited to the meeting that provided the information I'd been waiting for. That meeting was raided by the federal police.'

'There are terrorists in Richmond ...'

'I wasn't happy, I can tell you. I hadn't been home in months, which is where I was supposed to be that night, not bleeding to death in your garden.' He scowled at the French doors that led to the garden at the back of my house. I almost reminded him that it was my front yard, not the back, that he'd nearly died in.

I thought about the night I'd found Jack Jones, and the time he spent in my spare bedroom. He was badly hurt, and he had looked exhausted.

'So, did they get the guys? The feds?'

'Yes.'

I sat up straighter. 'Well, if the federal police are out there doing raids on terrorist groups, why do you need to do what you do?'

'Because they don't have the time, intelligence or legal capacity to find out what I can find out.' He added quietly, as though it was an annoying inconvenience, 'Albeit illegally.' He waved his hand. 'They may well have caught those guys, but they've since been released, and I know the police don't have the information I have.'

'What information?'

'Their next target.'

I felt a knot in my stomach and said, weakly, 'In, um, Sydney? Canberra?'

'In *Melbourne*, Erica.'

I swallowed bile. An instant vision of twin buildings crumbling to a pile of rubble and flesh invaded my thoughts.

I shook my head. 'And do you think these are the people who stole the fertiliser?' I glanced back at the newspaper headline.

'We believe so.'

'But how could they have done it if they'd been arrested? The fertiliser was stolen that same night.'

'There are a lot of people who work for these criminals. They're scattered all around Melbourne. Australia, probably. They pay ordinary people to do jobs for them.' As he said this, Jack Jones watched me carefully and I wondered why.

And then something occurred to me. 'Why are you telling me all this?'

He leaned forward, running his hands over his face. 'Erica, John Degraves and I have been observing you for a while now. JD's instructed me to invite you to join the Team. On a casual basis, of course. You'll keep your current job.'

'What do you mean, you've been observing me? What do you mean, join the Team? What do you want me to do?'

'I'll explain all that, if you'll give me a minute.'

'Why me?' I squeaked.

'Well,' he gazed right into my eyes, 'you're single and available, you don't have a social life, you live in a convenient location and work under John's roof. He believes you're trustworthy, and I need ... a female civilian to work with me.'

Jack Jones may as well have said: your useless husband left you; you have no social life (oh wait, he did say that); JD can make sure you don't screw up because you work in his building; and you must be trustworthy because you're stupid enough to trust a gambling, philandering husband. I wondered if I had a huge L painted on my forehead.

'Is that why you came to my house that night? You already knew me?'

'Yes.'

I felt like I'd been somehow betrayed; that I was being talked about behind my back, which I was.

I said, 'Why didn't JD say anything when I saw him after?'

'He won't. But he wants you in.'

'What if I say no?'

'Erica, we know you have debt issues —'

'It's under control.'

'Well, let's just say we know your life is controlled by your debt —'

'It is not!'

He sat back, hands up. 'We'll pay you a lot of money.'

I stared at him for a long moment. 'How much?'

He smirked. 'Let's just say for now, *a lot.*'

'Would I be safe?'

'I'll keep you safe.'

I sat back in my chair. 'So, what would I have to do?'

CHAPTER 10

*A*fter Jack Jones left with his gun, I stood quietly staring out the French doors for a while, thinking about what he'd said. It didn't sound so bad. He said he needed someone he could call on from time to time to help him with things. A bit like a personal assistant maybe. Doing undercover things. And I'd have to pretend to be his date sometimes, which would be all right. He was pretty cute. And I'd get a lot of money for doing it. I liked the sound of that, too. He said he'd contact me tomorrow with my first lot of instructions.

I called Lucy. I really wasn't sure how to lie my way around this with Luce, especially as she'd been so involved. Jack Jones said I mustn't tell anyone. So I told her about the cops looking for Danny, leaving out the minor detail of a physical struggle in my living room and the mistaken identity part. Still, it was good goss and I didn't need to tell her more than that. She wanted to meet for coffee.

'Are you absolutely out of your fucking mind? Have you completely lost the plot? Do I need to have you committed?'

'I think you've made your point, Luce.'

'Erica, just call the guy and tell him to shove it, take a long hike off a tall mountain, whatever. Do not, *please*, get involved!'

'I'm not supposed to have told you any of this.'

'Well, obviously!'

'It's just ... well, he was very convincing.'

'You're so bloody gullible when it comes to men. This is exactly why you marry losers!'

I gawped at her, offended. 'I've only married one loser, Luce.'

She looked away.

'Lucy, please, *please*, promise me you won't say a word to anyone.'

She glowered at the wall.

'Lucy, *promise!*'

She slammed her open hand down on the table, causing other people around us to jump. 'Okay, I promise. But that doesn't mean I like it!'

'I know, hon,' I said. 'Just forget about it for now. Let's go shopping.'

'Really?' Her face lit up.

'Yep. Wherever you want.'

She leaped out of her seat and paid for the coffees before I could change my mind. 'Let's go!' She suggested we shop for a new bed for my spare room.

'Bloody good idea.' I didn't mind spending some of my precious savings to keep Lucy happy. Also, I really did need some things. We headed for Victoria Gardens shopping centre and straight to Freedom Furniture where I ordered a queen-size bed for delivery the following week. Plus some new bed linen, towels, cushions for my sofa, curtains for my bedroom, light fittings, an entire set of bathroom accessories, Christmas decorations, a vase and some wine glasses.

'What else?' said Lucy.

'Actually, there is one more thing. I'd really like to get a cat.'

'A cat?'

'Yep. I want a cat.' I headed for the car park.

She grabbed my arm and spun me around, eyeing me. 'Erica,

buying a cat is just another reason to avoid going out at night. I know what you're like. You won't want to leave it home alone.'

'It's okay, really. I won't mind leaving it. Cats are independent. I wanted one for a long time but Danny was allergic.'

She narrowed her eyes.

'Look,' I said, 'I'll come to the pub next Friday night.'

'Promise?'

I nodded enthusiastically, pretending to be excited about it. 'Yep. I'll even buy a round of drinks.'

We drove to the animal shelter, not saying much on the way there. Lucy was brooding again. I hoped the cat-buying adventure would distract her. Now that I'd blabbed about Jack Jones, I was a bit worried about Lucy's ability to keep her nose out of it. But I was pretty sure she wouldn't tell anyone. I wondered briefly what the consequences might be if she did.

When we arrived, we went inside and I spoke to the receptionist. We followed her to the back rooms where cages lined the walls and cats meowed and howled. I wanted them all.

'I'd like one with personality,' I told the woman.

Lucy said, 'Get an adult, already broken in.'

'No, I'd really like a kitten.'

The woman said, 'I've got a kitten but we're not sure how he'll go in the future. He came in two days ago. We think the poor love was hit by a car.'

She pointed to a tiny black bundle in a cage. He was sound asleep.

'Oh my God, he's so cute!'

She nodded. 'He's a love.'

'But he seems so quiet.'

'We've noticed that he sleeps like the dead. But when he's awake, well, let's just say he's an entertaining little fella.'

I reached into the cage and picked him up. He was very small, and easily fitted in my palms. He was entirely black, sleek as a panther. His tiny pink tongue poked out of his mouth. He didn't wake up.

'Does he have a name?'

'Well, one of the volunteers named him Axle. Axle grease, you 'know.' I looked at her blankly. 'He was covered in grease when we got him,' she explained with a shrug.

'Ah.' Still, I liked the name.

LUCY and I drove back to my place with Axle in a cage on Lucy's lap.

'Do you think he's alive?' I said.

'Yes, I can see him breathing.'

I put Axle's new bed in the bathroom and lifted him out of the cage. He didn't stir or open his eyes. He was like a rag doll.

'I'm not sure about this little puss.'

I put some food and water on the floor and left him to sleep.

It was Saturday night and neither of us had plans; not entirely unusual for me, and Steve had his kids who didn't interest Lucy in the slightest. Lucy suggested 'Pizza & Hugh', which was shorthand for pizza delivered by our Brad Pitt lookalike and any movie with Hugh Jackman, preferably half-naked in the form of Wolverine. We were seriously considering patenting 'Pizza & Hugh' as an entertainment idea for single women. Anyway, we ordered, and soon there was a knock at the front door and we both ran to get the pizza. It was Brad Pitt. We fought each other to pay, just for the pleasure of brushing hands with him. We curled up on the sofa with a bottle of red wine, sighing over Hugh Jackman.

'Jack Jones looks a bit like Hugh,' I said. 'Did I mention that?'

Lucy was about to say something, probably nasty, when a black blur appeared at lightning speed from the hallway, launched itself in the air and landed on our pizza. It shook itself and took off up the drapes, leaving a trail of pizza footprints. Lucy and I sat, open-mouthed, staring at the tiny creature who was now perched on the pelmet inspecting us.

'Axle is awake,' I said.

CHAPTER 11

I watered my front garden the next morning, yawning from lack of sleep. Axle had spent most of the night sitting on the pillow next to me. I kept waking up and every time I looked for him, there he was, those green eyes staring, his pink tongue poking out at me. It was very disconcerting but I couldn't bring myself to lock him in the bathroom all alone.

My front gate swung open and Jack Jones walked through it. I jumped with fright and turned the hose on him, just for a moment, accidentally.

'Whoops.'

He stood gaping at me, water dripping off his chin.

'Well, I'm sorry, but you scared me!' I looked at the gate. 'Besides, that was supposed to be locked.'

Jack wiped his face and brushed himself down. 'I'm good with locks.' He frowned at the hose in my hand. 'There are water restrictions you know.'

'I'm allowed to water twice a week,' I said.

'I thought you had to water between six a.m. and eight a.m.'

'The garden-watering part of my brain doesn't work until ten a.m.' I turned off the hose. 'What, you're the water police too?'

He half smiled and said, 'Can I come in?'

I watched him open my front door and walk in. 'Sure. Go right in.' I followed Jack Jones into my house, and let out a small squeal when Axle flew out of my bedroom and attached himself to Jack's leg, climbing it like he'd climb a tree. Jack swore loudly and I laughed into my hand. I tried to scoop Axle off his thigh, but those needle-like claws dug further into Jack's flesh through his jeans. He swore under his breath.

'Ah, sorry, hold on.' I pulled gently at Axle's little legs. 'He won't let go.' I changed my tone to baby talk. 'Come on, Axle, sweetie.'

Axle unhooked his claws and I lifted him into my arms, where he promptly went to sleep. A picture of innocence.

'You need a bodyguard all of a sudden?' said grumpy Jack Jones.

'Aw, he's just a sweet little kitten. I got him yesterday.'

'Sweet? I could use him on my team.'

We walked down the passageway to the kitchen. I noticed Jack glance into the spare bedroom as we passed.

'Coffee?' I asked.

'Please.'

I pulled a jar of Nescafé out of the pantry.

'Don't you have real coffee?'

'No. Coffee police,' I muttered.

And Jack Jones muttered something that sounded like, 'Should've stayed in bed.'

We sat at the dining table with instant coffee and possibly stale biscuits, Axle asleep on my lap. Jack flicked a white business card across the table. I picked it up. It said, simply, *Jack Jones*, and a mobile phone number. Gold embossed.

'Is this for me?'

He nodded.

'So, what's the plan?' I said.

'You're taking me to the Melbourne Cup.'

'The Melbourne Cup? You mean, as a date?'

'Yes. And there might be other events I'll need you to attend.' He added, examining the contents of his mug, 'You'll have to get decent coffee.'

I said, 'Does this mean the Melbourne Cup is … a target?'

'Yes.'

Not one for sugar coating, I noticed. I wondered if it was too late to back out. 'What will I have to do?'

He pushed the coffee away and leaned forward. 'Erica, I won't ask you to do anything you're not fully qualified to do. And I won't put you at risk. Please don't worry.'

'Well, what if someone else invites me to the Melbourne Cup?'

'Like who? Your husband?'

'No,' I mumbled. Although, come to think of it, he'd probably be there. Danny loves to be seen in all the right places, wearing the right labels, with the best-looking girl and that's obviously not me.

Jack Jones said, 'I'll give you some money for an outfit and … hair-dressing.' His eyes flicked over me.

I gaped, blushing, while he looked around the room, seemingly bored.

I cleared my throat. 'So, how do I organise Melbourne Cup tickets? And do I just meet you there or do we go together or how would it work?'

He wiped a hand across his face. 'Jesus, Erica, with your interrogation skills, I seriously could've used you in Iraq.'

'You were in Iraq?'

'You won't have to organise it.' He looked at his watch. 'I have to go. Thanks for the coffee.' He made a face. 'And the injuries, hose-down, etcetera.' He rubbed his leg and wiped his wet T-shirt.

I stood, Axle in my arms for protection. 'Um, Jack, I have to tell you something.' I moved away from him. Still seated, he raised his eyebrows and waited. 'I told Lucy.' I flinched, waiting for his reaction. And he wasn't happy. He looked away from me and stood slowly. I took a quick step back, caught my foot on the rug, fell backward onto the ottoman and did a backflip over it, letting out a loud shriek. I landed on my knees on the floor. Axle flew out of my arms and up the passageway. I looked up at Jack, who was standing with his mouth open, staring at me.

'What the hell are you doing?' he said.

I stood and brushed myself down. I was blushing so hard my face burned. 'I tripped. You scared me.'

'Did you hurt yourself?'

'I don't think so.' My knees hurt, but I wasn't going to let him know that.

He looked at me for a long minute, frowning, fingers spread wide on his hips. 'Well, I am angry about this. Don't tell Lucy anything more.'

'Okay.'

He handed me an envelope – with some hesitation – and left with barely a nod. I followed him up the passageway, closed the door after him, waited a moment, and poked my tongue at the door.

'Shouldn't be watering, coffee not good enough, I'm angry about this ...' I mimicked.

I thought about being on a date with grumpy, gun-toting Jack Jones. He was also very good-looking and I wondered if I looked like someone a gorgeous guy would be attracted to. Apart from being an embarrassingly clumsy oaf, I scrub up all right. Thanks to my wicked grandmother who had a fling with a very smooth Italian – which produced my mother – I have long, dark eyelashes that don't need mascara, and I usually like my hair. And I get a great tan in summer. And, at thirty-two, I'm in my sexual prime. Apparently. I haven't put it to the test.

I stood in front of the bathroom mirror and smiled. I have nice teeth. But could I realistically look like I belong with him?

I opened the envelope and counted all the money.

AT WORK THE NEXT DAY, Rosalind called me in to tell me that the media and investor relations team had been invited to JD's marquee at the Melbourne Cup. With partners. Well, that was easy to organise, I thought. But Rosalind was miffed. Usually, she was the only one from our department to score a look-in.

She complained loudly, 'I don't know what JD's thinking!'

I knew.

She addressed her paperwork. 'John wants to see you, by the way.'

'Who's John?'

She looked up and rolled her eyes. 'John *Degraves*.'

'Oh! Now?'

'Yessss,' she said with the impatience of a prize princess and I left before I found myself accidentally making rude gestures.

As I walked with pad and pen through the cavernous executive reception area on the top floor, tiptoeing across the thick rugs and soft parquetry, two men emerged from JD's office. One grey-haired and distinguished-looking, about sixty, and I thought I recognised him, and the other much younger with blonde cropped hair and dark sunglasses. They didn't look happy as they strode by without acknowledging me. I knocked on John Degraves' PA's office door and poked my head in.

'Hi, Celia.' I liked Celia. She protected JD fiercely, but let people through if she thought they were important enough. I seemingly qualified.

'Hey, Erica, go through. He's expecting you.' She seemed distracted, agitated even.

'Are you all right?'

'What? Oh, yeah. Those guys who just left were a bit agro. They turned up unexpectedly.' She pointed at JD's office door. 'Go on in.'

I opened the door and saw John Degraves standing by the window, staring out of it. I could see his profile. He frowned at whatever he was, or wasn't, seeing. I cleared my throat.

'Mr Degraves? Should I come back?'

He turned and looked at me, his expression relaxing. 'Ah, yes, Erica. Take a seat.' He indicated his desk and I sat, feeling like a little kid in the principal's office.

As he sat opposite he studied me briefly. 'All fertiliser products containing ammonium nitrate have been recalled. They'll be banned;

from tomorrow it will be illegal to sell a product containing ammonium nitrate. It's the right thing to do.'

I nodded, listening.

He continued, 'This is a government initiative. The prime minister will issue information to the media but we need to do our own. Michael Barton's name will be on this one.' I knew that BIG stood for Barton Industry Group, and that Michael was the managing director. I wondered, suddenly and for no particular reason, how he felt about his family business being taken over by Dega.

I jotted some notes. 'Okay.'

'Rosalind has the details. And you might want to talk to BIG's PR people.'

'Okay.'

'We'll be re-branding BIG. Give them a friendlier face. Rosalind has those details too but talk to BIG. They'll want to feel involved.'

'Right,' I said. 'I'll see Rosalind right away.'

'BIG's share price has dropped. To be expected. Public confidence in the company will wane for a time.'

I nodded, trying to look like I knew why he was telling me all this.

He gave me a small smile. 'Everything going all right for you?'

The blush was crawling, starting at the base of my throat. 'You mean, in my role here?'

'Of course.'

'Yes, thanks, Mr Degraves.'

He smiled and nodded. 'Did Rosalind tell you I've invited your department to the Melbourne Cup?'

'Ah, yes. Thank you. I've never been.'

'Partners are invited.'

'Yes, I know. Thank you.'

'Will you bring your husband?'

That floored me. What was he doing? He must know I'm going with Jack. I gaped at him for a few seconds and he smiled back at me, waiting. 'Um, no,' I said. 'We're separated.'

'Ah. Well, I'm sorry to hear that.'

I nodded. 'I've invited ... someone else.'

'Good. Very good. Get a draft to me this afternoon, would you?'

'Sorry?'

'The media release.' He glanced at the notes I'd made.

'Oh. Right. Yes. Sure. I'll work on it straight away.'

I waited for him to give me a knowing wink or something, but his face was stony serious as though any thought of secret, illegal, anti-terrorist organisations wouldn't cross his mind.

I left JD's office and headed back downstairs, thinking about our conversation. Would I bring my husband? What the hell? And if Rosalind and no doubt BIG have all the details, why'd he called me to his office at all?

I stood at Rosalind's office door but she was on the phone, and shooed me away.

Marcus stuck his head over the partition. 'What did the grand poobah want?'

I whispered, 'Media release. They're withdrawing ammonium nitrate from the market.'

'Boring. I knew that.'

'And we're doing a new logo for BIG.'

'A stick of dynamite?'

I giggled. 'No!'

'What are you wearing to the Cup?' he said.

'Don't know. Actually, thanks for the reminder.'

While I was waiting for Rosalind, I googled 'Melbourne designers'. Another task in my new undercover role was to take the $3000 Jack had given me and find something fabulous to wear to the Melbourne Cup. Which made me wonder something else. What kind of women did Jack Jones have in his life if he thought I needed that much money for a new outfit?

After meeting with Rosalind, I called PR Susan in Sydney. Her snippy assistant put me through and Susan was a bit friendlier this time. We talked about BIG's new image. I guess JD wanted a logo that didn't look like its product could blow something up. Susan was actually happy for me to project manage that task, but I suspected she didn't have a choice.

She said, as a way of regaining control, 'We're having a function at the Opera House in March. It's an annual thing for our customers but we could expand it. Could be a good time to launch the new image.'

'I agree,' I said. 'Sounds ideal.'

AFTER WORK, I rehearsed a conversation with my mother all the way to her house for my usual Monday dinner. Unfortunately, I couldn't think of any way to keep her from finding out about Jack Jones. I was sure she had spy cameras in every corner of my world. Especially my bedroom. The whole sex issue caused her such angst, I sometimes wondered if it would be easier for me to never have sex again. Either that, or just marry someone to keep her happy. Or become a lesbian. She oscillates equally between horror at the thought of my being with a man, and utter distress that I'm not. When Danny and I separated, Mum spent a week in bed crying about her daughter's 'disastrous' life, and pondering the elusive answer to her favourite life question: Where did I go wrong?

Also, poor Mum's so devastated about being an illegitimate child, she tries to make up for it by living like a nun. I'm sure she'd insist that the only sex she's ever had was to conceive. (That makes twice, by my calculations.) Mum is a devout Catholic and goes to confession at least once a week. What she'd have to confess I have no idea, but I suspect it relates mostly to my shortcomings. My grandmother, on the other hand, tells everyone proudly about her daughter's illegitimacy. And all the details relating to the affair. I mean, *all* of them. Grandpa seems to be strongly in denial, though. He often marvels loudly about how two pale-skinned redheads could produce someone who looks like Sophia Loren.

I arrived at Mum and Dad's and as we sat at the dining table, I said, 'Guess what? I've been invited to the Melbourne Cup. On a date.'

Mum said, 'Praise the Lord!' and threw her hands in the air.

Dad farted and turned up the television.

My news about a new man plus the Melbourne Cup invitation gave my mother several new things to worry about, and I knew that would make her very happy. The long-term worry would be whether or not this guy would marry me; the short-term worries would be about my weight, my outfit for the Melbourne Cup, and the fact that I might have sex. In Mum's mind, if the short-term worries weren't dealt with properly, there's a good chance she wouldn't have a long-term worry. And if the long-term worry wasn't resolved and resolved well (i.e., marriage), then my purpose and worth were pretty much zero.

'Erica, you must go on a diet and don't let him kiss you yet. Men do not marry hussies!' To my mother, a girl can never be too thin or too chaste. She removed my half-eaten meal and crossed herself.

'Don't get excited,' I said. 'I don't know if I like him that much.'

'Sweet Mary, Mother of God.'

'He's a bit boring.'

'Bring him to dinner next week.'

'No!'

'Why not? Does your mother embarrass you?'

Yes. 'Of course not.'

'So, why not bring him to dinner?'

'Um.'

'It's settled then. We'll have curried sausages.'

On Friday night I went to the pub straight from work, as promised. Lucy was there, making a great show of being shocked that I'd turned up. Steve arrived with some mates and Lucy was suddenly a giggling, blushing teenager. Steve sat with us and I took that opportunity – the opportunity of Lucy being otherwise occupied – to casually announce to my small group of friends that I'd met a guy and I'd invited him to the Melbourne Cup with work. I quickly offered to buy a round of drinks to avoid further questions, but Lucy was fast. She nabbed me at the bar.

'This guy,' she said, 'is presumably the one I'm thinking of?'

'Phil from accounts? No.' I gave the barman my order.

'Erica, don't make me beat it out of you.'

I rifled in my wallet. 'I don't think I brought enough money.'

'You're not getting involved with that guy, are you?'

Lucy sounded really worried. I gave the barman my credit card and turned to her. 'I'm not supposed to tell you any more about it.'

She gripped my elbow. 'So, the Melbourne Cup. What's that about?'

I shrugged. 'Don't worry, hon. It'll be fine.' I think.

I walked away, back to our friends. More people had joined our group. The boys talked about football, Lucy was distracted by Steve, the noise in the pub got louder, and all this gave me an excuse to sit in quiet contemplation, wondering how the hell I was going to tell Jack Jones that he was invited to my parents' for dinner.

CHAPTER 12

'You told your *mother*? Are you serious?' I was glad Jack was on the other end of the phone, not standing in front of me.

'Only about the Melbourne Cup,' I said quickly. 'Not ... the other thing.' He blew out his breath. 'I couldn't get away with dating someone and not telling my family and friends.'

'Family *and* friends?'

'Yes. They'd find out and there'd be a lot of questions.'

Silence.

'And there's something else,' I said.

'I can't wait,' he grumbled.

'My mother's invited you for dinner. Tonight.'

Deafening silence.

I'd decided to wait until the last minute to tell Jack about the dinner invitation. My plan was that he'd rudely refuse, which meant I could tell Mum what bad manners he had and she'd hate him. Although, come to think of it, the idea of dating someone my mother hated was kind of tempting. I wondered how long we'd be 'dating'.

'Hello?'

'I wasn't expecting this,' he mumbled and I smiled smugly. 'All right. I'll pick you up.'

'*What?*' I felt sick.

'I'll pick you up. What time?'

'You don't have to do this,' I spluttered. 'You definitely don't have to do this!'

'It's okay,' he said and I think I heard him smiling, smugly. 'And you're right. It's reasonable that you told your family you're dating. I don't mind playing along. Besides,' he said conversationally, 'I don't get out very often.'

Oh. Shit. What if my mother liked him? Of *course* she'd like him! He was a man with a head, two arms and two legs. And money to throw around on expensive things. With that in mind, I said, 'What sort of car do you have?'

'I have a few. Why?'

'It's important.'

'Audi, Mercedes ...'

'Any Fords or Holdens?' The fact that Jack wanted to date me made him a saint in my mother's eyes before she even met him. Displays of wealth – such as expensive cars – would only make it worse.

There was more silence, and he said, 'Oh, you're serious?'

'Yes, but don't worry. I'll pick you up.'

'Erica, you drive an old Mazda. I don't think I'd even fit in it.'

'Yes, you will. I promise.'

I drove straight from work to where Jack had told me to pick him up on Nepean Highway in Brighton, and I wondered if that was close to where he lived. As I crossed the North Road intersection, I could see him leaning against a high brick wall. I pulled up at precisely 6pm and he strolled over. Through the passenger window I watched his groin getting closer, and suddenly the door opened and his face was there, mocking, like he knew I'd just been staring at his crotch.

'Is this car safe?' His eyes were smiling.

'Very funny.' I blushed. Again.

Jack climbed in and handed me a David Jones shopping bag.

'What's in here?' I said.

'Present for you. For me, actually.'

I looked in the bag. It was a coffee plunger and a bag of fair trade coffee. 'A subtle hint?'

He smiled and commented on the surprising amount of head and leg room in my car, and the ordinariness of this comment relieved my acute embarrassment. I didn't know what to say or where to look and I was starting to feel sick about the impending ordeal.

'I told you that wouldn't be a problem,' I mumbled.

He looked for the broken seatbelt and found it on the floor in the back. 'What year is this thing? 1960?'

I pulled out from the kerb. 'This car was born the same year as me.'

'And what year was that?'

He smiled and I looked back at him with narrowed eyes. 'I suspect you not only know exactly when I was born, you probably know how long my mother's labour was.' Which was not long enough.

He laughed and pointed at the floor. 'Why is there a hole there?'

'My friend Steve drilled a hole to let the water out.'

'Makes sense.' He clipped his seatbelt in place and tried unsuccessfully to tighten it, giving up with a shrug. 'Why don't you get a new car? This one can't be safe.'

'I love this car!' I tried to sound offended but the fact is I really should have a new car. A better one, at least. One with basics such as heating and windscreen wipers that work. I sighed. 'Actually, I would like a new car but all my spare money goes into my mortgage.'

He nodded and gazed out the side window and we drove without speaking for a few minutes. He seemed quite comfortable with the silence. As we passed a McDonald's he said, 'Do you think we'll eat straight away? I'm still full from lunch.'

I stopped at a red light. 'What time did you have lunch?'

'Lunch time.' He grinned. He really was extraordinarily good-looking. Even more so in this relaxed, happy mood, which I wasn't expecting. His eyes sparkled.

'Keep it up,' I said, relaxing. 'I don't want them to like you anyway.'

'Mothers love me.'

'Not if I can help it.' The lights changed to green and I moved on, grinding the gears and bunny-hopping forward in my usual style. I'd never quite got the hang of gears, and often thought longingly of owning an automatic car. 'By the way, will you have an English accent tonight?'

'No. That's only for people I want to confuse.'

'What about other languages?' I said. 'I think you were speaking Arabic.'

'Just then? I didn't realise.'

I laughed. 'No, at my house, when you were unconscious.'

'I was delirious.'

'Yes, you were,' I said, nodding and smiling. 'So, do you speak Arabic?'

'Sometimes.'

I kept glancing at him as I drove, trying to work out if he was joking or serious. I was delighted and relieved that he was in such a good mood. I'd been trying to avoid thinking about the possibility of my parents having dinner with an angry man with a gun. 'Any other languages I need to know about?'

'There's nothing about me you *need* to know, but I do speak six languages.'

'Six?' I nearly drove up the gutter. 'Are you serious?'

'Yeah.' He frowned, pointing ahead. 'Try to stay on the road.'

I tried to watch the road but it was hard not to look at him. Maybe he really didn't mind having dinner with my parents. Maybe he never goes out and he thinks this is fun? Amusing? Something to pass the time?

'How come? So many languages, I mean.'

Jack addressed the windscreen, nodding at it, hinting that I should be looking at it, not him. 'I grew up in Switzerland.' He shrugged. 'I speak Italian, French, German, some Mandarin and the others you know about.' He glanced at me and added by way of explanation, 'My father was Swiss.'

That accounted for the something else I detected in his Aussie accent – several something elses – but a Swiss father with the name

Jones? I also noted the 'was' in relation to his father.

'When did you come to Australia?'

'When I was sixteen. My mother was Australian, an only child, and we moved here when my grandmother became ill. She died soon after, and we stayed on. I live in her house.'

'In Brighton?'

'Yes.'

'Please don't tell my mother.'

I turned into the street where I'd grown up. My parents still lived there – a modest cream brick, typical 1950s house in Chadstone. Much to my mother's disgust. She'd always wanted to move to the next suburb, Malvern, which had much greater snob value. Personally, I loved growing up walking distance to Chadstone shopping centre.

I pulled up in front of the house. Dad was watering illegally.

Jack said, 'Now I know where you get it.'

I didn't park in their driveway because Dad likes to have 'vehicular access at all times', even though he only drives twice a week, to the supermarket on Friday and church on Sunday.

'Hi, Dad.'

Dad looked up from the watering and dipped his head to look over the top of his glasses. He never looks like he knows who I am.

'Dad, this is Jack,' I shouted. Dad's a bit deaf, especially to women's voices, he tells me. 'We've come for dinner.'

Jack held out his hand. 'Mr Jewell.'

Dad didn't suggest Jack call him Tom and I knew my mother wouldn't offer her first name, Margaret, either. They were only about sixty, but behaved like really old farts. Dad is a retired jeweller, which, considering our surname, is terribly funny. Well, I think so, anyway. I also think my mother would have preferred to marry a gentleman (of noble and wealthy means), but the fact that she scored some seriously nice pieces over the years kind of made up for it. I hadn't done too badly myself, although I'm not much into jewellery.

Dad shook Jack's hand. 'Brian, is it?'

'It's *Jack*,' I shouted.

'No need to shout, girl. I'm not deaf.'

'We'll see you inside.'

'What?'

I grabbed Jack's arm and dragged him to the house. 'Sometimes it's best just to walk away.'

THE RULE IS that you arrive and sit at the dining table immediately. I'm not allowed in the kitchen to help because I'm useless, apparently. Mum chats from the kitchen and you have to strain to hear her, especially over Dad's tiny old portable TV that lives on the buffet right next to the table. The buffet Jack now had his back to. He turned in his chair – out of politeness probably – to see what Dad was watching.

'Is this you?' Jack said, pointing to a framed photo. An incredibly embarrassing photo of Steve and me naked on the beach. We were about two, holding hands, facing the camera. With his other hand, Steve had a good grip on his willy.

Mum arrived with the first of the dishes. Dad grunted at the television. Jack was mesmerised by the photo. I attempted an out-of-body experience.

Jack said, 'Where was this photo taken?'

Mum said, 'Aren't they cute?' She sighed. 'They grow up so fast.'

'Mum,' I said, 'would you please update that photo? I'm sure there's a nice one of Steve and me wearing clothes.' I said to Jack, 'It was taken at Aireys Inlet. Mum and Dad have a house there.'

'What's that behind you?'

'In the rock face? It's the bum cave.' I smiled. 'We discovered it when we were older.'

As kids, Steve and I spent all summer at Aireys Inlet with our mothers, and our dads would visit on weekends. When we were about nine years old we were allowed to venture off on our own for the first time and we stumbled across the cave. We found it at low tide when Steve's frisbee disappeared through a narrow gap in the rocks. We'd laughed our heads off at the time because either side of the narrow gap were two bulging rock formations that looked like bum cheeks.

Which of course transformed the gap into a bum crack. And at the bottom of the bum crack was a gap big enough for a whole person to crawl through. Which is exactly what we did.

'The bum cave?' said Jack, smiling.

'You have to see it to understand why we called it that.'

Mum fussed and hummed, laying dishes out in front of us. The last pot arrived – Mum's masterpiece. She uses curry powder to make curried sausages, and the whole thing takes about twenty minutes, but she puts out curry condiments like banana and coconut as though it was some special dish she'd been cooking all day. There were a lot of dishes in front of us, and the table was tiny and we were all so close together and I had a feeling it was going to be worse than I'd anticipated. Jack sat opposite me and I wondered why a man like Jack Jones would agree to participate in such an agonising event as dinner with my parents. But, that said, his eyes gave away his mood, suggesting he was having a ball.

Dad stood to change channels, and farted loudly.

'Jesus Christ,' I muttered and dropped my face into my hands.

Mum came in from the kitchen with a jug of water. God forbid we be allowed to have wine. 'Erica, did you just blaspheme?'

'Yes, she did,' said Jack.

I glared at him and he smiled back at me. I complained to my mother, 'Dad farted in front of us. It's disgusting!'

Dad continued watching the news. Mum said, 'Please don't use the F word, Erica.'

I groaned into my hands. 'Fart isn't the F word, Mum.'

Mum tsked and sat at the table. What a happy little family. She patted Jack's hand.

'So, Jack, where do you live?'

'Jack lives in Footscray,' I said before he could respond.

'Footscray! Not far from Erica. She's in Richmond, you know.'

'It's on the other side of town,' I said. 'We hardly ever see each other. Jack's never been to my house.' I didn't want her to think there was a chance we'd had sex. On the other hand, if she thought we'd had sex, she'd hate him and might give up the idea he'd marry me. I'd have to think more carefully about my tactics.

'Oh, well, how did you meet tonight?'

'Jack caught the train to Richmond and I picked him up. He lost his licence for drink-driving.' I glanced at Jack. He sat back in his chair, arms folded across his chest, staring at me. I couldn't tell if he was annoyed or amused. Maybe annoyed enough to run away and leave me alone, I thought, and then retracted that thought.

'Oh, dear,' said Mum.

I waved a hand over the food. 'Jack, eat.'

Dad turned up the volume on the TV. *A Current Affair* was on. They were talking to farmers about the banned ammonium nitrate products.

'Wasn't that business about the fertiliser just terrible?' said Mum, addressing Jack. 'They make bombs from it!'

'Yes,' I said. 'We know, Mum.'

'It's the company Erica works for, you know. They make bombs.'

I sighed, again. I could tell that Jack was trying hard to keep an appropriately serious expression.

Mum said, 'You know Erica's been married.'

I coughed and sprayed food all over my plate. I clamped my hand over my mouth and mumbled through it, 'Sorry.'

Mum huffed but I didn't look at her.

Jack said, 'Tell me about your husband, Erica.'

The sausage I'd just hacked up was now back in my throat, choking me. I had another coughing fit, and Mum patted me on the back.

'Good Lord, dear, what a performance!'

'Sorry,' I said again and swallowed half a glass of water.

Mum said, 'Jack asked you about Danny.' She gave me a nudge.

'What about him?' I managed, my throat half closed.

'What does he do for a living?' said Jack. He seemed really interested. Maybe he was jealous? I gave myself a mental slap.

'He's, um, a salesman.'

'What kind?'

'Cars.' I shrugged and shovelled more food in my mouth.

Mum butted in and I loved her for it. 'And what do *you* do for a living, Jack?'

Jack was spooning food onto his plate. He opened his mouth to speak but I jumped in quickly, my mouth full. 'Jack's a panel beater.' Good one, I thought. Mum doesn't like 'smelly tradespeople', apart from Steve.

It was Jack's turn to have a coughing fit and I wondered if he'd brought his gun and if it was aimed at me under the table.

Mum said, 'Are you all right?'

He nodded, turning red. Mum poured him some water. There were tears in his eyes. From laughing, not choking, I hoped.

Mum turned to me. 'So, dear, you haven't told me where you two met.'

'Oh ... um ...'

Jack cleared his throat. 'In a bar in the city. Erica was drunk and made a pass at me.' He smirked. Magnificent payback on his behalf.

'Erica. I certainly hope you wouldn't act in such an unladylike way,' said my mother.

I avoided her glare and stared at Jack. 'No, Mum. He has it all wrong. He was the one who was drunk. I had to help him into a cab because he couldn't walk straight.'

Mum discreetly changed the subject, possibly sensing the onset of a lovers' tiff. She said quickly to Jack, 'Erica tells me you're thirty-five years old.'

He glanced at me and I shrugged. He cleared his throat again. 'I'm about to turn thirty-seven.'

'When?' I asked, interested.

'Next week.'

Next week. So that made him a ... Scorpio! I made a mental note to read his horoscope.

'What are you doing for your birthday?' I said.

He resumed interest in his meal. 'Not much.'

My mother nudged me again. She jerked her head at Jack, making strange faces and rolling her eyes to the side. I shrugged and gave her an 'I don't know what the hell that's about' face.

She eventually gave up and said, 'Well, Jack, maybe Erica will organise something for your birthday.'

Jack and I glanced at each other and I looked away. We all ate in silence for a while, the television noise thankfully filling uncomfortably quiet moments.

'And tell me all about your family,' Mum said suddenly.

Jack waited for me to speak on his behalf, but I waved my arm in the air. 'You have the floor.'

'My family. Well, when I was growing up in, ah ...' he glanced at me, '... Footscray, times were tough, you know?'

Mum looked at him with sympathy, and something else. I think it was adoration. I'd told her everything I could think of to put her off Jack, but she was in love anyway.

'Yes, go on Jack,' she cooed.

'I have a little sister, about Erica's age. She lives in New York.'

'And what about your parents?'

'My parents both died in 2001.'

'Oh, that's terrible!'

He said, 'Tell me about you, Mrs Jewell. What about your family?'

'Panel beater?'

We were back in my car, driving, dinner over. I shrugged. 'I did my best. She still loves you. I'll have to tell her we've had sex.' Whoops. I blushed.

'Sure,' he said, gazing out the side window. 'I can help with that.'

I could feel my face burning, and we drove on in silence. I stole glances at him. I decided his smiling eyes were now a permanent feature. They'd been laughing for most of the evening, in fact, and I hated to spoil the happy moment but I was now curious beyond good manners.

'Jack, can I ask about your parents?' His eyes were suddenly no longer smiling. I said, quickly, 'I'm sorry, forget I asked.'

'No, it's okay.' He took a deep breath, staring straight ahead. 'They were in New York on September 11, 2001.' *Oh, shit.* 'I was flying in that morning. We'd made plans to meet for breakfast at the building my sister worked at, but she was called to a meeting on the other side of town at the last minute. I suggested we meet anyway. The building had a great restaurant at the top with an amazing view. That's where I wanted to meet – the top of the World Trade Center. And my parents were there, waiting for me.' I pulled over. Jack held my gaze. 'But I was late.'

I looked away.

He said, 'I'll get out here.'

CHAPTER 13

My reflection in the full-length mirror in my bedroom was a strange sight. It had been a very long time since I'd made an effort with my appearance, and the result of this morning's work was intriguing. I even wore mascara and I looked pretty good, I thought, but I was regretting my decision to save money on hairdressing. Straightened, my hair was half-way down my back. But it was dull with split ends, and the small hat did nothing to hide this. I hadn't realised how much it had grown since – when? Couldn't remember my last hair appointment.

I practised walking around in my new high heels. That, too, had been a long time – my preference over the past year and a half was for comfort – but high-heel muscle memory must work a bit like riding a bike. I could still do it.

Jack Jones arrived early and looked me up and down, nodding with what I assumed was approval. He stepped inside and said, quietly, 'Are you ready?'

'Yes. I'll just get my bag.' I felt really nervous. As much about having a date as I was about the idea of a terrorist attack. I went into the bathroom and stood in front of the mirror. I couldn't remember the last time I'd done this. Got all dressed up. Actually, yes I could. It was the day of my friends' wedding. The day my husband left me.

'Are you all right?' I jumped. Jack was leaning against the bathroom door, watching me.

'Yes ... no. It's my hair. I should have made more effort.' That day, the day of my friends' wedding, I'd gone to the hairdresser as planned, dressed for the wedding and stood in front of this very mirror, practising my denial. Maybe that was my last hairdressing appointment?

'Your hair is fine, Erica. We need to go.'

'Right.' I stepped past him to the kitchen where I'd left my bag. I slipped my sunglasses on and walked back down the passageway to the front door. Jack held it open, watching me approach. I watched him back. Apart from the fact that his face looked so serious he seemed almost angry, he was very handsome in a pale grey suit. A beautifully cut suit. And he was clean shaven with his hair swept back. A lock fell across his forehead and I felt tempted to reach up and brush it back.

Jack took my keys to lock the gate behind us, and indicated a white Mercedes parked at the kerb with someone sitting behind the steering wheel. He held the door for me and I got in, glancing at the driver in the mirror, who smiled at me. Jack walked around to the other side and sat next to me. 'Joe, this is Erica,' he said.

Joe the driver looked at me again in the rear-view mirror. 'Hi, Erica.'

I felt shy. 'Hi.' I thought I recognised him. I suspected he was one of the men who'd picked Jack up off the park bench in South Yarra.

Joe pulled away and I whispered, 'How am I going to explain a chauffeur to my work mates?'

He whispered back, 'Tell them he works for me.'

'Does he?'

'Yes.'

I doubted my work mates would be convinced that I was dating a hot-looking guy with his own driver. I watched out the window in silence for a long time, then I remembered the money I'd put aside. I hadn't spent the entire $3,000, as much as I was tempted to. I pulled an envelope out of my bag. 'Here. I didn't spend all the money you gave me.'

He regarded the envelope. 'Keep it.'

'But it's almost a thousand dollars.'

He shrugged and looked out the window.

I alternated my glances between Jack, Joe, and the window view, all of which reminded me that I was heading for the site of a potential terrorist attack. Which in turn reminded me of Jack's revelation about his parents. Just over 11 years ago. Not that long, really. I wondered how he coped with such a devastating loss.

Our car joined the traffic on the Bolte Bridge, headed for Flemington Race Course. I said quietly, 'What do I need to do today?'

'You can speak freely,' Jack said, nodding at the back of Joe's head. 'Your purpose is to gain me no-questions-asked entry into Degraves' marquee and provide a reason for me to be there. I don't want to attract attention. Apart from that,' he said, turning to look out the window again, 'do what you'd normally do but don't wander too far from the marquee. And stay sober and stay alert.'

'Oh. Of course.' I thought for a minute about what I'd normally do at the Melbourne Cup, which was pointless because I'd never been before. Danny used to go to all the race meetings, but I was never interested. 'I don't really know what to do at the Melbourne Cup,' I said as a small joke, but he didn't respond.

We arrived at the racecourse and Joe parked the car. Jack and I walked the short distance to the Dega Oil marquee and I felt immediately more relaxed. Mostly because I was utterly distracted by the jaw-dropping spectacle of JD's efforts to out-do all other marquees. I stood at the entrance and my gaze slid up the length of the soaring cylindrical birdcage that seemed to be holding up the middle of the mammoth tent. The birdcage was maybe ten metres high and full of exotic-looking birds. As was the rest of the marquee. JD had wanted a 'bird' theme, and most women seemed to be wearing hats to suit. Jack had told me to wear a hat that wouldn't get in the way. In the way of what, I wasn't sure, but it was small and neat – unlike most of the ostentatious creations there – with a couple of emerald feathers to match the rest of my outfit. And my eyes.

My hand was being tugged gently and it took me a moment to realise Jack was holding it, and that he was watching me with a small smile as he encouraged me to follow him across the room. As we walked, I looked for my colleagues. It wasn't hard to spot them – mostly they were staring at us. So much for Jack not attracting attention.

On the way to the bar we made a subtle detour to where John Degraves was standing. At the bar, Jack ordered a beer and handed me a glass of champagne.

'I'm not good with champagne,' I told him.

'I'm sure one won't hurt.'

I took a sip. French. Yum.

JD quickly joined us. 'Ah, Erica, very good that you and your team could make it today.'

My face started to burn. I'm not great at cover-ups. I should never organise a surprise party. 'Thanks for inviting us, Mr Degraves.'

He looked at Jack, who introduced himself and held out his hand. I got the feeling they'd done this routine before. JD pumped Jack's hand with great enthusiasm and boomed, 'Real estate, you say? You and I shall have a long chat, Jack Jones!' And with that they strode away, JD's hand on Jack's back, guiding him through the crowd. They found a quiet corner to stand and chat in a friendly fashion about the outrageous price of property, I supposed. I wondered about John Degraves. A seemingly friendly, even jolly, chap who secretly employs cold-blooded killers. *Do not call me again unless the man dies.* I wondered if Jack knew how much he meant to JD. Probably. I went to find someone I liked.

Rosalind, who wasn't someone I liked, caught my attention by shoving her peacock hat in my face. 'Tell me, who is that divine-looking man?'

I plucked a feather out of my mouth. 'You mean my date?'

'*Your* date? *Really?*' Her eyebrows disappeared under her hat. 'And what does John want with him?'

I glanced at Jack and John Degraves, still in deep discussion. 'Um. Real estate conversation?'

'Really?'

I knew Rosalind would tuck that useless information away for some future purpose. A waitress walked past with a tray of drinks and I swapped my champagne for water. A feather floated from heaven and landed on my shoulder. As I flicked it off, I saw Marcus arrive. He spotted me and minced over to join us. He pulled me away from Rosalind, saying, 'Just need to talk work with Erica for a minute.'

When we were safely out of earshot, he said, 'God, you look gorgeous.' He took a step back and gave me the once over. 'What an outfit! I could change teams for you today, lovely.'

'In my dreams, Marcus.'

His eyes narrowed as they focused on my shoulder. 'Except this, sweetheart.' He pinched my hair between his fingers and inspected the ends. 'W.T.F.'

'I know, I know. Don't go there.' I smacked his hand away.

'Are you perfectly well?' he said. 'I mean, you're drinking *water* for God's sake!'

'Yes. I'm pregnant.'

Marcus laughed. 'Oh, you are my *favourite* person in the whole world. Pregnant! As if! So, what's news? Did you bring that feisty girl? What's her name?'

'Lucy? No. I've got a proper date today.'

'Really?'

'Yes, *really*, Marcus Blake. I do date occasionally.'

'Since when?'

Good point. 'Let's talk about you. Where's your man?'

'Oh, Roger.' Marcus frowned. 'He wouldn't come. Bastard.' Marcus's eyes suddenly glazed over as looked past me.

I snapped my fingers in front of his face. 'Hello? Earth to Marcus?' Before I could look around, I felt a hand on my shoulder.

'Here you are, darling. Who's your friend?' Jack was smiling, holding out his hand to Marcus, whose mouth was opening and closing.

I said, 'Er, Marcus Blake, this is Jack Jones, my, ah, date.'

Marcus kept doing the fish thing. Jack smiled, flashing his perfect teeth. 'Pleased to meet you.'

Marcus batted his eyes and took Jack's hand, leaned close to my ear and whispered, 'Clever girl.'

I rolled my eyes. I was sick of everyone being so shocked that I could hook a hot-looking guy, just because I'd married a loser and hadn't had a date since he left me. And then I remembered that I hadn't. Hooked a hot-looking guy, that is. This wasn't real. I felt depressed.

Jack said, 'Why don't you go for a wander outside? Watch the goings-on. I'm off to make a bet. Wish me luck.' He patted me on the backside and walked away. I glared after him and wondered if JD's sexual harassment policies extended to the Team.

I said to Marcus, 'Good idea. Let's get some fresh air.' I hooked my arm through his and we strolled out of the marquee to watch the passers-by.

'Tell me all about this gorgeous spunk of yours,' said Marcus. 'God, I didn't hear a word you said. What's his name again? I feel faint.'

Marcus pretended to swoon and I laughed. I needed to spend *much* more time with Marcus. He always managed to reduce me to tears when other men were, well, reducing me to tears.

Marcus sucked in his breath and pointed at an enormous-bottomed woman wearing a tight, pink satin dress. 'Oh my *gawd*, would you look at that? Those thighs are a moonscape!'

'Ssh! Marcus, she'll hear you!' But I was glad of the distraction. I really didn't have any answers ready for my nosy friends who might want to know more about the new man in my life.

We giggled at other fashion horrors and I was blotting tears and mascara when Marcus grabbed my arm and said quietly, 'Well, well, looky here.'

A familiar voice said, 'Still can't get a real date, Eric?'

I looked up, feeling ill. Danny Malleta stood before me, looking pretty damn good.

Marcus said, 'I'll see you inside, sweetie,' and threw a vicious look at Danny before turning on his heel.

I said to Danny, 'Don't call me Eric, you dick.' I smiled tightly at his girlfriend, who looked exactly the same as the one he left me for. Long white-blonde hair, fake boobs and an orange suntan. She was chewing gum and didn't look like she understood English. Or any spoken language, in fact. Danny didn't bother introducing her.

Instead, he said, grinning, 'You miss me.'

'Actually,' I informed him, 'life's pretty good without you.'

'Yeah, right.' He laughed. 'Hey, you look all right, Eric.' He stepped back and looked me up and down. 'You actually look like a girl.'

I was considering my options – verbal or physical abuse – when a posh voice behind me said, 'It's amazing what proper lovemaking can do for a woman's complexion.' From behind, British Jack Jones slipped his hands around my waist and kissed my neck. It was a soft, warm kiss. Then, with an arm around my shoulders, he held out his hand to Danny. 'Jack Jones,' he said.

Danny turned red and his girlfriend thrust her chest at Jack. She also seemed to be chewing more noisily. I wondered how Jack coped with the effect he seemed to have on, well, everyone.

Danny muttered something and stalked off, dragging the blonde behind.

Jack was talking. '... I'll be in and out of the marquee ...'

'What?' I could still feel his mouth on my neck.

'Erica, pay attention. It's important.'

'Sorry, that was all a bit unexpected.'

His face softened. 'I thought Danny Malleta was hiding from the police.'

I watched Danny as he walked away, glancing back over his shoulder at us. 'He's too arrogant to think they'll find him,' I said. 'And there's no way he'd stay away from this event.'

'They'll catch up with him,' said Jack. We watched Danny until he was out of sight. Jack then guided me with a hand on my back toward the marquee.

But his arm suddenly snapped up in front of me and I walked into it. It was like walking into a steel rod. A man blocked our path. Jack pushed me behind him and I peered around his broad shoulder.

'Well, well,' said Jack. 'The things you see when you don't have a gun. Shane McGann. I thought you were holed up in Sydney.'

Actually, I was pretty sure Jack *did* have a gun. And I wondered why he needed it now. Shane McGann was almost as tall as Jack. With cropped blonde hair and dark glasses he looked like he belonged in a commando movie. He was somehow familiar.

'No, I'm back in Melbourne,' he said conversationally. 'For good.' He looked at me. 'Not going to introduce us?'

'On the contrary,' said Jack, equally calm, 'I'd recommend any woman stay away from you.'

The man glanced over his shoulder at the Dega Oil marquee, seemingly unperturbed by that pretty blatant insult. 'On a case, Jones? Or just wanking off with Degraves' crowd?'

Jack took my hand and we walked past the guy.

'Not staying for a chat?' he said.

Jack ignored him, pulling me along.

McGann called after us, 'I like your lady, Jones.'

I looked up at Jack, trying to wriggle my hand out of his vice grip. His mouth was set in a hard line.

'Friend of yours?' I said.

'Not likely. I'll tell you later.'

PUNTERS MADE their way to the mounting yard and jostled for position as the Melbourne Cup runners paraded for the crowd. I watched from the giant screens inside the Dega Oil marquee. The race was due to start in twenty minutes. I wondered, again, where Jack was. And I was starting to wonder why we were even here. Nothing had happened.

And then I heard the explosion. Everyone in the room gasped or shouted in surprise and ran outside to see what had happened. I froze, not knowing what I should be doing. Then Jack walked into the marquee. He stood to one side, solid and still as people rushed past him. He saw me, held out his hand and I reached for it, pushing my way past Rosalind's ridiculous hat.

As he led me away from the tent, people were gathering, their heads all turned in the same direction to watch as a billowing mushroom of white smoke grew high and wide against the otherwise brilliant blue sky.

I ran to keep up with Jack's long stride, yelling after him, 'What's happening? Was that a bomb?'

'Keep up with me.'

I kicked off my shoes, picked them up, and ran after him. He glanced down at my feet. 'Watch for broken glass,' he said as though there was nothing more important to worry about.

Jack's car was waiting with the engine running. He put me in the front next to Joe and he sat in the back. 'Floor it,' Jack said. 'Get ahead of the traffic.' The Mercedes surged forward, weaving through a confused crowd that was still oohing and aahing and pointing at the cloud of smoke. I sat quietly, my mind racing through possible scenarios, none of them pleasant.

Jack was talking to Joe, giving instructions. I tuned in. '... and take Erica home.'

I said, 'Where are you going?'

'There's been an explosion on the Bolte Bridge. I'm going to help.'

I felt sick. 'Can I do something?'

'Nothing more today.'

'I can help,' I said in a really small voice, looking at him over my shoulder.

He didn't answer, changing out of his suit into jeans, T-shirt and runners. I looked away.

Jack instructed Joe, 'Get me as close as you can.'

Sirens came from every direction. We saw fire trucks, ambulances and police gunning down Racecourse Road toward the bridge. Joe followed them, and I could see the Bolte Bridge in the distance. Smoke still wafted from whatever was burning and the crowd of lights from emergency vehicles was growing as I watched.

The Bolte was always busy, feeding traffic north to south on

Melbourne's western outskirts, and it was accustomed to traffic jams, but nothing like this. We stopped, unable to go further, and Jack pushed the door open.

'I'll go on foot. See you at home,' he said to Joe and then looked at me. 'Go home. I'll call you.' He slammed the door shut, and sprinted toward the scariest thing that's ever happened in my beautiful, safe Melbourne.

I COULDN'T stomach food that night, so I poured a big glass of wine and settled in to watch the news reports on the explosion. No sooner had I flicked on the TV than the phone rang. I leaped on it, thinking it might be Jack.

'You haven't called me to tell me about your date!' said my mother. 'Did he hold your hand? I hope you didn't kiss him, Erica. He won't be calling you again if you did. Do you realise this? Well, a peck on the cheek, perhaps ...'

My mother would be the only person in Melbourne right now not interested in the bombing on the Bolte Bridge.

'I didn't kiss him, Mum. Don't worry.' I had an image of me chasing Jack along the Bolte, trying to kiss him. I refocused. 'And don't get excited. It was just a date.'

'Oh, but Erica. He's such a —' big sigh '— lovely man.'

'He's not that good.'

'Lord, have mercy.'

'And I think he's got a gambling problem. I hardly saw him all day.'

'Remember, Erica, some men have great stresses in their lives and they need a release. Perhaps Jack enjoys a flutter. So what? You're a very judgmental girl!' Her voice rose higher and higher until it was just a squeak.

'I don't think Danny's lying, cheating and stealing was just a *release*,' I retaliated. My mother and I were about to fight over something that was completely unfactual – Jack's gambling habits – and, therefore, not an issue. But I couldn't help it. Mum had that effect on me.

She didn't argue though. She tsked once. I pictured her disap-proving face; lips pursed so tight her mouth would look like a cat's bum. She said, calmly, 'Well, you should be able to help poor Jack if he has a problem. You've had practice with your first husband.'

'I know,' I said, equally calm, relieved our potential hang-up had been headed off at the pass. 'But Mum, I really don't want to get involved with anyone.' Especially someone who gets shot at as part of his job description. 'Not yet. I'm happy with the way things are. Please let it go.'

She sighed. 'God help us all.'

I returned to the television and watched as the media announced that Australia had suffered its first suspected terrorist attack. People were in shock, and traffic was a nightmare. All news channels reported on the explosion, with very little about the Melbourne Cup. They said a truck had blown up on the Bolte Bridge. Unbelievably, so far, only six lives had been lost including the truck driver's. There were many injuries. The authorities were yet to confirm the cause of the explosion, but they suspected the truck was filled with explosives. No one denied the terrorist rumours. There were suggestions that the stolen fertiliser had been used, and the public was reminded that if this was the case, Dega Oil, the owner of BIG Fertilisers, was respon-sible for never-before-seen death and destruction in Melbourne. I braced for a horror day at work.

CHAPTER 14

$\mathcal{A}$s well as Rosalind, Marcus and me, our department had two investor relations officers. The company's share registry was briefed to take calls from the public but we still got plenty. And the calls were nasty, to say the least. We also took calls from the media and major shareholders, and hand-balled to Rosalind any that demanded more senior authority. All I did that day was field phone calls; there was little point trying to get anything else done. On my desk were all the newspapers. I looked at the *Herald Sun* front page photograph, presumably taken from a helicopter, which showed a hole in the bridge, the scorched roadway around it, and two burnt-out cars nearby. It was also possible to make out a few people hovering around the devastation, and I wondered if one of them was Jack.

By mid afternoon, the event had been picked apart on every radio and television station, in every paper, on the internet, and the main thing that came out of all that discussion was that, considering its route and in terms of causalities, the truck couldn't have picked a better location to explode. Rumours filtered through that the driver's plan had been to blow up Flemington Racecourse, and that somehow that plan had been thwarted.

· · ·

TWO DAYS after a terrorist bomb exploded in Melbourne, I sat at my desk checking the new artwork for BIG, which was still at concept stage. JD wanted to see it, and he'd asked me to be the one to take it to him. I was about to head upstairs when my phone rang.

Jack's strained voice said, 'I should have called you before now. I'm sorry.'

I was about to say yes, well, I think you certainly should have called me by now, but I started to cry instead. I squeaked nonsense into the phone and spluttered, 'I don't know why I'm crying.'

'You're in shock. It's normal.'

'Okay.'

'I need to see you, Erica, for a debriefing. Can you be at home tonight?'

'Okay.'

'See you at eight.'

'Okay.'

It took me ten minutes to pull myself together, which made me late for my meeting with JD. I rushed upstairs to his office, apologising to Celia, and she sent me straight in. I laid the artwork out on JD's meeting table and he stood over it, nodding.

He said to me, 'What did you think of the Melbourne Cup, Erica?'

I blinked at him. 'Ah, it was nice. Except for ...'

'Yes, terrible business.'

He was watching me and I suddenly wished he'd just come out and say what he was thinking.

'It seems lucky that truck was stopped on the bridge,' I dared. What the hell.

'It was good work by the people involved.'

I nodded and he resumed his study of the artwork. JD made some suggestions, but said he was 'happy with my work'. Whatever the hell that meant.

WHEN I ANSWERED the knock on my door that night and saw Jack standing there, I burst into tears again. He stepped inside and put an arm around my shoulders, leading me down the passageway to the kitchen.

'Let's sit down and we'll talk,' he said.

When we reached the kitchen I moved away from him, embarrassed, and grabbed some tissues.

He put a bottle of whiskey on the kitchen counter. 'Do you want some?' he said.

I nodded and blew my nose and pointed to the glasses cupboard.

Jack filled two glasses with ice and whiskey and handed me one. We moved to the living area and sat on the sofa. I focused on the drink in my hand and said, 'Are you responsible for that truck blowing up?'

'I was involved.'

I looked up at him. 'All those people died ...'

'It was six people, including the bastard responsible. I know that sounds harsh, but it could've been so much worse.'

I nodded, taking a deep, ragged breath. 'Why didn't you just arrest the driver?'

Jack sat forward, elbows on his knees. 'Because he would have blown the truck the second he thought we were on to him, and many more lives could have been lost. Our intention was to disable the truck and hope he'd abandon it. But he didn't. He blew it, as we thought he would. We had people working to divert the traffic. There was little choice. The truck was en-route to Flemington, and I was there in case it got through.'

I thought about the possibility of Flemington racecourse being blown up on Melbourne Cup day, and shuddered.

'You have to understand the effect of an explosion like that in a crowded area,' he said. 'Out in the open on the bridge, where the space can absorb much of the impact, the damage was greatly lessened. That truck had enough explosives on board to match the Bali bombing, or worse. Do you remember how many people were killed there?'

I nodded. 'It's such a terrible thing.'

'Yes, it is.'

I sipped my drink and waited unsuccessfully to feel better about it.

'Jack, you knew what was going to happen and you knew who. Why couldn't you have done something before? Why couldn't you have stopped them?'

'We didn't know where they were coming from. We don't know where they've hidden the fertiliser. And, there are boys in the group – no more than fifteen or sixteen years old. Taking care of it before would have meant ... dealing with them all. I couldn't do that.' He ran his fingers through his hair. 'Besides, someone else would have stepped in to do the job. They don't care about their losses, but what we did on Tuesday sends a strong message that we're watching, that we're onto them.'

I thought about the young, impressionable boys who worked with the terrorists. And I thought about the innocent people who'd died. I tried to decide whose life mattered more. I shook my head. It was impossible.

'Will there be more?' I said. 'More attacks?'

'We think so. Yes.'

'Where? In Melbourne?'

'We don't know.'

Jack sat back and we were silent for a while. I watched the ice cubes bob around in my glass. Axle trotted into the room and crawled along the back of the sofa, settling on Jack's shoulder, purring like a chainsaw.

'This cat is not normal,' he said.

'Sorry. He likes you.' I wiped my wet face.

'Those claws are like needles.' He pretended to be annoyed, but he was smiling.

'I know. Sorry.' I left Axle there anyway. I stood and went into the kitchen, and came back with a small tray of cupcakes, a lit candle in one of them.

'I'm not sure when your birthday is, but I made you these cakes tonight. I hope you don't mind. They're probably not very good.' I put the tray on the coffee table.

He was touched, I could tell. 'That's really nice of you.'

'So, when's your birthday?'

'Actually, it's today.'

'Your birthday's today? What are you doing here? Shouldn't someone be taking you out for dinner or something?'

He chuckled. 'I haven't celebrated my birthday in a long time.' He moved Axle to his lap and leaned forward, picking up the cake with the candle and blowing it out.

'Did you make a wish?'

'No.' He looked up at me. 'Do you want another whiskey? Goes well with cake.'

'Sure. I'll get it. Can't disturb His Lordship,' I said, nodding at Axle.

As I walked into the kitchen, Jack called after me, 'Were you surprised to see Danny Malleta at the Cup?' I nearly dropped the whiskey glasses.

I stared at Jack for a few seconds, and he watched me too. I said, 'Oh. Well. Not really. I knew he'd probably be there.'

'Did you call the police? Tell them you'd spotted him?'

I blinked. 'No.'

'Why not?'

'I don't know. I ...'

Jack nodded. 'Do you see much of him?'

'No.'

'Most people don't seem to know you're divorced.'

'Who are most people?'

He adjusted his position on the sofa, moving Axle off his lap and sitting on the edge of the seat. 'I know a lot about you, Erica. Some of it by asking around. And most people don't seem to realise you're divorced.'

'Separated.'

He nodded. 'Why is that?'

I had no idea what to say. And I felt suddenly pissed off that he was hammering me with questions when he was supposed to be making me feel better or something. Discuss our first assignment together. Or something.

'I don't see why that's any of your business, actually.'

I poured more whiskey. My hands were shaking. I walked slowly back to the sofa, handed Jack a glass, then sat on the chair, away from him.

He said, 'Danny Malleta keeps some pretty unsavoury company. If you're going to work with us, I need to know how involved you are with him.'

'I'm not *involved* with him at all. Okay? I never see him.' And then, damn it, my bottom lip started to tremble. I stood quickly and walked to the bathroom, without offering excuses. I put my glass on the kitchen bench as I passed.

I'D THOUGHT in the ten minutes I'd sat on the edge of my bathtub, fiddling with soggy tissues, Jack might have discreetly left. But he was still there when I came out, watching television with the sound off. He flicked off the TV and watched me approach. I sat on the chair, glancing at him but mostly trying not to meet his eyes. Annoyingly, he seemed to have no issue with eye contact. None at all.

'So,' I said, 'tell me about that man at the Cup. Shane McGann.' I lifted my eyes and held his gaze. 'If I'm going to work with you, I need to know who to watch out for.'

There was a very small smile. 'You do indeed. All right. I'll tell you about Shane McGann.'

And for the next ten minutes, Jack explained to me about the very nasty, very evil, Mr Shane McGann. That they were in the air force together, the SAS, Iraq; that Jack was his leader and McGann didn't like this. That Jack suspected McGann of feeding weapons and information to the enemy in Iraq. And that he'd gratuitously raped and murdered people there. That Jack had him brought up on charges but McGann's father pulled strings to get him off. That in Melbourne he was charged with rape, twice, but let off because the women wouldn't testify. And that his father had sent him to Sydney while things cooled after the rape charges. And, finally, that he was back in Melbourne, saying things like, 'I like your lady, Jones ...'

While Jack talked, I listened, but something else occurred to me. I said, 'Who's his father?'

'Martin McGann. Head of —'

'Mintin Mining. You know, when we met Shane McGann at the Cup, I thought he looked familiar and I've just realised why.'

'Go on.'

'I saw him at work one day, coming out of John Degraves' office with an older man. They both looked really angry. It must have been his father.'

Jack nodded slowly. 'Shane used to work for Mintin, then he got into trouble here and moved to Sydney.'

I thought about that and why Shane McGann and his father might have been meeting with John Degraves. 'Does Shane know what you do? With the Team, I mean?'

'No, he doesn't – I hope. Why?'

'It's just that, at the Cup, he asked if you were on a case. I wondered if he knew.'

'I don't remember him saying that.' Jack stared off into the distance. 'I consult to a couple of government organisations. He'd know about that if he made enquiries.'

'I wonder why he was meeting with JD?'

'I'll ask.'

Jack stood to leave, and as I walked him to the door, I said, 'Does John Degraves call the shots? Tell you what to do?'

'Operationally?'

I nodded.

'No, I call the shots. Degraves pays for it, and makes the occasional recruitment request.' He glanced at me with what I thought was a look of absolute regret.

CHAPTER 15

The following Wednesday – my being-responsible-at-home night – I sat at the desk in my bedroom to check emails, pay bills and transfer money to my loan accounts. I accessed my savings account. I'm not brilliant with money, but I keep a close eye on how much I have. And my account said it had $10,000 more than expected. I checked out the details of the $10,000 transaction. The money came from Pee Wee Pies.

I rocked back in my chair and stared out the window at my front garden. That made $20,000 so far, for very little effort. Plus the $1,000 Jack let me keep from the Melbourne Cup. Less Lucy's share of the first lot. Not bad. I checked all my accounts to see where I stood – what I had and what I owed – and to estimate my current net worth. This was a weekly obsession but since property prices had dropped a bit, so had my net worth. Very frustrating considering almost every spare penny I have goes against my loans. I probably should stop with the net worth thing.

The home loan account said I owed just under $100,000. I opened the lying-cheating-bastard account, which showed how much I owed on Dany's debt. Depressing. Although I had to admit that I was still way ahead. Danny had agreed to hand over his share of our house in return for my taking on his debt, which was almost as much as my mortgage. Still, I reckoned my house would be worth over $800,000 by now, and, I thought, that makes me the winner – a nice change.

I had another look at the transaction details from Pee Wee Pies and had a quick fantasy about being debt free. I reckoned if I keep working for Jack Jones, I could own my home by the time I'm forty. A very attractive proposition indeed, except for the being forty part.

The Pee Wee Pies transaction said nothing more than who it was from and what it was for. I wondered about tax. I made a mental note to ask Jack about it. I preferred to leave illegal transactions to my ex-husband.

Speaking of whom. Through my bedroom window I watched my front gate swing open and Danny Malleta walk through it.

I opened the front door before he could knock. 'That gate's usually locked against unwanted slime bags,' I said with a casualness I didn't feel.

I waited for Danny's retaliatory insult but instead, he said, 'Can I come in? Please?' He looked anxiously over his shoulder. He seemed very nervous. In fact, I thought he might cry.

'Why the hell would I let you into my house?'

'Please. *Please*, Erica.'

I stepped back and he rushed past.

He said, 'Can you lock the gate?'

I walked to the gate, opened it, and looked up and down the street. Nothing unusual that I could see. I locked the gate and went back inside, locked the security door and front door. Danny was in the living room. I walked into the kitchen, keeping the bench between us, said, 'What's this about, Danny?'

'You don't wanna know.' From his favourite spot on the sofa, he flicked on the TV. I waited for more but that was the extent of his explanation. He relaxed pretty quickly, surfing Foxtel.

'Make yourself at home,' I said.

'Thanks, Eric.' He grinned.

I snatched a carving knife from the block on the bench and walked across the room. Danny scooted along the sofa, fear returning to his eyes. 'Hey!' he shouted, hands up.

In a low voice, I said, 'Whoever's after you, Danny, will be far less scary than me if you *ever* call me Eric again. Is that clear?'

'Friggin' hell! Okay!'

I went back to the kitchen and put the knife away.

'You're different, Eric — a.'

'Yes, my life's so much better without you. I'm fabulous.' I took a bow.

Axle trotted into the room and hopped onto the sofa. Danny shoved him so hard Axle landed on his side on the floor, and dashed back up the passageway.

'Jesus, Danny!'

'I'm allergic! You know that.'

'So leave!' I rushed down to the bedroom. Axle was fine, sitting on my bed cleaning himself, but I sat with him on my lap for a few minutes anyway, crooning to him and stroking his fur.

As I walked back into the kitchen, Danny said, 'So, who's the English guy you were with at the Cup? What's the deal with him?'

I could feel the heat rise up my throat to my face. I busied myself, pulling vegetables out of the fridge, avoiding his gaze. 'Oh, just a guy I met. Not that it's any of your business.'

'Well, I felt a bit jealous, actually.'

'Give me a break,' I muttered.

'It's true.'

I glanced up and our eyes met. He seemed sincere. A rare moment in time. In fact, when he was nice like that, I remembered why I'd fallen for him in the first place. Apart from his good looks, which, of course, get lost in the ugliness of his true nature. I reminded myself of this and dragged my thoughts back to the present.

'While you're here you can take all the crap you left behind.' I retrieved the knife from the block and attacked a carrot.

'There's only one thing in this house I want, Erica.'

'Bad luck. I drank it.'

'I'm not talking about the wine.'

I cleared my throat. 'The cops were looking for you.'

'Yeah, well, they need to take a number and join a queue.' He scowled at the television.

'What are you doing, Danny? Why are you here?'

'I can't tell you.' He looked at me pleadingly. 'Can I stay a couple of nights? Please, Erica? I'm trying to get myself out of trouble. Really. I just need a break.'

'No, Danny, no way.' I shook my head quickly, focusing on the vegetables.

He turned off the TV and walked over to me, holding out his hand for the knife. 'Here, let me do that.' I held the knife against my chest and we eyed each other, face to face. He stepped closer and I stepped back. He gently took the knife and turned to the vegetables.

'What are we having?' he said. Danny was proficient in the kitchen. A really good cook.

'Stir fry.' Although I really had no idea. I'd just been chopping.

'I'll do it.' He nodded at the sofa. 'Go sit down. Have a drink.'

Twenty minutes later we were opposite each other at the dining table, and I wondered how the hell I'd landed here. Which was stupid, of course. I'd opened my door and let my criminal husband into my house. That's how I'd landed here. Danny forked food into his mouth.

I asked, again, 'What's the deal, Danny? What trouble are you in?'

He stopped eating and addressed his plate. 'I really don't want you involved, for your sake.'

'Seems like I *am* involved.'

He shook his head, 'No. You're not. I just need a couple of days to get myself sorted, and I'll be out of your hair.' He looked up at me. 'Please, Erica. Please don't make me beg.'

I sat back in my chair and considered him. He was doing a good job of Mr Nice Guy. He seemed genuinely frightened, but I wondered if he was also genuinely keen to do the right thing, for once. I sighed. 'Okay, you can stay. Two nights. Then you're out.'

He grinned and resumed eating. 'Thanks, Eric. Erica!' He gave me a nervous look and I narrowed my eyes at him.

After dinner I set Danny up in my spare room, annoyed that he was the first person to use the new bed. He was exhausted, I could see that, and he went to bed early. I did the dishes, double-checked the doors and windows, and went to my room wondering if I'd made a huge mistake.

DANNY WAS in the kitchen the next morning when I walked out, ready for work. He'd made scrambled eggs, my favourite. He'd also set the table and was freshly showered, whistling, looking good. I didn't trust him.

'Sorry, I'm in a hurry. Can't stay for breakfast.'

He looked crestfallen. 'But, honey, I've made your favourite.'

'Don't call me honey.' I looked at my watch. 'I have to go.'

'Can I have a key?'

'No,' I said, and left, starving and way too early for work.

During my lunch break, I called home. No answer, but that didn't mean he wasn't there. I didn't have Danny's new mobile number, and didn't really want it.

I sent Jack a text instead: *Checkd my a/c. Tax? EJ*

I stayed late at work to avoid my husband, even though I was nervous about Danny being alone in my house. I wondered if I'd left any money lying about.

I got home at 7.30, walked through my front door and was aware of voices in the living room. I approached cautiously, wondering who or what I might find there. Criminals? SWAT team? Not quite as scary, but almost.

Danny was cooking and Jack was leaning against the kitchen bench with a beer in his hand. Jack watched me approach, his eyes dark. I dropped my bag on the bench.

Danny tsked and moved my bag. 'I'm just dishing up.' He looked at me. 'Is your boyfriend staying for dinner?'

Before I could answer, Jack said, 'Yes.'

'Well, this is all very friendly,' I said and opened the fridge, getting myself a beer. 'You two having a nice time?'

Danny mumbled something about Jack just walking in and Jack

turned off the television, found my CD collection, and chose something classical. How almost amusing. The boys were chesting up.

We all sat around the dining table.

Jack said, 'What's your line of work, Danny?'

There was that goddamn blush, working its way up my neck. I kept my eyes on my plate but imagined that Jack had locked eyes with Danny, and that Danny was looking away, his face burning like mine under that ice-blue gaze.

'Sales,' Danny said.

'What kind of sales?'

I looked up. Danny shrugged. He was fixed on his meal. 'Computer.'

'I thought maybe cars,' said Jack.

'Why?' said Danny.

'You seem the type.'

My mouth fell open as Danny's head snapped up. He gave Jack an angry look but only for a second. Whatever he saw in Jack's expression made him look away just as fast.

And then, in a moment of realisation, Danny said, 'Hey, what happened to your English accent?'

I glanced at Jack. His shoulders relaxed. He smiled slightly. 'I acclimatise quickly.'

Danny narrowed his eyes at Jack and I rolled mine, feeling almost sorry for Danny's lack of … sharpness.

After that, dinner was mostly silent. We finished eating, I cleared away the dishes and filled the sink to wash them. Danny went outside to make a call and Jack stood next to me, leaning back against the bench, arms folded over his chest. I focused on the mass of bubbles in the sink. Too much dishwashing liquid.

Without looking at Jack, I said, 'So you just walked in uninvited.'

And he said, 'You told me you don't see your husband.'

A couple of fast heartbeats later, I said, 'I don't. He just arrived on my doorstep. I don't know why.' I glanced up, knowing what to expect. Yep. Those cold baby blues were locked on my face. I looked away. 'I think he's in trouble.'

'No doubt.'

'He seemed really scared last night.'

'What about?'

'I don't know!' I threw the dish cloth into the sink and soap bubbles flew everywhere. All over my face. I wiped it with my sleeve and turned to Jack. 'Look, I don't know why he's here. I don't want him here. I'm just ... I'm just helping him out. He said he's leaving tomorrow.'

Danny opened the door and walked in.

Jack said to me in a low voice, 'Lock your doors tonight.'

Danny smiled brightly. 'Lemon Tart? Coffee? Liqueurs? I remember what you like, Erica.' He didn't look at Jack.

'No, thanks.' I pulled off the rubber gloves.

Jack said to me, 'You wanted help with your tax?'

I nodded. I'd forgotten about that. Is that why he was here? I said to Danny, 'Jack and I are, um ...'

'Going to bed,' said Jack and took my hand, walking me down the passageway.

Danny called after us, 'But I've made dessert!'

I snatched my hand from Jack's and stopped in the dark passage. I leaned against the wall, aware of my rapid heartbeat.

Jack stood a few feet from me and waited. He called out to Danny, 'Save us some. We'll be working up an appetite.' He held out his hand but I ignored it, walking past him to my bedroom.

Jack closed the door and I sat at my desk, turning on my computer. He sat on the bed and I kept my back to him, avoiding eye contact while I pulled up my tax information and a spreadsheet showing all my earnings and expenses. I asked him how I should handle the Pee Wee Pies income, and he showed me what to do. It was straight forward. The money Pee Wee Pies sent me was net income – they took care of the tax, so the money was all mine. Jack said they'd send me a formal statement showing my income and the tax paid. Pee Wee Pies employed the services of Erica Jane Jewell as a communications consultant. Simple as that.

There was a tap on my bedroom door.

'What!' I yelled.

Danny's muffled voice said, 'Um, is Jack staying the night?'

My mouth dropped open and Jack stifled a laugh. I walked to the door and yelled through it, 'Why the hell do you want to know?'

'Well, um, it's just that I'm cooking breakfast in the morning.'

'Cook for yourself! Then pack your bags!'

I heard him shuffle back to the kitchen. I looked at Jack with what I knew was a miserable expression.

'You're not feeling sorry for him, are you?' he said.

I sat heavily in the chair. 'A little.'

Jack stood in front of me, said, 'Don't trust him,' and left.

I went to bed, tired and emotional. I was woken at 2am by a movement next to me. Half asleep, I said, 'Puss?' and felt around sleepily for Axle.

An arm pulled me across the bed. Awake in an instant, I pushed away. 'What the—' I reached for the bedside lamp.

Danny was lying next to me, looking hopeful.

I flew out of the bed and spread myself against the wall. 'What the hell do you think you're *doing?*'

'Come on, honey, we belong together.'

'GET OUT! GET OUT NOW OR I'LL CALL THE COPS!'

Danny double-timed out my bedroom. He slammed the door shut, and I pushed a chair against it. I sat on the chair, my face in my hands, forcing my breath back down my throat.

The next morning, I was vaguely surprised I was still alive. I walked tentatively down the passageway to the kitchen, passing Danny's room on the way. It was empty. The kitchen was empty. His things were gone. I sighed with relief, realising in that instant how much I enjoyed my life without Danny Malleta in it.

I suddenly remembered my bag, and looked frantically around the kitchen. It was still where Danny had moved it to when I came home the night before. I checked my wallet. All my money and credit cards were gone.

CHAPTER 16

On Saturday morning I hauled my miserable self out of bed and into training gear, and dragged myself around the Botanic Gardens' running track – the Tan – but only at a walk. Not even my usual power walk. It was more like a ... shuffle. I was feeling especially sorry for myself, and chose to walk in the wrong direction, against the flow, because it was easier. Downhill. I watched a very tall, very sexy, very focused runner approach, and flash past.

I called out, 'Hey!'

Jack looked over his shoulder and stopped running. 'Hi,' he said, breathless, as I approached.

'Why are you running around the Tan?' I said. 'Don't you live near the beach?'

'I already ran on the beach.' He was bent over, hands on his knees, puffing hard.

'Today?'

'Yeah.'

'And do you leap tall buildings in a single bound?'

'Can we sit please?' He pointed to a park bench. 'It's hard for me to laugh at your jokes and breathe at the same time.' As we sat, he said, 'I was going to call in on you today.'

'Ask me out on another thrilling date?'

'No, to ask how things are going with your ex.' His breathing was already back to normal and he leaned forward, watching me.

I watched the sweat rolling down his biceps and I couldn't remember if I was meant to be saying something.

'Danny Malleta?' he prompted.

Ah yes. My ex. 'He left yesterday.'

Jack nodded, sat back, and we watched a flock of footballers jog past. Big, muscly, Collingwood ones. Nice except for being Collingwood. They weren't in uniform but I recognised them. Some were wearing running shorts over their skins, and some were wearing just the skins. I wondered if the ones who wore the shorts on top were hiding really small willies or really big ones. I glanced at Jack, saw him smiling and nodding at the players.

I waited for them all to pass before asking, 'Are you a Collingwood supporter?'

He looked at me, eyebrows raised. 'What if I am?'

'I don't think we can be friends.'

He grinned and stood, stretching his arms above his head. His singlet top rode up and I ogled his flat, muscled belly, and the sexy line of hair that ran down from his navel and into his running shorts. He, too, was wearing skins under the shorts.

I shook my head. 'Um, Jack, my friends want to meet you.'

His smile vanished and he looked down at me.

'I'm having a dinner party next Saturday night,' I said. 'Can you come?'

He sat next to me again. 'I have to tell you something.'

I searched his face. 'What?'

'The real reason the Team recruited you.'

I sat for a minute, letting his words roll around in my head. *...real reason.* I said, 'You mean—' I looked at him.

'Erica, we'd been watching you to get closer to Danny Malleta. You were never meant to be involved, but that night I ended up at your house, and you helped me ... well, JD thought it best to bring you all the way. You knew too much.'

I didn't know what to say. I felt like an idiot. Again.

'But you can't help us further,' he continued. 'We don't need you now.'

I felt like I was being dumped, which I was. And then something occurred to me. 'You don't think Danny's involved with terrorists, do you?'

'As I told you, he keeps some pretty unsavoury company. And it seems he'd do anything for a fast buck.'

'But terrorists?'

'We can't assume.'

I nodded, miserable, and Jack was silent as all that washed over me.

'What am I going to tell my friends?' I said. 'They think I've met someone.'

He smiled slightly. 'Tell them I turned out to be a jerk and you dumped me.'

'I'll tell them you're gay.'

He chuckled. 'If you like.'

'Marcus will want your phone number.'

He laughed some more and I forced a smile, then my smile dropped away.

I confessed, 'Danny did something terrible.'

'He cleaned you out.'

'How did you know?'

Jack reached into the pocket of his running shorts and held out his hand. In it were two credit cards. With my name on them.

I took the cards. 'How —'

'I grabbed Malleta last night. We searched him, questioned him for a while. He's an errand boy for the people we're watching but he won't be doing any more of that now. He doesn't know anything. We let him go.'

My mouth was hanging open and I forced it shut. 'Did you hurt him?'

'No. Didn't need to.'

I nodded. Sighed. Felt like crying. 'Thanks for getting my cards back.'

'He said you gave them to him.'

Bastard. 'No, he stole them.'

'Sorry I didn't know about the cash.'

I got up early to get ready for my dinner party. I'd had a miserable week after saying goodbye to Jack Jones at the Tan. He'd squeezed my arm and asked if I would be all right. He suggested I have nothing more to do with Danny and, by the way, he'd know if I told anyone about the Team. He gave me a peck on the cheek before turning and jogging away. I'd watched him until he was out of sight, then I'd shuffled home and gone back to bed.

I was going to cancel the party but Lucy bullied me into having it. She, for one, was delighted that Jack was out of my life. She'd wanted to bring one of her doctor friends for me but I'd said no to that. I wasn't ready. I hadn't told my mother yet. I'd probably tell her that Jack had died or moved to Italy. I hadn't told any of my other friends either. Yet.

I cleaned the bathroom and stood at the French doors eating toast, gazing at my weedy garden, making a decision to clean it up. But before I tackled that particular job, there was something else I needed to do. I took two giant garbage bags to my bedroom, emptied the wardrobe of all Danny's clothes, and trudged down the road like Santa to my local op shop. I knew the ladies there and they were surprised I was making a deposit rather than a withdrawal. They looked at the clothes I'd delivered, and gave each other a knowing look.

'About time, don't you think?' I said.

They smiled.

I called in at my hairdresser who pretended to faint, then pretended that she didn't know who I was, and I asked if she could fit me in during the week. But she shoved me in a chair and wrapped me in a cape before I could escape. I asked for the works. Cut, colour, highlights, blow dry – hundreds of dollars worth.

Three hours later, on the way home, I stopped at the tiny plant nursery in my street and bought some pots of colourful annuals, which I placed around the garden, moving and swapping until I thought they were in the right place. When I finished, I stood back and wiped the back of a grimy hand across my brow, delighted with my efforts. The garden looked lovely! I decided to save up and buy a new outdoor setting so I could sit out there in the summer and enjoy it. I even spent some time reading with Axle purring on my lap. I never read any more. The afternoon passed by gently, and I liked it.

I WAS CHOPPING vegetables for the salad when someone knocked on my front door. I glanced at the clock. My friends weren't due for another hour. I ran to answer it, still holding the knife. As soon as I opened the door Axle dashed through it and ran up the leg of my visitor, attaching himself to Jack's bicep like a koala. I gawped at Jack and he looked at the knife in my hand, at the kitten on his arm, and said, 'I wasn't expecting an ambush.'

I stammered, 'What are you doing here?'

'You invited me.'

We stood like that for a few more seconds. Jack stepped hesitantly forward, keeping an eye on the knife. He was holding two bottles in his left hand and a box of something in his right.

He indicated the cat. 'Do you mind?'

I lifted Axle off Jack's arm and put him in my bedroom, closing the door behind me. I headed back down the passage to the kitchen with Jack following.

'I hope it's all right that I'm here,' he said.

'Oh. Sure.' I couldn't look at him because I didn't want him to see my smile.

'Where are your champagne glasses?'

I pointed. 'Same place as my whiskey glasses.'

He uncorked a bottle of Bollinger and poured. He handed me a glass and I shoved it in my face to hide the stupid grin. He sat on a stool at the kitchen bench opposite me and nudged the box of chocolates. 'For you,' he said.

Not just good old Cadbury Favourites from the supermarket – these were hand-made truffles from some posh shop in Brighton. He probably paid five dollars each for them.

'Thank you.'

'What are you cooking?' he said.

'Burnt lasagne and salad. And chocolates.'

'Burnt lasagne?'

I shrugged and checked the clock. 'You're very early.'

'I'm always early.'

I pushed a plate of cheese and biscuits at him. 'So,' I said, recovering some composure, 'Are my friends on your hit list or is this purely social?'

He flinched but covered it with a smile. 'Social.'

'You didn't have a better offer for tonight?'

'I rarely go out.'

He topped up my champagne. I hadn't realised I'd already drunk it all.

'I'm not good with champagne,' I said and guzzled some more.

'I'd prefer something other than panel beater as a profession,' he said. 'For tonight's conversation, I mean.'

'What would you prefer? Hired killer?' Guzzle.

'Very funny. I've got a couple of legitimate businesses.'

I looked at him, surprised. 'Really?'

'Yes. You can tell your friends I'm an accountant, if you like.'

'Are you?' I don't think I'd ever met anyone who looked less like an accountant, except maybe Pamela Anderson, but I'd never met her.

'Not a practising one,' the mercenary informed me. 'Mostly I employ people to run my businesses, but I'm involved with them.'

'Right,' I said, sceptical. No one will believe me. I regarded Jack Jones as he looked around the room. 'You seem different tonight,' I said.

'How?'

'You're nice, happy, relaxed.'

'As opposed to?'

'Bossy, officious, scary.'

He nodded in apparent agreement with that annihilation of his character. 'Well, I'm out with friends.' He tipped his glass. 'Cheers.'

Steve and Lucy arrived. I noticed Lucy's step falter when she saw Jack, surprised he was here, probably, but also because of his appearance, which was very different to the only other time she'd met him. She nodded curtly as he shook her hand.

Jack held her hand and looked deeply, comfortably into her eyes. I think that was his way of saying, *Thank you for saving my life*. Or it might have been, *Tell anyone and I'll take out a contract on you*.

Steve was delighted. I hadn't considered what Lucy might have told him, whether she'd said anything at all or that the 'new man' in my life had already dumped me.

'At last, someone I can eyeball.'

He gripped Jack's hand. They were a similar height and, in true bloke style, they moved to a corner of the room. The fact that Jack was a Collingwood supporter and Steve, like me, was a Richmond supporter made sure their conversation would be interesting. Lucy and I stood in the kitchen, watching across the room.

She whispered, 'What's he doing here?'

I shrugged. 'Dunno. What did you tell Steve?'

'Nothing yet. I didn't know what to say.' She stared at me for a few moments. I was grinning like the proverbial cat. She said, 'Are you sure you know what you're doing?'

'No.'

'Well, as long as you're sure.'

Emma and Ben were old school friends of mine. They started dating at thirteen and seemed to be over each other by the time they were fourteen. But they got married anyway and now had three kids with another on the way. When they arrived, Ben joined the blokes and Emma hung out in the kitchen.

'Why do guys do that?' Emma said.

Lucy and I shrugged.

Emma said, 'God, my tits are leaking,' and went off to the bathroom.

Marcus and Roger arrived and Marcus threw his hands in the air. 'Darling, your hair! It's *fabulous!*'

Roger went to the boys' corner and Marcus stayed in the kitchen, making faces about Jack's hotness, then regaling us with stories of their recent holiday in Bali. Within minutes we all had tears streaming down our faces. I walked over to the boys with the cheese and biscuits, chuckling, wiping my face.

'Marcus is telling us about your holiday, Roger.' I tried not to laugh.

Roger said, 'The part about the monkey?'

'Yes!' I shrieked laughing.

Roger glared at Marcus. 'Not funny!'

Jack took the plate from me and draped an arm over my shoulders. I stood like a frozen lump, my arms crossed. He chatted with Ben, running his hand up and down my arm and across my back. He played with my hair.

I snatched the plate back. 'Well, that's enough cheese for you fatties.'

As soon as we sat down to eat, my friends started hammering Jack with questions about what he does, how we met, etc, etc. I left him to it, listening with great interest to his responses. He lied very easily, glancing at me occasionally with lovey-dovey eyes and I wondered why he was bothering. Maybe he just felt sorry for the poor, boring girl with the crappy husband and bossy mother and bossy boss and bossy best friend. Let the friends all think she'd scored well, for once, before he goes on his merry way, having realised, with relief, his true homosexuality.

Steve brought up the Bolte Bridge bombing. 'They say the truck was supposed to reach the racecourse and someone stopped it.'

Ben said, 'I reckon we've got our own Batman in Melbourne.'

'Well I'd like to meet him, shake his hand,' Steve said.

I glanced at Jack and he was watching Steve with admiration. Maybe he was considering recruiting Steve to the Team.

Lucy said, 'Six people were killed, Steve.'

'Including the prick driving the van.' Harsh words from Steve.

'And someone's grandmother.'

Jack flinched. Lucy looked upset and angry. Steve was revved up, something I'd rarely seen.

Jack spoke up. 'They say if the truck had made it to Flemington, several hundred people could have been killed.' Everyone looked at him. 'Including our darling Erica,' he said, looking at me and giving my hand a squeeze. I blushed. 'And even if the truck had made it just as far as Racecourse Road, imagine all the shoppers there with their children ...'

Steve and Ben nodded in agreement. Lucy's eyes were on me. I wasn't looking, but I could feel them. She knew.

'I wonder how they did it,' said Steve. 'Stopped the truck, I mean.'

Ben said, 'Batman would have used his bare hands.'

'I'd like to see that,' said Marcus, pretending to swoon at the thought of being man-handled by Batman.

'Probably a sniper rifle,' said Jack and the table went quiet.

Ben said, 'But they didn't say the driver was shot.'

'No,' said Jack. 'There's a fifty-calibre bullet that can stop an engine.' He looked around the table. 'I was in the air force,' he said and shrugged.

'Might be Batgirl,' I said and everyone looked at me. 'It might be a girl watching over Melbourne.' I smiled and went to get more drinks and while I was doing that, I was happy to hear that Emma had changed the subject to her two-year-old's toilet training success.

Two hours later we were still sitting around the table, the meal over and a mess of dishes all over the kitchen bench. The conversation, after a ridiculous amount of drinks, turned to sex.

Ben complained, 'We haven't done it since she conceived this one.' He indicated Emma's bulging belly.

Emma retaliated, 'You know I like it in the morning and you're never there.'

'Well, sorry if someone has to get up and go to work!'

Marcus said, leaning on the table with his chin in his hand, making gooey eyes at Jack, 'So, Jack, of course you know Erica prefers it in the morning.' He batted his lashes.

I choked on an olive. No one seemed to notice. Jack said, 'Actually, I didn't. Thanks for the tip.'

Emma said, 'I suppose you guys'll be lying around all morning tomorrow, bonking.' She humphed. 'Unlike us. We'll be up at five, cleaning shit and snot.'

'Charming,' said Marcus. He turned back to Jack. 'Are you staying here tonight?'

Jack said 'Yes' as I said a resounding 'No'.

Everyone looked at me. 'Jack has to work or something. He can't stay.'

'Yes, I can.' Jack wagged his eyebrows.

'Marcus, darling, change the subject please,' I said, taking a big gulp of wine.

'Okay, sweetie. So, Jack, what turns you on about Erica?'

I sprayed red wine all over the white tablecloth. Everyone glared at me except Jack, who seemed amused. Marcus said, 'For God's sake, E!'

'Sorry.'

Jack wiped a drip of wine from my chin with his thumb, and licked it off. My face was a permanent blush. I didn't need the wine stains.

Jack said, 'Well, there's the way she concentrates when she's chopping vegetables.'

Everyone chuckled, even though it wasn't funny.

'And she gets a little frown line right here.' He indicated the space between my eyebrows. More chuckling.

'And I like the way she blushes when she's embarrassed, and falls over when she scared.' Raucous laughter. I blushed.

'And the curls that fall across her face – I can't help but want to push them away from her eyes so I can look into them.' He did it. Intakes of breath.

'And those lips that pout so lusciously I want to kiss them forever.' Audible collective sigh.

'And of course there's that incredibly sexy bod with legs that go up to here and —'

'*Enough!*' I glared at my friends. They were all sucked in. Even Lucy.

Marcus jumped in. 'Erica, what is it that turns you on about Jack?'

Everyone looked at me. I glanced at Jack. 'Well, have a look at him, for God's sake. Coffee?' I stood and stomped into the kitchen.

EMMA, Marcus and Roger had cornered Jack. Lucy was arguing about something with Ben. Steve dragged me away from the dishes. 'Smoke?'

'Thought you'd never ask.' I dropped the dish cloth, grabbed a glass of wine and headed for the back door. I knew I was drunk, but I seem to have this enviable ability to be able to walk straight, no matter how much I've consumed. On the way through the living room, I tripped over the rug, spilling wine, and the ottoman jumped in front of me and I fell over it. Steve stood me up and I swore at the ottoman, saying also that I needed a new rug. I continued on my way with Steve's hand firmly around my upper arm.

Outside, Steve gave me a cigarette. He was an ex-smoker who smoked occasionally at parties. I'd never been a smoker but was known to light up when drunk. I sucked on the ciggie and coughed, then I sucked on my empty glass and inspected it.

Steve said, 'I really like Jack, but are you sure you're into this guy?'

'Sure,' I said. 'Why?' I tossed the glass over my shoulder into the garden and Steve cringed.

He said, 'It's just that he seems to like you much more than you like him.'

'No,' I slurred. 'He's just a better actor.'

Steve looked puzzled. Jack walked outside.

'Come here, *darling*.' I beckoned and nearly fell over.

Jack strolled across my tiny terrace. 'What is it, pumpkin?' He took the cigarette from my hand and butted it out.

'Hey!'

'Stunts your growth.'

I hiccupped and hung on to Jack's arm.

'I don't like you,' I said, poking his chest.

'I don't blame you,' he said.

Steve mumbled something and disappeared inside.

I slung my arms around Jack's neck, swaying, hanging on. 'Kiss me.'

'I thought you didn't like me.'

I shrugged. 'So what?'

He rested his hands lightly on my hips, the corners of his eyes creased. 'You don't want me to kiss you.'

'Yes, I do.'

'Everyone's watching.'

'That's the idea.'

'You're very drunk.'

I hiccupped again. 'I *dare* you to kiss me.'

'You dare me?'

'Yep.'

'You should never dare me.'

'I *double* dare you.'

'Okay, then.' Even though they were blurry, I could tell his eyes were laughing. 'Are you ready?'

'Ready.' I threw back my head and closed my eyes, my arms draped loosely around his neck. I waited, swaying against him in a mellow fog, aware that nothing was happening. I was tempted to peek, see what he was doing, but then his hands moved to my waist, tightened slightly.

His body was closer now and his warm breath was at my ear. He whispered in it, 'Irresistible,' and I giggled, squeezing my eyes shut. His lips moved from my ear across my cheek and his breath was on my mouth. He ran the tip of his tongue lightly, slowly, along my bottom lip. 'You taste like an ashtray,' he muttered.

'Just don't think about it,' I muttered back and his mouth pressed softly onto mine. He gently sucked my lip. I shivered and the alcohol haze lifted, all my senses snapping to attention. I moaned, pressing into him, and I could feel his smile. Should I be embarrassed? Should I stop? What the hell. I clutched him, my arms tight around his neck, our lips pressed together. His hands slid around my back and he pulled me harder against him, and my feet barely touched the ground. His tongue probed gently, and then Jack's mouth covered mine in a deep, wet, orgasm-inspiring pash that lasted at least twenty seconds.

He released me gradually, his mouth lingering then easing to a feather-light touch, and I landed back on earth. I opened my eyes and blinked up at him.

'Is that what you wanted?' he said, smiling.

And I said, 'I'm never going to see you again, am I?' just before I passed out cold.

CHAPTER 18

Sunday night and still nursing my hangover, remembering being kissed by Jack but not remembering why he did it. I flicked through four million channels hoping to find something of interest. No luck.

There was a knock on the front door and I cursed myself for leaving the gate unlocked. But then I thought it might be Lucy and maybe even Steve. Or Jack! That made me feel better and I walked quickly to answer it.

An Asian woman, gesticulating, distressed, asked for my help. Something was wrong with her car, she said in broken English, and she had children at home alone. I was following her to the gate when a hand closed tightly over my mouth, an arm around my shoulders. I froze, confused. The owner of the hand was pressing into my back, holding me very tightly, and I didn't understand why. A joke? The woman turned and rushed back past me, and I heard my front door slam shut. Panic was just starting to register when a stinking wad of cloth replaced the hand, and I struggled for a few seconds, clawing at the cloth, before sinking involuntarily to the ground.

. . .

I LAY ON MY SIDE. I had a thumping headache and fuzzy eyesight. I blinked at the furry scene before me while I struggled to remember where I was, and why. My eyes focused on the few square centimetres of grubby mattress in front of my face. A cockroach scuttled past my nose, and I jerked my head back; I wanted to brush it away, but I couldn't move my hands. It took me a moment to realise they were tied behind my back. And my feet were bound. I tried to call out, but my mouth was taped. And then, panic. I kicked wildly and screamed under the tape. I started to cry and my nose blocked. I could no longer breathe.

A figure appeared in front of me and slapped my face, hard. I froze, staring up at the man, trying to draw air through my nose. Then a woman, speaking harshly to the man in a different language. She ripped the tape off my mouth. I gulped great lungs full of air and, as my vision cleared, I realised why I knew her. It was the woman at my front door with the broken car and children at home alone.

She pushed a mobile phone at my face. 'You call husband! Tell him he pay money or we kill you!'

'What? I don't know what you mean!'

She punched my face. Pain seared my cheek. I stared up at her, shocked.

'You tell Danny Malleta he pay now or we kill you,' she said. She pushed the phone at me.

'I don't know his number! We're not married any more!'

The man raised his arm to hit me and I cringed, turning my face into the stinking mattress. The woman shoved him away. 'I have number.' She pushed buttons and held the phone at my face.

Danny answered, shouting, 'Look, I'll get your money, just back the fuck off!'

'Danny!' I screamed. 'Help me!' Silence. *Danny!*

'Erica? What ... what's going on?'

I sobbed, 'They're going to kill me!'

'Erica! Jesus. Fuck!'

The woman took the phone and spoke into it. 'Get money today or we kill her.' They both left the room. They didn't replace the tape over my mouth. I leaned over the edge of the bed and vomited on the floor.

To distract myself from the fear and relentless pain in my head, I spent hours staring at the paint peeling off the walls – at the way it hung in sheets – and I thought that if it were my house, I couldn't help pulling at those sheets of paint. I couldn't just leave them hanging like that. I traced the faded carpet patterns and the criss-cross of threads in the worn parts, and I examined the bare light bulb hanging from the centre of the room. Dust covered the bulb like fur and I wondered absently if it had ever had a shade fitted. I inspected my own vomit, trying to remember what I'd eaten to make it look like that. And through a tiny gap in the boarded-up window, I watched the light change as the sun moved across the sky. I tried not to think of the friends I'd seen just last night. Last night? Maybe the night before. I might never see them again. I didn't dare scream or yell; terrified they'd tape my mouth again. Cockroaches scuttled over my body and past my face on the lumpy mattress. I focused on that so I wouldn't think about dying.

At one stage I thought I heard Danny's voice and I started to cry. I thought I was about to be saved. I could hear his panicked yelling. But then his voice was gone and everything went back to the way it was.

The woman didn't come back to the room, but the man spent a lot of time in there with me. Every time he opened the door, a rush of dank air would cause the bulb to swing a little. He sat on a chair in the corner with a knife in his hand, running his fingers up and down the blade. His mouth hung open. His teeth were missing or black. He smoked. The room was thick with smoke.

'Water, please?' I said hoarsely.

He shook his head.

'I need the toilet.'

He smiled. 'You piss your pant, lady.'

Time rolled by. My body ached. Stress caused me to sleep regularly, and escape my prison. I had a dream. A woman was yelling in the distance. I couldn't see her, but I was quite happy to stay there, in my dream with an invisible woman yelling. It was the closer scraping and banging sound that dragged me back to consciousness.

The yelling was real. Was Danny back? The man was standing in the corner now, fear in his eyes, his chair on its side. The woman's shouting got closer and closer. The door to my room crashed open and the woman flew backward through the air, arms and legs splayed like a starfish. She thumped onto the floor and howled, clutching her arm. The man shouted, waving the knife frantically at the door. I was surprised to see Jack standing there, gun hanging by his side. Our eyes met – tears sprang from mine and fury flashed in his. Danny stood behind Jack, crying.

Jack strode across the room to the man. The man dropped the knife and pressed himself into the corner, knees buckling. He looked terrified and sounded like he was pleading. Jack raised his arm, fist closed, speaking angrily, but I didn't understand what he was saying. The woman screamed and crawled to the man. Jack backed away, pushing his gun down the back of his jeans. He turned to Danny.

'Give them the money.'

Danny was snivelling outside the door, staring at me.

Jack lunged at Danny, grabbing his shirt and hauling him into the room. 'Give them the money, you piece of shit!'

Danny stumbled and cried harder. He pulled a roll of notes out of his pocket and threw it on the floor.

Jack snatched up the knife and sliced the tape around my hands and feet. He threw the knife; it stuck in the wall above the man's head. The man and woman cried out. Jack picked me up and carried me out of the room. Danny reached out to me with a shaking hand, but Jack shouldered him away. 'Don't touch her,' he said.

He carried me out a door and across a small backyard. I wrapped my arms around his neck and pushed my face into it, crying softly. His body jerked as he kicked something that cracked and crashed – a gate in a fence maybe – and he put me in the front seat of a four-wheel drive that was parked in a dark lane. I heard Danny shouting,

'Wait, please, wait!' He got into the back of the car and the door slammed shut.

Jack drove fast. It was dark, street lights flashed past, and with my face turned to the window, I caught a glimpse of my shattered reflection. I turned away and closed my eyes. I didn't know how much time had passed, but I assumed about twenty-four hours. I'd been given no food or water, and I could still taste vomit in my mouth. I smelled of my own pee.

Jack pulled up at the kerb of a busy road. He said to Danny, 'Get out.'

Danny said, weakly, 'Erica ...'

'Now!'

I heard the back door open and shut softly. Jack reached across to lay my seat back a little. He drove away and held my hand.

'So thirsty,' I said.

'I know. Won't be long.'

I gazed past Jack at an ocean of lights, all twinkling.

I pointed. 'What's that?'

'Footscray docks.'

I nodded, willing myself to associate those pretty lights with something nice. Something like Christmas maybe. Something other than this night.

He held my hand for the entire trip, releasing it only to make brief calls. On the phone he said, 'I've got her,' and I wondered who he was talking to. Once he held the phone out to me and said, 'It's Lucy,' but I turned my head away. I had nothing to say to anyone.

When we pulled up, two people were waiting for us. Joe opened Jack's door and a woman opened mine. She handed me a bottle of water.

'Erica, I'm Kate Grigg, Jack's doctor. I just want to check that you're okay.'

I nodded and chugged down all the water. Jack helped me out of the car and I stood, but my legs gave way. He picked me up and carried me into a huge house and up the stairs to a bedroom. He sat me on the bed and handed me some more water. I gulped some of it down and lay on my back. Jack sat next to me, holding my hand. Kate was in the corner, pulling things out of a bag.

'Is this your house?' I said eventually.

Jack nodded. 'Yes.'

I looked around the room. 'Is this your bedroom?'

'No. It's yours.'

It was a big bedroom. I wondered what his was like. 'I stink,' I said.

There was a brief smile. 'This is nothing. I once spent a week lying around in my own shit.'

He left the room and Kate spent some time examining me. I thought she looked lovely. Kind face, no make-up, mousey hair – fragile.

She said, 'Erica, did they do anything else to you I should know about?'

'No, they didn't.' I shuddered at the possibilities.

'It sounds like you spent some time unconscious.'

I thought about that. I knew my body, and I knew where I hurt. 'I'm sure, thanks, Kate.'

'Okay. You've got severe bruising and swelling on your face, and I can give you something for that. Everything else seems to be all right. Anything else worrying you?'

'Just the embarrassment. I wet myself.'

'It doesn't matter,' she said, kindly. 'Most people would under such circumstances.'

'Not because I was scared. They wouldn't let me use the bathroom.'

'Good for you. I hope it made a stain.'

I couldn't imagine those people noticing a stain on that bed. I don't think they'd even noticed my vomit on the floor.

Kate said, 'Let's get you into a bath.'

I tested my legs and walked with Kate's help next door to Jack's bedroom – it was even bigger – and into his bathroom. The tub was full of bubbles. I pulled off my clothes and asked Kate to throw them all away. She left a pair of pyjamas folded on a foot stool for me, and as she was leaving the room, she said, 'There's a toothbrush and some toiletries in your bathroom.'

I sank into the deep bath, sighed, and gazed around the room. There was a shower big enough for at least two. A long vanity with twin basins. The floor and walls were lined with huge, rectangular slabs of chocolate-coloured stone. The room was gorgeous, luxurious. I felt safe.

After the bath, I checked the mirror. The left side of my face was swollen and bruised. I smiled at the image. It was definitely me. I walked gingerly back to my room wearing Kate's pyjamas, and stopped in surprise. Curled up on my bed in a dead sleep was Axle, and on the floor by the bed was my handbag. I picked Axle up and hugged him to my chest, then crawled into the bed, exhausted.

Kate arrived with a plate of sandwiches and cooed over Axle, tickling him under the chin. She asked, 'Is he all right?'

'Yes, this is how he sleeps, like he's dead.' I picked up a sandwich, took a bite and spoke to Kate with a full mouth. 'I can't thank you enough for coming out tonight to see me.'

She smiled at my bad manners. 'You're part of the Team, Erica. It's what we do for each other.'

I smiled back. Part of the Team. She obviously didn't know I'd been sacked.

CHAPTER 19

Kate had given me a strong sedative. Axle was curled up on the pillow next to me, and I was drifting off to sleep when I heard Lucy's hysterical voice downstairs.

'Where is she?' I couldn't hear a reply, but Lucy said, 'Well, I'm taking her home with me!'

Jack's voice was now raised enough for me to hear. 'Erica's not going anywhere tonight, Lucy.'

'This is all your fault! She hasn't been safe since you came along!'

I didn't hear what he said, but Lucy shouted, 'Someone needs to protect her from *you*.' There were footsteps banging on the stairs, and my door was opened gently. 'Erica? Sweetie?' The room was very dark.

I whispered, 'Hey, Luce.'

She threw herself on me, sobbing. 'Oh my God, I can't believe what happened to you. Do you want to go home tonight? I can take you home with me.'

'No. I want to stay here.'

'Do you want me to stay with you? I'll just tell Jack Jones that I'm staying too, whether he likes it or not.'

'Stay if you want. Jack won't care. And Lucy, if you care about our friendship, you need to be much, much nicer to Jack.' I rolled onto my side, my back to her, and slipped into a deep sleep.

IN THE MORNING Lucy was next to me, asleep, breathing softly. I watched her for a while, rolled onto my back and looked around the room. Bright morning light sliced through the heavy drapes, and Axle was a gargoyle on the pelmet. I used my bathroom and peeked in the wardrobe. There were some clothes in there. Women's clothes. I found a dressing gown and put it on.

I stood under the pelmet, my arms outstretched. Axle leaped into them. I walked slowly down the stairs, gazing around, admiring Jack's home. Light filled all the spaces and there was a silence that made me want to tiptoe. The house was big, old and solid. Jack's grandmother's, I remembered. It had been restored and enhanced. Edwardian, I thought. Presumably the two bedrooms upstairs used to be four or even five separate rooms. The bottom of the stairs faced the double front doors that Jack had carried me through the night before. To my right was a closed door and a small passage that led around the back of the stairs, and to my left another set of double doors opened to a formal looking living room with a big old fireplace. Between that room and the stairwell, a much wider passageway led to what I assumed was the rest of the house. Jack's home was elegant, like him. I found my way to a modern room that was the kitchen and living area with a ceiling as high as the two levels of the house. The entire wall to the outside was glass, and it was open to the garden outside. It was a beautiful day.

Jack sat at a large stone table on the terrace, reading the paper, drinking coffee. He smiled up at me, but then he looked concerned. I'd caught a glimpse of myself in a mirror on the stairwell. The swelling had gone down but the left side of my face was black.

He said, 'Hey.'

I said, 'Hey.'

I set Axle down and he dashed past Jack, leaping into the air, chasing invisible butterflies. I sat at the table.

'Cereal? Toast? Kangaroo?' said Jack.

''Roo.'

Jack called out, 'A whole kangaroo for Erica, please, Joe.'

I looked over my shoulder at Joe, who had magically appeared in the kitchen. He smiled and pulled eggs out of the fridge. His massive arms were heavily tattooed and his hair was standard army issue. He was a big, scary man in an apron.

'Joe,' I said, 'did you bring my kitten here last night?'

'I did. I hope you don't mind. He's an interesting little devil.' Joe rubbed his arm.

'Thank you. That was really nice. I would have worried about him.'

'He ate a big can of tuna.'

I nodded, felt a stab of guilt. 'He would have been hungry.'

We all looked at Axle. He was way up the trunk of an oak tree that dominated the vast, manicured backyard. He spotted something worth risking his life for and leaped, flying through the air, landing on the ground several metres below. I cringed and Jack made a hissing sound.

Jack and I looked at each other. I wasn't sure what to say.

'How did you sleep?' he asked.

'Like the dead. Lucy's still asleep.' I fidgeted with the salt and pepper shakers. 'I'm sorry about the way she spoke to you last night.'

'She's just watching out for you.'

I fidgeted some more. I could feel him watching me. 'I'm not sure if I want to talk about it,' I said, glancing up.

'That's entirely your call, but I recommend you do. Preferably with a professional.'

I nodded. 'How did you find out?'

'Malleta called Lucy, and Lucy called Degraves.'

'Really? What did JD say?'

'He told me he'd had a call you'd been taken.' Jack hesitated. 'Of course, we assumed it was something to do with me ... us. That wouldn't have been good for you.' He looked away for a moment and cleared his throat. 'I phoned Lucy. She was very distressed. Malleta had told her it was something to do with me.'

Bastard. 'He's a low-life.'

'Yes, he is, Erica. You need to stay away from him.'

I nodded my absolute agreement on that particular matter. 'How did you find me?'

'Malleta knew where you were. I picked him up and we drove there together.'

I remembered hearing Danny's voice earlier in the day at that house. Maybe I hadn't imagined it.

'What about those peo—' I broke off and Jack leaned across the table, squeezing my hand.

'Eat now,' he said. 'We'll talk more later.'

Joe appeared with a plate of eggs, bacon, mushrooms, spinach, tomato – all sitting on a fat piece of toast. I looked up at him. 'God, Joe, thank you. I'm absolutely starving.'

'Coffee? Tea?'

'Tea, thank you.'

I watched Joe walk back to the kitchen and I whispered to Jack, 'He looks more like he'd kill people than cook for them.'

Jack whispered back, 'He does both.' And winked. And I wondered if he was serious.

I tucked into my breakfast and looked around while Jack read his paper. The house folded around the terrace on both sides but one side was longer with tinted windows all the way along. I tried to see through the windows, but the morning glare made it impossible.

'That's Joe's wing,' said Jack.

I blushed at being caught. 'Does he live here too?'

'He does. He works for me, but he's also a friend.'

Lucy walked into the room and cleared her throat. I glanced over my shoulder. 'Hey, Luce.'

She seemed horrified, presumably at the sight of my face. She said tightly, 'Good morning.' She nodded briefly at Jack.

Jack said to her, 'How did you sleep?'

'Okay, I suppose.'

Joe asked Lucy if she'd like some breakfast. She said, 'No, I'm leaving. I just came out to say goodbye.'

'Come and sit,' I said to Lucy and pulled out a chair.

She came without argument and sat, hands folded in front of her, staring at them.

'Luce, what happened to me had nothing to do with Jack.' She glanced at me and at Jack. 'Danny owed money to those people and they took me to force him to pay. He lied to you, Lucy. Danny not only put my life in danger but also Jack's. In fact, I strongly suspect it was Jack's money he gave them.'

I looked at Jack and he shrugged. 'Doesn't matter.'

'So, do you understand? I said. 'Jack probably saved my life and Danny's too. And on top of that, he's put himself at risk with those people, and involved himself in something that the police would possibly like to know about.'

She sat slack-jawed for a moment, then dropped her head and whispered, 'I'm so sorry.' She looked at me. 'Oh, honey, your beautiful face ...' She started to cry, which made me cry, and we hugged until Jack interrupted by swearing loudly.

Axle was sitting on his shoulder, claws digging in to keep his balance. I wiped my face. 'He totally loves you,' I said.

'Yeah, well, I wish he wouldn't.'

Lucy stood and walked around the table to Jack. She gently lifted Axle off his shoulder. 'Jack, I'm truly sorry for the things I said.'

'It's okay,' he said. 'I understand where you're coming from.'

She looked at me and tears welled in her eyes again. 'I don't know what I'd do without my friend.'

I walked with Lucy to the front door. I asked her if she'd come and stay with me for a few nights until I felt better, safer, whatever. Of course she would, she said.

I asked her not to tell anyone about what had happened, mainly because I didn't want to have to relive it over and over as friends questioned me about it.

I looked at my watch. It was 8am. 'Is it Tuesday morning?' I asked Jack.

'It certainly is.'

'I'm not sure what to do. I don't know what to tell my boss.' Obviously I hadn't turned up to work yesterday.

'JD's taken care of that,' he said. 'Apparently Celia took a call from you saying you're unwell.'

'Oh, well, I'd better call Rosalind. She won't be happy.'

Jack nodded.

I said, 'And then, I guess ... can you drive me home?'

'You're welcome to stay here.'

'Oh, thank you, but Lucy'll stay with me until ... anyway, I should go home. Back in the saddle and all that. Can't hide here forever.'

He nodded slowly. 'I've organised for someone to change your locks and install a security system.'

'Really?'

'Is that all right with you?'

'How much will it cost?'

He smiled. 'You don't have to worry about that.'

'Right. Well, I'll get my bag and ...' I looked down at the dressing gown I was wearing. 'Do you mind if I borrow this?'

'Have a look in the wardrobe in your room. My sister visits every year. She keeps some things here.'

I went upstairs to change but first I checked my mobile phone. It had two missed calls from Lucy, one from Jack and four from a number I didn't recognise. Probably Danny's.

Rosalind didn't answer but I left her a message saying that I'd had a fall down some stairs and probably wouldn't make it into the office for a couple of days. I suggested she email me any work she wanted done. I knew she wouldn't hesitate to do so.

In the wardrobe I found jeans, a T-shirt and an old pair of runners that were half a size too big.

Back in the kitchen, Jack and Joe were bent over an iPad on the bench. Axle was also on the bench, eating what looked like red salmon from a very expensive dish. Jack looked up when I walked in.

'You found something to wear,' he said.

'Yes, thanks. I'll clean and return them.'

He turned back to what appeared to be a map on the iPad. 'Joe and

I'll visit that house in Footscray today, make sure they don't come near you again.'

My heart rate picked up. 'What will you do?'

'Just talk to them.' Jack and Joe glanced at each other and Joe smiled a little.

CHAPTER 20

We left Jack's house in his Mercedes with Axle standing on my lap, watching out the window like a dog. As we drove I realised that we were in one of the most exclusive parts of Brighton. We turned into North Road and passed the church Danny and I had been married in. My mother couldn't afford to live in Brighton, but that didn't mean she couldn't use one of their churches for her only daughter's wedding. I watched the gorgeous old building slide by and an involuntary shiver ran up my spine. I remembered that day, walking down the aisle and feeling so happy.

'Are you all right?' said Jack.

'What? Oh, yeah. I got married in that church.'

He nodded. As we turned onto Nepean Highway, he said, 'Erica, I need to know if you want to involve the police.'

I stared out the window, considering it. 'That wouldn't be good for you, would it?'

'No. But I'll handle it.'

'Then there's nothing to consider. No police. In fact, I'd rather not tell anyone.'

'All right, but I want you to see the Team's counsellor. I think you should work through this with a professional. I'll give you her number. You won't have to pay.'

I nodded reluctant agreement. 'This team. It's pretty substantial, isn't it?'

'Yes.'

'There must be a lot of people who believe in what you're doing.'

'There is.'

I thought about all the people secretly running around Melbourne doing secret anti-terrorist things. And not just anti-terrorist; all kinds of bad guys, it seems.

We met Richard the security guy at my house. He was parked out the front in his van that advertised a security system business. Richard seemed like a normal kind of guy, but I noticed he didn't bat an eye at the sight of my bruised face. Being battered and bruised was probably normal for Team members.

Jack and Richard followed me through my front gate. But I took two steps and stopped, staring at the space where I'd been grabbed. I broke into a sweat and started shaking. Jack guided me to a chair and sat me down. He took the house keys and opened the front door for Richard, then squatted in front of me.

'Okay?' he said softly but I shook my head, stood and walked across the tiny courtyard to the garden where I threw up all over my geraniums. It occurred to me that this was also the spot I'd found Jack with his bullet wound, but he didn't seem to have an issue with being here again.

While Jack worked with Richard I cleaned up the kitchen and checked my message machine. One from my mother, of course, because I hadn't turned up for Monday dinner. 'Are you dead?' she said. I didn't call her. Not yet.

The boys installed sensor lights in my small backyard and I made cups of tea and coffee, sat on a rickety old chair and watched, thinking that it was very nice of Jack to be doing all this for me. I also thought about the fact that the last time Jack and I were in my backyard together he had kissed me. I wished I could remember more about the night.

'Erica?'

I looked up. Jack was standing in front of me, smiling.

'Sorry, did you say something?'

'You were pretty lost in thought there.'

I could feel the blush starting. I'd probably had a smile on my face while I was lost in that thought.

'We've done as much as we can today,' he said. 'Richard will need to come back tomorrow. Is that all right?'

'Yes, of course.'

Richard left and I walked Jack to the front door where he said to me, 'Time will fix this. You won't always be afraid.'

I nodded. 'Thank you.'

'You've got my number.'

'Yes.'

'Feel free to call me if you're ever concerned about anything. Anything at all.'

'All right. Thanks, Jack.'

'Kate's coming to see you today.'

'I know. Thank you.'

He gave me a smile and a small chuck under the chin, and left. And I felt like crying. I went back inside, locked the front door, checked it three times, ran to the back door, locked it, shut everything up, all the curtains and blinds, then I turned all the lights on and stood in my living room and said, 'Oh, for God's sake.' So I opened all the curtains and blinds again, and my French doors so the sun and fresh air could come in. Axle wound around my legs and I said to him, 'I need something to do.'

I went back out the front to check my mail. There was a newspaper stuck in the street side of the letterbox so I went out my gate to get it. A tall man stood in front of me suddenly, blocking the path. I blinked up at him. The sun was behind his head so it was hard to make out who it was. Jack?

'Hi, Erica.'

Not Jack. It took me a moment to realise that it was the man from the Melbourne Cup – Shane McGann. I was frozen to the spot.

'What happened to your face?' he said.

'Are you looking for Jack?'

'Not necessarily.'

I pointed down the street. 'He just left.'

McGann reached up and ran a finger lightly down my face. 'Nasty bruises.'

I pulled back, surprised. And then, seemingly from thin air, Jack appeared, shoving McGann so hard his feet left the ground. He flew through the air, landing hard on the pavement. Jack rushed at him and hauled him to his feet. I heard McGann's T-shirt rip.

McGann held his hands up; Jack's nose was an inch from his.

'You're causing a scene, Jones.'

I looked around. Cars were stopping and people stared.

Jack shoved him away, saying nothing.

McGann scooped his car keys off the footpath and sauntered to his car. He looked back once. Smiled. We watched him drive away in a black BMW with a number plate that said GUNN1.

Jack's chest was heaving as he stared after McGann's car. I tugged on his arm, pulling him through my gate and into the house; I closed and locked the door.

'Oh, my God,' I said.

Jack ran a hand through his hair, agitated. 'I'm sorry.'

'What was that about?' My heart was racing, but not as fast as his, by the look of it.

He shook his head. 'I'm sorry, Erica, but you can't stay here.'

'What?'

'You need to come with me. Pack some things.' He strode back out the front door and stood on the footpath, looking up and down the street.

I didn't argue and as I threw some clothes in a bag, I got teary. Not teary upset; teary relieved. I wasn't ready to come back to my house. Not yet. I gathered up Axle, his things, my laptop and bag and once we were in Jack's car and moving, I said, 'Why did you come back?'

'I wasn't happy about leaving you there. Not at all.'

'Why was Shane McGann at my house?'

We stopped at a red light and he looked at me. 'To frighten you, maybe. I'm not really sure. What I do know is what he's capable of.' The red light changed and as we moved on, Jack said, 'Tomorrow I'll have Richard beef up the security system. We'll install panic buttons and cameras.'

Great. I'm being stalked by a psycho. And murderous kidnappers. Maybe I should feel flattered.

'You're safe from them all at my house,' he said, reading my mind.

Back at Jack's we unloaded my things and Jack told Joe what had happened with Shane McGann. The look on Joe's face and then the fact that he quickly tried to cover up that look added to my worry.

Jack said, 'Joe and I are going to see those people in Footscray, have a chat with them. Okay? You'll be right here for an hour or so? You've got my number.'

I nodded but I was still scared, and I was nervous about Jack and Joe going to that house. I wanted to throw my arms around Jack and beg him not to go. But they left, and I walked around the house making sure everything was locked. I cuddled Axle and it was comforting to hold him. He was getting bigger.

I took deep breaths, pulled myself together, and called Lucy to cancel her overnight visits. I couldn't tell her about Shane McGann. I just said Jack had offered for me to stay and I carried on about what a nice house it was and all that.

'You fancy him,' she said.

'I don't!'

'Are you okay?'

'Yeah. I guess. I feel safe here.'

And then I knew I had to call my mother. I found the kettle and made a cup of tea before picking up the phone.

'Hi, Mum.'

She was frosty. 'I do think you might have called me before now, Erica. I thought you were dead!'

'Really? I didn't see a missed call on my mobile.'

'It's not a mother's place to call a daughter's mobile telephone.'

'Who made up that rule?'

'I really don't think you ever consider your mother, dear.'

Big sigh. 'I've been really busy, Mum.'

'Doing what?'

Kidnapping, bombs, work, secret vigilante stuff, dinner party I'd rather Mum not know about. 'Well, I ... fell down some stairs and I've got a big bruise my face.'

'Heavens!'

'So I can't go to work for a few days.'

'Your father and I will visit you tomorrow. I'll make chicken soup.'

'Ah ... you can't come because ... I've got fleas in my house. And cockroaches.'

'Goodness!'

'And so I'm staying at Jack's.'

I heard a sharp intake of breath. 'Erica, what will people say? They'll say you're a hussy, that's what!'

'I don't think anyone apart from you will think I'm a hussy, Mum, but don't worry because I've got a chaperone.'

'Who's the chaperone?'

'Joe.'

'Joe? A man?'

'No. I said Joe ... anne. Jack's Aunty Joanne. She's staying with him at the moment.'

'Oh, well, I suppose. We'll come and visit you in Footscray, tomorrow.'

I flinched at the mention of Footscray. Not only because of my recent experience there, I'd forgotten I'd told Mum that's where Jack lives. 'Er ...'

'And I think you should invite Jack to Christmas lunch.'

What! 'Ah, Jack can't come. He's going to, um, New York.'

I managed to end the call without handing over an address, Footscray or otherwise.

The doorbell rang. There was a security system monitor next to the phone and I checked out the two people standing at the front door. It was Kate Grigg and another woman. I let them in.

Kate said, 'Hi, Erica. Jack said you were staying here a few days.'

She introduced the other lady as Gail, the Team's shrink. Well, she didn't say 'shrink'.

Kate said, 'Jack and I thought you and Gail should meet and have a chat.'

'Thanks. But I think I'll be okay.'

I made coffee and we talked for a while about other stuff. They were delighted with Axle. I told them where Jack and Joe had gone, and I got teary. I pretended I had something in my eye, but trying not to cry made it worse. And the fact that I was crying made me feel so upset, I started sobbing. And then I was laughing with embarrassment, and sobbing at the same time, which possibly made me seem like a lunatic.

Gail said, 'Why don't you and I go have a chat right now? Just to gauge where you are about it all.'

I thought that was fairly discreet of her, considering it was pretty obvious where I was. I found some tissues and followed Gail to the formal living room at the front of the house. We talked and I cried and found I did feel much better after verbalising my fears. Not only in relation to the kidnapping, but also in relation to Jack Jones. I hadn't realised how much I'd come to care about what happened to him. Afterward we moseyed out to find Kate sitting on the terrace, playing with Axle. A book was open on the table.

'Did you read your book, Kate?' I said.

She laughed. 'Not a chance. Not with this little monkey wanting attention.'

Kate checked out my face, gently prodded and poked, and we talked about things, and I cried a bit more. She handed me a bunch of tissues and I said, 'Thank you. I'm glad you both came by.'

'And here's some more Valium,' she said, handing me a small packet. 'Take one before bed. It'll help you sleep.'

I lay in a coffin. Two Asian people peered over the edge at me. They lowered the lid and I heard the screws turning. I tried to move my arms but the coffin was so narrow my arms were pinned. I tried kicking my legs but there was no room to move them. I tried lifting my head but the lid was too low. My breathing became shorter. I screamed and screamed and screamed.

I sat up, sucking in air.

My bedroom door opened and Jack's silhouette appeared. 'Are you okay?'

I nodded, trying to breathe, but he couldn't see that in the dark. He walked into the room and sat next to me on the bed, gently gripping my shoulders. 'Are you okay, Erica?'

'Yes.' It was barely a gasp.

He turned on the bedside lamp. 'Bad dream?'

'Yes.' My breath was coming back. 'I was in a coffin.'

'I'll get you a drink.' He left the room and came back a minute later with a glass of water. I gulped some of it down and lay on my back, staring at the ceiling. And started to cry.

He turned off the light and walked around to the other side of the bed. He lay beside me, on top of the covers, and gathered me into his strong arms. And I let him, falling instantly into a deep, dreamless sleep.

I WAS ALONE when I woke in the morning, and wondered if I'd dreamt the whole thing, including the coffin dream, which of course I had. I got up and went to the bathroom, then opened the drapes to let in some light. I looked up at Axle on the pelmet. 'Hi, baby.' I had a Valium hangover. I crawled back into bed. I hoped all the crying had finished. It was embarrassing.

There was a soft knock on my door and Jack walked in carrying a tray with a pot of tea for me, a coffee for him, and a rose from his garden. He was wearing running shorts, a singlet and a warm smile. I sat up as he put the tray on my bedside table, picked up his coffee and walked around the bed to sit on top of the covers, propping himself up with pillows.

'Good morning,' he said.

'Thanks for rescuing me, again.'

'My pleasure.'

'You're probably getting sick of it.'

'It's fine.'

'You know what?'

'What?'

'I feel okay.'

He seemed impressed. 'That's good. That's really good.'

I poured my tea. 'This is what girlfriends do,' I said. 'Sit up in bed together and gossip.'

Jack said, 'I could probably come up with some gossip.'

'Okay, tell me some gossip and it'd better be bitchy.'

He thought for a minute. 'All right, here's some gossip. I know this girl, let's call her Erica, who's staying in a big house in Brighton with two blokes, let's call them Jack and Joe. That's all very well, except Erica's mother is planning a visit, and she – the mother – thinks Erica is staying in Footscray with Aunty Joanne.'

I grimaced. 'What do you think Erica will do?'

'I think Erica will eventually see the sense in either calling off the visit or telling her mother the truth about where Jack lives, and dealing with the consequences.'

'She's waiting for me to let her know the address.'

'I know,' he said. 'What will you do?'

'I might confess. I'll tell her you won Tattslotto and bought a house in Brighton, and that I fell down your stairs trying to escape your advances.' I indicated my bruised face. 'Do you think Kate would mind posing as Aunty Joanne? I'll buy her a grey wig.'

Jack laughed. He apparently thought I was joking. He and Joe had laughed last night too, when I'd told them about my conversation with Mum, and Jack had said something about weaving tangled webs.

'Seriously though,' I said, 'I don't think I can get around it. Do you mind if my parents come here? Really?'

He kept chuckling, shaking his head.

'What's funny?'

'I don't mind at all,' he said. 'But I'm thinking this isn't exactly what I had in mind when I first started surveillance on you. Sitting up in bed discussing afternoon tea at my house with your parents, I mean.'

'I know. Sorry.'

'Why don't you just tell your mother you broke up with me?'

'You don't understand. My mother still hasn't recovered from my broken marriage. She blames me for Danny leaving. Couldn't possibly be a man's fault.' I shook my head. 'No. Eventually I'll tell her you died. Or got a job overseas or something.'

'Turned gay?'

'No. Because she'd blame me for that too.'

Axle leaped from the pelmet onto the bed. It was a long leap. He sat on Jack's lap and clawed it. 'God, that hurts!'

'He's making a nest.'

'Why does he always want to do it on me?'

'He loves you.'

'I wish he wouldn't.'

There was a minute of comfortable silence while I smiled at Axle and Jack winced and swore softly, before I spoiled the happy moment by saying, 'Jack, do you know who those people are?'

He knew I was talking about the kidnappers and he hesitated before answering. 'They told us their boss is an "Aussie man". They don't know his name. He tells them what he wants them to do and he pays them a small amount. Their contact is by phone; an untraceable mobile. They didn't know much else.'

'So ... do you think Danny owed money to this man?'

'Yes.'

'Could be anyone.'

'Yes. If I can find Malleta, I'll be asking him.'

'I might have his mobile number.'

Jack nodded and said, frowning, 'There's something else. Something the woman told me.'

'What?'

He looked at me for a long moment. 'She told me that Malleta grabbed the money back before he followed us out of the house.'

I felt sick.

Jack said, 'Do you think he would do such a thing?'

I didn't hesitate. 'Yes.'

'Which means there's still someone out there wanting his money.'

My stomach lurched. 'Okay.'

'I'm sorry to tell you that but you need to know.'

'Okay. I understand.'

I called my mother. Jack, Joe and I were sitting around the outdoor table, drinking coffee. Axle was chasing a fly.

I turned my back on the boys. 'Hi, Mum.'

'Oh, good, Erica. Now where does Jack live? Your father and I want to visit you today.'

'Well, Mum, here's the thing.'

'What thing, Erica? Do you know the address or not?'

'Well, it's just that Jack kind of lied about where he lives.' I heard

Joe snort with laughter. Jack walked around the table to stand in front of me, hands on hips, pretending to be cross.

I turned away from him, facing Joe again, who was chuckling.

Mum said, 'What on earth do you mean?'

'Well, it's just that Jack has so many women chasing him ...' More laughter from Joe. Jack went into the kitchen and started banging around.

'What is all that noise, Erica?'

'Oh, that's, um, Aunty Joanne. She's baking a cake.'

'Go on. What were you saying?'

'Well, it seems Jack lives in Brighton, not Footscray, and I really don't think you'd want to see my bruised face, Mum. It might upset you.'

'Well, I can understand why that poor darling man would tell a small lie about his wealth. There are so many hussies looking for a rich husband.'

'Yes.' I smiled at Jack. 'So many hussies.' He shook his head. 'Did you hear what I said about my face, Mum?'

'Yes, dear. Now give me the address.'

I handed over the vital information, hung up and looked at Joe. 'They're coming at two thirty.'

He said, 'I'd better bake that Aunty Joanne cake.'

'Really? You bake cakes?'

'Yep.'

'Thanks, Joe.'

Jack was making coffee on his big Italian machine. I walked up behind him and tickled his ribs. He moved away, his back to me.

'Are you ticklish?'

'Stop it.'

'You *are* ticklish!' I kept tickling. He laughed, giving in. He put his coffee down, turned and grabbed my wrists.

'And *you* are a little cow!'

I shrugged. 'I know. Sorry. But she still loves you and doesn't blame you for telling lies.'

'*I* didn't lie, *you* did!'

'She feels sorry for you being chased by women all the time.'

He threw his hands in the air, laughing, shaking his head. He picked up his coffee and walked back to the table where Joe was still smiling away.

I said, 'Now, you guys have to go somewhere when my parents come to visit. You could go see a movie or something? My treat.'

Jack glanced at Joe then back at me, mischief in his eyes. 'No. Joe and I are staying.'

'*Pleeeeeeeease*, Jack. Please go away. They'll be here any minute!' He was in his office upstairs, shuffling paperwork around on his desk. He ignored me. I got down on my knees next to his chair. 'I'm begging you.'

He looked down at me and smiled. 'No.'

'I'll cry.'

'Won't work.'

'You should be nice to me because I was kidnapped!'

The doorbell rang and I ran to answer it. 'Hi, Mum, hi, Dad. Look at my face. Aren't I clumsy?'

Mum touched my face, inspecting it briefly. 'I'm sure you'll live, dear.' She handed me a Tupperware container. Chicken soup, presumably.

Dad kissed me on my unbruised cheek and they walked into the house.

Mum said, 'Oh, how lovely! What a lovely home! Now, don't outstay your welcome, Erica. Remember what your grandmother used to say: fish and visitors go off in three days.'

I wondered if my grandmother had applied that rule to her lover, my biological grandfather. 'Come into the kitchen and have a cup of tea,' I said and led them through the house to where Joe was waiting, sitting on the sofa, reading. He'd had the decency to wear a long-sleeved shirt that covered his tattoos.

I put the soup in the fridge and introduced them. 'Mum, Dad, this is Joe. He's, um, Jack's cousin. Aunty Joanne's son.'

Joe shook hands with Dad.

'Brian, is it?' said Dad.

Joe said, 'It's Joe.'

I explained, 'Dad's a bit deaf.'

Mum asked, 'And where is your mother, Joe?'

'My mother? Oh, ah, Joanne. She's out this afternoon. She was sorry to miss you, but she made you a cake.' Joe was blushing. I felt bad about him having to lie for me. Not quite bad enough, though.

'Oh, well, that's very nice, and we'll meet another time, I'm sure,' said Mum.

Jack walked into the room and Mum gushed. He gave her a kiss and shook Dad's hand.

Mum said, 'Oh, Jack, you poor thing. All those hussies chasing you!' Her eyes cut to me. 'I bet you can't sleep at night. I'd lock my bedroom door if I were you.'

Jack said, 'I sleep all right, Mrs Jewell. Thanks for your concern.' Our eyes met briefly. His were laughing. Actually, they were in hysterics.

'Cup of tea, anyone?' I said and walked into the kitchen to put the kettle on.

Dad sat on the sofa and picked up the remote. Jack showed him how to turn on the monstrous TV, and asked, loudly, 'Would you like a whiskey, Mr Jewell?'

Dad smiled and nodded. Joe sat next to Dad and showed him how to use Foxtel. Dad was officially in heaven.

Mum stood with her back to me, looking at the television. I was pouring the tea when she said, 'Jack, such a shame you'll be in New York for Christmas.'

I poured tea all over the bench as I looked up, desperately seeking Jack's eyes. He handed Dad his whiskey, glancing at me, clearly understanding that there'd been yet another lie. He ignored my silent pleas.

'Actually, my plans have changed. I'll be in Melbourne at Christmas time.'

'Wonderful!' said Mum. 'Will you come for Christmas lunch? The whole family will be there.'

I shook my head, mouthing *No! No! No!* He smiled, still looking at me, and replied, 'I'd absolutely love to.'

Mum turned to me and said, 'Isn't that wonderful — Erica! Look at the mess you've made!' She marched over to the bench and picked up a cloth, mopping up the spilt tea. 'Goodness me. What man would marry such a clumsy girl?'

I thought I might vomit. Or cry. Or faint. Maybe all of them.

Mum delivered cups of tea to everyone, and said, 'So, dear, are there terminators at your house?'

Jack and I glanced at each other.

'Terminators?' I said.

'Yes. For the fleas. I assume you'll get in the terminators.'

CHAPTER 22

The next morning, I lay awake thinking about Danny. I'd had a pretty confronting dream about him being beaten to death by a gang of Asian people. Can't imagine where that came from.

I got up and rifled around in my bag, looking for my mobile phone. I found it and scrolled to the missed calls log, looking for the unknown number that had called me four times. I found the number, sat on the bed and dialled. Surprisingly, he answered.

'Erica.'

'Where are you, Danny?'

'Not in Melbourne, but that's all you need to know.' I could hear the ocean in the background. Actually, I could hear the crash of surf.

'You're on the Gold Coast.' It was his favourite haunt, and now I thought it suited him perfectly. Surfers Paradise was glittery on the surface, but when you scratched away a bit, its true nature showed itself and that wasn't always nice. Just like Danny Malleta.

He said, 'Are you okay?'

'As if you care.'

'I *do* care. I can't tell you how I feel about what happened. I thought they were going to kill you.' I could hear the distress in his voice, but

143

that meant about as much as if he'd said, 'I didn't mean to sleep with that blonde.'

'Yeah, well, if you were that concerned you wouldn't have snatched the money back, you bastard.'

Silence.

'Who'd you owe it to?'

'What —'

'We know it's not the kidnappers. We know they're working for someone else.'

He hesitated. 'I can't tell you.'

'Well, I want that money. It's Jack's. You have no right to keep it. Not to mention what you stole from me.'

I heard him take a deep breath. 'I *want* to give you the money, but I can't give it to you now. I'm in really deep shit.'

'No shit.'

'But I'm glad you're okay.'

'I will be.'

I listened to Danny's heavy breathing. 'Erica,' he said, finally, 'I was an idiot to let you go. But you deserve someone much better than me.' He was right. I did. And it felt good to acknowledge that to myself. 'And I'm glad you've got someone like Jack to look after you.' His voice faltered slightly. 'I have to go.' Maybe he really was as distressed as he sounded.

'All right, Danny. Just stay away from Melbourne, and from me,' I said, not very convincingly.

'Bye, Erica.' His voice broke and he hung up.

I chewed on my thumbnail; dug around in my bag again and found the card for Mr Bill Lucas, Senior Detective. I held the phone in my right hand and Bill Lucas's card in my left, like a scale, weighing my options. If Danny went to jail, he might survive the ordeal, but not well. Then again, he might be safer in jail than on the streets with very bad people hunting him. Maybe I just needed to leave it to the Universe to sort out, and get on with rebuilding my own life, Danny Malleta finally out of it.

I dialled Bill Lucas's number and left a message saying who was calling, and that Danny Malleta had been spotted on the Gold Coast. I walked into the bathroom and tossed the card at the small waste bin, thinking that I really needed to do something about a divorce.

FOR THE REST of that day and on Friday I sat at my computer in Jack's formal dining room, working on all the stuff Rosalind sent through to me. Not once did she ask how I was, but I didn't expect it anyway.

Joe was generally home and Jack generally wasn't. Tending his other businesses, Joe said. At night we were all there and I offered to cook but Joe, thankfully, wouldn't let me.

On Saturday morning I walked into the kitchen – last one up as usual. Jack was sitting at the dining table reading the paper, home already from his 2000 kilometre run to Sydney and back. He looked up at me as I approached.

'Morning,' I said, smiling because I felt like I was living in a resort.

'Good morning.' He smiled back.

I sat opposite him, looked at the paper and asked, 'Any news? No, don't tell me. I'd rather just pretend that the whole world is like this.' I swept an arm through the air.

He smiled some more and said, 'The cleaning lady found something in your room yesterday.'

I had a sudden horrible thought that I'd left my vibrator lying around, but then I remembered I didn't have it with me at Jack's.

'You're blushing,' he said.

I cleared my throat and looked away. 'What did she find?'

Jack tossed Mr Bill Lucas, Senior Detective's card on the table.

'Are you spying on me?' I said, surprised to hear myself say that.

'Absolutely not. It was on the floor in the bathroom and she thought it might be important. That's all.'

I nodded. 'That's fine, but it was supposed to be in the bin.'

'I assumed that, but my concern is *why* it's in the bin.'

I sighed heavily. 'I spoke to Danny two days ago. He's on the Gold Coast.'

'So, why aren't you calling Senior Detective Lucas and telling him that?' Jack watched me over the top of his reading glasses.

'I did. I left a vague message for him, but I feel bad about it. Actually, Jack, I'm really worried about Danny. He wouldn't cope in prison. And I think he really is desperate.'

Jack continued with the intent gaze, possibly wondering if I'd totally lost my mind. He didn't ask me if I'd totally lost my mind, but he did say, 'Do you remember what he put you through recently?'

A small shudder ran up my spine. How could I ever forget? 'About the money Danny took; I can pay you back but not straight away. Is that okay?'

'I don't care about the money, Erica. That's not a problem. But Danny Malleta *is* a problem.'

'I know.'

'I'd like to know who it is he owes.'

'He wouldn't tell me.'

Jack nodded. 'I won't be nice if I ever meet him again. You do know that, don't you?'

'Yes, I know.'

'All right. Nothing more to say on that subject.'

I looked at him appreciatively. 'You're a good person, Jack Jones.'

He turned a page of his newspaper and huffed. 'There are plenty who wouldn't agree.'

THAT AFTERNOON I sat at my computer, but this time not working on Dega stuff. I googled 'Shane McGann' to see what I could find out about him. If I was going back to my house I needed to know who I was dealing with. With Danny out of the picture, this reduced the potential threat to just one stalking psychopath.

I couldn't find much information about the rape cases – the ones that were dropped because the women were obviously too scared to testify. But I did find something important. The name of one of the women: Eloise Degraves.

· · ·

THE NEXT MORNING, Jack and Joe were already up and about when I decided to grace them with my presence.

Joe went to make breakfast for me but I told him I'd do it, so I made toast and a cup of tea while Joe made coffee, and we all sat at the dining table.

'Eloise Degraves,' I said.

Jack and Joe glanced at each other.

'I googled Shane McGann,' I told them.

Jack nodded. 'JD's daughter.' Nothing more to say about that.

I said, 'I couldn't find the name of the other woman.'

'Why do you want to know?' Jack asked.

'You know why.'

He nodded again. 'Yes, she was associated with John Degraves.'

Why did I feel so sick suddenly? This is what I expected, after all. 'And, so, do you think this is why Shane McGann's interested in me?'

Jack sat back. 'To be honest, Erica, I don't know.'

Joe kept his eyes down.

'Anyway,' I said, 'I think it's time for me to go home.'

The boys stared at me. 'Why?' said Jack.

'Because as long as Shane McGann is alive and kicking in Melbourne, I'm a potential target. And I can't hide here forever, as much as I like the idea of it.' I gazed around at the beautiful home and its expensive interior, and sighed.

Jack said, 'You're welcome here, you know that.'

I nodded. 'Yes, thank you. Both of you. For everything.'

The weeks leading up to Christmas flashed by. I'd had a week off work to let my bruised face heal and then I worked late to make up for it. Things had quietened down about the stolen fertiliser, but I had to other things to do, including BIG's new image.

Jack called me every day for a week and told me he was having me followed to and from work. Lucy stayed with me every night for the first week, then cut back to a couple of times a week until I finally said I thought I'd be all right. I told her about Shane McGann because it wasn't fair on her to not know the potential danger. Of course Lucy hated Jack again, blaming him for my position. And of course she wasn't the least bit afraid of Shane McGann and any nasty thing he might consider doing.

Jack had told me to set my house alarm when I went to bed – reminded me I now had panic buttons – and to call him if there was anything, even a minor suspicion, that McGann was sniffing around.

Then I didn't hear from Jack for ages and I assumed he'd forgotten about Christmas Day at my parents'. Well, I hoped he'd forgotten.

But one morning, a week before Christmas, he called me and said, 'Just letting you know McGann's been spotted in Sydney.'

'Oh! That's great!' I felt hugely relieved.

'Yeah. He's up to something though.'

'What?'

'We don't know. Shady meetings with shady people.' And then his voice brightened considerably as he changed the subject to something much more horrifying. 'So,' he said, 'I'll pick you up on Christmas Day. What time?'

Oh, bugger, bugger, bugger!

'Jack, please don't come. My family is weird and it'll be awful and you'll hate it and I'll hate it even more than usual because I'll be worried about you.'

'You don't want me to be on my own on Christmas Day, do you?'

I hadn't thought of that. I suspected he was bluffing and I was sure I could hear him smiling but I mumbled anyway, 'S'pose not.'

'So, what time should I get you?'

JACK ARRIVED EARLY to pick me up for Christmas with my family.

I complained, 'You're early! You're always early. I don't even know what I'm wearing yet.' I was dressed in a sarong, and my hair was still wet. Axle leaped from my bed and Jack caught him mid-flight at the bedroom door. They made a good team.

Jack put Axle down, turned and reached for something on the ground outside. It was a big box-shaped gift, covered in gold wrapping and with a giant gold bow. 'Merry Christmas, Erica.'

'Oh ... Jack ... oh. I didn't get you anything.'

He smiled. 'I didn't expect you to.'

'I mean, my family does a Kris Kringle. That's usually the only thing I buy.'

'Let's open it,' he said and walked with the box to the kitchen, and Axle and I followed. He set it on the bench.

As I was pulling at the paper, he said, 'You could say this is really a gift for myself.'

'Oh?' It was a coffee machine! An expensive-looking Italian one. 'Wow! Jack, thank you!' We smiled at each other and of course I needed to properly show my appreciation. I leaned toward him and he leaned in to me, and I went to kiss his cheek but he turned his head at the last second and somehow I managed to plant a big wet kiss on the corner of his mouth.

We both laughed, embarrassed. Well, I was.

'So,' I said. 'Can I assume you're planning on having the odd coffee here?'

'Sure, I might be passing some time. You never know.'

I finished getting ready while Jack watched Foxtel with Axle sitting on his shoulder. I grabbed my food contribution for the day: king prawns bought the day before at Queen Victoria Market. Jack had offered to bring champagne.

We left my house and while Jack locked the front gate, I stood on the pavement looking up and down the street for his car.

'Where's your car?' I said.

He pointed to the old convertible in front of me. It was a white Mustang.

'This is yours?'

'This is my sweetheart,' he said, patting the fender. He opened the boot. There was an Esky in there, whose lid he opened for the prawns.

'Jack! Oh my God!' There was a dozen bottles of Bollinger in there. 'You've spent way too much on all this.'

'Well, there's a big crowd, and you'll drink two bottles.'

'No way! Absolutely *no* champagne for me today.'

He opened the door for me and I sank into the soft red leather. I was relieved he was bringing this car. I couldn't bear the thought of my family making a fuss about a Mercedes or some expensive thing, and this old one was the kind any car lover might have.

'My brother will love this,' I said. I could imagine him getting excited about having such a car to pick up girls in.

Jack started the engine and its throaty gurgle vibrated through me. He gave it a small rev, and the whole car shook. As we pulled out from the kerb, he said, 'They don't make V8s like they used to.'

Traffic was typically heavy for lunchtime on Christmas Day, but I didn't mind because I was in no hurry. Sitting in that open car with

Jack made me think that life probably couldn't get much better, but as we pulled up outside my parents' house, I started to feel sick. Oh well, I thought, the good life didn't last long.

Jack popped the boot to unload the stuff saying, 'You know, when I recruited you, I really hadn't given much thought to this whole scenario.' He glanced over his shoulder at my parents' house. 'At the time, I was thinking only about our needs, and how we could, well, use you. I really didn't consider you or your family. And I'm sorry about that now, Erica. I don't want any of you to be hurt in any way.'

'Thanks, Jack, but it's okay. They'll get over you. Or not.'

He smiled, opening his arms wide and I stepped into them. We hugged each other and as I stood there with my arms around his neck, feeling very happy and smoochy, I glanced at the window of my parents' living room. Eighteen pairs of eyes stared out at us.

I OPENED MY PARENTS' front door and reminded Jack, 'No champagne for me, remember?'

'I remember.'

We walked in and stood at the wide entrance to the lounge room. Every person there was gawking at us. Some were smiling. I thought I heard a pin drop. My cousin's six-year-old son walked up to Jack and said, 'Are you going to marry Erica?'

Jack grinned and ruffled his hair. The crowd held its breath.

I looked up at Jack. 'Well,' I said, 'let's open that champagne, shall we?'

CHAPTER 24

*A*fter the events of Christmas day, I had assumed Jack would move overseas, have plastic surgery, fake his own death, anything to get me – and my family – out of his life. I mean, the day had gone exactly as expected, with Grandma telling Jack about her affair and Dad farting in front of everyone and my uncles having a punch-up in the backyard and my mother giving me a lecture about sex and me getting drunk and beating up my brother, and my mother wondering where she went wrong. In relation to me, I mean.

But Jack called me on Boxing Day, thanked me for 'a fantastic day' and sounded like he quite liked me. I'd thought we'd said goodbye forever, again, when he dropped me home and kissed my cheek.

'What are you doing New Year's Eve?' he said.

'Maybe something with Steve and Lucy. Why?'

'JD's having a party. Would you like to come?'

I didn't say anything. Was he asking me on a *date*?

He continued, 'I want to return the favour. You treated me to a wonderful Christmas, and I think John's party'll be fun.'

Was he on drugs? 'Hang on a minute. First, *I* didn't treat you to anything. My mother invited you to Christmas, not me. Second, it wasn't wonderful. It was typically awful.'

'I don't get to do that kind of thing very often,' he said. 'I thought it was a nice family get-together.'

And now I felt guilty and unappreciative. And, yes, he was clearly on drugs.

'So,' he said, 'would you like to come? I've got some guys on security so I'll be working, but not so much I won't have time for a dance. Joe'll be there. And Kate's invited. She's JD's doctor, too.'

'Well, all right then. I'd love to!'

I SPENT the entire day getting ready for JD's New Year's Eve party. But when I pulled my dress out of the wardrobe – the only dress that could possibly be suitable for a party at John Degraves' house – I saw the red wine stain that I'd completely forgotten about from the last time I wore it, probably two years earlier. I stared at it in dismay, visualising my New Year's Eve now spent at home with Foxtel instead of foxy people. And I was absolutely *over* the whole never-going-out thing. I called Lucy, not knowing how she'd react to my dilemma. I'd already told her how I was spending New Year's Eve and she'd been annoyed that I was still seeing Jack but delighted I was going on a date.

'Luce, my dress has got a stain. It's totally wrecked and I've got nothing else to wear!'

'Sweetie, get ready for your party. I'll be there in ten!'

Lucy arrived eight minutes later, rushed in the door and threw a piece of silver foil at me.

'Here you go. You'll look gorgeous in this!'

I held the tiny, weeny snippet of material between two fingers. 'You have got to be joking.'

'Oh, c'mon. Just try it.'

Apart from clothes, I was ready to go. I looked at my watch, knowing that Jack would be early. I reckoned I had time to try Lucy's dress and reject it.

I threw off my robe and Lucy rolled the sheath over my head, tugging it down past my hips. I gasped, trying to breathe. 'Keep pulling it down.'

'That's it, honey. It's down as far as it's going.'

'What!' I spun around to check out the full-length mirror. The dress sat mid-thigh and clung to my body like Glad Wrap. I was about to shriek my protest when there was a knock at the door. Lucy and I stared at each other, my face expressing horror, Lucy's delight. She ran for the door.

'No!' I squealed as she yanked it open.

From my bedroom, through the wide-open door, I watched Jack step into my house. Lucy turned him immediately to face me. I stood with my mouth hanging open and he mirrored my expression. His eyes slowly travelled the length of my body. I waited for the laughter.

He blew out a long breath. 'You look —'

'I know! I look ridiculous. Just give me a minute to change.'

'What? Don't you *dare* change out of that dress!'

I stared at Jack and Lucy, who was beaming at me. I looked from one to the other, waiting for one of them to burst out laughing. Surely they couldn't seriously think I looked ... good?

Joe was driving the Merc and they'd already picked up Kate. We were getting there early because Jack had to discuss security arrangements with JD. I sat in the back with Jack.

Kate said, 'I'm so glad you're coming tonight. I don't know many people.'

Joe said over his shoulder as he pulled away from the kerb, 'You look very lovely, Erica. You'll have to save me a dance.'

I said, 'Why, thank you, Joe. I will. You look very dashing and it's nice to see you off duty for once.' Which of course he wasn't.

Kate laughed and Jack said, 'Are you two right?' He leaned toward me. 'But Joe's right. You look lovely, and sexy. Are you looking forward to it?'

'Yep. I am, as a matter of fact.'

He smiled. 'Me too.'

I said, 'It was very nice of you to send my mother flowers. She needed three vases to fit them all.'

'It was a pleasure.'

'You know she's planning our wedding.' Which was probably a stupid thing to say but everyone laughed and Jack gave me a warm smile.

'No champagne, no way.'

'Boring,' said Jack.

'I want to remember the night.' I also didn't trust myself not to drink too much and vomit or pass out on JD's expensive-looking furniture – or worse, try to kiss someone.

I looked around the ballroom of John Degraves' magnificent Toorak mansion, which was at the top end of a secluded, leafy court. The room was decorated with helium-filled, colourful balloons that bounced on the ceiling in the breeze caused by the air-conditioning. Everything looked gorgeous, festive. There was a band set up at one end with a dance floor, and the French doors at the other end of the room opened onto a terrace garden. It was a balmy night and I felt terribly happy.

Joe had parked inside the grounds of JD's home and when we walked inside, JD didn't seem surprised to see me. We'd arrived a half-hour earlier than everyone else and Kate and I had been fussed over by Mrs Degraves and the staff while Jack, Joe and JD discussed security arrangements. Jack had told me that JD had received some threats after the stolen fertiliser business, but I already knew that. The threats and anger from the public had been pretty loud and widespread.

Jack's security team arrived and so did Rosalind. She headed my way without bothering to hide her annoyance.

Jack said, 'I'll leave you to chat with your boss. I need to go see my guys.'

'No! Don't leave me with her!' I grabbed his arm.

He laughed and walked away.

Rosalind arrived and demanded to know how I scored an invitation.

I said, 'Oh, you know, Jack and JD have become friends since the

Melbourne Cup.' I added, 'We spend quite a bit of time with John and Sue.' And smiled.

Her eyes narrowed and she wafted away.

Kate was chatting with Sue Degraves and I looked for Jack. His guys were standing around him, listening as he pointed and gave instructions. Richard the security van man was there, and someone who looked like Rambo. I gazed around the room, smiling, happy, looking for someone else I might know. A very good-looking man approached. I recognised him.

He said to me, 'I'm hoping you're not involved with anyone here so we can elope tonight.'

I giggled.

He took my hand and kissed it. 'Charlie Heiner at your service,' he said. 'Any service at all.'

'We've met before,' I said with a giggle. Charlie Heiner was JD's nephew, a society A-lister, and a playboy, but that's not how we met.

'Surely you're not one of my past conquests. I'd remember you,' he said just as Jack arrived at my side. Charlie grinned broadly and with just enough cheek to let me know his tongue was firmly in it.

I looked up at Jack, who was rolling his eyes.

'Hello, Charlie,' said Jack.

Charlie said, 'Jack,' and they shook hands briefly.

I said, 'No, I met you a couple of years ago at a Dega function. I was with ... my ex-husband.'

He frowned.

'Danny Malleta?' I said. 'You and he got on quite well, I think.'

His smile returned. 'Well, I don't remember him, but now I remember you.' He stepped back and looked me up and down. He did it in a way that made light of the action, not to offend. 'You've changed, Erica.'

'Well, I'm impressed you remember my name!'

He stared into my eyes. 'As I said, I remember you well. But you have changed. You seem more ... worldly.' This time he kissed my palm.

'Well, it's amazing what divorce can do for a woman's complexion,' I said, glancing at Jack.

And Jack was eyeing me with suspicion, like he'd just noticed I'd grown talons or something.

I WAS in full flirt mode, having the time of my life. I danced a lot, mostly with Charlie when he wasn't on the terrace glued to his mobile phone. Jack seemed especially occupied with a particular leggy blonde, whom I was yet to meet.

Charlie asked me very early in the evening how involved I was with Jack. I told him that we were just friends. He wanted my phone number so we could go out. I considered it. Why not?

At the stroke of midnight I was standing on the terrace, talking to Kate. Charlie found me and tried to kiss me on the mouth. I turned my head and let him kiss my cheek. 'You'll have to give me your phone number,' he slurred and staggered away.

Kate said, 'He's a charmer but I wouldn't get too close if I were you.'

'Yes. I'm starting to realise that.' Actually, I'd been trying to avoid Charlie for the past hour. He wasn't a nice drunk, and I'd changed my mind about going out with him.

Someone called, 'Speech!' and everyone moved inside.

A hand grabbed mine from behind. I turned angrily, expecting Charlie, but it was Jack.

'Whoa!' he said, ducking. 'Were you about to hit me?'

'Sorry, I thought you were Charlie.'

'Is he giving you a hard time?'

'Well, let's just say he's very persistent.'

'You want me to take out a contract on him?' he said but his eyes were smiling, and I smiled back.

'Everything tight and secure?' I said.

'Seems to be.'

'Are you going to have a drink?'

'I will. In a minute.' He put his arm around my waist. 'Happy New Year, Erica.'

I put my hands on his chest. 'Wait a minute,' I said. 'Are you going to kiss me?'

He chuckled. 'I thought I might. It's tradition, isn't it?'

I didn't say anything but I could feel the blush grow on my face as his moved closer. I closed my eyes. His lips pressed softly onto mine and I waited for the kiss to end but it didn't. In fact, he put his other arm around me and held me against him, and my hands found their way around his neck, and just as the kiss was about to get pretty serious, there was an earth-shuddering explosion. We pulled apart and blinked at each other. Fireworks, I thought. Private, expensive, New Year's Eve fireworks organised by John Degraves, just for us.

The next explosions came in quick succession. BOOM! BOOM! BOOM!

'Fireworks?' I said, but Jack was already running away from me. There were two more blasts as I followed him through the house to the front door. As I ran out onto the street, Jack, Joe and many of the other party guests were standing on the footpath, surveying the devastation. The cars parked down one side of the street had blown up – pieces of metal flung about like confetti. Flames spiked from the burning vehicles and black smoke puffed straight up into the still night air, which was now filled with the stench of burning rubber. A couple of Jack's guys were running down the street, guns drawn. People were appearing tentatively from inside their homes, and John Degraves was striding toward a bewildered-looking neighbour.

I stood next to Jack staring, disbelieving, at the scene. This was not something you'd expect to see in your average Toorak street.

Jack turned to the growing crowd of party guests and shouted, 'Everyone inside, *now!*'

Wives tugged on husbands' arms. People shuffled back into the house.

Jack said to Joe, 'Get the neighbours inside. Clear the street and secure it. Be forceful. No guns. See if anyone's hurt.' Joe ran off, issuing orders to the men and women who seemed to be familiar – comfortable even – with this kind of horror.

Jack turned to me, handing me his mobile phone. 'Call emergency. Tell them we need everything including the bomb squad. More detonations likely.'

'More? Are you serious?'

'Do it!'

I walked away from Jack and the noise, dialling 000.

Charlie Heiner was standing near Jack when I returned. Jack was pointing, snapping orders, directing his team. I stood between Charlie and Jack, watching the far end of the court where onlookers were appearing for a stickybeak. A man emerged from a house and ran toward an undamaged car. I grabbed Jack's arm and pointed. 'Look!'

Jack's voice boomed over the noise and confusion. '*Joe!*'

Joe was hustling people along the street. Jack pointed to the man, now climbing into his car, and Joe bolted across the street as the car pulled out of its parking spot. He opened the driver's door and dragged the shrieking man from the car, abandoning it in the middle of the street, sending him back inside his house. A crowd was building at the end of the court. Some of the Team took up post there, stopping further intrusion by onlookers; some guarded front doors preventing neighbours leaving their homes; others jogged back up the street to where we were standing to receive more orders. Kate was running around, looking for wounded people. I thought maybe I could help her. I turned to ask Jack if I should do that but he was jogging down the middle of the street. I saw him walking through the crowd at the end of the court, seemingly looking for someone.

I said to Charlie, 'I wonder what he's looking for?'

But Charlie was watching too intently to notice or hear me.

Jack came back and pushed me toward the house. 'Go inside,' he said.

'But I want to help.'

He pointed at the house, his arm fully extended. '*Now!*'

I jumped with fright, feeling like a naughty child, and Charlie took my hand.

'Come on, Erica, I'll look after you.'

He turned to the house, pulling me away. But Jack grabbed Charlie's arm and they glared at each other.

Charlie said, 'What's your problem?'

'You don't seem too concerned about any of this.' Jack jerked his head at the devastation.

Charlie shrugged. 'Not my car.' He tried to shake off Jack's hand.

'Mind your manners,' Jack said, glancing at me.

'Erica's a big girl. I'm sure she can look after herself.' Charlie snatched his arm away, and grinned boyishly at me. 'Let's get a drink,' he said and led me toward the house. I didn't look over my shoulder to see if Jack was watching us, but I suspected he was. That is, until I heard another explosion, followed by another and another. I threw myself on the ground, arms wrapped around my head, curled up on John Degraves' front lawn through two more booms.

I stayed like that for a few moments until I felt a hand on my shoulder, and Jack's concerned voice saying, 'Are you all right?'

I peeked out from under my arm. 'I think so.' I sat up and looked around. A car's side mirror was growing out of the perfectly manicured lawn nearby. 'More cars?' I said unnecessarily, trying not to visualise the new garden ornament embedded in my ribs.

'Yes.' He helped me up. 'You need to go inside.'

I SENT Charlie to get me a drink while I watched through the window as emergency services, including the bomb squad, arrived. Lights and sirens from every direction. A few of Jack's men had injuries from flying debris and Jack had some minor cuts, but he brushed the ambulance fuss away, sending them to tend to others. Charlie appeared with two glasses of champagne and tried to drag me away from the window. But I wouldn't leave. I wanted to watch Jack, make sure he was all right. Charlie went to find someone more interesting to play with, and that suited me just fine.

I watched JD and Jack having what looked like a fairly heated discussion. JD seemed angry. Did he blame Jack for the explosions? They eventually came inside and I could see Jack searching the room.

I went up to him, tugged on his sleeve. 'Are you looking for me?'

'Yes.' He put his hands on my arms and looked me over. 'Are you okay?'

'Yes, are you?'

He nodded and looked around. 'It's over. Nothing more we can do.'

'Do you know who did it?' I said and he shook his head, frowning, about to say something, when Charlie appeared.

He said, 'Come on, Erica. I'll take you home.'

'I'm not getting in a car with you, Charlie. You're drunk.'

'You can drive. It's a Porsche.'

Whoop-de-do, I was thinking as Jack put a hand on my arm. 'Fuck off, Heiner,' he said, which surprised me. Jack was usually so cool, and he rarely swore. 'Where were you, by the way? Ran inside and left Erica out there?'

Charlie glared at Jack, then stalked away.

Jack said, 'I need a fucking drink.'

Jack, Joe and I sat around a table on JD's terrace while his staff fed us expensive booze. Kate was still tending to minor injuries. The security guy who looked like Rambo joined us, and Jack introduced me. 'Erica, this is Brad. From Sydney.'

Oh! The Team has a Sydney branch. 'Hi, Brad.'

Brad looked slightly in my direction, which I guessed was his way of saying hello. He wore sunglasses even though it was the middle of the night and this made it hard to gauge his thoughts, assuming he was having some.

Jack said to Brad, 'What's the latest?'

Rambo's lips barely moved. 'Prick met with the Fed.'

'What prick?' I said, leaning in so I could hear properly even though it wasn't my business.

Jack said, 'Your friend, McGann.'

'Oh. Sorry I asked.' But I wasn't really sorry because I wanted to know what that particular prick was up to.

Jack elaborated, but quietly. 'McGann has a mate with the federal police in Sydney. Brad used to work for this guy and Brad reckons he's dirty. We think they're planning something.'

'Right,' I said, nodding as though I knew what he was saying. Dirty. 'What do you think they're planning?'

Brad piped up, but I had to strain to hear as he muttered, 'Somethin' big. Somethin' bad.'

'In Sydney,' I confirmed, relieved and straight away guilty that I felt pleased about something bad in Sydney instead of Melbourne.

'Yes,' said Jack and gave me a raised-eyebrow look as if to say: Happy now? Do you have all the information you need, Ms Jewell? 'This is not for general discussion, you understand.'

'Of course,' I said.

Brad checked his watch and moved on without another word. To where, I couldn't imagine. A swag in some jungle? I pictured him walking out JD's front door, stripping off his shirt, and strapping on a bandana.

Jack nodded to the waiter and held up three fingers, which presumably meant another three of the same. He was drinking whiskey, Joe was having Coke, and I was on my second champagne for the night. I looked around and said, 'I haven't seen Charlie for a while. He's really drunk and I'm worried he's driven somewhere.'

Jack was in a much better mood. Something to do with a bucket-load of whiskey, presumably. He smirked at Joe, who smirked back.

'Don't worry,' said Jack. 'Charlie might find his car's not working tonight.'

I looked from one to the other. 'So, boys, are you saying you've tampered with Charlie's car?'

Jack feigned offence. '*I* didn't touch Charlie's car.' He looked at Joe. 'Did *you* touch Charlie's car, Joe?'

'Not me.' Joe sipped his Coke.

I looked from one to the other, then gazed around at all the other potential car tamperers – party stragglers, mostly Team members, wiping dirt, sweat and blood off their faces, talking about the night, slugging back booze.

'It's amazing no one was killed,' I said, 'especially that guy you dragged out of the car, Joe.' That guy's car had been one of the second lot to blow. If Joe hadn't got to him, he would've blown up somewhere down the road.

Joe nodded. 'It's good to save a life.'

Jack said to me, 'Well spotted.'

I leaned toward Jack and said quietly, but loud enough for Joe to hear as well, 'Bet you're glad you didn't park on the street tonight.'

Jack looked at me, trying not to smile. Joe looked away, also trying not to smile. I could tell.

I looked from one to the other. 'What?'

'Losing a car is hardly important when lives are at risk, Erica,' said Jack. He was still trying not to smile.

'I agree,' I said in a low voice, and then I realised. 'Aha! You guys have already had this conversation!'

Jack grinned. 'Maybe.'

I watched Jack throw down a few more whiskeys. He was getting pretty drunk. Joe made the call to leave and once he'd found Kate, we all piled into the Merc and drove slowly past the smoking wreckage. All the media had gone but there was still a good number of sticky-beaks, tow trucks, etc. As we drove by, Jack sat forward, his head swivelling as he scanned the crowds.

'Who are you looking for?' I said.

'The bombers. They like to hang around, see the results of their work.' He flopped back in the seat, took my hand and squeezed it.

'Did you see them?' I wondered what a bomber would look like.

'No.' He then announced, slurring slightly, 'Joe, I'm staying at Erica's. Someone has to protect her from Charlie Heiner.'

Joe looked at me in the rear-view mirror, eyebrows raised, and I shook my head, smiling. He said, 'I don't think so, man.'

'Yes, I am. She loves me.'

I elbowed him. 'I do not!'

'Ow! Yes, you do.' He grinned, eyes sleepy, rubbing his arm.

'Don't be silly.'

Kate laughed.

Joe said, 'Erica, I promise you don't want Jack in your house when he's loaded.'

Jack undid his seatbelt, lay across the seat and put his head on my lap. He wrapped his arm around me, gave me a squeeze, and fell asleep, snoring softly. I played with his hair and asked Joe, 'How did Jack know more cars would blow up?'

'He didn't, but there was a chance, and we never assume anything in a situation like that.'

'Oh. Okay.'

When we got to my house, Joe opened the back door and hoisted Jack off me so I could slip out of the car. I said goodnight to Kate and Joe walked me to my door, waited while I opened it and disarmed the alarm.

I said, 'Thanks Joe,' and gave him a kiss on the cheek. These Team guys have such nice manners, I was thinking, when the gate swung open. Jack staggered in and stood grinning at us. 'What's going on?' he said.

Joe said, 'Uh-oh.'

I said, 'Uh-oh?'

'Yeah, this'll be fun.' He tried to turn Jack, saying, 'Come on, buddy. Back in the car.'

Jack pushed Joe away. 'I'm staying here.'

'No way, man. I'm taking you home.' They wrestled with each other, fell into my garden and rolled around.

'Boys!' I yelled. 'My geraniums!'

Now Kate was standing at the gate, hand over her mouth, looking both worried and amused.

Joe helped Jack up and I brushed them both down. Jack pushed away from us and headed for my open front door.

Joe made a move to go after him but I said, 'Don't worry about it, Joe. I'll bring him home in the morning.'

'Are you sure?'

I laughed. 'Yeah, it'll be fine. I think.'

I said goodnight to Joe, locked the gate and walked into my house. Jack was lying face-down on my bed with Axle standing on his back, kneading it. I picked up Axle, grabbed my robe and walked down the hall to the spare room.

I spent fifteen minutes trying to get out of my dress, gave up and climbed into bed still wearing the silver sheath. If the dress had been mine and not Lucy's, I would have cut it off, although it did have grass stains so it was probably ruined anyway.

As I tried to sleep, I heard what I thought was thunder rumbling overhead, or possibly an outbreak of war, but realised it was Jack snoring. It was so loud I thought the ceiling might cave in. I got up and followed the noise to my bedroom. He was now lying on his back in his shirt, socks and undies. I dragged my eyes away from the lower half of his body and shook him. He wrapped his arms around me and pulled me onto the bed.

'Jack, stop it!' I wriggled out of his arms and he started snoring again. I tried to turn him onto his side. Not a chance. I sighed, found some earplugs and went back to the spare room.

CHAPTER 25

My mobile woke me in the morning and I was disorientated for a few seconds while I remembered that I was in the spare room and why. I squinted at my watch. Nine o'clock. Way too early.

'Hello?'

'I'm hoping you're somewhere in this house so you can bring me coffee.'

'Happy New Year to you too.'

'Please?'

'All right,' I grumbled. 'You'll have to wait.'

As I was walking out of the kitchen ten minutes later with coffee for Jack, my mobile rang again. I picked it up and continued down the passageway.

'Why does everyone think this is a reasonable time to call me on New Year's Day?' I shouldered open the door and walked into the bedroom containing a bleary-eyed but still handsome face peering at me over the doona.

'What. The. Fuck,' said Lucy.

'And a Happy New Year to you.' I was already bored with my own response to everyone so far this morning. I put the coffee on the table next to Jack, and noticed that *all* his clothes were now spread around the floor. I walked to the other side of the bed and sat on top of the covers. Jack pushed a pillow behind my back.

'Erica, if my dress has grass stains, I'll ... I'll ...'

I felt suddenly very uneasy. 'How could you know about that?'

'The photo!'

'Photo?' I felt sick.

'The one on the front page of every newspaper this morning! *You*, sitting on the *grass* in *my* dress!'

Shit, shit, shit! 'Not *just* a photo of me. Please tell me it's not.'

'Of course not. It's a shot of the blown-up cars, but you're in it.'

'How can you tell it's me?'

'Your head's turned away but I know it's you.'

'Will my mother be able to tell it's me?'

I could hear the rustle of paper. 'Hmm. Maybe.'

'Fuck.'

Jack tsked at my bad language. I'd forgotten about him. His naked torso was propped up next to me and he was sipping his coffee. It was difficult to look away, and difficult to remember what I was talking about. Lucy helped. She said in a weak voice, one that was preparing itself for the worst news, 'So, has my dress got grass stains?'

'It does. I'm really sorry.'

'Okay.' She huffed a big sigh. 'Are you all right? The paper said no one was badly hurt.'

'Yep, all good.'

'Can I ask the *real* reason for the cars being blown up? I assume it's got something to do with what Jack does.'

I got quickly off the bed and made my way back to the kitchen. I didn't want Lucy guessing that someone was listening to our conversation. I especially didn't want her guessing that that someone was Jack. In my bed. She said the papers were making all kinds of provocative claims. 'Experts' said it was the work of anarchists. Kids, they said. They avoided the T word in relation to anything Australian.

There was also talk about whether or not the stolen fertiliser had been used and discussions about whether or not it was an attack on John Degraves personally. I told Luce I really didn't care what the papers said, because I needed more sleep. She said she'd call again later and we hung up. I turned on the TV. The bombs in JD's street made top story. I flicked through all the news channels, carefully watching the repeating images. I couldn't see me anywhere, thank God. The cameras scanned the crowd, showing the horrified faces.

I took a cup of tea back to my bedroom. Jack was under the doona, dozing. I sat on the bed and he stirred.

'Do you want me to turn on the telly?' I said. 'The bombings are all over the news.'

Without opening his eyes, he said, 'I'm not ready to face that reality just yet.'

'Well, I need to talk. I think I'm traumatised.'

He opened one eye. 'Did you take advantage of me?'

'Certainly not!'

He lifted the doona and looked under it. 'So why am I naked?'

'You got yourself naked, friend. I slept in the other room. Or should I say, *tried* to sleep.'

He rubbed his face with his hands. 'So, you're traumatised.'

'Yes, by your snoring.'

'Sorry.'

'It's okay. I found earplugs.'

He nodded, sleepy.

'Lucy said the bombings are all over the newspapers. Front page. And I'm in the photos.'

His eyes flashed open suddenly and he sat up. 'Have you got any newspapers here?'

'No, but I've got this.' I reached for my iPad on the bedside table.

He snatched it from me.

'What are you looking for?'

'Photos of the crowds.' He tapped the screen and scanned.

'Last night? It's on the news.'

I picked up the remote and turned on the small wall-mounted TV.

'Are you looking for the bomber?'

'Yes.'

We watched the various news channels and Jack changed to a kneeling position, intent on the screen, leaning closer and closer, eyes narrow, checking the crowds. As he shuffled down the bed to get closer to the TV, clutching the doona in front of him, he clearly wasn't considering the view from behind.

Of course I averted my eyes. Of course I did! I cleared my throat.

'Find what you're looking for?'

He covered himself. 'No. Sorry.' He sat back against the pillow, picked up his coffee, ran a hand through his hair. 'Why do I have leaves and dirt in my hair?'

'Long story, but you probably should be nice to Joe.'

'He's a good mate.'

'Yes, he is.'

'So are you.' He reached out and patted my knee, inspecting me. 'Why are you still wearing your dress?'

I shrugged. 'I can't get it off. I'll have to get Lucy to come over and unglue it.'

'I can do it.' He grinned.

'I don't think so.'

'I can.'

'No doubt.'

'Don't you trust me?'

'Who do you think was responsible for the bombs?'

He sighed. 'I don't know. 'The police think kids – politically moti-vated – sending a message to Melbourne's wealthy. But I'm not so sure it's not a message for JD.'

'About the stolen fertiliser?'

'Yes.'

'He's really copping it over that.'

'He is.'

'It doesn't seem fair. Dega only bought the company a week before it was stolen.'

'I know.'

'You're not thinking the stolen fertiliser was used?'

He considered it. 'Don't know. It'd be sweet justice though, wouldn't it? If they'd used the company's product.'

'Yes, it would.'

We talked a while longer, or rather, I talked and Jack lay back down and drifted in and out of sleep. I lay on my side, on top of the covers, and watched him, eventually falling asleep myself. When I woke I could hear the shower running. I went to the kitchen and put the kettle on again, and let Axle out the back door.

Jack walked out of the bathroom with a towel around his hips, his hair wet, droplets of water rolling off his shoulders and getting caught in the hair on his chest, I noticed.

'Sorry, Jack, what were you saying?'

'I asked if you'd mind driving me home.'

'No problem. I told Joe I'd deliver you home, anyway.'

He took a seat at the dining table. 'I'm trying to imagine how that conversation came about.'

'Which one?'

'Between you and Joe about delivering me home.'

'Oh, well, you see, you wanted to stay here, and Joe wrestled you to the ground trying to get you back in the car, but you won the battle and ended up in my bed. Alone. My geraniums are squashed.'

He looked sheepish, and a bit embarrassed, for the first time since I'd known him.

'Sounds like I owe you both an apology,' he said.

'Not really. You were very funny.' I added, 'Just a very loud snorer.'

We smiled at each other and he reached a hand toward me. 'Come on, I'll make it up to you. Let me help you out of that dress.'

'No way!' I stepped back.

He stood and walked down the hall, adjusting the towel around him. He came back with another towel and handed it to me. 'Here, wrap it around yourself when I get the dress off.'

I considered his innocent, smiling, handsome face. He wanted to help me out of my dress. What an offer.

'All right. And don't you dare look!' My undies were no more substantial than dental floss, and my bra was completely see-through.

Jack put the spare towel on the kitchen bench and held his hands out to me. I turned my back, lifted my arms over my head like a little kid. 'Go on, then. And don't look!'

He grabbed the bottom of my dress and pulled it up in little jerks, causing me to stagger about. 'Here we go!' he said and whipped it right over my head. I looked quickly over my shoulder as I reached for the towel. Jack was grinning at me, the dress swinging off his index finger.

'You're looking! I can't believe it!' I snatched the towel off the bench.

'Sorry. I forgot.'

I stormed out of the kitchen and down to my bedroom, listening to the merry chuckles behind me.

ON THE WAY to Jack's house, he said, 'You and Charlie seemed to get along well.' He was looking at me with raised eyebrows.

'And, so?'

'Are you planning on seeing him again?' He waggled his eyebrows.

I said, 'I'm just trying to imagine why that's any of your business.'

'Well, did you know he's JD's nephew?'

'Yes, but I don't see what difference that makes.'

'And he's got a reputation. Women, drugs. You know. I'd hate to see you get hurt.'

'Don't worry. I could never be hurt by a man like Charlie Heiner, and you'll be the first to know if I meet someone else I'd like to bonk. I mean ...' My face burned at that Freudian slip – third degree burns, in fact – and I hoped Jack didn't notice. Of course he noticed.

'Okay,' he said. 'That's sorted.'

I cleared my throat. 'Yes, that's sorted.'

'By the way,' I said, 'I told Charlie that if he wants my phone number, he'd have to get it from you.'

Jack smiled.

'And I'd prefer it if you didn't give it to him.'

He laughed. 'No worries.'

I pulled up at Jack's house.

'Thanks again,' he said, 'and sorry about last night.'

'No problem.'

He got out of my car, closed the door and leaned in through the window. 'See you later.'

'Is this goodbye forever?' I said. 'Again?'

He grinned and turned to walk away, stopped and came back. 'You can't blame me,' he said.

'For what?'

'Did you look in a mirror last night?'

I smiled.

'See you later.' He winked and walked away.

I GOT home and thought about all the housework I'd been neglecting. My washing machine had been playing up and so I'd ignored my dirty laundry, thinking the fairies might take care of it. They hadn't. I emptied the hamper onto my bed to sort through it, thinking about when I'd hidden Jack's gun in there and that made me smile. Something else of Jack's fell out of the basket – his watch. An elegant Longines.

'Well,' I said to Axle, 'I could tell him I've got it and wait for him to get it, or I could take it to him, or I could sell it.' Axle wanted me to sell it.

I shoved a load of washing into the machine and turned it on. Nothing happened. *Shit.* I hate laundromats.

I called Lucy on her mobile. She said, 'Sorry, sweetie, I'm not home and I can't get a key to you.'

I sighed. 'No worries. I'll go to Mum's.' But I didn't want to go to Mum's. Going to Mum's meant sitting around for a couple of hours while she lectured me about sex and my weight.

I called Jack's house. Joe answered and I said, 'Hey Joe, did Jack apologise to you?'

He laughed. 'Yeah. He's promised me a big, fat bonus. It was worth it, I reckon.'

'I found his watch in my laundry basket.'

Joe roared laughing, and that made me laugh too.

'I thought I might bring it around this afternoon,' I said.

'I'll come get it. Or Jack will.'

'Actually, I've got a favour to ask.'

'Shoot.'

'My washing machine's broken.'

'No problem – come on over. I'll be here all day.'

The security gate was ajar when I got to Jack's and Joe opened the door as I walked up the steps. He took my basketful of washing and carried it to the laundry for me.

'Jack's with the police at JD's,' he said. 'I don't know when he'll be back.'

'That's okay. I've seen enough of him lately.'

We grinned at each other, brothers-in-arms. I shoved all my whites and coloureds in together and moseyed back to the kitchen where Joe was baking cupcakes. He made me some lunch and we yakked about the party, and laughed so hard about Jack being drunk I had tears streaming down my face.

When the washing machine finished I unloaded my clothes and went back to the kitchen to finish my cup of tea. I heard the front door open, and Jack appeared with the leggy blonde from the party. I could feel my face heating up.

Jack said, clearly in a very good mood, 'Hey! I saw your car out there.'

I smiled tightly back. I was annoyed with him but couldn't remember why. 'My washing machine broke.' I pointed at the basket of washing, suddenly feeling very boring and housewifey. Frumpy. Short. Brunette.

Jack turned to the blonde and said, 'Caroline, this is Erica.'

Caroline smiled warmly and said, 'Hi, Erica. I saw you last night but we didn't get to meet.'

'Oh, right, nice to meet you, Caroline.' I forced another smile.

Jack said, 'Well, I'll see you later.' He smiled and Caroline smiled and they walked up the stairs to his bedroom.

Joe pushed the plate of cakes across the bench, but I leapt off the stool, saying, 'Can't sit around here all day! Back to the housework. Thanks so much, Joe. I'll see you soon!' I waved and ran out of the house with my washing, and drove home really fast.

CHAPTER 26

The next day I went back to work and I was the only one in my department not still on holidays, which suited me fine. Rosalind was at a health spa and I felt sorry for all the other people there. They'd have a horrible time, not really knowing why.

Post-Christmas and New Year was usually a great opportunity to catch up on stuff, but with the events of New Year's Eve, another round of abuse from the public and demands from the media were expected. All calls were supposed to be diverted to BIG in Sydney and the company's share registry, but some slipped through to me.

Apart from fielding calls, there was nothing much else for me to do. Usually I'd start thinking about the annual report, the annual general meeting, that kind of thing. The ad agency was still working away on BIG's new brand.

I spent time on Facebook, searching for Jack, but apart from the fact that there are forty million Jack Joneses, I couldn't imagine him playing around on Facebook anyway, telling his friends what he had for breakfast.

Then, as though he knew I was thinking about him, Jack called me. And he sounded really happy. Of course he was happy – he was getting laid. He told me that the New Year's Eve bombs had been analysed and that they were made from fertiliser. He thought I'd like to know ahead of the announcements about it.

'The stolen fertiliser?' I said.

'Unlikely. This was vandalism, not terrorism. Ammonium nitrate was readily available until recently. My guess is it's unrelated.'

'And you're still thinking the terrorists you've been watching stole the fertiliser?'

'Yes.'

'Okay. Well, thanks for letting me know.'

'How are you?'

'What? Oh.' I remembered then that I was supposed to be shitty with him, so I gave him my shittiest voice. 'I need to go. Got work to do.'

'Right. And Erica?'

'Uh huh?'

'Charlie Heiner called me. Asked for your number.'

'Well I hope you didn't give it to him.'

'No, but I assume you told him you're available?'

'Of course. Because I am.' I hung up.

ON SATURDAY MORNING I headed out for a power walk. On the way to the Tan I passed a couple of sporting fields. There were lots of people around. I liked watching people as I walked. I liked watching them play with their dogs, and families having fun on bikes, and I *especially* liked the big, handsome football players training on the oval. I was surprised to see them there today though, in January. A charity match? I wandered over to the fence and watched for a while. Lines of fans were thick around the periphery, yelling and shouting.

'Don't tell me you're a Collingwood supporter,' a voice behind me said.

I whipped around, ready to clobber whoever was using such insulting language. It was Charlie Heiner!

'No,' I said. '*No!* Are you?'

'I am.' He was grinning, so handsome.

'Well, that does it. I'll never go out with you, Charlie Heiner.' I stamped my foot and pouted. How does he do it? Cause me to flirt like an idiot simply by smiling at me?

He made a sad face and I giggled.

'There's a charity dinner on Saturday night at Crown. It's to raise money for kids with cancer.'

'Thanks, but I don't think so.'

'Please? It's a great cause and I'd love it if you'd come. Jack won't give me your number.' He made another sad face and I felt suddenly annoyed with Jack for being such a meany. And he had Caroline. And Charlie was so handsome and nice and, well, he seemed kind of upset that I'd said no.

'Well ...'

A huge grin broke across his face. 'I'll pick you up at seven. What's your address?'

I NOW HAD a formal dinner to shop for, and this occupied my thoughts all the way around the Tan and home again. I called Lucy and told her about Charlie Heiner, and she squealed so loud I had to pull the phone away from my ear.

'Charlie Heiner won that bachelor of the year competition,' she said. 'He's such a spunk.'

'I don't think he works.'

'His family's so rich he probably doesn't need to!'

The next morning, Lucy and I discussed Charlie all the way to Chapel Street, Prahran, where I wanted to shop for something to wear to the dinner. It was a formal event and I wanted elegant, and not cheap. Although cheap was possibly more appropriate.

We strolled up the street, window shopping. Lucy said, 'I haven't grilled you about New Year's Eve yet.'

'About the bombs?'

'No. About ...'

'I know. I owe you a new dress.'

'Not that, you goose. I mean Jack. Did you have a good time with him?'

My mouth turned down of its own accord.

'Why are you looking like that?' she said.

'Like what?'

'All shitty.'

I sighed. 'I'm kind of annoyed with him.'

'Why? What did he do?'

I shrugged. 'Nothing, really.' I couldn't tell Lucy I was shitty he had a girlfriend. 'He got drunk and passed out on my bed.' My very independent mouth smiled at the memory.

'On *your* bed? Why haven't you told me about this?'

I shrugged again. 'Nothing to tell. He snored all night in my bedroom and I slept in the spare room.'

Lucy seemed disappointed, which surprised me. We stopped in front of a shop and looked in the window. Lucy oohed and aahed over the dresses while I commented on the prices. I tugged her arm and we kept walking. I found a shop advertising 'UP TO 80% OFF!!!', which annoyed me because this basically says they're ripping off the people who pay full price.

While I was in the change room, Lucy called out, 'Make sure you don't drink too much and get all the goss. God, I wish someone would invite me to a night like that.' She was green with envy. And so was the dress. Emerald green. Long, softly figure-hugging with not too much cleavage. And it was 80 per cent off. Perfect.

 spent all Saturday afternoon getting ready. It was a very high-profile event, I'd discovered. JD was going and there'd be lots of celebs. Rosalind was back from the health spa but not looking any healthier, and she was pissed off that I got an invitation to the charity dinner and she didn't. I found this very satisfying.

I felt nervous about the date with Charlie and what he might expect afterward. During the week he'd sent me a Facebook friend invitation and I'd accepted. I was interested but not totally surprised to see that about 90 per cent of his friends were female.

I was pleased I hadn't heard from Jack. I didn't want him to know I was dating Charlie. My first date, really, since Danny. New Year's Eve didn't count.

Charlie picked me up in his silver Porsche. He tooted his horn and I could see him from my bedroom window, parked in front of my gate. He was sitting in his car, mobile phone at his ear. That annoyed me, a lot, so I ignored him, forcing him to knock on my door.

But he looked great in his tux, standing at my front door, smiling away. I forgave him immediately. He tried to kiss me on the mouth but I gave him my cheek instead.

Charlie walked ahead of me and got into his car. I locked my gate and when I realised he wasn't going to open the door for me, even from the inside, I let myself into his car and he roared away from the kerb before I had my seatbelt on. I was already missing Jack and his nice manners.

'What do you think of my car?' he said.

I looked around the interior. 'Not bad.'

'Not bad? This is a fine piece of machinery. Cost me a shitload!' He screeched around the corner, way after the light had turned red. I clung to my seat, wondering if it was too late to change my mind about this date. Maybe I could just step straight into a taxi at the other end?

He said, 'Baby, when you're with Charlie, you're with the best.'

I squeezed my eyes shut as we shot across the Punt Road intersection. Would I hurt myself if I jumped out now? I wondered. I think you're supposed to roll when you hit the ground.

To distract myself from thoughts of fatality, I said, 'What do you do for a living?'

He looked at me, incredulous. The traffic ahead was stopped. Charlie roared up behind it, stopped, and I started breathing again. 'I don't need to work.'

'Don't you get bored?'

'Nup.' He gave my leg a rub.

'Where do you live?' I said, pushing his hand away.

'Toorak.'

'You've got your own place there?'

'I live with the olds but I've got my own wing.' He laughed. 'Get to do whatever I want. Come and go. Don't pay for anything.' He gave me a nudge with his elbow. 'I'm out for a good time, baby, not a long time.'

Once we were there, Charlie buggered off, schmoozing, I supposed. I didn't care. I was happy to sip champagne and people watch. I wished Lucy was there so we could gossip about the fake boobs and suntans.

We were on a table next to JD, and he seemed surprised to see me there, and smiled. When he saw I was with Charlie, though, his smile turned to a frown. Didn't he think I was good enough for his nephew?

A very good-looking blonde woman sat to my left – she reminded me of Caroline – and Charlie was on my right, and as everyone started taking their places, I realised Charlie was the only man on our table. By design? All the women were drop-dead gorgeous. Like models. I felt very unattractive.

As soon as I had a chance, when Charlie disappeared for a smoke between courses, I asked the blonde next to me if she knew him. She laughed, but it was a laugh full of irony. 'We all do,' she said, waving her hand around the table.

'How?'

'He hired us.'

'What?'

'Well, I should say that he paid for us all to be here. He's a very generous friend.'

She seemed amused at my reaction, which was one of absolute shock.

'Nothing wrong with that,' she said.

I nodded dumbly. Generous friend indeed! Generously looking after his own image, more like it. So, what was he doing with me? He could have any one of these women, probably. And they were all so, well, *gorgeous*. Why me? It's not like we were soul mates or anything.

When Charlie came back for main course, he slid his hand up my leg, trying to get under my dress, but I pushed him away, wondering if the models would have let him grope them under the table. He laughed.

There was a charity auction with some very valuable items up for the taking, including around-the-world first-class air tickets, six weekend packages in one of Crown's best suites, and a very beautiful Aboriginal painting that had clearly attracted JD's attention. As soon as bidding started, his hand was up. Followed immediately by a counter bid. I craned my neck to see who it was – Martin McGann, head of Mintin Mining and Shane's daddy. I looked around nervously to see if Shane was somewhere in the room.

There were four people in the original bidding but it was quickly down to just two, Martin McGann and John Degraves. It seemed that as soon as JD put his hand up, Martin McGann made an immediate bid. JD looked exasperated. He wanted the painting. He started hesitating before each bid, and finally threw his hands in the air, giving up, pissed off.

The applause was thunderous and Martin McGann seemed very pleased. He smiled across the room at JD, but even with the distance between us I could see his eyes weren't smiling. JD turned away.

By midnight I'd had enough. I wanted to find Charlie to let him know I was going. I hoped he wouldn't insist on driving me home.

I searched the room and headed for a door that had a *Smokers* sign on it. I walked outside, saw no one and was about to head back in when I heard hushed voices from a dark corner. I could see cigarette smoke curling into the still night air from behind a pillar. I walked a bit closer and heard Charlie's voice, and was about to make myself known when I heard another man's voice. Instinct told me to be quiet. I stepped up to the pillar and leaned against it, my heart rate picking up as I listened.

'I need more, man.' That was Charlie, sounding desperate.

The other voice said, 'You'll get it, for fuck's sake. After Sydney.'

'What am I supposed to do till then?'

'Just cool it. I'll cover you.'

There were a few moments of silence. Sucking on cigarettes.

'Take her now and park out the back. I'll meet you there.'

'How long will you be?'

'Not long. Warm her up for the video if you want.' There was some quiet chuckling.

I broke into a sweat and pressed my back into the pillar, holding my breath as the two men – Charlie Heiner and Shane McGann – came out from behind it. They were walking away from me – Charlie to the door that led back inside, McGann to the car park stairwell – when McGann glanced over his shoulder and saw me. He signalled Charlie and they both came to stand in front of me. I looked from one to the other; Charlie looked very worried, his eyes darting around. I was trying to think of something that might get me out of the predicament when the door to the ballroom opened and a couple of guests walked out with their cigarettes. I pushed quickly past Charlie, McGann and the smokers and into the room. Charlie was beside me in a moment. I looked around for McGann; he was gone. I walked through the ballroom toward the exit with Charlie in step beside me. JD was still there, and Martin McGann, but what could I say to them? That JD's nephew and Martin's son were planning something terrible?

Charlie said, 'Slow down, Erica. There's no point running off.' He grabbed my arm and I snatched it away.

'Go ahead, Charlie, and I'll scream rape so loud you'll need a hearing aid.'

He looked around nervously. I'd attracted some attention from guests at a table nearby. 'Calm down and I'll take you home.'

'Just fuck off.' I walked quickly to the front of the hotel where a queue of taxis waited. Charlie stayed in step with me until I approached two security guards and said, 'This man is threatening me. Can you please help?'

The guards looked at Charlie and each other, clearly unsure what to do. Charlie held up his hands and backed away. His eyes bore into mine for a moment, then he turned and walked away, pulling his mobile phone out of his pocket.

I ran outside and pushed to the front of the taxi queue, shouting, 'Sorry, it's an emergency!' I jumped into a cab ahead of a few dozen annoyed party-goers. I gave the driver my address and asked him to hurry, watching over my shoulder as he drove out of the hotel driveway and into the traffic. He sped toward Richmond but what was I thinking? I couldn't go home. I tapped the driver on the shoulder. 'Turn here and stop.' He turned into a narrow street, pulled over and looked at me. I threw a fifty dollar note at him and leaped from the car. 'Go. *Now!*' I slammed the door shut and he sped away. I flung myself behind a bush and watched the main road. A black BMW blew past.

My mobile rang. Charlie. What a dickhead. I waited for the ringing to stop then dialled Jack's mobile. It went straight to voicemail. 'This is Jack. Leave a message.' I didn't have his home number in my phone, and I didn't have Joe's mobile either. I walked back to the main road, crossed it and headed back toward the Casino. I flagged a taxi and gave the driver an address near Jack's house.

As we approached, I told the driver to pull over. I got out and waited for the cab to move on, looking up and down the street for any sign that I'd been followed. No one about. No black BMWs and no silver Porches. If they'd followed me I'd be in deep shit right now, but I felt a need to protect Jack's home as well. I didn't know if they knew where he lived.

I kicked off my shoes and jogged barefoot to Jack's street, about five hundred metres up the road. I stood at the locked gate and rang the doorbell a dozen or so times before I accepted that either no one was home or they were sound asleep. There was loud music or something, but I couldn't be sure where it was coming from.

I couldn't climb over Jack's gate; no footholds. So I walked the length of the high front wall to the neighbour's property, whose gate was unlocked, and where a Jacaranda tree overhung Jack's fence. I threw my shoes and bag into Jack's front yard, slipped quietly through the neighbour's gate, hoisted up my dress and scampered up the tree like a twelve-year-old. If I hadn't been so frightened, I would've enjoyed the reminder of good times with my brother.

I crawled onto the overhanging branch and over Jack's wall, then slipped and fell with a squeal into the bushes. At least I fell on the right side, I was thinking, when the entire front of Jack's house lit up like the MCG, floodlights blinding me and every creature within a kilometre's radius. Before my vision could fully adjust, I realised I was staring at the nasty end of a shotgun.

'Erica! What are you doing?' Joe held out his hand and pulled me out of the bushes. My dress was torn and my hair was tangled with leaves and twigs. Something wriggled inside my dress and I started squealing and jumping around. Joe stepped back and whatever it was fell out.

'I tried calling Jack and I rang the doorbell,' I said, inspecting the ground. 'I thought you guys must've been out.'

'No.' He frowned. 'Jack's on a bender. He's not good.'

'What do you mean? What's wrong with him?'

I realised suddenly that Joe's face was very drawn.

'You'd better come in,' he said.

Joe opened the door and the loud noise I'd heard before blasted out of it.

'What the hell is that?'

He closed the door again. 'On second thoughts, we'd better talk out here.'

I looked around, feeling like I was on stage. 'Joe, can you kill these lights or can we go somewhere else to talk?'

He nodded, looking concerned, and opened the front door again, leading me to a small storage room under the stairs. He turned on the light and closed the door. 'Sorry, this is the best place to talk so we can hear each other.'

I asked again, 'What's wrong with Jack?'

Joe seemed to be considering his answer. 'Has he told you about his wife?' he finally said.

'Jack has a *wife?*'

'Had. Eva. She was killed in the towers in New York on September 11.'

I took a sharp breath, shocked. 'He only told me about his parents.'

Joe nodded. 'Yeah, they were all together. Jack's wife and parents. He was supposed to meet them for breakfast, but his flight was late. You know.'

I looked around for a seat. Joe cleared a spot on a small box and I sat, putting my face in my hands. I wiped my face and looked up at Joe, who didn't seem to know what to do with me.

He said, 'Today's Eva's birthday. It's the same every year and on September 11. And their anniversary. He can't handle the guilt of surviving and he feels responsible. I think he thinks if he'd been there, he might've been able to do something.'

'But that's crazy! No one could've done anything for anyone that day!'

'I know it and deep down he knows it.' He gazed down at me.

'Erica, Jack needs a reason to keep going, new things to look forward to. He really likes hanging out with you. It might help him to see you tonight.'

I nodded and stared at the floor. I had a million questions that needed to wait. I asked, 'Doesn't Jack ever have ... women in his life?' I wondered about Caroline. Why wasn't he with her tonight?

'Only briefly. He's not good with commitment since September 11.'

'Tonight gets worse, Joe. You'd better take a seat.' Joe remained standing, but as the story of my evening unravelled, he slunk to the floor, his back against the door. He didn't say anything for a long time.

Eventually he focused and said, 'Are you all right?'

I nodded.

'You can't tell Jack about this tonight. I don't know what he'll do, but it won't be good for anyone. And he can't go out.'

'I know McGann and Charlie will go to my house,' I said. 'I'm really worried about my cat. I know that sounds stupid.'

'No, it's not stupid. But they'll set the alarm off, and that'll trigger the security company to call here. I'll forward the house phone to my mobile, and I'll go over there now to check on the cat. Call the cops in the meantime if you want; tell them someone's breaking into your house.'

I gave Joe my house keys and a kiss on the cheek. 'Thank you, Joe.' I rang the police and reported intruders at my house.

VIOLENT DIN from the giant TV shuddered through the living room. Jack was slouched at end of the sofa, feet on the ottoman, head bowed, eyes closed, empty whiskey glass in his right hand, remote perched on his left leg. I crossed the room and picked up the remote. His eyes flew open, angry, and he grabbed my wrist. I stood motionless, staring down at him. His face softened in recognition. He released my arm and his hand flopped onto the couch.

I pointed the remote at the TV and turned it off, picked up his whiskey glass and put it next to the empty bottle. I sat on the coffee table in front of him, said softly, 'What are you doing, Jack?'

'Ah, Erica ...' He reached for me with both hands and pulled me onto his lap. He buried his face in my hair. 'I'm a friggin' mess.'

'I can see that.'

He said, slurring, 'What are you doing here?'

Joe was right. There was no way I could tell Jack what was going on. Not tonight. 'I came to see my friend.'

He squeezed me again, his face in my neck. 'You smell nice.'

'You need to go to bed.'

'Come with me?'

'I'll help you.'

'Sleep with me.'

'I'll tuck you in.'

'Okay.'

I stood and helped him up. I swung his arm around my shoulders and we walked – staggered – to the stairs, and slowly up to his room.

'You look pretty tonight,' he said on the staircase.

'So I should,' I said, my breathing laboured. 'Spent enough time on it.'

Jack collapsed onto his bed and pulled me down on top of him. 'Stay with me.'

I rolled off him and lay with my head on his shoulder, my arm around his middle. He gave me a squeeze and I felt his body relax.

'Go to sleep.' I kissed his cheek and wondered if, with his senses blurred and his face turned away, he might imagine it was his wife he held in his arms. But if he was fantasising it didn't last long. Jack's freight-train snoring started within a minute, so I slipped off the bed and went back downstairs. I was worried about Joe. I made a cup of tea and sat up for a while, but weariness overwhelmed me and I climbed back up the stairs and into the guest room. I stared in dismay at the bare mattress. I sighed and went back to Jack's room, lay beside him and drifted in and out of a fitful sleep.

CHAPTER 28

I got up early still wearing my dress from the night before, and realised this was becoming a habit. A bad one. Jack hadn't moved, except he was now sleeping quietly. I crept downstairs and across the living room to Joe's wing. The house was still. I knocked softly on Joe's door and heard a muffled grunt from the other side. I pushed the door open slightly. It was dark in there.

'Joe?'

He turned on his bedside lamp and sat up. Axle was asleep on the pillow next to him.

'Oh! Joe, thanks so much. Sorry to wake you but I was really worried.'

'It's fine.' He yawned.

'Do you want me to take him?'

'No, he's okay.' Joe gave the comatose Axle a tickle under the chin.

'Any sign of Charlie or Shane McGann?'

He shook his head. 'No, but that doesn't mean they won't be hanging around. Police were there, a bit confused. I told them to keep an eye out. You should stay here for a few days. Sorry. The guest room isn't made up.'

'That's okay. I bunked in with the snoring one.'

"

He chuckled. 'You'll be needing some sleep, then.'

'Yeah.' I backed out of the room, saying, 'Thanks, Joe,' and thought bleakly about how much my life had changed.

I padded back out to the kitchen, lost in thought about whether or not it was too late to resume my boring, cheapskate lifestyle. The sound of a cupboard banging shut brought me out of my reverie, and I looked up with a start. Jack was standing at the kitchen counter, dressed in the jeans and T-shirt he'd slept in. He was staring at me. Frowning, actually.

I said, gently, 'Hey, how are you?'

'Awful.' Now scowling.

I stopped, hands on hips. 'Are you frowning at me?'

His eyes cut to a space behind me.

'What ...?' I looked over my shoulder at Joe's bedroom door. 'Oh! No, Jack, I slept with you last night!'

His frown changed to a look of surprise. 'You did?'

I feigned hurt, my hand clasped over my mouth. 'You don't remember?'

He froze, staring at me.

'Just kidding.' He blew out the breath he'd been holding and I said, 'Well, you don't have to look so relieved!'

'Erica,' he said, resuming interest in the coffee machine, 'if you and I were ever going to have sex, I'd at least like to remember it.'

'Oh.'

'How do I keep ending up in bed with you and *not* remembering it?' he muttered.

'Well, minor correction on that. Last week you ended up in my bed, alone. And that, too, coincided with three gallons of booze down your throat.'

He looked me up and down. 'Why are you here and why are you dressed for a ball? And why is your dress torn and, most importantly, why were you just coming out of Joe's bedroom?'

'Huh. You think a ball? It was just a dinner.' I looked at my reflection in the window. 'Maybe this was too formal.'

'And ...?'

'I fell into your garden climbing over the fence.'

I could see confusion mounting. 'Right. And ...' He glanced at Joe's bedroom door.

'And, oh, well, I was worried about Joe after he went to rescue my cat. I wanted to see if he'd made it home alive.'

'I suspect I'm missing some information here.'

'Yes, Jack, I've got some terrible news. You'd better sit down.'

'YOU DID *WHAT*?' I'd just dumped the best part of my news. My date with Charlie. 'Erica, Charlie Heiner is a dickhead!'

'And a wanker.'

'And a brainless fool!'

'And a Collingwood supporter.'

Jack narrowed his eyes.

I said, 'I know all that, but that's not my terrible news.'

We were sitting opposite each other at his vast dining table, and I was now afraid to tell him; more for his sake than anything. I knew this would be awful news, and I couldn't imagine the implications. Right now though, his concerned eyes were fixed on my face. I hid behind the vase of flowers in the middle of the table.

'Well, um, I think Charlie Heiner is friends with Shane McGann,' I said really fast. 'Actually, I'm 99 per cent confident about that.' I cringed, waiting for his reaction.

His expression darkened. He said, slowly, 'That's a serious accusation.'

I nodded. 'I know.'

'And a frightening thought.' He looked off into the distance for a few moments and I thought how scary he would be if he was really angry. He said, a little too calmly, 'Tell me.'

I moved out from behind the flowers, hesitantly, and told him everything that had happened, including the conversation I'd overhead that mentioned Sydney, and about warming me up for 'the video'. And then Jack *was* really angry. He snatched up the vase and flung it across the room. It smashed into the wall by the television and fell in a shower of glass, flowers and water all over the floor. I slid down in the chair, covering my ears. Jack sat with his face in his hands. Joe walked into the room.

Jack glanced up at Joe. 'You know about this?'

Joe nodded, serious. 'Yeah.'

Jack said, 'This is Sydney. And Heiner's involved.'

'I reckon.'

'You should have called me, Erica,' said Jack. 'I would've come to get you.'

'I *did* try to call you.'

He closed his eyes. 'I'm sorry.'

'It doesn't matter. I came in a cab and Joe helped.'

Joe said to me, 'I need to give you my mobile number.'

Jack shook his head, muttering, 'I should've been there for you.'

'You are human, you know,' I said. 'I think you're allowed time off. And, well, I'm sorry I didn't tell you about the dinner with Charlie. I should have, but I knew you wouldn't like it.'

'Yes, you should have told me and no, I wouldn't have liked it.' He added quietly, 'But it's important information, so in a sense, it's good you were there.'

He stood and walked to the kitchen, opening the pantry door and pulling coffee out of it. But then he slammed the door shut and punched it. 'No! It's *not* good you were there!' He glared at me across the room. '*Anything* could've happened to you, Erica!'

I was stuck to my seat. The pantry door now had a fist-sized hole in it. Joe walked into the kitchen, took the coffee and put a hand on Jack's shoulder. 'Mate ...'

Jack smacked Joe's hand away and strode toward me, yelling, 'Do you realise what they could have done to you?'

I shot out of my chair, shouting back. 'Yes, but right now I don't know who's worse – Shane McGann or *you!*'

Shock replaced the rage and he stopped, hanging his head. He looked up at me again, worried.

'You're bleeding,' I mumbled, indicating his hand.

Blood ran from Jack's knuckles, down his fingers and dripped onto the floor. He wiped the back of his hand on his jeans and walked across the room, gently gripping my shoulders.

'I'm sorry. I truly am. But I feel sick about what could have happened.' His voice was hoarse. 'And still can.'

Jack begrudgingly let me tend his injured hand and sat looking ashamed while Joe dealt with the mess on the floor – glass, water, blood, flowers and bits of timber from the pantry door. A regular war zone.

Jack said to Joe, 'I think Erica should make a complaint to the police. Warn off Heiner and McGann.'

Joe didn't say anything.

I said, 'But isn't that putting the Team at risk? They might expose you if we threaten them that way.'

'*You've* been threatened, Erica. I can't let them get away with that.'

'No, Jack! When you were bleeding in my garden, you said "death is better". Better than exposing the Team!'

'That was me; this is about you.'

My voice rose a few octaves. 'What the hell's so special about my life compared to yours? That's very selfish, Jack!' I realised I sounded like my mother and I snapped my mouth shut.

He looked at me, eyebrows raised. I hoped he didn't want me to explain how I came to that ridiculous conclusion.

'And how did you come to that conclusion?'

I blew out a sigh. 'I don't know. Sorry. I'm stressed.'

Joe said, 'We could pay Heiner a visit. Have a chat.'

Jack nodded slowly. 'That would send a message to McGann. Okay, let's do it.'

THE BOYS LEFT and I called Steve about repairing the pantry door. Lucy was working and he didn't have his kids, which meant he was happy for a distraction. He said he could come straight away. When he arrived, I opened the front door and he was holding a newspaper, eyebrows raised, giving me a strange look.

'Why are you looking at me like that?'

'Have you seen this?' He held up the newspaper. The *Herald Sun*.

'Don't be ridiculous. Jack wouldn't have a tabloid in his house.'

Steve followed me through to the kitchen, commenting, 'Nice dress.' He tossed the paper onto the counter with a low whistle. 'Nice house.'

'Yeah. And there was a nice antique vase until this morning.' I indicated the newspaper. 'What's in there, anyway?'

With an uncharacteristic flourish, Steve flipped open the paper to the social pages. Of course, there was me, centre stage, seemingly enjoying Charlie's attention. I felt the blood drain from my head as I pictured my mother's cat's bum mouth. On cue, my mobile rang. I ignored it.

'Holy fucking hell,' I whispered and flopped heavily onto a stool. In the photo, Charlie was kissing my neck with vampiric enthusiasm and I was laughing, my head thrown back. I remembered that shot being taken. The laugh was fleeting – the kiss not only surprised me but tickled my neck. One second later, I'd pushed him away.

Steve said, 'Why would you go on a date with this guy?'

I stared at the paper. 'Ah ...'

'What does Jack say about it?'

'What?' I looked up at Steve.

'Does Jack know where you were last night? What's going on with you two?'

I sighed. I hadn't been sure if Steve knew about my true relationship with Jack, via Lucy, but clearly not. 'I'm an idiot.'

'I already know that.' He nudged my arm.

'It wasn't really a date. It was just ... I don't know what it was.'

But Steve wasn't listening. He was staring at the hole in the pantry door.

'Did Jack do this?'

'Yeah.'

'Because of this?' He pointed at the newspaper.

'No.' I thought about how to explain to Steve why my date with Charlie had caused Jack's violence. 'Sort of.' I couldn't explain. 'Yeah.' Sigh.

He shook his head. 'The whole door will need to be replaced. I'll take it to my cabinet maker.'

Steve went out to his car for some tools while I attempted an out-of-body experience, which never seems to work. When he came back, I said, 'Can you stick around until Jack gets back? I don't want to be alone with him when he sees this.' I stared at the photo, wondering about time travel.

He put his drill on the bench and looked at me, worried. 'Are you saying that Jack is violent toward you?'

'Oh, God, no! It's just ... I don't know. It's his eyes, the way he looks when he's mad. He's very scary.'

Steve turned back to the job of removing the pantry door. 'Well, if you were my girlfriend and I saw this pic, I'd have scary eyes too. You're on your own with this one, buddy.'

'Gee thanks, *buddy*.'

OF COURSE JACK had seen the photo. He had a newspaper in his hand when he arrived home. Someone had dobbed on me. Charlie, most likely. Or my mother.

Jack tossed the paper onto the kitchen counter and opened it to the defamatory page. I avoided his glare.

'Steve came. He's going to fix the door,' I said, indicating the now open pantry. There was no response and I was too scared to look at him. 'Where's Joe?' I asked, picking fluff off my dress.

'Joe didn't want to stick around for this.'

'For what?' I swallowed hard, glancing up at Jack and his angry eyes.

'Have you seen this?' He stabbed the photo with his finger.

I shrugged. 'What of it?'

He took a deep breath. 'I thought you didn't *enjoy* your date with Heiner.' Were his teeth clenched?

'I didn't! Don't you remember what I told you?'

'Well, this picture tells a very different story,' he said, his voice low and even a bit menacing.

And that made *me* mad. This wasn't what I was expecting. I thought he'd be angry that I'd somehow risked exposing the Team. Or something. I stood and looked up at him, hands on hips, my chin jutting. 'What are you suggesting?'

He looked away.

'Jack? What the hell are you suggesting?'

He looked at me again, eyes dark and accusing. 'That you gave Heiner reason to think you wanted him.'

I slapped his face. Snatched up my handbag and marched to the front door, throwing it open and storming through it in bare feet, my dress hitched up around my thighs.

'Erica, stop.' Jack was behind me.

I kept walking, tears burning my eyes. He held my arm and stood in front of me, blocking my path. I looked at the ground.

'Come back inside. Please. It's not safe for you out here.'

I heard the words and I believed him, but I was too upset to care. 'Leave me alone.' I tried to push past him.

His tone softened. 'Please. Please come back inside and we'll talk.'

'WHY WOULD you say that to me?' My turn to shout and storm around while he sat at the kitchen bench.

'Because Heiner told us —'

'What? What did that bastard tell you?'

'Look, it doesn't matter what he said. I'm sorry for what *I* said. It was ... thoughtless.'

'Damn right it was!'

He walked across the room and stood in front of me. He reached for me with one hand but then fixed both on his hips. 'It was stupid. I'm sorry.'

'Why would you doubt *me*, Jack?' I shouted, not letting it go. 'Why believe a lying bastard like Charlie Heiner over me?'

He looked at the ground. 'I think ... I don't know.'

I was hurt and furious, but in the back of my mind I couldn't help wondering what his real problem was.

LATER THAT AFTERNOON I moved temporarily into Jack's house. I hadn't wanted to be forced out of my home, again, but he offered either that or 24-hour babysitters. 'You choose,' he'd said. He didn't tell me the content of his 'chat' with Charlie, but we forgave each other and he took me to get my things. I forwarded my home phone to my mobile so my mother hopefully wouldn't find out where I was.

Of course she phoned me. And she was close to tears.

'What on earth?' she said.

'It was just a date, Mum.'

'Why are you going out with other men? What about Jack? Oh, you are a *hussy*!' She howled into the phone. 'What will I tell Mary?'

I sighed. I didn't know what to say. Would it help if I told her Jack has a girlfriend? That we're not together really but that I'm staying at his house because my life has been threatened? No. That wouldn't help.

'Don't worry, Mum. I'm not seeing that guy again.'

'Well, I should hope not. And I wouldn't blame Jack if he broke up with you!' She slammed the phone down.

Jack looked at me with pity. He'd probably heard everything she said.

I shrugged. 'She'll get over it.'

That night the three of us – four including Axle – sat around watching television. Someone had decided on *Muriel's Wedding* – one of my favourite Aussie movies – and I wondered if this was Jack's way of sucking up to me.

'Thanks for the chick flick, guys.'

Jack said, 'I like the sister who sits around all day —'

'You're terrible, Muriel,' Joe finished and chuckled.

I'd decided to paint my toenails – one of my favourite movie-watching chores. With my foot propped on the coffee table, I scrubbed the nails with polish remover, threaded rolled-up tissue between my toes to keep them separated, and carefully painted the nails, glancing up at the television as I dipped the brush. I suddenly had a feeling I was being watched. Joe was staring at my toes. Jack was sitting back, arms stretched along the back of the sofa, Axle sprawled across his broad shoulder. They, too, were watching my performance; Axle with a twitching tail.

I looked from one to the other. 'What?'

Joe cleared his throat and resumed his television watching.

Jack said, 'I've never seen anyone do that before.'

'Paint their toenails?'

He nodded, amused.

'You've got a sister haven't you?' I said. 'You've lived with ... women. Surely you've seen this before.'

'Well, I think the women I know pay to get that done.'

'That'd be right,' I muttered, picturing Caroline at some expensive salon.

Joe changed the subject, tactful as always, suggesting he add his mobile number to my phone. I pointed to my mobile on the kitchen bench and he left the room with it.

Jack bravely ventured further conversation about the previous night. 'Now that we've all calmed down a bit, can I ask why you agreed to this date with Heiner?'

'You're the only one who needed calming down.' I painted my pinky.

'Don't change the subject,' he said in a bossy voice.

I glanced at him. 'You're not very scary with a kitten sitting on your shoulder.'

'And you're avoiding the question.' Jack scratched Axle behind the ear, which started the chainsaw purring.

I shrugged. 'Well, I don't see why it should bother you. Me going on a date, I mean.' I looked at him with raised eyebrows and a smile. 'Unless you're jealous?'

He waved his hand, huffing. 'Of course not. Ridiculous. It's just, Charlie Heiner of all people.'

'Yeah, well, you've got your blonde friend. What's the big deal?' I slipped and painted a smudge on my big toe.

'Blonde friend?'

'Yes, whatsername ... Caroline.'

'Caroline, the art dealer?'

I shrugged again. 'I don't know what she does. None of my business.'

Silence. I looked up. He was smirking. I narrowed my eyes. 'You're smirking.'

'You're jealous.'

I sat up straight. 'I most certainly am not!'

He chuckled. 'Caroline is helping me find a piece for my bedroom wall. That's all. I have no interest in Caroline otherwise.'

'Oh. Well. As I said, none of my business anyway.' I bent over my big toe again, turning my head slightly so that Jack couldn't see that my face was now the colour of beetroot.

CHAPTER 30

For the next week Jack wouldn't let me out of his or the Team's sight. I didn't mind at first, moving back into Jack's place. Actually, it was kind of nice to be fussed over. I was driven to and from work and escorted on all outings, and it was exciting to think about having someone who carried a gun watching over me. Like a celebrity.

But pretty soon it started to annoy me. Imagine being a famous person! There was no point trying to catch up with my friends because I couldn't explain why I was being shadowed by a tough guy. Jack was out every night and I didn't want to burden or bore Joe with extra babysitting time. But Joe was out a lot of nights with Jack anyway. They wouldn't say where. Jack would line up babysitters who wanted to know if I was going to the toilet and they'd hang around outside my room when I went to bed.

On the Saturday following the dinner with Charlie, Joe was out but Jack was home, preoccupied with paperwork. I sat at my laptop and logged on to Facebook. I checked on Charlie but there was nothing recent from him. I went upstairs and knocked on Jack's office door.

'Jack?'

'Uh huh?' He didn't look up, his fingers flying over a calculator.

'Do you want to come for a walk with me?'

'Can't.' He looked up. 'I've got to get this done. Sorry.' He gave me a small smile.

I sighed and went back downstairs. I did laps of the formal living and dining rooms, which were separated by a pair of ancient glass doors that were always kept open. I poked around, opening and shutting things, and then, in the bottom drawer of a beautiful old bureau, I found a flat, white box with gold embossing on the lid: *Jacques Phillipe Junod and Mei-Ling Qin*. Inside was a photo album covered in white suede and gold embossed with the same names. I sat cross-legged on the floor and pulled the album into my lap. I opened the cover of the album and let out a gasp. The bride was beautiful, exquisite. Her face filled the entire page.

The sound of a throat being cleared made me look up quickly. Jack stood there, looking embarrassed rather than annoyed.

With mouth hanging open I stared up at him, then back at the album. 'Oh, shit. I'm so sorry.' I carefully put the album back in its box and returned the whole thing to the drawer. Jack sat on the edge of the sofa and I said, 'I wouldn't usually ...'

'It's okay,' he said. 'I don't mind.'

'I'm really sorry, Jack. I wasn't thinking. I'm just bored, that's all.' I sat opposite him on the other sofa, my hands clasped together.

'I haven't looked at that album in years,' he said. 'I try not to think about her too much.'

'That was your wife? Joe told me ...'

'Eva changed her name when she got her American citizenship. And I changed my name when I moved here from Switzerland.'

Mei Ling and Jacques. 'Where was she from?'

'China.'

'Why did you change your name?'

'Imagine being a sixteen-year-old new kid at a private boys' school with the name *Jacques*?'

'Right.' Especially a pretty-faced new kid, as he would have been.

He said, smiling, 'So, has your curiosity been assuaged?'

'Well ...'

He laughed. 'What else?'

'Can I ask about Eva? In all fairness, you grilled me about Danny.'

He nodded once. 'Quite right.' He stood. 'But let's walk.'

'Really?'

'A quick one.'

'Great!' I raced upstairs for my runners. And off we went for a walk along the beachfront. Jack kept looking over his shoulder and I gave him twenty questions. It probably wasn't the most relaxing half-hour he'd ever spent. He told me a bit about Eva, though. That they'd met at the hotel where he was staying. She was working as a waitress while she studied, and I wondered about Jack falling in love with someone who served him drinks. I decided it was feasible; Jack was a snob when it came to material things, but not with people. He told me also that her family had moved to America and she wanted to move to Australia but Jack didn't want to leave her family behind so they stayed in New York. That she was a student of politics when they first met and by the 'end' she was working for the then presidential candidate.

'Who?' I asked but he shook his head, frowning.

'I need to get back,' he said, checking his watch, and we returned home in silence.

Jack's temporary good mood had disappeared. He returned to his office and I realised I now needed to grill Joe about Mrs Eva Jones. Jack hadn't told me nearly enough.

I CAUGHT up with Joe that afternoon. He was in the kitchen, as usual, but this time not baking cakes. He was cleaning his gun.

'Hey, Joe, want a coffee?'

'Sure. Thanks.'

But me trying to work the coffee machine was useless. Joe ended up doing it. He also got some cake out of the cupboard. And while he was doing that I ran to the bottom of the stairs to check Jack's office door. It was shut against unwanted nosy parkers.

'Jack told me about Eva,' I said.

'Really?' Joe seemed surprised. 'He won't usually talk about her.'

'Maybe he should.'

'I agree.'

'Did you know her?' I asked.

'Yeah.' He frowned.

'Did you like her?'

He glanced toward the door.

'He's in his office. Door's closed.'

Joe nodded, pushed his gun to one side. 'She was all right at first. Really nice. But she changed after a while.'

'How?' I leaned in.

'Well ...' He was hesitant.

I said, 'You don't have to say if you don't want to.'

'No, I reckon you should know. It's a good sign he talked to you about it.'

I nodded encouragement.

He said, 'Just before she died, Jack found out she was having an affair with her boss.'

'Oh my God! What woman in her right mind would cheat on Jack?'

Joe shrugged.

'Hang on,' I said. 'Jack said she was working for the presidential candidate. She was having an affair with *him*?'

'Yeah.'

'Wow,' I whispered.

'But there was other stuff before that. I think Eva really liked having money and position, but things went downhill pretty soon after they got married. Jack loved her family, but Eva wanted to move away from them. She was really into her new western life, practising her American accent and all that, but her family was very traditional and I think they embarrassed her. So, she wanted to move here. I think she thought here, she'd be a big fish in a little pond.'

'How?'

'Well, New York's a big place with a lot of competition. Americans are very competitive. And so was Eva, but I think she just wanted to win. In Australia she could have moved up the political ladder pretty fast. That's what she really wanted. And Jack was happy to move here but he wanted her family to come too. Eva wanted to leave them in New York.'

'So, what happened?'

He shrugged. 'They all stayed in New York. Jack's parents spent a few months there every year anyway, and his sister lives there, so it seemed like the best option. Jack didn't want to just dump her family and leave.'

'How long were they married?'

'Just over a year.'

'And what happened to Eva's family after ... September 11?'

'They wanted to go back to China. Hong Kong, actually. Jack gave them a lot of money and they left the US.'

Joe looked at me suddenly, all worried as though he'd said too much.

'I won't say a word,' I said. 'Thanks for telling me.'

'Maybe Jack will tell you more some day. I hope he does, Erica. He needs to.'

The next morning, Sunday, stretching, yawning and feeling great from a good night's sleep, I was lured down the stairs by the most beautiful music. Jack was sitting in one of his favourite spots: morning paper and coffee in front of him at the dining table.

He beckoned me over and pulled out a chair for me. 'Close your eyes,' he said softly.

I did it.

'Listen.'

So I did. I sat through the entire piece of music with my eyes closed. Exquisite piano permeated the room. When it finished I looked at him.

'That was beautiful, really beautiful.'

He nodded, pleased. 'That was Beethoven's *Piano Concerto No. 5.* Here, watch this some time.' He handed me a DVD. *Immortal Beloved* – the story of Beethoven's life. 'The most tragic love story ever told.'

'All right, I will. Thanks.'

'Actually, you might want to watch it today,' he said, looking at his watch. Jack told me then that he and Joe had some surveillance work. He said he had some guys watching McGann and Charlie, but he wanted someone with me anyway.

But I didn't want a broody gun-toting babysitter, and the only way Jack would accept that was if I asked Steve and Lucy to come and spend the day with me. So I picked up the phone, pretending to call Lucy and have a conversation with her while Jack watched.

'All done. They're coming over in an hour. I'm sure I won't drop dead in the meantime.'

I was clearly convincing because he didn't question it. But the truth was, I was getting sick of being watched 24/7. I'd even been aware of Jack opening my bedroom door in the middle of the night, presumably to check I was still there and still alive. One night I'd sat up, turned on my lamp, threw back the covers and said, 'Would you like to sleep here?' He'd muttered an apology and left. I felt bad for him but I was a bit over it.

So, instead of catching up with my mates, I looked forward to some alone time and with that freedom, I went straight back to the photo album. As I gazed at Eva's photo, I found I was hoping it had been digitally enhanced. I turned the page. There was a full-length shot and I couldn't drag my eyes away from her magnificent form. Her long, slender figure; the glossy black hair. She was awesome looking but then, so was her groom. Traffic-stopping handsome. What was wrong with that stupid cow?

It was easy to see where Jack got his good looks from. His parents both looked like movie stars; tall and elegant and also, well, rich. A plain-looking blond stood by his mother in the family shot, and I assumed it was Jack's sister. She looked like Jack, but not a feminine version of him. More like ... exactly like him. She had his straight, sharp nose.

Eva's parents looked so humble, like they didn't feel deserving enough to be included in the shot. Eva had her back turned away from them, facing Jack's family. What a bitch! And at the very back of the album, a wedding certificate. *Jacques Phillipe Junod and Mei-Ling Qin.* Jacques Junod. Jack Jones. I supposed 'Eva' was an invented name to fit with her preferred western lifestyle. Typical bitchy behaviour, was my overly biased opinion. I checked the date. Jack, *Jacques*, would have been twenty-six years old.

I'd exhausted my snooping, watched the movie and cried for half an hour afterward, and it was only just 3pm. I gazed out the front window of the house, thinking about thwarted love, and about how angry Jack would be that I'd exposed myself to danger by standing in front of the window, but I didn't care. I felt like I was pining for something. The outside world. Fresh air. Independence. Freedom.

I gave myself no time to consider consequences as I changed into training gear and snuck out to the garage, surveying his collection of cars.

It was the first time I'd seen inside it – his garage. He'd told me that when he'd renovated his house he'd removed the pool and extended the garage to cater for his cars and bikes, but I hadn't expected this. From the front it looked like a normal two-car garage. But it was long enough for six cars plus a few motorbikes, plus a heap more space at the back.

One was missing – Joe's LandCruiser – and the two cars now in front were Jack's Mercedes and an Audi. And that was an easy choice for me – the Merc was automatic. I ran back inside and rifled through the rack of keys in the kitchen, back out to the garage and into the shiny car.

I PULLED up at my old stamping ground, the Tan, which I missed dearly, and strode off happily against the flow of running traffic. But I hadn't planned on Charlie Heiner having the same idea. I was humming my way anti-clockwise along the river when Charlie jogged toward me and blocked my path.

'Hey, Erica.'

I stopped and glanced around. Lots of people.

He smiled, friendly. 'I was really upset about what happened last Saturday night. I didn't understand what the problem was.'

I fumbled in my head for words. Finally, I shrugged and settled on, 'What can I say? You're a boring date. Now, get out of my fucking way.'

I pushed past him but he grabbed my arm. And out came the fangs.

He hissed near my ear, 'That's not what I told Jones. I told him you wanted to go down on me in my car.' I tried to struggle out of his grip. 'I told him I thought you wanted to come home with me. You should have. I would've shown you a nice time.'

I snatched my arm free. 'I couldn't think of anything more revolting, actually.'

'Well, maybe you won't have a choice about it in future.'

So I kneed him in the balls. A couple of people walking past gasped and stepped back, but hung around, probably not sure who needed more help.

Charlie crumpled, groaning, hands at his groin.

'That might spoil those plans for you, Charlie.' I stepped quickly over him and continued my walk at a much faster pace, shaking, watching over my shoulder.

When I got back to Jack's my mobile was ringing, and I ran to answer it. It was Jack.

'Hi!' I said with forced enthusiasm.

'I've been calling.' He sounded relieved. 'Where were you?'

Whoops. 'Oh, sorry, I was ... in the bath.'

'With Steve and Lucy?'

Whoopsy whoops. 'Ah ... no, Steve had to go somewhere for an hour and Lucy ... fell asleep so I took a bath.'

'I'm sending someone over,' he said in a flat voice.

'No! Jack, please. I don't want babysitters. Steve and Lucy are on their way now.' I cringed at the lie. 'I promise it's fine. They were held up. That's all.'

He sighed. 'All right.' He breathed loudly, huffing into the phone. 'We need to stay out longer. Probably late into the night.'

I processed the possibilities. 'That's okay, I'll see what Steve and Lucy are doing. Don't worry about me.'

'Oh, but I do.'

That evening, I snuck out again. I took a taxi and met up with Roger and Marcus at a tiny restaurant near their house in South Melbourne. It was lovely, right up to coffee, when the restaurant door swung open and Jack walked in. His eyes were fixed on Marcus and

Roger as he approached our table.

'Sorry I couldn't make dinner, fellas,' he said, shaking hands, then took a seat next to me.

I sat there with a sweet smile, wondering if he'd murder me in the car or wait till we got home. But in the car, he was silent.

'You had me followed?' I said.

'Uh-huh.'

'Are you angry with me?'

'No, not angry.' He sighed. 'Just worried, I guess. How were you planning on getting home?'

'I ... ah ...'

'Yes?'

'I hadn't worked that out.'

Jack nodded and looked anxious, all the way home. He also looked very, very tired. In the wee hours of the morning my bedroom door creaked open and his silhouette appeared in the soft light from the landing.

I switched on my lamp, sat up, said, 'Are you all right?' A clear case of role reversal.

He shrugged. 'Not really.' He wasn't embarrassed this time, standing there in T-shirt and boxers.

'Have you had any sleep?'

He shook his head. 'Sorry. I don't want to worry you.'

'What will be will be,' I huffed dismissively, possibly boosted by false confidence after my afternoon's encounter with Charlie. 'I'm not worried. You shouldn't be either.'

'Easier said than done, for some reason.'

We looked at each other. I tried to come up with a reasonable solution and he was probably doing the same thing. He flopped into the armchair next to my bed.

'You know,' I said, 'this could really cramp your style. I mean, if you keep having to get up in the night to check on me.'

'Yeah, well, I don't exactly have a style to cramp.'

'Why, Jack? Why don't you have a girlfriend?'

He stared at the floor.

'None of my business,' I said.

He looked away.

'Sorry,' I whispered.

'No, it's all right.' He ran a hand over his face. 'I'm just not sure how to answer that.'

'Is it because of what happened to Eva?'

He sighed. 'Maybe ... I don't know.'

I felt like saying some nasty things about Mrs Eva Jones, the two-timing cow who caused poor Jack to have trust issues and then she went and died and that's caused him to live with extreme guilt and fear of getting close to someone again. But instead, I said gently, 'I can understand why you'd feel afraid to get close to someone else.'

'You have no idea.' He stood suddenly and walked to the door. 'Sorry to wake you.'

I felt strangely dissatisfied with how that all ended and I called after him, 'I *do* have an idea.'

He stopped and turned.

'Jack, I haven't suffered the horror you have, but I *do* have an idea. I was married to a gambling, cheating, lying son-of-a-bitch who stole all my money and left me for another woman before I had a chance to kick him out. I know a bit about it.'

He nodded. 'Fair enough. Goodnight, Erica.' And he left.

I flopped back onto my pillow. I lay there for a while thinking about how to distract Jack and give him something else to focus on. Maybe I should just jump his bones, right now, I thought. *That* would distract him.

I ran through some other ideas – yoga classes, meditation, move to Greenland, have a party – and an idea popped into my head. I got up and barged into his room, snapping on the light. 'Are you asleep?'

He sat up, blinking. 'And if I was?'

'I've got a great idea!'

'We should swap rooms?'

'No! Let's have a barbie here on Australia Day. We can invite everyone from the Team. What do you think?'

He stared at me for a minute. 'I can't remember the last time I threw a party. Not since I moved back from New York, anyway.' He nodded. 'Good idea. I'll organise caterers tomorrow and we can send out invitations.'

'Caterers? Jack, you've got to be kidding. It's a barbie! *You* have to be the tong-master at your own barbecue! Joe and I can make salads. Everyone can bring their own drinks. You won't need to do anything except flip the snags!'

He was staring at me like I was speaking a language he hadn't yet learned. 'A party without caterers,' he mused. 'All right. I'll give it some thought.'

THE FOLLOWING MORNING I got ready for work and ventured into the kitchen where Jack was drinking coffee and reading the paper. The *Herald Sun*. Strange. I put the kettle on.

'I didn't ask how you spent your day yesterday,' he said, pleasantly.

Uh-oh. I considered him with narrowed eyes. I clearly needed to tread carefully. 'Oh, well, I had a bath, just hung out, you know.'

'With Steve and Lucy.'

'Uh-huh.'

'Here.'

'That's right.'

'So you wouldn't know anything about this.' He spun the open newspaper on the dining table.

'I had nothing to do with that tabloid being in your house!' I joked, wondering what on earth could be in there.

But he didn't laugh, and I felt I had no choice but to walk across the room and look at the paper. More photos of Charlie and me? Surely not. But the paper *was* open at the society pages and I was worried for a moment. A quick scan showed no pictures of me.

'What am I looking at?'

He tapped the gossip column. I read the heading of the first item: PUMMELLED PLAYBOY.

I blushed and looked away, saying casually, 'Who takes notice of society gossip?'

'Read it.'

I pretended to be bored, gazing longingly over my shoulder at my brewing cup of tea. I yawned and sighed, and started reading the article to myself.

'Out loud.'

'Bossy.'

'You haven't seen bossy. Read.'

'Bachelor of the Year playboy Charlie Heiner copped a knee to the groin yesterday —' I glanced at Jack.

'Go on.'

'Witnesses say that Heiner was attacked by a dark-haired woman on the Tan jogging track ...' I looked up. 'Couldn't happen to a nicer guy.'

'Read.'

'One witness said that the woman appeared to be the same one he was pictured with ...' I laughed lightly. 'Maybe an old girlfriend attacked him.'

Those ice-blue pools were watching me, unblinking. 'So, Erica, would *you* happen to know anything about that attack on Charlie Heiner?'

'*Moi?*' I said, spreading my fingers theatrically wide on my chest.

'*Oui, vous.*'

I sighed. 'Maybe.'

He tried to look cross. 'I don't know whether to be proud of you, or angry that you put yourself in danger like that!'

'Be proud!'

He put his face in his hands. His shoulders were shaking.

'Jack Jones, you're laughing!'

He looked at me with a stern expression but his tell-tale eyes were still enjoying the moment. 'How did you get there, by the way?'

I grimaced. 'I, um, borrowed one of your cars?'

He sat up straight. 'Which one?'

'Ah, the, ah, Merc?'

He relaxed. 'Okay, fine, now tell me about it.'

I didn't ask which car would have upset him; the Mustang probably. I sat opposite him and stared into my cup of tea. 'Charlie doesn't frighten me, Jack. He's all talk and no balls, so to speak.'

'Charlie's a mate of McGann's, and from what you heard, it sounds like he's somehow indebted to McGann. Erica, look at me.'

I looked up. Jack was leaning toward me, his eyes as serious as I'd seen them. 'I believe Shane McGann is capable of anything,' he said. 'Do you understand that I mean *anything?*'

I nodded and looked down at my lap, thinking about going home one day and feeling vulnerable there, all by myself apart from a killer kitten. I mumbled, 'Charlie threatened me, and he told me what he said to you. That's why I did what I did.' I glanced up.

'When Heiner said those things, Joe had to hold me back. I wanted to ...' Jack's fists balled on the table in front of him. 'I don't want to frighten you but until I can figure out how to deal with all this, I need to keep you here, protected. Understand?'

'Yes. Okay.'

'And I need to say, you have no idea what it would do to me if something happened to you. Especially if it was because of me.'

'Okay. I know where you're coming from.' I thought about his wife and the guilt he'd been carrying all these years, and made a mental note to be much more considerate of Jack and much more patient about being under house arrest.

But then, in the following week, everything changed.

CHAPTER 32

I hardly saw Jack for a few days. He was gone every morning by the time Joe took me to work. He was out every night.

When Joe was out with Jack I had a babysitter, usually Richard the security man, and he didn't have much conversation, watching dumb old sport on telly.

On Wednesday night, Axle and I went to bed early leaving Richard in front of the TV. At 3am something woke me and I heard soft voices at the bottom of the stairs. I crept to my door and opened it a crack, peeking out. From there I could see the downstairs foyer where Richard was talking quietly with Jack and Joe, who were dressed in black from top to toe including black beanies. I heard a car pull up. The boys slipped through the front door, and Richard closed it. I heard doors opening and closing and then a car drove slowly away.

The next morning Joe was yawning as he drove me to work.

I asked him, 'What did you and Jack do last night?'

He shook his head. 'Nothing.' And stared straight ahead.

But something was going on, and when I saw the headlines in the morning papers, I knew. TERROR SUSPECTS MURDERED.

Three men on the government's terrorist watch list had been

murdered in their sleep. An execution-style killing, the reports said. The same men had been arrested in early October in relation to the stolen fertiliser and again following the Bolte Bridge explosion, but had been released due to lack of evidence. A number of federal policemen and women were being questioned over the murders.

So. Now I knew. Jack and Joe had gone out last night and murdered three men. That's what all their mysterious surveillance had been about. I ran to the bathroom and threw up my breakfast.

My plan was to get Lucy to pick me up and take me somewhere after work. How could I sit at Jack's, making idle conversation over dinner, knowing what I knew? And I knew they'd be home tonight, Jack and Joe. After all, their work was done now, wasn't it?

At one stage during the day John Degraves walked past my desk and we locked eyes in a serious moment of understanding. No. Not understanding; shared knowledge. It lasted only briefly then he smiled and said, 'Good morning, Erica.' I didn't respond.

But Jack spoilt my plans. He not only picked me up; he came to my desk to do it. Stood there in front of me and said, quietly, 'Let's go home.'

I couldn't think of a single thing to say. I picked up my bag and left with him, not saying goodnight to my colleagues even though they were all hovering, wanting to check him out.

He had a parking fine that he peeled off the window and pocketed without comment. We were both silent during the drive except for my phone call to Lucy to cancel my evening with her. When we got to his house, I ran upstairs to my room and stayed there. He allowed me exactly one hour alone before knocking on my door. I didn't answer or open it, but he came in anyway.

'I need to tell you about it,' he said.

I was standing at the window, gazing out. I turned and when I spoke, my voice trembled. 'Oh, no, you don't. You're not using me to make yourself feel better about what you've done.'

He approached slowly. 'Not for my sake. For yours. You need to understand why.'

'Why? I mean, why do you care what I think or feel?'

'Because I do.'

He stopped a couple of metres away from me, possibly sensing he shouldn't come closer.

'Okay, then.' I waved a hand in the air. 'Do tell. Why did you murder three men in cold blood?'

There was something, a part of me, that wanted Jack to say he regretted it. Or that he hadn't actually pulled the trigger. Or even that it wasn't him. But he didn't.

'Because they were going to blow Southern Cross Station. In peak hour.'

I couldn't speak.

He continued, 'We know how and when they were going to do it.' He paused to let that sink in. 'Do you know anyone who might be at Southern Cross Station at 8am on a Monday?'

I looked at my feet. My brother. Marcus. Half the people in my office.

'If you could go back to September 10, 2001,' he said softly, 'and kill the men involved in the massacre the following day, would you?'

No. But I wouldn't mind someone else doing it.

Jack's shoes appeared in front of me and I looked at them for a while.

'And so,' he said, 'a mass murder here in Melbourne is now averted. Three criminal lives have been sacrificed to save ... how many, do you think?'

He put his hands on my shoulders, gently, testing my reaction. I leaned into him and he put his arms around me. My head was on his chest.

He whispered in my ear, 'What do you think happens when people go to war these days, Erica? Protect the women and children? Honour among soldiers? No. This is a modern war. Whoever kills first, wins.'

· · ·

THE CONVERSATION over dinner was respectfully subdued. The television was off. Jack and Joe didn't eat much and neither did I. Axle sat on the kitchen bench eating red salmon.

After dinner I helped with the dishes and put Axle outside. I watched him through the glass door. He crouched, slunk along the ground and disappeared into the darkness of the garden. Prepared for the kill. Learning bad things at this house, I thought.

Behind me, Jack was moving about in the kitchen. I could hear the quiet opening and closing of cupboards, the fridge. He was suddenly still. I glanced sideways at his reflection in the glass. He was standing there, both hands on the kitchen bench, staring at my back. I was mesmerised, watching him watching me. He closed his eyes then, bowed his head, and left the room.

I let Axle in and took him upstairs. Went to bed without saying goodnight to anyone.

I woke at eleven. Couldn't sleep. Tossed, turned – I needed to talk. I remembered the other night when Jack had come to my room, unable to sleep, and sat in the chair and we'd talked. I liked that. I wanted to do that now.

And then it was 1am and I heard soft footsteps on the stairs. Jack's bedroom door opened and closed quietly. I lay there for a while, wondering how he'd spent the evening. Wondering how he was feeling and if he thought much about ... it.

I needed to talk.

I waited a few more minutes then crept to his bedroom door. In my mind he'd be in bed by now, but not yet asleep. I had a mental image of his dark room before me, the shape of him in bed. When I saw that I'd whisper, 'Are you awake?'

But when I opened his door, the room wasn't dark. It was lit softly by the bedside lamps. And two people were standing by the bed, embracing. Jack was facing me, his head bent to the shoulder of a woman whose dark hair tumbled down her naked back. He looked up and we stared at each other for a full two seconds before I backed out of the room, quietly closing the door.

.   .   .

WHILE ROSALIND RANTED about my commitment to my job – because I'd arrived at 10.30, not wanting to get out of bed – all I could think about was escaping to my parents' beach house at Aireys Inlet. Aireys was always so safe and quiet and normal. If I went there I'd be away from everyone who made me feel bad: Jack, Shane McGann, Rosalind, my mother.

I called Lucy and told her, 'I'm desperate to get away. Come to Aireys for the weekend? Please?'

'Really?' she said. 'Aren't you, like, under house arrest or something?'

I'd told Lucy pretty much everything about my date with Charlie and what had happened. Again she blamed Jack, but this time she was entitled to do so.

'Not really. I just need to get away.'

'Well, okay, but what does Jack say about it?'

'Luce, I really need you to not talk about Jack. Okay?'

LUCY and I were on the road, trundling along in my old car at about the time Joe would be leaving home to get me from work. I'd taken the train to my house and Lucy had met me there. I hadn't even bothered looking over my shoulder – I was beyond caring.

But now I felt happy and free. It was a warm day, and it was good to be with just Lucy. I dug my phone out of my bag and handed it to her. 'Can you text Jack for me? Just say, *Taking a break with Lucy. Back Sunday night. Please feed Axle.* Add some kisses.'

'You didn't tell him you were going?'

'Actually, no kisses.'

Moments later, she said, 'Okay. That's done.' She dropped my phone into my bag and we heard it beep almost immediately in response.

'That was quick,' I said.

Lucy picked it up and read, '*Where are you?* What do you want to say?'

'Don't worry. I'll be fine.'

Lucy sent the message and hung onto the phone, expecting a response. This time, it rang. She jumped and held it out to me. 'Here, I'm not talking to him.'

'Well, I'm not talking to him!'

She threw the phone into my lap. I threw it back at her. She squealed and threw it on the floor.

My phone stopped ringing and then Lucy's rang. She searched through her bag and found it. 'It's Jack.'

'See what my life has been like? What a nightmare! Don't answer it.'

'Sweetie, isn't he just kind of protecting you?'

Lucy's phone stopped ringing, and after a minute a message came through on mine. Lucy read, *'Please tell me where you are.'*

But I turned up the radio and sang so loudly and out of tune that Lucy had to laugh and join in.

About an hour later we stopped at the tiny IGA supermarket in Anglesea for supplies. We threw the shopping bags onto the back seat, jumped in and I started the car. Then I noticed a black BMW cruise past the supermarket car park, heading in the same direction as us. And another black BMW. Their windows were darkly tinted, so I couldn't see inside, but I knew one of the plates. It was GUNN1. I froze, staring, and felt sweat bead on the back of my neck.

Lucy said, 'What's wrong?'

My eyes were following the two cars, which had driven ahead and pulled in at the pub's car park. I had no idea if they'd seen us.

'Erica, what are you looking at? You're scaring me!'

I stared out the window. 'I think that might be the bad guys in those BMWs.'

'Oh, you're fucking joking!'

'I don't know what they're doing. They're not getting out.'

We watched for a while longer, until the two cars left the car park and continued on the road toward Aireys Inlet.

I said, 'Let's just keep going. They probably haven't seen me and I don't think they even know my car.'

Lucy said, 'I think we should head back to Melbourne.'

I ignored her, the thought of going back to Jack's making me feel instantly sick.

'Nope, we're gonna have F-U-N, Miss Lucy Collins!' I forced a laugh and pulled out onto the road, driving slowly, not wanting to catch up to the black cars. 'Besides, even if they are looking for me, we won't be leaving the house. I'll park out the back and they'll never find us.' We cruised out of Anglesea and I started to feel more confident that they'd gone ahead. But as we neared Urquhart Bluff, my gaze was so fixed ahead that I hadn't checked my rear-view mirror at all. When I did, I nearly drove off the road.

'Bloody hell!'

GUNN1 was tailing us. As I watched, it accelerated until it was so close I couldn't see the front grille of the car. The other BMW overtook both of us and sat in front. We were wedged between the two black cars.

Lucy's head swivelled back and forth. 'Jesus, Erica, do something!'

I didn't know what to do, but that problem was fixed because the bastards in front shot out a tyre. I watched the guy lean out of the passenger-side window, not understanding what he was doing until I heard the loud *bang*. My car slid out of control. Lucy screamed and I hit the brakes, hard. In my mirror I saw GUNN1 swerve violently and it clipped the corner of my car. The impact forced us off the road. We crashed sideways through the barrier, where the ground dropped away to a steep slope. As we slipped over the edge, I watched GUNN1 spin over the same embankment and roll slowly onto its roof. My car stayed upright but slid backwards down the slope. I cut the engine but I had no brakes. Lucy yelled, 'Oh my God! Oh my God!' I wrapped my arms around my head and screamed until we crunched into dense bush, way down the bottom, almost to the beach.

One of the things I've always loved about Lucy is her ability to keep her cool in an emergency. Probably her training as a nurse, but whatever caused it, I was happy about it now. While I was frozen with shock, stuck to my seat, Lucy released both our seat belts, grabbed our handbags and said, 'Come on!'

She dragged me out of the car and we ran, slipping and sliding, down the remainder of the slope through bush that scratched our faces and arms and grass that whipped our bare legs. We hit the beach and stopped, crouching and panting, looking back up to the top. There were four people way above, staring down.

I said, 'That's Shane McGann and Charlie Heiner. I don't know the other guys.' There was no one else around, absolutely nobody.

Lucy said, 'Where now?'

I pointed to where the beach disappeared around the cliff. 'Tide's out. We can work our way around there to my house. Or I know where we can hide if we have to.'

We started jogging and the sand to the right of us exploded. We both screamed and dived to the left. 'Jesus! They're shooting at us!' I yelled.

Lucy grabbed my arm and yanked me toward the cliff face, out of their line-of-sight. As we made our way over rocks and sand, I called Jack. The signal was weak, but the call went through.

He picked up on the first ring. 'Where are you?' He was really angry.

'Running from Shane McGann,' I gasped.

'Goddamnit, Erica! Where?' Now he was angry *and* running.

'I'm sorry —'

'Where!'

'Aireys Inlet. On the beach,' I puffed.

'Can you get away?'

'I think so.'

'I'm coming.' And he hung up.

Lucy said, 'What did he say?'

'He's coming.'

She called Steve. 'Hi baby, how are you? Really? Oh, great! Yeah, fine … at Aireys … Bit of a problem though … Um, some guys chasing us … They've got guns … I'll explain when I see you … You can come? Great, we're running … Hold on, Erica's talking – what's that, E?'

'Tell Steve if we're not at the house we'll be in the bum cave.'

'Erica says ... Oh, you heard? Okay, kiss kiss ...'

'Bloody hell, Luce, you could've cut to the chase.'

'What's the bum cave?'

'You'll see.' I glanced at my watch. Seven thirty. I estimated we had about an hour of daylight left, and probably not much more than that before the tide wasn't so low. The bum cave was only accessible, safely, at low tide.

We rounded a rock face and I looked back to see Charlie and McGann behind us on the beach, a couple of hundred metres away, taking their time, which made me think that the other two guys had gone ahead to cut us off. This cancelled any thoughts of making it to the house.

I pointed ahead. 'There's the cave.'

'I can't see it.'

'I know. That's why it's so good.' I pointed above and to the left. 'There's also a track here leading up to the road, but I don't think that's a safe option. I reckon they'll think we've gone up there.'

'So let's go in the cave.'

There it was, my old friend. Two rounded rock faces with a narrow slit between them that concealed a spacious cave. The slit was wider at the bottom, making the cave accessible at low tide, but only at a crawl. In the distance I heard sirens – more than one – and I wondered if Jack had called the cops. What the hell would I tell them?

I slithered on my stomach through the opening and Lucy followed. We sat on the wet sand at the very back of the cave, our breathing shallow. I whispered, 'Turn off your phone,' and sent a quick message to Jack – *Steve knows where we are*, along with Steve's number – and turned off my phone. I reached for Lucy's hand and held tight. We sat in the most perfect silence apart from the swish of the approaching tide and our ragged breathing. I tried not to think about the other things that might be sharing our cave.

'The tide's coming in,' I whispered. 'If we have to wait too long, we'll be swimming out.'

Lucy blew out a big sigh.

'Luce, I'm so sorry.'

She squeezed my hand, and I squeezed my eyes shut.

We waited and waited. It was getting dark. Lucy muffled a sneeze and at the same time a flash of light invaded the cave. I gasped, quickly smothering my mouth with my hand. I heard movement outside. Cops? Or bad guys? My pulse pounded in my ears, making it hard to hear anything else. I heard voices but couldn't make out what was being said. In the weak light through the gap, I could see two pairs of feet, then three, then four. They were silhouettes and I couldn't work out if the shoes belonged to uniforms or not. Whoever it was, they were no more than ten metres from where we were sitting. I started to shake, and Lucy squeezed my hand a little tighter.

They moved away. I watched two pairs of feet walk off to the right, and two to the left. After a short while, Lucy whispered, 'Do you think it's safe to go out there?'

'No.'

'Okay.'

Another hour or so passed and the water was rising. It was so dark. I turned on my phone and quickly adjusted it to silent mode. One message from Jack. *Call me.*

I was punching in his number when a wave rolled in and washed around our feet. I jumped back, hitting my head on the roof of the cave, and my phone fell into the water. I rubbed my head and whispered to Lucy, 'I dropped my phone.'

'Oh, fuck!'

'Ssh!'

Lucy turned on her phone. 'I don't have a signal.' We waited.

Lucy said, 'I'm getting a bit nervous about the tide.' The sea was washing around our knees.

'Don't worry. It won't go above waist height. We're safer in here than out there. I think.'

I heard splashing. The sound of something splashing noisily through water. My heart pounded. Lucy grabbed my arm and I held my breath.

Torch light filled the holes in the cave wall. 'Lucy! Erica! Are you in there?'

Steve! We waded to the cave entrance, babbling like idiots.

He called out, 'Remember how to swim out, E?'

I said to Lucy, 'We'll have to swim through the gap.' I pointed to the invisible gap below the dark water.

'I'd swim through piranha to get to Steve right now.'

I yelled, 'Okay, we're coming!' I said to Luce, 'You go first. Wait for a wave to come in and swim out with it. Stay close to the bottom.'

'I don't know what to do with my bag.'

I took Lucy's bag and yelled, 'Handbags coming through above!' I pushed them both through a head-height hole in the rock.

'Got 'em!'

We waited for a wave and I said, 'Now.'

Lucy took a breath and ducked under the water. I pushed her down so she'd clear the rocks, and I felt her slip through the gap.

Then a familiar, deep voice said, 'Okay, Erica, now you.' My heart did a little flip and I didn't say anything. 'Are you in there?' said Jack.

'Yes,' I squeaked.

'Are you coming out?'

'No. I'm scared of you.'

'You should be.'

I considered my options, which of course were non-existent.

'You need to come out, Erica.'

'All right.' I sighed. 'Coming.' I waited for a surge of sea, took a breath and ducked under the water. Another wave followed quickly and I struggled against the flow, clawing at the rocks and sand. I floated back to the surface, still inside the cave. I spluttered, 'Give me a minute,' and stood there for two minutes, trying to think of some magical alternative to facing Jack.

Something brushed my legs and I screamed, jumping back, falling into the water.

'It's just me,' said Jack.

'Bloody hell! I thought you were something scary under the water!'

'I am.' He hoisted me to my feet as a swell rolled in. 'Go now.'

I took a deep breath and he pushed me down. I stretched my arms out in front as the ocean sucked me through the hole. A pair of hands found mine and dragged me to my feet.

Steve said, 'Been a long time since we've done this.'

Lucy was standing behind Steve, Jack's phone in one hand, his gun in the other like she'd been born with it, poised to shoot a star. Jack appeared, retrieved his gun and phone and said, 'Let's go.' He took my hand and we made our way in the dark over rocks and through water to the beach near where my car had landed. As soon as we hit sand, Jack released my hand and strode stiffly ahead. We crossed the beach to the car park.

I pointed to the bushes to our left. 'My car's in there, somewhere.'

Steve said, 'We'll look for it tomorrow.'

Jack said nothing and walked on. As we left the sand, I noticed Steve's truck but couldn't see Jack's car. I called out, 'Where's your car?' But he didn't respond. He was way ahead of us and the car park was otherwise empty. Jack strode toward the darkness at the far side of the car park. I could make out a shape in that space: motorbike.

I ran after Jack and grabbed his arm as he mounted the bike. The moonlight softened his furious glare a bit, and I was glad we weren't standing under the bright lights in his kitchen.

'Where are you going?' I said.

'Home,' he grunted. He pulled on a leather jacket and shoved a helmet on his head.

'Please don't go without me.'

He started the bike. I jumped on the back of it, shivering in my wet shorts and T-shirt. I wrapped my arms around him, my cheek pressed into his back.

He turned off the bike and sat silently. I clung to him, unmoving. Finally, he took off his helmet. 'I can't go anywhere with you on the back, dressed like that.'

'I know.'

'So you need to get off.'

'If you make me get off and leave me here, I'll cry my heart out. It'll be worse than being kidnapped by Shane McGann.'

Jack dismounted with me attached to his back; I slid to the ground and stepped away. He turned, putting his helmet on the bike seat, and we stared at each other in the moonlight. His face was so angry, so dark, I wondered if he might actually hate me.

'Yell, shout, hit something,' I pleaded. 'But please don't look at me like that.'

He stood with fists on his hips, his mouth tight. He stared at the ground.

'Jack, please.'

He took a deep, slow breath and said quietly, 'Erica, I'm so upset, I don't know what to say.'

'Say what you're thinking.'

'What I'm *thinking*?' he shouted, and I jumped. 'You want me to say what I'm *thinking*?'

'That's better. Shouting is better.' I nodded encouragement, wringing my hands.

'I'm *thinking* thank God I don't have to deliver your raped or dead body to your parents tonight!' He waved his arms and paced away from me.

I swallowed hard. 'Okay. I understand.'

He turned sharply. 'Do you? Do you understand what I went through not knowing where you were? If you were safe? Do you know what it was like when I got here and had to wait another half-hour for Steve, not knowing if you were lying hurt somewhere?'

He looked at the ground. He was breathing so hard and I felt absolutely terrible.

'Jack, I'm sorry. I'm truly sorry.'

And then he said, so quietly, 'Why did you come into my room last night?'

'I didn't know. I'm sorry ...'

He looked at me. 'But why did you come in?'

'I ... I wanted to talk.'

He nodded. Looked away.

I said, 'Is she ... someone ...'

'No.'

I shivered. And I really needed to pee. I bounced up and down, rubbing my arms.

Jack pulled off his jacket and wrapped it around me, leading me with an arm around my shoulders toward Steve's car. 'You need to warm up,' he said. 'I don't know what the hell I'd say to your parents if you died from hypothermia.' His tone was much gentler.

As I got into Steve's car, I said to Jack, 'Can we go to my parents' house? It's just around the corner.'

'Does Heiner know about it?'

'No, I told him nothing about me.'

He said to Steve, 'Take the girls to the house and I'll follow, see where it is, then I'll ride around and see if they're still in the area.'

'No worries.' Steve started the car.

Jack looked at me. 'Stay low.'

I nodded and slumped down in my seat.

'You too, Lucy.'

'Okay, Jack. Hide from the bad guys. Got it.'

Jack shut my door and Steve drove away. Five minutes later, we pulled into the driveway of my parents' beach house and Jack cruised past on his motorbike, disappearing into the darkness at the end of the street.

'Nice bike,' said Steve. 'Expensive.'

'What kind is it?' I said.

'Ducati. Italian.'

'Of course it is.'

I unlocked the door and ran around closing the drapes before turning on lights. Then I headed for the toilet, with relief.

Steve brought firewood inside and Lucy checked out the pantry and fridge. 'There's canned soup, frozen bread, chips, and plenty of booze.'

'Perfect.'

Steve loaded up the fireplace and threw in a match. The dry kindling crackled and smoked, and the fire sparked to life. He crouched, staring into the flames, and said, 'Can I ask why my friend and my girlfriend were being chased by men with guns today? And can I also ask why Jack has a gun?' He looked from Lucy to me, eyebrows raised.

Lucy said, 'Am I your girlfriend?'

Steve turned quickly back to the fireplace, embarrassed. 'Only if you're comfortable with that,' he mumbled.

She threw herself across his back, arms around his neck. 'Very comfortable with that.' She kissed his ear. 'Let's go to bed.'

Steve stood, grinning, sweeping Lucy off his back and into his arms.

I said to Steve, 'I'll ask Jack how much you're allowed to know. Do you mind waiting?'

'No worries.' Steve was suddenly far too interested in Lucy to worry about blokes with guns.

I pointed to the stairs. 'Why don't you go raid the wardrobes in the meantime. My brother and I always leave stuff here. Actually, Steve, there's probably some of your clothes up there.' They ran up the stairs. 'And stay out of the beds!'

I stood by the fireplace, adding bits of wood, warming my cold, wet, barely clad body until Steve and Lucy returned wearing dry clothes. I went upstairs for a shower.

Jack arrived about twenty minutes later and when he walked in the door, I greeted him with a tight hug around the waist. He was cold and soggy.

'Are you sucking up to me?' he said, one arm lightly around my shoulders.

'Yes.' I released him and pointed to the stairs. 'There are dry clothes up there. First door on the right. And towels in the bathroom cupboard if you want a shower.'

'Thanks.' He pulled off his wet boots.

'There's another problem.'

He looked at me, concerned.

'Instant coffee.'

He sucked in his breath. 'You owe me big time,' he said and headed up the stairs. I put Jack's boots in front of the fire.

Lucy sat on Steve's lap in my father's big old armchair. We all had beer. Jack appeared wearing dry jeans and a T-shirt, and I handed him a beer. He took a seat on the sofa, and I stood in front of the fire.

'Did you see them?' I said. 'Charlie and Shane McGann?'

'No, but that doesn't mean they're not around. I saw McGann's car on its roof. Presumably they got out of that all right?'

I nodded. 'Yes, they all seemed to be okay. There's four of them.'

'And your car?'

'Down the bottom of the slope. I don't know how we'll get it out of there.'

'Joe will sort it.' He leaned forward, elbows on knees, his eyes demanding my full attention. 'Now, tell me what happened.' He was still frowning, but in a much better mood.

I glanced at Lucy and she kept her mouth tightly shut, but she and Steve were both attentive. I told Jack what had happened – everything – how one of them had shot our tyre and shot at us on the beach.

He was thoughtful. 'McGann's a loose cannon, but if he'd wanted to shoot you, he would have.'

Steve asked, 'Who are these guys, Jack? What do they want with Erica and Lucy?'

Jack seemed momentarily surprised. 'I'll tell you.' He gave Lucy an apologetic look. 'I assumed you would've told Steve. Sorry to judge you like that.'

Lucy smiled. 'Thanks, Jack, but Steve just thinks you're Erica's *boyfriend*.' She grinned at Steve, who gave her a squeeze.

Jack told Steve about the Team and his role in it. He explained how we met, and about my brief role with the Team and why.

At the mention of Danny, Steve scoffed, glancing at me. 'Nothing that bastard's into would surprise me.'

Jack told Steve about Shane McGann and Charlie Heiner. He didn't mention the kidnapping and I was grateful for that. And through it all, Steve watched Jack impassively, listening carefully, and when it was over he stared off into the distance.

Jack said, 'If you're worried about Erica's safety, you have good reason to be. I never intended for her to be so ... close to me.'

Steve said, 'No, actually, that's not what I'm thinking about.' He looked at Jack. 'The Bolte Bridge?'

'That was my team.'

'Congratulations,' Steve said, but not in a light-hearted way, and Jack didn't respond.

I wondered if Steve would ask about the murdered terror suspects. He didn't and I was glad. I didn't want to hear Jack say, 'that was my team' or worse, 'that was me'.

Steve turned to me. 'I'm a bit disappointed.'

'Oh?' I said.

He nodded. 'Yeah, I thought you'd met someone really great, Erica. Someone worthy of you.'

'Aw, shucks, Steve.' If he'd been within reach, I would've punched his arm.

'And, actually, you two kind of behave like a couple.'

Everyone laughed a bit.

Jack said, 'I think Erica can do a lot better, and safer, than me.'

Really?

'So, guys,' I said, changing the subject, 'are we all staying the weekend? Surf's up!'

'Erica,' said Jack, 'there are men out there with loaded guns, looking for you. And you want to go surfing?'

'Sure!'

He chuckled, much less grumpy, shaking his head. 'I was wrong. I won't be the death of you. You'll be the death of me.'

After a feed of canned soup, toast and a few more beers, sitting around the dining table, Lucy and Steve announced it was time for bed and rushed up the stairs.

I told Jack that I wanted to go to bed too and asked if he would stay the night. I said he could sleep in my brother's room.

'Yes,' he said. 'I'm tired. Didn't sleep much last night.'

'Neither did I,' I said and we looked at each other.

'I mean ... not because ...'

I held up a hand. 'Not my business.'

He leaned across the table and took my hand, squeezing it. 'I'm glad you came into my room last night, Erica. You stopped something I would have regretted.'

I withdrew my hand and covered my mouth with it – there was an inappropriate smile lurking.

CHAPTER 33

$\mathcal{I}$ woke with a start and yelped at the dark shape looming over me.

'It's me,' said Jack. 'Let's go.'

'You scared the hell out of me!' I scrambled out of bed, still dressed from the night before, and followed him down the stairs. 'Where are we going? What about Steve and Lucy? Why the hurry? I thought we were going surfing.' I stumbled after him into the kitchen, where Steve was drinking coffee.

'Morning,' Steve said, grinning. Steve was always grinning. Even at 3am. It's very annoying.

'What's going on?' I demanded.

Jack asked Steve, 'Has she always been an interrogator?'

Steve nodded. 'You should have seen her in maths class, challenging some of the most ancient formulas. Very frustrating for poor Mr Pitts, wasn't it, E?'

'When you two have finished discussing *me*, I wouldn't mind knowing what's going on. *Please.*'

'You and I are leaving,' said Jack. 'Steve and Lucy are staying. Get your stuff.'

I yawned and looked around the room. 'I don't have any stuff apart from this.' I picked up my handbag.

'Then let's go.'

'On your bike?'

'We're going in a car.'

'What car?'

'See you guys later,' said Steve, still smiling.

Jack said, 'See you, mate, and thanks.' They shook hands.

I said to Steve, 'Can you do me a favour and make sure the house is tidy?'

'No worries.'

I flipped a wave and followed Jack. As we walked outside, I saw a dark car in the driveway and gasped, squinting at the number plate. 'Where the hell did *that* come from?' It was the second BMW – the one McGann's mates were driving.

'I'll tell you in a minute.' We got into the car and Jack backed out of the driveway without headlights. We drove slowly up the street to the main road, turned right and headed for Melbourne. He flicked on the headlights and cruised up to the speed limit.

'What's happening with your bike? Why are Steve and Lucy staying? Why do we have to leave?'

'Hammering me with questions won't get you answers, Erica.'

'And not answering my questions won't make me shut up, Jack.'

He sighed. 'Obviously, I can't have this car sitting around in the driveway all weekend, which is why I have to leave, and I'm not leaving you behind. Steve and Lucy are coming back to Melbourne later this morning. Steve's riding my bike.'

I nodded and checked out the speedo. 'I thought you might drive faster than this.'

'Don't want to attract undue attention. I think there's enough on us already, don't you?'

As we passed Urquhart Bluff, Jack slowed and we checked out GUNN1 on its roof.

'I'm a bit scared,' I said.

'I know.' He patted my knee.

'I mean, I'm scared of my mother.'

He burst out laughing. 'Why?'

'Because she'll think I slept with you in their house.'

'Well, she doesn't need to know I was there.'

'She *will* know. I don't know how. But she will.'

We cruised through Anglesea, and Jack opened it up on the road to Geelong. For someone who'd probably had very little sleep, he looked pretty alert.

'So,' I said, 'tell me about this illegal acquisition.'

He smiled. 'I went for a walk to see if I could find McGann and his mates at the local motel. I passed the general store and two guys were parked in this out the front. I don't know where Heiner and McGann were – probably getting some sleep.'

'Bonking each other.'

Jack pretended to be shocked at my crudeness, tsking like my mother.

'Who were the guys?' I said.

'Don't know them.'

I felt suddenly nervous that Shane McGann was still at large and I glanced at the back seat. 'So, what happened?'

'Well, I jumped in the back and grabbed their guns, told them to take me for a drive. We drove a few miles into the bush and I relieved them of, well, everything actually, and left them there. It'll take them a couple of hours to walk back to town.' He seemed very pleased with himself.

I wanted to ask Jack why he didn't just kill the guys but I thought he might not appreciate the suggestion he's into gratuitous murder. Although ...

'Jack, why don't you just sneak into Shane McGann's house one night and take him out?'

'*Take him out?*' He shook his head. 'I want McGann in jail. Death is too good for him.'

Jack called Joe and told him briefly what had happened, and where to meet us. 'Bring something to torch the car,' he said and hung up.

'Are you going to blow up this car? Can't you just dump it somewhere?'

'No.' He poked my leg. 'Spoilsport.'

It was about 4.30 and still dark when we met Joe at the agreed scary place, and I sat in the back of his four-wheel drive while the boys played with fire. As I watched, looking nervously around, the BMW erupted in a fireball. Jack and Joe ran back to the car. Jack watched the inferno over his shoulder as we bolted out of the abandoned warehouse car park, and they performed one of those complicated high-five/handshake things. I sat in the back, sweating and worrying, and they laughed all the way home. Boys.

WHEN WE GOT to Jack's, Joe went back to bed and I went to find Axle, forcing him to acknowledge me.

Jack said, 'Thank God,' and rushed to the kitchen.

'Thank God, we're alive or thank God, decent coffee?'

'Coffee.'

I sat at Jack's dining table and Axle moved around my legs, purring his chainsaw purr. I suspected his empty dinner bowl had something to do with the sucking up. Jack brought me a cup of tea and sat opposite.

'So, now what?' I said.

'I'm not sure.'

'What do you mean, you're not sure? You're always sure.' He looked at me thoughtfully and I said, 'You're not actually looking at me, are you?'

'Huh?' Jack focused.

'What are you thinking?'

'Options.'

'Do any options involve feeding my cat?'

'Yes.' He grinned. 'To the fish.'

'Hey!'

'Just kidding.'

I trudged across the room, pulling Axle's open can of food out of the fridge and spooning the remnants into his bowl.

'Speaking of fish food,' I said, 'I need a new phone. Mine's probably in Tasmania by now.' I sighed. I really wanted to just go home to my own bed, sleep until midday, sit around for the rest of the day reading, maybe take in a movie, or walk around the Botanic Gardens. But the reality was that Shane McGann probably wanted to hurt me to get at John Degraves, and Charlie Heiner wanted revenge because I walked out on him, or, if I were to be really negative about it, they both probably wanted to kidnap and rape me, and then swap me for Jack, who they would possibly torture before killing in some sadistic, horrible way.

Jack said, 'I think it's time you had lessons in self-defence. Joe and I will teach you.'

How could I possibly have been happy with my life before Jack Jones? 'I really need more sleep.' I lay on the sofa. 'Oh, God, this feels so good.'

He walked over and held out his hands. 'Come on.'

'Where?'

'Upstairs. Joe'll be up again soon. You won't get much sleep here.'

I let Jack haul me to my feet and up the stairs. I headed for my room and he followed, and when I flopped onto my back on the bed he pulled off my shoes.

'I should lock this door,' he said, 'so you can't escape.'

'Don't you get any ideas, Jack Jones.'

'About locking you in or the fact that you're a temptress, lying there like that, a wanton wench.' He tickled my foot.

I giggled, pulling my foot away. 'Both.'

'Don't worry. I have a cast-iron will. Besides, I'm too tired.'

Jack left and I lay on top of the covers, curling onto my side with a contented sigh, wondering briefly what my mother would think if she was here. Surely she'd advise Jack to put a lock on *his* bedroom door to keep out the resident hussy. Maybe I shouldn't think about my mother so much. I smiled in amusement and fell into a deep, lovely sleep.

CHAPTER 34

I asked if Jack would wait for Lucy and Steve before beginning the self-defence lessons so they could join in. Lucy had called on her way from Aireys saying that she was on Geelong Road, and that Steve had just passed her, going 'way too fucking fast'. When I told Jack that, a grin spread across his face.

Steve arrived half an hour before Lucy and the three boys spent an hour in Jack's garage – doing what, I couldn't imagine – then we were ready for our lesson.

'I can't *wait* to learn how to kick a guy's butt,' said Lucy.

Jack and Joe were dressed in training gear. They'd moved the furniture out of the way to make space and so we could use the rug.

Jack said, 'We'll show you first, then you can try it. Okay?'

I said, 'Okay.'

Steve, Lucy and I sat on stools and watched.

'I'm going to come up behind Joe and grab him. Joe will show you what to do, then you can have a go.'

'Okay.'

Jack stood behind Joe and wrapped his arms around him. Jack started to say something, but he suddenly hit the floor with a thump. He rolled around, laughing and groaning at the same time.

I jumped off the stool. 'Can I have a turn?'

Jack stood. 'Hang on a minute. We haven't started yet.' He grabbed Joe in some kind of wrestling hold. Then they were both on the floor, rolling around, laughing. Steve slapped his leg, laughing too. He probably wanted to jump in there with them.

'Come on, guys!' I said. 'You're being silly.'

Finally, Jack stood behind me with his arms around me, pinning mine down. Lucy and Joe were in the same position, facing us. Steve watched, his face serious.

Jack said, 'The most important thing to remember, always, is to run when you can. That's your goal in any situation like this. Okay?'

I nodded once. 'Okay.'

Lucy said nothing.

Jack said, 'Okay? Lucy?'

Lucy stared at Jack, her lips pursed, but didn't respond. Jack released me and stood in front of Lucy, hands on hips.

'I'm thinking about it,' she said.

'And what is the alternative action you're considering?'

'Kicking his butt.'

'Well, I can tell you now, Lucy, you're not going to kick Joe's butt.'

Lucy stomped hard on Joe's foot. He let out a shout, releasing her, and started hopping around the room. She watched on with great satisfaction.

Steve said, 'Jesus, Luce.'

Jack was trying not to smile when he said, 'Are you all right, Joe?'

Joe hobbled back into position looking warily at Lucy. He nodded at Jack and we all resumed our original positions.

'You've got her?' Jack said to Joe. 'You're sure?'

Joe gave Jack an *I'll get you for this* look.

'Now, can we just try this my way?' said Jack. 'If someone grabs you like this, he'll be expecting a struggle.'

'That's a bit sexist,' I said. 'What if it's a woman?'

'Unlikely.'

'But it might be.'

Jack sighed. '*She'll* be expecting a struggle.'

'Thank you.'

'So the first thing to do instead is to relax against him – or her. Do it, Erica.'

I relaxed my body, leaning into Jack. He staggered back a step and said, 'Do you see what happened? Erica's body weight threw me off balance.'

'Watch your mouth!'

'This also relaxes the attacker a bit. He thinks you're not going to struggle, and so he'll loosen his grip.' Jack demonstrated. 'This gives you a bit more freedom of movement, and this, Lucy, is when you step into action.'

The boys showed us how to use our elbows, fists, knees and feet to temporarily disable an attacker, giving us time to run away. Lucy didn't want to run, however. She wanted to stay and fight. It was a trying lesson for Jack and especially Joe, and Steve was looking worried.

ON SUNDAY I slept all morning, until Jack made me get up so he could take me to get a new phone, and then Lucy arrived to help me prepare for the Australia Day barbie. First we had another self-defence lesson. Lucy loved it so much she was thinking about taking up some sort of martial arts. She'd started watching the Ultimate fighting shows on telly.

After the lesson, Lucy and I did some cooking. She was making coleslaw and I was cooking the spuds for potato salad. Jack and Joe were outside – Joe sweeping and cleaning up the garden and Jack fiddling with the barbecue, pretending to know what he was doing. Joe came in and pulled a large, green garbage bag out of the kitchen drawer.

I said to Joe, 'Jack isn't very domestically inclined, is he.' We all looked at Jack, who was puzzling over some tricky barbecue business.

'Nah,' said Joe as he wrestled with the opening of the bag. 'But if you ever find yourself in a jungle surrounded by snakes and snipers, with leeches crawling over you, and you're on your knees praying, then he's what you want to pray for.' Joe snapped open the bag and walked back outside to gather up his pile of swept leaves.

'I'll try to remember that,' I called after him, thinking about being surrounded by snakes and leeches and maybe even spiders. Snipers I could live with.

Lucy told me that she and Steve were coming to the party in a cab so they wouldn't have to worry about drinking and driving.

'Why don't you stay here tomorrow night?' I suggested. 'You can have my room and I can just bunk in with my good friend, Jack Jones.' I grinned at Jack, who was walking into the house with the barbecue grill. He nudged me out of the way to get to the sink.

'Jack? Is that okay with you – if Lucy and Steve stay?'

'Erica,' he said sternly as he washed the grill, 'I don't know how strong you think my self-control is.'

'Well, you said you have a cast-iron will.'

'Yes, but even cast iron is destructible at certain temperatures. If you're going to hop into bed with me, something's gonna give.' He gave Lucy a wink and said to her, 'You're welcome to stay, by the way.' He walked outside with the grill. Lucy fanned her face.

I called after him, 'Well, I'll just bunk in with Joe!'

Joe dropped the broom and Jack laughed.

CHAPTER 35

I was excited about the party. By the time I got up, Jack and Joe had already filled tubs with ice, beer and champagne, and Joe had been to the bakery for fresh bread and cakes. The wall of glass was open and it was a gorgeous day. It was going to be hot.

Jack walked into the house and I laughed, surprised. He tended to dress elegantly – always fashionable – but today he wore board shorts, bare feet and a gimmicky singlet with a picture of a scowling Daffy Duck and a slogan that said *Nobody upsets this little black duck*.

'Are you wearing that today?' I said.

'Sure! Why not?' He grinned at me.

Joe finished preparing the food and I finished decorating the tables with Australiana before running to my room to get ready. I wore a white strappy sundress and sandals, hair out; unusually girly for me. Jack gave me an admiring look and I tried not to stare at his perfect arms. The singlet was very, well, flattering.

People started arriving after midday with arm loads of drinks, and some brought gifts – chocolates and flowers. I'd asked a few others to bring salads. I'd invited Steve, Lucy, Marcus and Roger. Kate arrived with her kids – she said her ex-husband was picking them up at two o'clock and she was looking forward to letting her hair down. Caroline the art dealer arrived with an extremely good-looking date and I greeted her with a big hug. She seemed surprised by my enthusiasm.

Several champagnes into the afternoon and Kate, Joe, Marcus and I were talking in the shade of Jack's big old oak tree. A horrible sound made everyone jump. It was Kate's daughter, screeching at her brother, who had thrown her doll into the tree. It was stuck in the lowest branch, but still out of reach. Kate said, 'Sorry, Joe. Have you got a ladder?'

Joe didn't need a ladder. From a standing start he jumped and caught the branch. His tattooed biceps bulged as he hoisted himself up, snatched the doll from its leafy nest and jumped down again. Joe handed the doll to the little girl, who suddenly had a very sweet, musical voice. 'Thank you, Uncle Joe.'

I was reminded of what Joe had said about being in a jungle, praying for Jack, and I suddenly found myself wanting to be in a jungle with Jack. Marcus, flushed from the display of muscles, said, 'I can't stand this,' and walked away.

The party rolled on and people were having a good time. Everyone was happy. There was a lot of laughing. Joe cooked and Jack filled glasses and handed out beers. He and Steve were becoming really good mates, which I thought was nice. I passed around sun cream and wondered if any of the women at the party had a gun strapped to her thigh under her dress. Like Lara Croft. In a jungle.

At around three o'clock, Kate's ex-husband arrived to pick up their kids. He walked into the house like he owned it, nose in the air, and I hated him immediately.

'What does he do for a living?' I asked Jack.

'Surgeon,' answered Joe in a snarly voice and I looked up at him in surprise.

Kate was quickly gathering up her kids as the ex stood by, tapping his toe and making a great show of checking his watch. I was sure she said he'd be there at two.

We were close enough to hear their exchange, although he didn't bother to keep his voice low.

'Jesus Christ, Kate, I'm late.'

'Sorry. Richie! Molly! Daddy's here!'

'What the hell have you dressed them in?' He pinched his daughter's dress between two fingers like he was holding something poisonous. 'With all the money I fork out you'd think you'd find something better than these rags.'

Joe actually growled. He made a move toward Kate and the horrible husband, but Jack stepped quickly in front of him, hands on his chest, pushing back. Nothing was said between them – Jack and Joe – just a warning glare from Jack. And the way Jack pushed against Joe's chest made his arm muscles bunch, I noticed.

Someone was saying my name.

'Huh?'

Jack said, 'Why don't you see if Kate will help with the cakes?'

'Oh. Sure. Good idea.'

Jack turned an unwilling Joe and, with an arm around his shoulders, walked him down the backyard. Joe looked like he'd rather follow horrible husband to his car.

I ran off to distract Kate, who looked close to tears. I knew if she started crying, I'd go out in sympathy.

'Kate! Will you give me a hand with dessert?'

She smiled, relieved. 'Of course.' She followed me to the kitchen and helped me pull things out of the fridge. She took my hand and gave it a squeeze. 'Thanks, Erica.'

I squeezed her back. 'Are you all right?'

'Sure. Actually,' she said brightly, 'I need a drink.'

'Now *that* I can help with.' I ran outside to open yet another bottle of Jack's delicious French champagne.

A couple of hours and lots more champagne later, I was watching Jack across the room, admiring his muscles. My gaze followed the lovely lines of his arm to his shoulder, neck and chin, and I eventually found his eyes, which were smiling back at me. Whoops. I refocused, pretending to look at something past Jack, and saw Joe standing by himself. I made my way across the room to talk to him. But as I approached I saw that he was focused intently on something in the garden. I followed his gaze to where Kate was chatting with Marcus and Roger. I had to assume it wasn't Marcus or Roger Joe was looking at with such ... love?

The day wore on into night and the champagne started to taste like water, so much so I used it to quench my thirst. My focus slowly but surely narrowed to one tiny speck and that speck was talking to a blur on the back lawn away from the lights of the house. In the darkness, with the stage-lit sky creating mysterious silhouettes, the garden morphed into a jungle. Someone cranked up the volume for Kings of Leon's 'Sex On Fire'. The blur was snagged for a dance, and I slipped into its spot. I clasped my hands behind Jack's neck.

'Hey, Tarzan.'

He gave me a puzzled look, his hands on my waist.

I shimmied against him. 'Dance with me.'

'With pleasure.' He wound his arms around me and I swayed to and fro, which was all I could manage.

'Say something in French,' I said.

'*Qu'est-ce que tu veux que je te dise?*'

I sighed and lay my head on his chest, and he chuckled and held me tighter.

'I think Joe loves Kate,' I told him.

'I think you're right,' he murmured into my hair.

'And I love you.'

He squeezed me. 'Well, I'd be very touched if you hadn't already said that to everyone else here.'

My head fell back and I hiccupped. 'Kiss me.'

His eyes crinkled at the corners. 'You're very demanding tonight.'

'I dare you.'

'Hmm. *Déjà vu.*'

I shrugged and twirled my fingers in his hair. 'Double dare.'

'You don't really want me to kiss you, Erica.'

'That's right. I don't,' I whispered, pressing into him. 'What I really want is your body, naked, right now.'

'Stop that.'

'No.'

He frowned and a little dent appeared between his eyes, and I thought that was very sexy.

'My friend,' he said, pretending to be cross, 'I've had way too much to drink to be as responsible as I need to be at this moment.'

'Then don't be.' I stood on tiptoes and gently bit his chin.

'Teasing is dangerous,' he said.

'I never tease.'

'Erica ...'

'I want you.'

'You're drunk ...'

I wrapped my arms around his neck and pulled his face down to mine. 'Come on, Jack.' I ran my lips over his neck and chin with soft kisses and bites. His breathing quickened. 'Let's go to your bedroom. I'm *desperate* for you.' I pressed harder against him. 'Jack Jones! Is that your gun?'

He shook his head slowly. 'Erica ...'

'Jack ...' I reached for his lips and he held back for one more second before surrendering finally to my irresistibleness.

'Bitch,' he moaned and kissed me briefly but deeply. He whispered against my lips, 'You might regret this.'

'No, I won't.' Famous last words. I released him and walked away, not looking back as I made my way into the house and up the stairs to his bedroom. And with my peripheral vision temporarily out of order, I had no idea who was watching my performance. Nor did I care.

I kicked off my sandals and threw off my dress and perched on the end of his bed in lacy underwear, legs crossed, leaning back on my hands as I watched the door. But he didn't come through the door; he stepped into the room from the balcony and I wondered how he'd climbed up there. Swinging on a vine? I wished I'd seen him do that. But never mind. He was here now, and I stood and walked across the room to meet him.

There was no hesitation or resistance in his lustful eyes as he strolled toward me, pulling off his singlet and tossing it away. I held out my hands and he snatched me into his arms, unsnapped my bra and threw it over his shoulder. I untied his board shorts and they fell to the floor. Just as I suspected – no undies. Jack walked me backward, holding me as the floor gave way to the bed. He supported me with one arm, kissing me, crawling up the bed, and I slid along it under him with my arms around his neck.

I moaned softly as Jack's warm mouth moved down my neck and across my breasts, but mostly his kisses made me feel mellow and smoochy. I lay on my back with eyes shut as he pulled my knickers off. I giggled and shivered with anticipation, at the same time feeling more and more relaxed and, actually, overwhelmingly sleepy. I was tempted to curl up on my side under the doona. I yawned loudly and then my face was being kissed all over, and Jack's deep, soft, slumber-inducing voice whispered, 'No, no, no, baby, don't go to sleep.'

I smiled as unconsciousness folded around me like a warm, soft blanket. And just before my internal lights snapped off, I was fuzzily aware of something landing heavily on the bed next to me, and a noise that sounded a bit like an animal in pain. A lion perhaps. Or a bear?

CHAPTER 36

*A*wareness came upon me at about the same speed as an old woman moving backward with a walking frame. After a couple of minutes I was vaguely conscious, but my eyes weren't ready to open. I groaned as I tried to lift my head with absolutely no success, wanting to understand the cause of the pain in my ear, which was squished between my very heavy head and the extremely hard pillow. Stopping the burning sensation became my focus and I rolled my face into the pillow, feeling my ear pop back into shape.

I sighed with relief but realised I was too hot under the doona and I tried to lift my leaden arm to throw it off. Something tickled my nose and I sneezed. The hard pillow shifted slightly and something stroked my arm. I forced one eyelid back and bright light flooded my vision. Forgot to close the drapes? After a while I focused and stared for a long time at a hairy nipple. I knew that nipple. I'd just never been this close to it before.

Old-woman semiconsciousness was body-slammed awake. I was naked, sprawled across Jack's chest, my leg hooked over his. I pushed away, groaning, rolling, landing face-down at the edge of the big bed. I turned my head slowly and stared through a tangle of curls at the face smiling at me.

'Good morning,' it said.

'Holy shit,' I croaked.

'It's not that bad is it?'

I snatched the doona over my head and searched my memory in panic. I remembered only a little of my performance in the garden. There was my favourite song. There were snippets of other images. Mostly about me being naughty. Did he come through the balcony door? There were kisses. All over my body. Oh, God. I had sex with Jack!

Did I?

I slid the doona down my face just enough so that I could see. And breathe. I watched him though my hair. 'Did we ... do it?'

He flipped onto his side, facing me. 'Well, that depends on how you define "it". If you call "it" getting naked together right before one of us fell asleep and started snoring, then yes, we did it. But if you need actual penetration and orgasms as part of your definition, then no, we didn't.'

I blew out a sigh. I wasn't sure if I should feel relieved we hadn't had sex – especially sex I couldn't remember – or mortified that Jack had seen me naked, or guilty that I'd lured him to bed and passed out before he had a chance to enjoy himself. I chose mortification, and lay silently while it swept through me, trying to recall other details.

'So, now what?' I whispered.

'That depends on what you mean by "now what".'

'What do we do now?'

'Right now? Well, we could have wild sex.' He gave me a wink.

I groaned and pushed my face into the pillow. I'd fantasised about sex with Jack so many times and now I was naked, in bed with him, and all I could think about was vomiting in his bathroom without making too much noise.

'I'm joking ... sort of,' he said and I kept my face in the pillow. 'Erica, you're not upset about this, are you?'

I turned my head, peeking through my hair. 'I can never look you in the eye again.'

'You're looking me in the eye now.'

'I mean later, tomorrow, you know.'

'No, I don't know.'

'You've seen me naked. Up close.'

'I certainly have. Very nice.'

'Oh!' I threw my pillow at him and he deflected it like it was no more than ... a pillow.

'You saw me naked too,' he reminded me.

'But I don't remember!'

'I'll show you now if you want.'

'No! I mean, it's just, everyone will know.'

'Who's everyone?'

'Everyone at the party.'

'And that's bad because ...'

'I don't know,' I mumbled into the mattress.

He poked me in the ribs and I squealed a muffled squeal.

He chuckled. 'I'm going for a cold shower. Another one.'

I watched through my hair as he walked to the bathroom – magnificently, beautifully naked.

WHILE JACK WAS in the shower I gathered up my scattered clothes, put them on and crept downstairs. On the way I noticed that the door to the guest room – my room – was closed and I assumed that meant Steve and Lucy were in there.

As I emerged from the downstairs bathroom, I gazed around the living room. The wall of glass was wide open and all the lights were still on. Axle was stalking a dead moth, oblivious to the magpie that was picking through leftovers on the kitchen bench. It snatched up a half-eaten sausage and flew out of the house. Someone was snoring on the sofa on top of someone else. I wasn't sure who they were.

I walked around flicking off lights and a movement in Joe's wing caught my eye. I watched Kate sneak out of his bedroom wearing yesterday's clothes. I stared at her, my mouth hanging open. She smiled a sheepish smile and tiptoed past me and out the front door whispering, 'Good morning. I'll see you later.' I smiled back.

'Did someone put something in the water?' I muttered and went to make coffee on the machine. I put bread in the toaster and drank a big glass of water. My toast popped up and I spread a thick layer of Vegemite on it, and sampled the coffee. Not bad. I felt instantly better with rehydration, caffeine and the vitamin B hit.

Axle hopped onto the bench and butted me with his head, disapproving.

I tickled him under the chin and confessed, 'Mummy's never drunk so much before.'

'I don't think anyone has,' said Jack, walking into the room and surveying it, inspecting the couple on the sofa with his head cocked to the side. He smiled and walked past me to the coffee machine, giving my arm a squeeze on the way. He examined the kitchen bench. 'Is that bird shit?'

'Yes.' I moved closer to whisper in his ear. My need to gossip far outweighed my earlier embarrassment. 'Kate just came out of Joe's bedroom.'

He looked surprised. 'Really?'

I nodded. 'Yep.'

He looked at the sofa couple and Joe's bedroom door. 'Am I the only one who didn't get laid last night?'

I giggled and gave him a shove. 'I think it's nice about Kate and Joe.'

He smiled. 'Yeah, it is.'

THAT AFTERNOON, the house all clean and tidy, Jack, Joe and I sat around watching TV, nursing our hangovers, and I made a scary decision.

'I'm moving back home today,' I said.

The boys glanced at each other. Joe stood and walked into the kitchen, pretending to do something before slipping discreetly out of the room.

Jack flicked off the television and turned to me, sitting forward on the sofa, elbows on his knees. 'I can't let you do that.'

'Yes, you can, and you will.'

Frowning, he said, 'Can I ask why?'

'You know why.'

'Because of what happened last night?'

'I can't stay here now that we've ... done it.'

He tried not to smile. 'We didn't actually do it.'

'We may as well have.'

'*Now* you tell me.' He smiled but I didn't, and he watched me for a long time. It annoyed me that he had no issue with lengthy eye contact, while my face grew hot and I glanced all around the room. 'What's this really about, Erica?'

What's it really about? Probably about me feeling overwhelmingly tempted every night to crawl into his bed and fall asleep in the crook of his arm. Terrified that I might start cooking and knitting, staring out the window and caring only about when I get to see him next. It wasn't even about sex. But I couldn't say any of that.

'I need my space, that's all. And my things. I miss having my things around me. I miss my house.' This wasn't a lie. I did miss my house.

He nodded, understanding, but said, 'I don't believe you'll be safe at your house on your own.'

'Actually, I'm probably more concerned about your lack of sleep than my safety.'

'All right, you know I won't get a minute's sleep.' He was trying to keep it light, jolly me out of leaving.

I leaned toward him. 'So take a tablet.' I stood and left the room, trying very hard not to feel guilty. It was, after all, my fault. I walked up the stairs and into my room, where I packed my things and stripped the bed. I went back to the living room where Joe had resumed his television watching and Jack was leaning against the kitchen bench, arms folded, presumably waiting for me.

'I'm off.' I tried to smile. 'I need some help with my stuff and can I borrow a car?'

'All right,' said Jack after a long pause, 'but I'll follow you, check out your house, and you *will* allow me that.'

I nodded. 'Okay.'

'And there's something I want to give you.' He glanced at Joe, walked around the bench and opened a drawer. And pulled out a gun.

'Jesus,' I whispered.

Jack approached me slowly with the gun, holding it out on his palm like he was showing me something interesting he'd found in the garden. 'This is a Walther P99 40 calibre semi-automatic; very easy to use, extremely accurate and reliable. I want you to take it. I'll show you now how to use it.'

I stared at the weapon. 'I think I need to sit down.'

He guided me with his hand on my back to the sofa. Joe turned off the TV, but he stuck around while Jack showed me how to fatally shoot someone who might be coming at me in my bedroom with a knife.

'And what if I do?' I swallowed. 'Shoot someone, I mean.'

'You call me.'

I nodded and reached out to poke the gun with the tip of my finger. 'What sort is your gun? The one I kept for you?'

'I'll show you.' He left the room and came back with it.

'This is also a Walther P99, but full size.'

'I thought it was bigger than that.'

'It's longer with the silencer.'

Of course. Silly me. Jack showed me how to use that one, too, probably trying to help me feel comfortable. Then he offered me the other gun – my gun.

'Here, hold it. See what you think.'

I leaned away from it, frightened that it might possess me if I got too close. Like Christine in the Stephen King novel.

'It doesn't bite, Erica.'

No, it doesn't bite, just blows a big hole in someone. I picked it up by the skinny bit around the trigger and let it swing between two fingers of my left hand before transferring it clumsily to my right hand. My writing hand. My gun hand. 'Is it loaded?'

'No.'

Jack showed me how to hold it, how to aim, how to shoot.

'Does it come in any other colours?' I said but no one laughed, including me, because, well, really. And while Jack took me through the idiot's guide to killing someone, I made a decision that my gun was going straight into my laundry hamper, never to be touched again, and Shane McGann could do whatever the hell he wanted. There was no way I could shoot someone. Not anyone. No way.

CHAPTER 37

'Before we go to your place, I need to take you somewhere,' said Jack, holding a small leather bag in one hand and my suitcase in the other.

'Where?'

'The shooting range.'

We were standing at the entrance to his garage and I looked up at him, trying desperately to think of something to get me out of that particular task.

'I don't want to,' I said. 'You showed me how to use the thing. I don't need to go to the shooting range.'

'The *gun*. That's what the thing's called.' He opened the rear door of the Merc, putting the bags inside. Then he held the passenger door open. 'Come on, Erica,' he said. 'Let's just get it over with and I'll feel happy you know what to do.'

I shuffled over to the car. 'But what about Axle? He thinks he's going home.'

'Joe will look after him until we get back.'

I couldn't think of anything else. I slumped in the seat as Jack shut the door and walked around to the driver's side. He called Joe on his

254

mobile, telling him where we were going and asking him to give Axle all the love and attention he thought he might need.

We drove down Nepean Highway and took the turn-off for Moorabbin Airport. Drove past that and down Boundary Road. Jack pulled into the car park of an ordinary-looking three-storey brick building. Head office for Pee Wee Pies.

'Oh!' I said. 'This is —'

'Yes.'

Pee Wee Pies of course is a front for the Team's secret operation. I knew nothing more than that about it, apart from the fact that I love their pies. Everyone I know loves Pee Wee Pies.

Jack parked in a spot labelled 'Managing Director', took the small bag from the back seat, walked around the car and opened my door, which I was perfectly capable of opening myself.

As I took my time getting out, I said, 'You're parking in the boss's spot.'

'Yes, I am. It's my company.'

'You *own* Pee Wee Pies?'

'Yes.' He led me by the elbow to the front doors, which opened automatically as we approached.

'How come you don't give me free ones?'

He chuckled. 'I'll organise something.' He said to the receptionist, 'Afternoon, Honey,' as we walked past her desk.

She gave him a provocative smile and, believe it or not, a wink. 'Hi, Jack.' Her voice actually sounded like honey. She ignored me, of course.

'Did you just call her Honey?' I whispered as we walked down a long passageway, Jack nodding and smiling at people as we went.

'Yes, that's her name.'

'Who calls their baby Honey?'

'Honey's parents, I suppose. Here.'

He pushed open a stairwell door and led the way down two flights of stairs.

'Do you come here very often?' I said. 'For normal business stuff, I mean.'

'Of course.'

'Oh.' I'd thought Jack Jones spent his life sneaking around at night, running a thousand miles and reading the newspaper by day.

He opened the door and I walked through it into a narrow passageway with a series of doors along it.

'Offices and meeting rooms,' he said in answer to my unasked question. *Secret* office and meeting rooms, I thought. He led me to the end of the passageway and through a very heavy door into a small room that overlooked a shooting range. There were a couple of people in there firing guns.

I suddenly had damp armpits. Jack handed me some ear muffs. He helped me adjust them to fit properly, gave me some clear safety glasses, and decked himself out as well. He opened a second heavy door and led me past the other two shooters to the very end of the range. I recognised one of them. John Degraves.

I tugged on Jack's sleeve. 'That's JD!' I shouted, a bit worried because I was taking a sickie.

He put a finger to his lips and said in a normal voice. 'You don't need to shout.'

'Oh.' The ear muffs blocked the gun shots but allowed normal conversation.

Jack put the small bag on the ground and unzipped it.

'Why is JD here?' I said.

'He likes guns.'

And I remembered something else. JD is chairman of Pee Wee Pies. With a smile, I thought that Celia probably had 'Pee Wee Pies board meeting' in JD's diary for today.

Jack lifted two guns out the bag – mine and his. Sweat beaded on my top lip. He turned me to face the target way at the other end of the range – I could hardly see it, let alone shoot it. But the target – a silhouette of a man's body – started to get closer. It stopped about ten metres in front of me. I looked up at Jack, who was standing behind me, his finger on a button on the wall.

'Too close?' he said.

'No, but have you got one that looks like Rosalind?'

He laughed but only briefly. Things were serious here at the shooting range.

'All right,' he said. 'Here's your gun. And remember, it's now loaded.' He handed it to me. It felt heavier now.

I pointed it at the target, my right arm raised, shaking slightly. I was trying to remember what he'd told me, and what they do in the movies, but then Jack's arms came around me and that made me feel light-headed.

His left hand raised mine as his right hand gently held my wrist. Again, he showed me the safety thing and how to hold the gun, how to sight down the barrel.

'Relax your shoulders,' he said. His mouth was right next to my ear and I could feel the hard length of his body behind me. I forgot why we were here.

'Erica?'

'Huh?'

'Stand with your feet apart, your left leg slightly in front of your right. When you fire the gun, you'll need to absorb the impact. Prepare for the kickback.'

'Okay.'

'Lock your arms. Sight down the barrel. Aim for the largest body mass – his chest.'

'Okay.'

'Are you ready?' He released my hands and stepped back.

'Yes.'

'Squeeze the trigger. Just squeeze it.'

I squeezed. The gun fired and I screamed as it jerked up and back and right out of my hands. Jack caught the gun with his left hand and me with his other as I fell backward.

I got such a fright I burst into tears like a little kid, which turned out to be a good thing because he gave me a big hug. But I could tell he was laughing.

I pushed away, removing my glasses and wiping my face. 'Okay, I can do it. Give me the gun.'

We turned back to the target. I squinted at it. 'Did I hit it?'

'No. But you've cleared the room.'

I looked around. He was right. Imagine if I'd accidentally shot JD!

Jack said, 'Here, watch me.' He took his gun and aimed at the target. 'Stand back a bit.' I did. 'See how I'm placing my feet? Watch how I hold the weapon.'

Jack's gun was bigger than mine. And heavier.

I said, 'You know how I got your gun out of the rubbish bin?'

He lowered it, looked at me over his shoulder. 'Yes. Why?'

'Why didn't you send Joe to do it?'

He looked down at his feet for a few seconds, then back at me. And even with the goggles I could see that his eyes were smiling. 'Because I wanted to see what you were prepared to do for me. And whether or not you'd keep quiet about it.'

'It was a mean, nasty test.'

'It was a test, yes.'

'That's pretty gutsy, admitting that now when I've got a gun in my hand.'

He smiled and turned back to the target. I watched as he fired off six shots, looking just like they do in the movies. He made it look very easy. And sexy. There was a jagged hole in the target's chest. Jack pulled that one in and put up a fresh one.

'Come on,' he said. 'Try again.'

We stood in position. I knew what to expect now when the gun fired, and I had the added incentive of not wanting to be the laughing stock of Pee Wee Pies. Jack's arms were around me and this time he stayed behind me, supporting my body with his. He murmured instructions again and I took careful aim and squeezed the trigger, bracing my arms and legs in position, ready for the impact.

It worked. The gun fired. It kicked back but I stood my ground, with Jack's help. I looked up at him, but he was inspecting the target with his finger on the button, bringing it in. As it moved toward us, I could see the light shining through a hole, right between the eyes!

'Is that good?' I said.

He chuckled. 'Yes, that's very good, but I wanted you to aim for his chest.'

'Can I do it again?'

We practised for another half hour or so and I got the hang of it. It was kind of fun, in fact.

Back in the car, Jack said to me, 'You're a good shot. A natural.'

'Are you just saying that to be nice?'

'No. I wouldn't. Not about something like this.'

And I knew that was the truth. Jack doesn't sugar coat anything. I felt quite pleased with myself. Which was a nice change.

WITH MY CAR recovered but still off the road, Jack was (surprisingly) happy for me to borrow one of his. We stood again at the entrance to his garage and I gazed at the collection of cars. The choice was easy, but it was his turn to sweat a bit, I reckoned.

'I think I'd like, ah ... that one.' I pointed to the Mustang. My favourite by a long shot.

He clasped his hand to his heart, rather theatrically I thought, and gasped. 'Not my sweetheart!'

'Yep, that's the one I want.'

'What about the Audi? Come on, Erica, I'll already be losing sleep without that added stress.' He seemed really upset.

I huffed and mumbled, 'All right, I'll take the stupid Audi.'

'Don't listen to her,' he said, addressing the stupid Audi.

I drove the Audi and had to admit that it was very nice. And fast, except that I stalled at every red light and bunny hopped most of the way home with a few fast bits in between. Jack followed me in the Merc and pulled up across the driveway once I'd reversed into my carport. He grumbled about my driving and told me to wait in the car while he checked out my house, the alarm system and all the locks; I suppose making sure no one had been in there tampering with things.

As I walked through the French doors into the living room I screamed much louder than was probably necessary, and Jack nearly hit the ceiling.

'What? What's wrong?' His eyes flashed around the room.

'How could you inspect my entire house and not see *that?*' I pointed to a hairy spider on the wall.

'Jesus,' he muttered and I ran into the bathroom.

I yelled, 'You have to take it down the street but don't kill it!' I didn't like killing things, even spiders. Well, cockroaches and mosquitoes – they deserved to die.

After that, Jack hung around and kept finding things to do. Finally he sat on the sofa with the television remote. I stood in front of him, my arms crossed.

'I'm a big girl, Jack, and you're going to have to leave at some stage. You can't sit there all night.' As much as I liked the idea of it.

He sighed and turned off the TV. 'Where's your gun?'

I looked around the room, trying to remember where I'd put it. 'I think it's in my handbag.'

'Erica,' he ran a hand over his face, 'you need to *know* where it is. You also need to remember you have it illegally. You can't be so casual about its whereabouts.'

It wasn't in my handbag but I finally found where I'd put it. My gun was in my toiletry bag, nestled among the tampons. Jack checked out my bedroom. He wanted to have Steve build a small shelf with a drawer under my bed for the gun, but in the meantime he decided I should keep it in the bottom drawer of my bedside table.

I agreed with everything he suggested and he made me show him again that I knew how to use my new P-thingy pistol. He sat on my bed and filled it with bullets, then he said he would leave.

I felt instantly terrified but managed to avoid falling at his feet, begging him to stay. He also seemed to have trouble dragging himself away, and pulled me into a tight hug. We clung to each other and I felt like one of us was going off to war or something. Why was I doing this again? Why didn't I want to stay at Jack's gorgeous house where there were lots of guns and two big, strong men who were perfectly comfortable with shooting people and who were quite happy to stand guard over me 24/7? Not to mention a cleaning lady.

After he left, I took my gun from the bottom drawer and inspected it. I aimed it at my bedroom door, trying to imagine shooting someone who was rushing at me. 'I can shoot you, bloody Shane McGann,' I said to the wall but Axle suddenly appeared in the doorway and I screamed, nearly wetting my pants. Axle ran away and I sat on the bed, my heart thumping, telling myself not to be a cry baby. I dropped the gun into my laundry hamper and covered it with dirty washing. And that, I decided, is where it would stay.

I DIDN'T SLEEP much that night, tossing and turning and jumping with fright every time Axle stretched or yawned. At around 3am my mobile buzzed. A text from Jack: *I can't sleep. Hope you're happy.*

I messaged back: *A&E sleeping like logs*

– *Axle misses Jack*, wrote Jack.

– *A luvs E's bed*

– *Erica loves Jack's bed ;)*

– *Gnite!*

I think having the gun in my laundry hamper made it worse – like the Law of Attraction might think I *wanted* murdering, raping type people to come to my house. I finally fell asleep for an hour or two and in the morning I got up and went to work, trying to concentrate on not-so-scary things. Rosalind kept spoiling that by, well, being there.

I called Lucy at lunch time – she'd sent a text saying she was desperate to gossip about what had happened – and I told her I'd moved back home. I asked her to come over and keep me company that night, which she agreed to do, and she asked if Steve could come too. I was very happy my friends were coming to visit me; mind you, I had to promise to tell Lucy every detail of my romp with Jack, or at least, the ones I could remember.

Jack called me at work that afternoon. 'How are you? Did you get any sleep?'

'A bit. You?'

'No. Do you want to come here tonight?' He sounded hopeful. I wondered how many women had fantasised about having Jack Jones say that to them.

'Thanks, but I'm okay. Lucy and Steve are coming to keep me company.'

'Good. And just so you know, I've got two guys watching McGann and Heiner. We'll know if they come near your house.'

'Thanks, Jack.' I felt relieved. I didn't want babysitters but that didn't mean the bad guys couldn't have them.

The next few days passed by uneventfully. To keep Jack happy I got Steve to build a small drawer under my bed – I told him it was for my vibrator and he said he was sorry he'd asked – but I kept the gun in a sock in my laundry hamper as planned. One day, Jack said he was coming by to see me so I put the gun in my new secret drawer. He inspected the drawer and the gun, asked why it was in a sock, then he emptied the bullets and loaded them all again. Counting them in case I'd used one and forgot to mention it?

Jack had me followed to and from work, and called me every day. He mentioned on one occasion, with a smile in his voice, that it wouldn't hurt me to pick up the phone and call *him* some time. He asked if I was still feeling upset about what had almost happened between us, and I said that I thought I was nearly fully recovered from the ordeal. He said he was offended that I referred to it as an *ordeal* and I said he needed to get over that. One day I left a voice message on his mobile saying, 'I haven't not called you because we nearly had sex or because I'm dead. I've been very busy. Please don't worry.'

CHAPTER 38

The Monday after I'd moved back home, at lunchtime, the phone on my desk rang interrupting my Facebook chat with Marcus, who was sitting at his desk. I called out to Marcus, 'Hold that convo!' and picked up the phone.

'Media relations. Erica Jewell speaking.'

'What are you doing about the stolen fertiliser?'

I sighed. Another angry member of the public, one with a muffled voice. 'May I ask who's calling?'

'If you're looking around Melbourne, you won't find it.'

And he hung up.

I quickly jotted his words down on a scrap of paper. And stared at them.

I called Jack.

'Hi!' he said, happy.

'I just took a call you need to know about.' I told him the exact words, keeping my voice low.

He mulled that over for a few seconds and I stayed silent. 'What was the guy's accent?' he said.

'Oh. Um. Well it was hard to hear him. The voice was muffled. But it was an Aussie accent.'

'Definitely?'

'Yeah. Yes.' I nodded to myself. 'Definitely an Aussie accent.'

'Okay, well, that probably rules out the group I've been watching.'

'The ones you...' I nearly said murdered '... thought stole the fertiliser?'

'Yeah.'

'So... what does this mean? The people you've been watching are innocent?' My voice had raised an octave or two.

He gave a brief, humourless laugh. 'No. They're not innocent, Erica. It means they've used something other than the stolen fertiliser to make their bombs.'

'Okay.' Phew.

'And the guy you spoke to is the thief or knows the thief.'

'Right,' I said. 'And he wants Dega to know he's the thief.'

'Yes. He's playing with you.'

'Well, I'm not having fun.'

'Erica?'

'Uh huh?'

'You need to tell the police.'

I SPENT most of that week working on an information kit showing off BIG's new image. It was supposed to be handed out at the Opera House function, which was now bigger than Ben Hur. Everyone was invited: media, celebs, politicians. It was a very expensive PR exercise. Rosalind told me I'd need to fly to Sydney for it, which I didn't really want to do.

The police had come to the office and interviewed me, extracting every morsel of information they could get about the caller, his voice tone, his accent, anything that might have rung a bell. They didn't necessarily believe that the fertiliser wasn't 'around Melbourne', and they also thought this guy was just toying with Dega, and basically they said it could be anyone, even a practical joker. So, in other words, not really that helpful.

On Friday, Rosalind walked out of her office and plonked a pile of paperwork in front of me.

'BIG's shareholder list is in here. Make sure the share registry's invited all the people who were supposed to get an invitation. And *our* shareholders, of course.' She rolled her eyes and wafted back to her office.

I glanced quickly down the list to determine who BIG's major players were. No surprise to see Mintin Mining Industries in there with its substantial shareholding. Another one stood out, making me shiver: GUNN International Ltd. I couldn't help investigating further and then was sorry I had. It was Shane McGann's company. And not only that, the company had sold some of its shares in early October, and bought back roughly the same amount three weeks later at a lower price. I read and re-read the details, and a terrible sense of dread crawled up my spine and settled in the middle of my chest.

I sent Jack a text: *Will u b home 2nite? need 2 c u*

He came straight back: *At last, you realise you need me.*

I did a Rosalind eye-roll. *Y or N?*

– *Bossy. You sound like me.*

– *Ur ment 2 abrev 8 when txtng*

– *An abomination. I refuse.*

– *So? Y or N?*

– *Yes. Dinner? I'm cooking.*

– *No thx*

– *Here's an abbreviation for you :(*

– *OK then*

– *:)*

I stuck my head in Rosalind's office. 'I'm going now. Just letting you know I'm taking the BIG shareholder list home to work on. You don't need it, do you?'

Rosalind shook her head and waved me away without looking up.

I gave her the finger – she wasn't looking – and left. I intended driving home to feed puss before heading to Jack's, but I was lost in thought and found myself in Brighton before I realised what I was doing. I wondered if the Audi had a preference for Jack's place over mine. What car wouldn't? I rang the doorbell just after 6pm and waved at the security camera. He opened the door, gave me a kiss on the cheek.

'You're early.'

'Well, you didn't say what time, and your car kind of drove itself here straight from work.'

He grinned. 'It misses me.'

'It misses your garage.'

We walked through to the kitchen and Jack said, 'I was going to vacuum and buy flowers.'

'Yeah, right. You've never vacuumed in your life.'

'How did you know?' More grinning. Mr Happy. 'Do you want to stay the night? Your room's made up. I could do with a good night's sleep.'

'No. Thanks anyway.' I looked at the pot on the stove. 'Your special spaghetti sauce?'

'Yep.' Jack lifted the lid and stirred. 'It's the only thing I do well apart from barbecue, as you know.'

'Sounds like you and I should never live together without Joe. We'd die of menu boredom. Where is he, by the way?'

'Joe? Had a last-minute invitation to Kate's. The kids are with their father.'

This caught my interest. 'Is he staying the night?'

Jack waggled his eyebrows, smiling, and I smiled too, and I thought it was nice that we were all smiley and happy for the next one second.

'Jack, I need to show you something, and you're not going to like it.'

'All right. Drink?'

I nodded. 'Yes, please. Beer.' My favourite straight-from-work-with-bad-news drink.

We sat on the sofa and I pulled the BIG Fertilisers shareholder list out of my bag. I put it in front of him and let him scan the page. 'Mintin Mining. McGann's company.' He looked at me. 'Is that what you wanted me to see?'

'No.' I pointed to GUNN International, and told Jack that Shane McGann owned it.

Jack stared at the paperwork in silence, then looked at me. 'He knew BIG's share price was about to drop.'

'I think so,' I said. 'Do you know why the share price dropped? Have a look at the dates of those transactions.'

He checked the details, looked out the window, and back at me. 'It's about the time you and I met.'

'That's right. And something else.'

'The fertiliser was stolen. So – oh, fuck.'

'It's like he *knew* the fertiliser was going to be stolen.' I watched Jack as he gazed through me to a distant place. 'So,' I said, 'are we both thinking that Shane McGann knows who stole the fertiliser?'

Jack kept staring. 'No.'

'Then what are you thinking? Jack?'

He focused. 'That Shane McGann stole it.'

'WHY WOULD HE? What's his purpose? What's he trying to prove?' I paced around the room. How could this happen? In Melbourne? In Australia? 'Didn't Shane McGann just have a normal kind of upbringing? I mean, what went *wrong*?' I wanted Jack to provide all the answers but he was standing at the window overlooking his back garden, hands in pockets, frowning.

'New Year's Eve,' he said. 'McGann blew up those cars. And Heiner probably.'

'Why would they?'

'Because they're scumbags.' Jack looked at me. 'I reckon this is the Sydney thing we've been investigating.'

'What do you think they're going to do?'

'Blow something up.'

'*What?* Why?'

'I don't *know*, Erica. That's the problem. If I knew why, I'd be able to work out the rest.'

It was his slightly cross voice but I didn't care. I wanted answers. I couldn't understand how a normal Aussie bloke from a normal Aussie family could get involved in something so heinous.

'It'll be big,' said Jack.

Big. Great. I hoped they didn't do it while I was there ... Oh. I felt the blood flood from my face to my feet. I sat on the sofa.

'Jack.'

He looked at me.

'It's the BIG function,' I said. 'BIG Fertilisers.'

'What function?'

'Dega and BIG are having a function at the Opera House.' I swallowed hard. 'Next month. Everyone's going. Absolutely everyone. The premier. The media. JD. And me.'

Jack stared at me for a long time. Finally, he said, 'You're right. This is it. And no, you won't be going.'

'AND CHARLIE HEINER'S INVOLVED,' I said.

We were sitting at Jack's dining table, eating overcooked, cold spaghetti. Well, I picked at mine. For some reason I'd lost my appetite. Jack had spent a half hour on the phone with JD, Joe, Brad.

'Appears to be.'

'Why would he, do you think?'

Jack shrugged. 'Seems he doesn't like his uncle.'

'From what I overheard at the charity dinner, he seemed pretty desperate.'

'Maybe McGann's got something over him.'

I pushed my plate aside. 'So,' I said, 'if they're planning on blowing up the Opera House ...'

Jack looked at me, waiting for me to finish.

I said, 'I can't believe I'm actually saying those words.'

'I know,' he said. 'What were you going to say?'

'Why don't you just call the police?'

'And tell them what?'

'That Shane McGann is the one who stole the fertiliser.'

'And the police will do what? Search and not find the fertiliser.

Question McGann and get no answers. McGann will go into hiding again and if he can't go ahead with this plan, he'll do something else.'

'So, what will you do?'

'Catch him in the act.'

'But how?'

'We've got someone on the inside. Now we know what and when, we can find out how.'

'Okay. Well, you seem pretty calm about it.'

'I have to be.'

AFTER DINNER, Jack made coffee and we sat on the sofa. 'I'm not happy about you going home tonight,' he said.

I shrugged. 'No different to any other night.'

'No, but now I feel McGann truly *is* capable of anything. And I don't know where he is. Haven't seen him for a couple of weeks.' He reached out and gave my hand a squeeze. 'And I'm worried about you.'

I nodded. 'Good. You can do all the worrying. I don't have time.' I checked my watch. 'I should go. Axle will be starving.'

Jack sat there looking at me, all worried, and I thought how nice it would be to just take his hand and walk upstairs to the safety of his big bedroom. His big bed. Him. Definitely time for me to go.

At the front door, he said, 'I'll walk you out. I want to say good-night to my car.'

But he would have walked me out anyway.

We stood on the road next to the Audi. Jack gave it a pat. I put my bag and paperwork in the car.

I said, 'If this is all true, it's so ... so *awful*.'

'It is,' he said gently and put his arms around me, giving me a hug. I returned it, my arms tight around his waist. 'Be careful,' he whispered and leaned back against the car, still holding me. We stood like that for a while, me with my head on his chest.

And then, he nuzzled my hair. I looked up at him and we gazed at each other, not moving, and he had no choice but to kiss me. It was a nice kiss, tender, lasted a while. Our mouths separated but our bodies didn't.

'Oops,' he said, softly.

'How dare you,' I whispered, thinking about cooking and knitting and waiting happily for him to come home every night.

'As I said before,' he murmured, 'your room's made up if you want to stay.'

'You'd have to lock your bedroom door.'

'It doesn't have a lock.'

The voice in my head then was so loud I jumped, and I was surprised Jack didn't hear it. It said, 'WHAT THE HELL ARE YOU DOING, ERICA?' I stepped back and wiped a hand over my face. I really felt like smacking my face, but that would have probably looked weird. This kiss had no excuse like the others. This was a proper, sober one with emotion and no Christmas or New Year's Eve or Australia Day party to excuse it. What was I thinking? I was thinking about making love with a *man*, that's what. And we know what men do. They leave us and hurt us.

I opened the car door. 'I should go.' I couldn't look at him.

'All right.'

I dropped onto the seat and tried to close the door, but he held it, which forced me to look at him.

'Sorry,' he said, concerned.

Sorry? What for? God, I didn't know what to say or do. I shook my head, attempted a smile. 'I'll see you.'

And I drove away. Correction. I bunny hopped down the street and he probably cringed, watching me mishandle his precious Audi.

CHAPTER 39

*A*fter that kiss I didn't hear from Jack for nearly two weeks, and I didn't call him either. I knew what I was thinking but I didn't know what he was thinking. I knew I was being watched by his guys.

One Monday evening, just home from my parents' where my mother practically tied me up and tortured me for answers about my *boyfriend*, my mobile rang but I didn't recognise the number.

I said, 'Hello,' and someone was sobbing into the phone. It was heartbreaking.

'Erica ...'

'Danny! What's wrong?'

'I've been arrested.'

I felt instantly relieved. This was the best thing that could happen. For everyone. 'It was inevitable, Danny.' But I was trying not to cry.

'I have to tell you something ...'

'Tell me what?'

'When you were kidnapped. The guy I owed the money to ... it was Charlie Heiner.'

'What?'

'I tried to pay him, Erica! He loaned me ten grand but he wanted another ten in interest!'

'Jesus, Danny.'

He sobbed, 'I'm sorry,' and the line went dead.

I sat heavily on my bed and stared at the phone, feeling nothing but sadness. A single tear slid down my face. I was surprised Danny hadn't asked me to bail him out, and the fact that he didn't said something about him. Was he growing a conscience?

I lay on my back. Was I going to cry more? No. I sat up and dialled Jack's number.

He said, 'How are you?' in a voice that maybe indicated minor guilt he hadn't called me.

'Um, not great, actually. Danny's been arrested.'

'I know. I was going to call you,' said Jack.

This stunned me. I didn't say anything.

'I spoke to Bill Lucas,' he said.

'The policeman? Why?'

'Because ... he's a mate of mine.'

Speechless again. What did that mean? The cops who burst into my house that day Jack came to get his gun ... It meant that Jack knew them, or at least one of them, which meant ...

'You set up that whole thing at my house.'

'I did.'

'Jesus Christ, Jack, why?'

'You know why. We were after Danny. Bill wanted him for different reasons. But in the end you couldn't help us.'

'Excuse me? I think I *did* help you.'

'You know what I mean.'

I was about to just hang up because I was too mad to say goodbye, but then I remembered why I'd called him. I said, tartly, 'Danny told me Charlie Heiner was behind my kidnapping. He's the one Danny owed the money to. Or did you know that already too?'

And *then* I hung up.

· · ·

I HALF EXPECTED Jack to call me back at some stage, but he didn't and three days went by. I found dozens of reasons to be furious with him and I kept thinking of reasons to call him to tell him why I was so furious with him, but good old common sense prevailed. For once. And the fact that I really couldn't think of what to say.

So I focused on work and the rest of my life, which, I was delighted to realise, was returning to its usual boring and pleasantly dull state. Then, one morning, my usual weekday wake-up call – the 7am news – gave me such terrible news I wondered if I was still asleep and having a nightmare. I lay on my back in bed for probably an hour, listening to the same information being played over and over.

'... Bachelor of the Year Charlie Heiner was found murdered in his Docklands apartment this morning. Police say the execution-style killing was possibly the work of professionals ...'

I stared at the ceiling, trying to work out how I should feel. I imagined Charlie on his knees, with a gun pressed into the back of his head. He'd probably pleaded with the murderer. I wondered how his mother was feeling, thinking about her boy pleading with a killer.

I got up and moved robotically around my bedroom, dressing in tracksuit pants and a T-shirt, making my bed. Charlie didn't deserve to die, I thought, did he? No matter how badly he behaved. He was just a spoiled brat. That's all.

There was an urgent knock on my front door. I roboted to the door and peered through the peephole. It was Jack. Jack the murderer. Anger, fear, horror, guilt, shock all roiled inside me and I screamed at the door, 'Get away from me!'

'Let me in,' he said.

'Get away!'

'Erica, please. Open the door!'

I ran down the passage to my living room. I could hear him at the front door. He was breaking in! I rushed out the back, struggled with the roller door. I pounded on it, sobbing. My throat was tight, couldn't scream.

He was in my house, running! I clawed at the door. He was behind me, arms around me, holding me tight.

I struggled, screamed, '*How could you?*'

He spun me around, held my shoulders. 'Erica —'

'How *could* you!' I thumped his chest with my fists.

'Erica, stop!'

Hysteria swept through me. I swung my arms and fists, not caring where they landed.

'Murdering bastard!'

'Stop!' He shook me. 'Look at me!'

I was crying so hard I could barely see him. Jack walked me inside and sat me on the sofa. He crouched in front of me, gripping my arms. 'It wasn't me.'

I blinked at him through my tears. 'What?'

'Joe and I found Charlie. He called me, wanted a meeting.'

'Why?'

'I don't know. Erica, it was Shane McGann. He killed Charlie, I'm sure of it.'

'Why?' My crying subsided but I was now shaking. 'Why would he?'

'I don't know, but he's disappeared again.'

I took a deep, shuddering breath. Jack went in to the kitchen and came back with a glass of water and a box of tissues. He sat beside me on the sofa.

'I'm sorry I thought it was you.' I took some tissues and looked up at him. His lip was bleeding. Did I do that? 'Oh, Jack.' I pressed a tissue gently to his mouth, and he folded his big hand around mine.

I hiccupped, more sobs coming, and he put his arm around me. I rested my head on his shoulder, feeling terrible, but also relieved that Jack hadn't carried out this particular cold-blooded murder.

CHAPTER 40

Charlie's funeral came and went but I didn't go. I'd spoken to the police; told them what I knew. They didn't want to see me again. My car was repaired and returned and Joe arrived to pick up Jack's Audi. Life was suspiciously quiet. And then one day at work I got a call from Celia.

'John would like to see you. Now, if you can.'

'All right. I'll just let Rosalind know.'

'No, don't tell Rosalind.'

Wow. Was it something about Rosalind? Maybe he needed evidence against her. Proof that she really is a vampire.

Celia sent me straight into his office. I'd sent a card to the Degraves family after Charlie died, but this was the first time I'd seen JD since.

He waved at the chair opposite him and I sat, saying, 'I'm so sorry for your family's loss, Mr Degraves.'

He nodded. 'You knew Charlie.'

'Only briefly. We just went on that one date.'

'Well, I was very pleased when I knew you were no longer seeing him. I'm afraid he wasn't always a nice person, Erica. And you are.'

'Oh. Well, thank you.'

'He was desperate for money, you know,' he said suddenly.

'Oh?'

'Yes. The family cut him off because he refused to work.'

I nodded.

'But that's not why I called you here. Our friend has told me about your discovery and what he suspects is planned for Sydney.'

Our mutual friend, Jack? I nodded, held my breath. We're not supposed to talk about this stuff.

He continued, 'He's advised me to stay away, but I won't, of course.'

'Right.'

'He also told me that he doesn't want you there, exposed to danger. But I don't agree, Erica.'

Well, what could I say to that? Nothing.

He glanced at his closed office door and leaned in. 'I'm concerned that Shane McGann won't show his face in Sydney. That he'll run the operation from somewhere else and we won't have a chance to catch him. But it seems to me that you draw him out. Jack's told me a few things, including the phone call about the fertiliser.'

'Yes, that must have been him.'

'What interests me is that he called *you*.' He sat back in his chair. 'So. Think about it. And let me know what you decide.'

'I don't need to think about it. I'll go.'

He smiled. 'That's very brave.'

'I want to help.'

'I was hoping you would.' He pushed an envelope across the desk. 'Just go there with the intention of doing your job. Jack will look after you. Keep you safe. He cares for you. A great deal, I think.'

I took the envelope. 'Jack knows about this?'

'No. But I'll tell him once you're gone.'

I left JD's office. He actually walked me to the door and gave me a reassuring pat on the back. At my desk, I opened the envelope he'd given me. It was a gold American Express card with my name on it. And a handwritten note saying I should use it for 'necessary expenses'.

I already had a company credit card but JD clearly didn't want me to use that for – for what? My imagination raced with the possibilities. A new gun perhaps? So, what did this mean? It means, I said to myself, that I've been reinstated as a member of the Team.

Whether Jack Jones likes it or not.

I flew to Sydney on the Tuesday night after work. The Opera House gig was on Thursday. All the information kits had been couriered the week before. I'd barely given Jack or even Shane McGann a moment's thought because I'd been too busy.

On Monday I'd gone for my usual dinner at Mum and Dad's, this time taking Axle to be babysat while I was away. I'd wondered if Mum would look after him well enough if I got blown up. Maybe Lucy would be a better foster mother? After dinner I'd sat with a cup of tea, checking my watch, while Mum lectured me about my priorities. She hated that my job caused me to 'go gallivanting around the place', especially in the future when Jack and I are married. What husband would tolerate such carrying on? Who will cook for him if I'm not around? Some other hussy, that's who.

When I got to the hotel, I was starving. I hated airline food almost as much as I hated flying. I checked in and asked about room service. The reception guy said, 'Your friend's waiting in the bar for you, madam. You can get a snack in there if you like.'

'My friend?'

'Yes, he said to tell you.'

'Thank you.' I left my bag with the porter and walked hesitantly across the lobby to the open bar. I wondered if Jack would be cross with me for coming to Sydney. Near the back of the dark, almost empty room, I saw him sitting in a lounge chair, reading a magazine under a circle of soft lamp light. A waiter hovered nearby.

As I approached Jack looked up at me. Uh-oh. If I thought I'd seen him angry before, I was wrong.

'Hi!' I said with a big smile.

Jack glanced at the waiter and said, 'Whiskey.' He tossed the magazine onto an adjacent chair.

The waiter looked at me. I said, 'What the hell. I'll have one too.'

I sat opposite Jack, still smiling, said, 'How are you?'

He sat forward, right on the edge of his chair. 'Do you think this is a game?'

'No, I —'

'What the *fuck*, Erica?'

'Don't be mad with me! JD sent me.'

He sat back and glared at me for what seemed like a full minute. The waiter arrived and put the drinks down, offered Jack the docket to sign.

Jack waved him away. 'Later.'

Wow. I'd never seen Jack be rude to anyone. I gave the waiter an apologetic smile.

Jack took a deep breath. And another. 'Well,' he said, 'it's too late to send you home tonight. I've booked you on the seven a.m.'

I sat a bit straighter. 'Actually, that's not your call to make.'

'Like hell it isn't.'

'Like hell it is! I remind you that this is my job. I'm needed at the function.'

'They don't need you.'

'Yes, they do.'

'They don't, and neither do I. You'll be in the way.'

I could feel a blush crawling up my neck, but not from the usual embarrassment; this time, from my brewing anger.

He swallowed his whiskey in one go and stood over me, ice in his eyes. 'You can pick up the tab with your new credit card.'

I muttered, 'Bastard.'

As he walked away, he said, 'Be in the lobby at five thirty tomorrow morning. There'll be a car waiting.'

'Fuck you, Jack Jones!' I called after him, way too loudly. He didn't stop or turn to look at me, but the waiter certainly did.

I WAS WOKEN by a shuffling sound and it took me a moment to remember that I was in a hotel room overlooking a brick wall in Sydney. But what was the shuffling? Something by the door. I turned on the light, got up and checked the time: 3am. There was a note on the floor. It was in scrawly handwriting on blank paper, not hotel stationery, which told me it had been hand-delivered to the hotel, not called in over the phone. And it wasn't in a hotel envelope with my name and room number, as you'd expect. The note said: *Welcome to Sydney. Look forward to catching up with you. SM.*

That's okay, I thought. This is the reason I'm here. To draw out Shane McGann. It's fine, I told myself. Just be calm. Call reception. I did.

I said, 'You just delivered a note to my room. I'm wondering about the person who dropped it off.'

'One moment, Ms Jewell.' He put me on hold for a few seconds, then he was back. 'I'm sorry, no one here has delivered a note to your room.'

'Oh. Well, can you check with the concierge?'

'I just did. She's right here. No one from the hotel has delivered a note to you.'

'Thank you.' I hung up. And that's when the shaking started.

I double-checked the locks on my door. Turned on all the lights. Made a cup of tea. Called Jack's mobile.

He answered immediately, sounding extremely awake and still grumpy. 'Erica.'

'Shane McGann just paid me a visit.'

'*What?*'

'He didn't actually come into my room. He put a note under the door.'

'I'll be there in five.'

'I'm in room —'

But he'd already hung up.

Jack knocked on my door 90 seconds later. I checked the peep hole and he was staring right back at me.

I opened the door and he barged in, saying, 'Show me the note.'

I handed it to him and couldn't help adding, '"Please" would be nice.'

He read the note, started pacing around the room. He waved the paper in my face and said in a mildly nicer voice, 'Does this prove the danger you're in?'

And I said, 'Does this prove you need me to draw him out?'

Jack blinked, didn't answer. He paced a bit more. Stared out the window at the brick wall.

'Would you like coffee?' I said.

'No.'

I sat on the bed with a fresh cup of tea and watched him.

Finally, he said, 'Get your stuff together. You're coming with me.'

'Where?'

'My room.'

'Well! What girl could refuse such an offer?' I jumped off the bed and grabbed the few things I'd unpacked so far.

Jack took my bag. He stuck his head out the door, looked up and down the corridor, took me firmly by the upper arm and marched me to the lifts.

Jack's suite was cavernous. And the view was to die for, except that it contained the Opera House. It annoyed me that Jack got such a good room and mine was so crappy.

'Who's paying for this room?' I demanded.

'I am.'

'Oh.'

I looked through the double doors into the bedroom, where one side of the monstrous bed was immaculately unused, I was pleased to note. Where did they find sheets to fit that thing?

'You can have the bed,' he said. 'I'll sleep out here.' I checked out the two white leather sofas, which didn't look very comfortable. Whereas the bed looked very comfortable.

'Okay,' I said and walked into the bedroom. I sat on the bed and bounced. It was *so* comfy.

Jack found a blanket in the dressing room and took his pillow, and just before he pulled the bedroom door closed he said, 'I'll see you for breakfast. We'll talk then.'

I smiled. 'Okey doke.'

'Goodnight, Erica.'

'Nighty night.'

CHAPTER 42

*O*f course I didn't sleep. I wondered if Jack still planned on putting me on a plane in the morning. I was supposed to be in the lobby at 5.30 for the car to take me to the airport. I rolled across the bed to see how many times I had to turn to get to the other side. Three. I lay on Jack's side and decided that before I went back to Melbourne, I was going to have him. In this big bed. Whether he liked it or not. If we survived the Opera House being blown up.

At 5am I listened for him. I thought he might knock on the door, make me get up and push me downstairs and into the car. But there wasn't a sound. Not even snoring.

At 6.30 there was a soft knock on the bedroom door.

'Erica?'

'I'm awake,' I called out.

'Breakfast's here.'

I got up and wandered out to the living room in my PJs. Jack was still wearing the same jeans and T-shirt.

He glanced at me. 'Good morning.'

I nodded at him and checked out the breakfast table. 'Is there enough?' I said.

'I changed the order.'

Actually, there was a lot of everything. Fruit, muesli, eggs, toast. We sat opposite each other.

'So,' I said.

'Yes,' he said.

'I think Shane McGann likes me.'

'I wish you wouldn't make jokes about this,' he grumbled.

'Why not? It's better than being grumpy and scared.'

We ate. Jack didn't speak but glanced at me occasionally.

I tried to think of more jokes.

His phone rang. He spoke into it for a few seconds and returned to his breakfast.

I said, 'I'm supposed to go to the office.'

He looked at me but didn't comment, and I thought how nice it would be to go on a ferry trip instead. A romantic cruise with French champagne.

'Originally,' I said, 'I was just coming up on the day of the function itself but JD sent me a memo saying he wanted me here a couple of days early. To supervise the preparations. You know.'

He nodded slowly, said, 'I've got some guys coming here soon.'

'Okay.'

'Just letting you know.'

'You don't want me sitting here in my PJs when the big tough guys come?'

He almost smiled. 'You can sit there if you want. I'm just giving you a heads up.'

'So your manners have returned. That's nice.' The almost smile disappeared and I said, 'Sorry. That was unnecessarily bitchy.'

He buttered some toast. 'I'm not bothered by your bitchiness, Erica. I'm bothered by your naiveté.'

'Ouch.'

He sat back and crossed his arms. 'We'll work together then.'

I smiled. 'All right. Better than fighting.'

There was a knock on the door. Jack opened it and Joe walked in, followed by Rambo.

Joe said, 'Hey, Erica.' He looked surprised to see me sitting there, although he was too polite to say anything.

'Hi, Joe. I didn't know you were here.'

Jack said, 'Erica, you remember Brad.'

I smiled at Rambo. 'Hi, Brad.'

Brad turned his head so that his face was pointing in my general direction and I knew that was as much greeting as I'd get. He was still wearing dark sunglasses.

While I munched on toast, Jack filled in the guys about what had happened with Shane McGann. Joe looked worried and Brad's eyebrows raised a millimetre above his glasses.

I said, 'Shane McGann's in love with me.'

Jack rolled his eyes and Joe looked even more worried.

The boys then sat on the white sofas and talked in muted tones while I scarfed down the rest of my eggs. Brad gave Jack a pile of stuff, then Brad and Joe left.

I said, 'Do you want the bathroom first? Or should I go? Or should we go together?' I was full of it this morning.

He seemed to be considering all the options. 'You go.'

Eventually we were both showered, dressed and ready for action without any embarrassment or awkwardness. I asked Jack what he wanted me to do.

He said, 'Sit down,' and pointed at one of the sofas. The one without his pillow and blanket.

He sat opposite me and we looked at each other across the coffee table.

'I want to be very clear,' he said.

'I'm listening.'

'You'll do *exactly* what I tell you and when. No questions. No arguments. If you can't agree to that now, I'll have you delivered to the airport. Understood?'

I nodded. 'You're the boss.'

'Do you understand, Erica?'

'Yes.'

He kept staring at me. What did he want me to say?

'Loud and clear,' I said. 'I understand.'

'All right.' He looked at his watch. 'You're going to the BIG offices?'

'Yeah. I need to find out how to get there.'

He made an exasperated tsking sound. 'You won't be going anywhere without me or one of the boys. I'll take you this morning.'

I sighed. This again.

WE PULLED up in front of the BIG Fertilisers' office building in Jack's rented Lexus.

'I'll pick you up at four,' he said. 'I'll park right here.'

'How will I explain leaving the office so early?'

'You'll think of something. Don't be late.' He shooed me out the door without even a kiss goodbye. But then he called through the window, 'Don't even think about going out at lunchtime.'

I rode the lift to the 25th floor and said to the receptionist, 'I'm Erica Jewell, from Dega in Melbourne.'

'Oh, yes, Erica, we've been expecting you. Take a seat.'

I'd been sitting for about ten minutes before a phenomenally attractive, thirty-ish streak of blonde strolled through reception in four-inch heels and looked down her nose at the top of my head.

'Come with me,' she said.

Goodness. Someone was already having a bad day. I stood and followed the unfriendly, nameless girl down a corridor until she stopped in front of a door and pointed at the office beyond. 'That's yours.' She pointed to a desk in an open area. 'I sit there.'

Right. I was beginning to get the picture. She hated me before she even met me. Fair enough. I probably would too. 'I'm Erica,' I said, not offering my hand.

'Rebecca.' She looked me up and down and I tried not to feel insecure about her gorgeousness.

'I think we've spoken on the phone,' I said.

She shrugged.

'We'll be working together?'

Rebecca nodded. 'Apparently.'

'And you're not very happy about that.' Maybe she could work with Jack and I'll stay here at the office?

She looked away. 'I don't need any help.'

'Well, you know what? I'm not all that thrilled about being here, so let's just try to get along, okay?'

She shrugged. Miss Shruggy.

'Excuse me, Erica?' It was the receptionist, walking quickly toward us. Rebecca took the opportunity to turn on her pretty heel and skulk away to her corner. 'Mr Degraves wants you to call him.'

'Okay. Thanks.' I threw a glance at Rebecca, but she was sitting with her back to me. I closed the office door, picked up the phone and spun my chair to face the harbour view. Celia put my call straight through.

'Good morning, Erica!' said JD like my call was a lovely big surprise.

'Hi, Mr Degraves. Were you looking for me?'

'Yes, yes, dear girl. Just to say that I might need you to run a few personal errands for me while you're in Sydney.'

Ah, my cover for leaving the office early. 'Of course. Er ... anything in particular?'

'No, nothing special. Just errands. No one needs more than that.'

'Okay. Thanks, Mr Degraves.'

'Goodbye, Erica. God speed.'

God speed.

A few pro-Dega people called by my office to introduce themselves. I'd participated in corporate take-overs before, and I understood the dynamics and politics involved when a small, happy, independent company suddenly has Big Wealthy Corporation looking over its shoulder. The people who welcomed me were the ones who were looking for a fast climb up the corporate ladder. They saw the size of my office and knew they needed to be nice. Of course, if I'd never been recruited to the Team, I might still have been sent to Sydney, but I would have been assigned a much smaller desk, probably next to Rebecca. This office was a gift, and a message, from JD.

My visitors eventually included Susan, the glamorous public

affairs manager with whom I already had an iffy relationship. She was a little more friendly than Rebecca, but clearly offended that I'd been sent to help, and she was not overly interested in sucking up to JD.

Susan said, 'It's lovely to meet you, Erica, but we really don't need you. However, I'm sure we can fill your time here.'

I assured her I was here to help, not hinder, and happy to do whatever needed to be done. In an effort to smooth the way, I tried to convince Susan and Rebecca that John Degraves was a bit of a micromanager until he'd worked with you for a while.

'Give him six months and he'll stop looking over your shoulder,' I said.

They seemed to accept that and Rebecca was a tad warmer toward me. In fact, she suddenly realised she could use me to do all the awful jobs no one else wanted. She started by dumping the guest list and name tags on my desk.

'You'll need to check the spelling and *all* the details,' she said, smirking.

Fine by me. I'd rather have something to do than nothing. I ran my eyes over the list, stopping to inspect the names marked as VIPs and trying not to imagine them bobbing around in the harbour, lifeless and limbless.

Susan stuck her head in my door and announced, 'Wonderful news! We've just received confirmation from the prime minister's office. Add him to the list!'

At 3.50pm, starving because I'd had no lunch, I knocked on Susan's door and told her I'd been asked to run some errands for John Degraves.

'That's fine, Erica,' she said with a sweet smile. 'We don't need you anyway.'

I left without telling Rebecca.

When I walked outside Jack was already there, leaning against the car, arms folded across his chest. I couldn't tell if he was still grumpy or not. If he didn't put a smile on his face soon, I'd blow up the Opera House myself just to get it over with.

He opened the door for me and as soon as he got in the car, I said, 'The prime minister's coming tomorrow night.'

He nodded.

I said, 'Aren't you concerned?'

'His life is no more important than anyone else's.'

'Good point,' I said. 'I'm starving.'

'Me too.'

'I wasn't allowed to get lunch.'

'You'll live.'

So much for sympathy. As he drove into the hotel car park, he said, 'You'll need to get changed quickly. We're walking from here.'

'Where are we going?'

Jack parked, turned off the engine. 'Time to lay the bait.'

'Bait?'

He looked at me. 'That's you, sweetheart.' And he got out of the car.

CHAPTER 43

On the Opera House forecourt we strolled among the tourists; lots of Asian people following their guides like sheep.

Jack held my hand. He was carrying a digital SLR camera with a small telephoto lens. He stopped suddenly. He was saying things that made no sense. I looked at him and started to speak, but he silenced me with a hand signal. He wasn't talking to me – he was talking to a hidden microphone, presumably.

He turned me to face him and stood with his hands on my shoulders, gazing at me, chatting with someone else. Brad? I smiled and tried to look lovingly back at him, assuming I was meant to be playing a role.

He whispered suddenly, presumably to me, 'Sorry, I've got an opportunity to ID someone involved.' And in a more normal voice again, 'Thanks, mate.'

'Are you talking to Rambo?'

'If you mean Brad, then yes.'

We started strolling again, hand in hand. It was terribly romantic: Jack, me, Brad the microphone.

Jack said, 'There he is. Twelve o'clock.'

'Are you talking to me?'

'Who else?'

'Which guy?'

'Blue jacket. Army haircut.'

'I see him.'

'Very, very bad dude.'

And then *I* saw a guy. A big, blonde one standing on the Opera House steps, head and shoulders above all the black-haired people around him.

I said in a low voice, 'Jack. It's Shane McGann.'

'Is he watching us?'

'No.'

'Where?'

'Um. Ten past two.'

He stopped walking. 'This isn't a driving lesson.'

I blinked up at him.

He said, 'Ten o'clock or two o'clock?'

'Is it when the big hand —'

'Never mind, I see him. They're casing the place.'

'Do you think he's seen us?'

'Don't know. Come over here.'

He guided me to a space by the harbour wall where we'd be in clear view of Shane McGann, away from the flocks of sheep. I leaned against the wall and looked over it. Water rolled in giant ripples away from passing ferries; small waves smacked the wall. Jack turned me to face him, put his hands on my shoulders. He pushed my hair back from my face.

'This is very romantic,' I said.

'You can pretend you like me if you want.'

'But I don't.' I stood like a statue, arms by my side.

He leaned in, kissed my forehead. 'Fair enough.'

I put my arms around his waist, but kept a gap between us. 'I want a souvenir. One of those snow globes. With the Opera House inside.'

'I'll get you one.' He closed the gap, arms around me.

'Why will Shane McGann think you're here?' I said, head on his chest.

'He'd know by now that I head up JD's security.' I felt his shrug. 'Maybe I'm here with my lover.'

'In separate rooms.'

'My very chaste lover.'

'Who realised she was being silly and moved to the enormous suite.' I looked up at him. 'He might think you're onto him.'

'He can't know that I know what he's planning.'

'He knows you know he's here. He might know you know he knows ... something.'

Jack smiled down at me.

'Maybe he won't go ahead with it,' I said but Jack was looking past me.

He gave me a gentle push and said, 'Stand over there now, darling. I'll take your photo.'

I walked. 'Here?'

'Good.' I heard the camera's motor drive working.

He walked up to me, inspecting the shots he'd taken, and said, 'Let's go,' giving me a little shove. So much for the romance.

Once back on the street we walked quickly to the hotel, mostly in silence. Except, of course, for Jack's chitty chat with Brad the microphone. Jack held my hand, dragging me along. He was laughing with Brad now, sharing a joke I didn't catch. Was it about me? I was trying not to stumble, and I was trying not to be pissed off. Too late. I snatched my hand out of his and walked faster.

When we got back to the room, Jack slipped into something more comfortable – a new personality. He sat at the desk, whistling, and loaded the photographs onto his laptop.

'Can I see?' I said.

'Sure.' He patted his knee. Mr Happy.

'I'm not sitting on your knee.'

'Why not?'

'That's very patronising, Jack.'

'Well, you're very grumpy.' He grinned at me.

'You can talk!' I stomped off to the bathroom and locked the door.

I ran a bath and sat in it, huffing. After about half an hour, there was a soft tap on the door.

'I'm not here!' I got out of the bath.

'Let's go out for dinner.'

'Go out for dinner with Brad!'

'I don't want to go out with Brad. He doesn't say anything. Besides, you're prettier.'

I jerked open the door; a towel around me. He was leaning against the doorjamb, smiling.

'*You* are being patronising and stupid,' I told him.

'Sorry.' He didn't look sorry. He looked amused.

'God, I can't read you at all. It's so hard to keep up with your moods.'

He shrugged. 'This job's a worry.'

'Don't you think I know that?' I waved one hand around while I clung to my towel with the other. 'Jack, I hauled you half dead into my house and since then I've watched you do things that anyone with a heart just shouldn't have to do!'

He dipped his head for a few moments, then looked at me again. I huffed and waited.

'Sometimes ...' he began. He sighed. 'Look, sometimes, I just feel if there's a chance to enjoy a moment, I need to grab it. Even when things are looking as bad as they can.'

Which I assumed meant right now. I pushed past him and marched into the dressing room. Then I marched back out, still waving my arm. 'Why don't you go play golf? Travel the world? Have affairs with blonde women? You've got plenty of money. You don't *need* to work.'

He watched me; his expression now a mix of amusement and concern. I was basically suggesting he become a playboy. An international one, no less.

'Or be an accountant. A financial adviser!' I ranted on. 'Something nice and safe. You can't save the whole world, Jack!' I blinked at him, waiting for a response. There wasn't one.

'Okay.' I sighed. 'Let's go for dinner.'

He smiled. 'I'm starving,' he said. 'I haven't eaten since this morning.'

'Then I'd better hurry.'

'Take as much time as you want, baby,' he said and walked out of the bedroom, patting my backside as he passed.

I shouted after him, 'I'm adding sexual harassment to my list of complaints about you!'

He seemed to think that was funny, and so did I when I thought about JD reading that list. We left the hotel and strolled toward The Rocks. We passed a small, intimate restaurant and I stopped to look in the window.

'I've read about this place,' I said. 'It's meant to be really nice.'

'I don't think so. Candlelight.'

'Candlelight is flattering,' I said, fogging up the glass with my breath.

'Candlelight is foreplay.'

'It's not!'

'Yes, it is. Candlelit dinners are foreplay. Always.' He grinned and kept walking. I followed, thinking about the candlelit dinners I remembered, and felt I had to concede on that particular point.

We sat at the bar in a big, bright, noisy restaurant, waiting for a table. Jack said, 'I haven't asked about your day at the office.'

I pulled a face. 'Ice-queen city. They hate me.'

'Did you attack anyone?'

'I resisted. Lucky I've got you.' I punched his arm. We smiled at each other but then I spoilt the happy moment by asking, 'How are you feeling about tomorrow night?'

Jack took a long pull on his beer. He glanced around and said quietly, leaning in, 'It's the most perfect target. The Opera House. Farmers. The foundation of Australia's economy. The PM's just a bonus.' He took another long drink. 'Of course, the greatest insult is that they're using the company's own product.'

I nodded slowly. 'If they're successful ...' I shook my head, struggling to comprehend the enormity of it. Even putting the physical toll aside, the psychological impact of such an attack would be devastating.

Jack seemed so calm about it. I asked, 'How do you *know* what's going to happen?'

He gave me a considered look, went to speak then hesitated. Finally, he said, 'Our informant is very close, Erica. She's married to one of them.'

'She?'

'Yes. Her husband's the federal cop involved; the guy I pointed out to you at the Opera House.'

'The very bad dude?'

'Yes. She's also Brad's girlfriend.'

'*Really?*' I could feel my eyes grow wide. I couldn't imagine Brad having a girlfriend, especially a married one. Brad seemed more the lonely-wanderer-plus-dog type.

'Yes. It's all very … delicate. Aida's husband would probably kill her if he knew.'

'*Kill* her?'

Jack nodded. 'He's a very violent man.'

'But *why*, Jack? Why would they do this? Blow things up. Kill people. What's in it for this guy anyway?'

He shrugged. 'We don't know.' He looked at me. 'And now you know why we can't involve the federal police. I don't know who's clean.'

'So, you won't involve the police at all?'

'Yes, but the state police. They're already involved, unofficially. I've got some mates.'

I whispered, 'What will happen to her, Aida, after tomorrow night?'

'If we're successful, Brad will leave, take her away. If we're not, well, it depends on who's still alive.'

'Jesus.'

'Yes,' he said, nodding, and I felt an overwhelming desire to meet Rambo's mistress.

The waiter called us to our table and we followed him with our drinks. I gazed out the window at the view which included the Opera House. I looked away.

'Have you got something to wear tomorrow night?' Jack asked after the waiter had moved away.

'You're asking what I'm *wearing*?'

'Yes.' He picked up the menu.

'Well, whatever you'd expect someone in my position to wear to some posh cocktail function.'

He nodded. 'You'll need to buy something different.'

'Hold on. You don't actually know what I'm wearing.'

'I'm guessing a dress and high heels.' He looked at me with raised eyebrows over the top of the menu, as I thought about what I'd brought with me to wear. He was right.

'Have you got the credit card Degraves gave you?'

'Yes. Actually, I'm impressed he trusts me with a gold Amex.'

'It's got a limit of twenty thousand. Can't do much damage with that.'

'But I *could* go out and buy a twenty-thousand-dollar dress.'

'You could, but then you'd have nothing left to buy shoes. By the way, buy something you can run in.'

There was that impending vomit feeling again. I put down my drink and watched Jack as he inspected the wine list with great care. I thought how nice it would be to do this every night – watch Jack across a dinner table.

'Jack, how did Brad and Aida meet?'

He looked up. 'Brad was a cop. He worked for Aida's husband.'

'The bad dude.'

'Uh-huh.'

'And how long have they known each other? Brad and Aida?'

'Couple of months I think.' He gazed back at the list. Maybe he thought this would be his last bottle of wine?

'Do you think they'll get married?'

'Don't know.'

'How old is she?'

'I'm not sure.'

'Does she have kids?'

'Don't think so.'

I leaned in. 'Can I ask something?'

He glanced up again. 'You're stopping your interrogation to ask if you can ask something?'

'What? Oh. Sorry. I was just going to ask if you ever think about having kids. You know.'

He sat back in his chair and regarded me. 'No.'

'You don't want kids?'

'No, I mean I never think about it.'

'Oh.'

He resumed his inspection and I picked up the menu.

'So,' he said slowly. 'Do *you* want kids?'

I almost said, 'Yes, yours', just to be funny but thought he might not think it was funny. So instead I said, 'No. I mean, I don't think about it either.'

I INSISTED on taking the sofa. We argued back and forth about it and I knew we were both thinking the same thing: the bed was plenty big enough for us both. But I won, arguing that he would need more sleep because he had to save the world, whereas I just had to worry about myself. I sent him off to use the bathroom first. I wanted to sit up and watch telly for a while, knowing I wouldn't sleep, knowing I'd be thinking about bombs, death and mayhem until the wee hours.

I woke sometime in those wee hours. The TV was still going softly in the background. My back ached and I was cold, and I hadn't cleaned my teeth yet. I turned off the TV and crept to the bedroom, which was the only access to the bathroom. I opened the door quietly and peeked in, waiting for my eyes to adjust to the darkness. But Jack wasn't in the bed. I let out a silent gasp when I saw him silhouetted, naked, against the backdrop of star-studded sky. I couldn't help gazing at his exquisite shape as he gazed out the window. I knew what had his undivided attention. Those Opera House sails positively glowed in the moonlight.

I slipped through to the bathroom, cleaned my teeth, and changed into my pyjamas in the dressing room. By the time I'd finished, Jack was back in bed. I padded across the room and sat beside him. He lay on his back, hands behind his head. I could see his face, lit gently by the moon.

'Nightmares?' I said.

He reached for my hand, lifted it to his mouth and kissed my palm.

'If you weren't naked in there,' I said, 'I'd climb in with you.'

He smiled.

'But I don't think I can trust you,' I said.

'You definitely can't trust me.' His voice was hoarse.

'Maybe tomorrow night?'

'Definitely tomorrow night.'

'We'll be celebrating, for sure.'

'Without a doubt.'

He gave my hand a squeeze and I stood, waiting for him to release it, which he did, eventually.

'Goodnight, Jack.'

'Goodnight, Erica.'

CHAPTER 44

When I woke I could hear the shower running. I used the toilet in the powder room and raced back to my makeshift bed to pretend everything was lovely. I lay staring at the ceiling, thinking that I really should get up and deal with the day. But I didn't want to. I wanted to go to fairyland where everything is pink and nice, all the time. I checked the time. Not quite 7am, which meant there was time for a small escape. I closed my eyes and visualised a pristine, deserted beach, palm trees, blue sky, me frolicking with dolphins and Jack Jones doing push-ups on the sand.

I opened my eyes as Jack walked out of the bedroom, body wet and glistening, towel low on his hips. Who needs an imagination? He pointed his toothbrush at me. 'You need to get up. I have to go soon.' Frowning. Serious. What happened to Mr Vulnerable, naked in the moonlight?

I sat up. 'Okay.'

'Good girl.'

'I feel sick.'

'So do I.'

I spent the morning at the office helping with final details for the big event, and by lunchtime I was so sick of feeling sick, I marched myself into the bathroom and had a good yak with the mirror. We (the mirror and I) discussed the uselessness of negative feelings such as fear and anxiety, and so I decided to pretend that I was in Sydney for romantic reasons rather than scary ones. I felt immediately better. Denial, I decided, is a good thing.

Jack had said he'd pick me up at 12.30 to go shopping for something suitable to wear for an evening bombing. I told Rebecca that I'd see her at the Opera House in the afternoon. When I left the office Jack was already waiting, of course. On the way to Paddington I asked how much time I had for shopping.

He checked his watch. 'An hour or so.'

'Two hours?'

He hesitated. 'We'll see.'

'This might be the last time I ever go shopping. I want to make the most of it. God, I wish Lucy was here.'

'Let's try to be a bit more positive,' he said, frowning.

We parked and walked. First stop was a lingerie shop. Jack stayed on the street, pacing around, talking on his mobile. My gold Amex and I found something French, white and lacy.

Jack asked what I'd bought and I said, 'You'll have to wait and see.'

Then we found a nice local fashion designer who happily sold me some hand-made wool evening pants, a lovely silk shirt and a to-die-for jacket that was an absolute steal at $1200 (it was on sale). I also bought a gorgeous, shimmery cocktail dress that fitted beautifully, showing off all my good bits and hiding my not-so-good bits. It wasn't on sale.

When I came out of that shop, Jack was sitting on a bench seat, his face in his hands.

'Haven't you ever been shopping with a woman?' I said.

He shook his head. 'I don't know. I don't think so.'

'You could come into the shops with me if you want.'

He groaned.

I then went back to the lingerie shop to get something more suitable to go with my new outfit (the white was completely wrong), and just a few doors down from that was a shoe shop with a pair of sensational Manolo Blahniks in the window, but as I thought attending the cocktail function might involve a lot of walking and standing (denial kicking in magnificently), I settled on a stylish but sensible pair of Bruno Maglis. I bought the sexy Manolos as well, just in case the event was a fizzer and Jack decided on a candlelit dinner instead.

My chauffeur then took me directly to the Opera House to help Rebecca set up for the function. On the way, he glanced over his shoulder at the pile of bags on the back seat.

'You did shop for just tonight, didn't you?'

'Yes, but I've covered myself, just in case. I shopped for the worst-case scenario, and the best-case scenario.' I smiled. 'You know. Just in case.'

He nodded slowly. 'And did you spend twenty thousand dollars?'

I looked at the shopping bags, made a mental calculation. 'I think I came in under.'

'Well done.'

BIG Fertilisers' cocktail party was being held in the Concert Hall foyer, a visually amazing space, right on the water with a spectacular view of the harbour including the bridge. After cocktails, a few speeches and a display of fireworks from a boat in the harbour, our guests were being treated to a special concert by some singers from Opera Australia. I was hoping that Shane McGann would have done whatever he was planning to do before then. I hated opera.

Once Jack saw that the foyer was full of non-murdering types – Rebecca and the caterers – he let me go ahead while he did whatever he needed to do somewhere else.

I helped Rebecca by setting out name tags and erecting the banners with the new logo. After an hour or so Jack came looking for me. Rebecca saw him approach. She tossed her hair and pushed me out of the way, thrusting her cleavage at him. He raised an eyebrow, glancing at me over her shoulder.

'Hi,' purred Rebecca, 'are you the sound guy or the lighting guy?'

'Neither. I'm her guy.' Jack smiled and pointed at me.

Rebecca's mouth dropped open. She looked like she wanted to accuse me of something.

I said, 'Rebecca, this is Jack, my, ah ...'

'Boyfriend,' said Jack. 'And I need to borrow Erica for a minute.' He reached out his hand for me to take and added, 'If you don't mind, that is.'

Rebecca was flustered it seemed. Very satisfying. 'I suppose it's okay,' she said but we were already walking away. Jack led me to the far side of the function area and we stood by the glass wall that faced the harbour bridge.

'What's happening?' I said.

'Nothing. How long will you be?'

I looked across the room at Rebecca, who was stealing glances at us. 'Another hour, maybe, then I need to go back to the hotel and change.'

'Okay. I'll come back for you.' He looked around the room and lowered his voice. 'This is where they're planning on doing it. Here, at interval, when everyone's close together. More damage that way.'

I gazed across the vast space that would be crowded with people later. I had a sudden, unwelcome vision of glass walls blowing out across the harbour. And body parts. I blew out a nervous sigh. 'God, Jack, I just can't imagine what it would mean if —'

'I know.' He looked at me seriously, lifted my chin with his finger, bent his head and kissed me. It was a soft, lingering kiss.

I blinked up at him. 'Do you think Shane McGann is watching us?'

'No. But Rebecca is.'

'You're terrible, Muriel.' I gave him a gentle shove.

He smiled and walked away, and I watched him, wondering how late the candlelit restaurant stayed open.

JACK and I returned to the hotel and had a quick bite to eat in the room, not that I could stomach much food. There was a moment in the dressing room when we tried to pass each other, kept stepping to the same side, then gazed at each other and I wondered if he was thinking the same thing as me. That we should just go to bed right there and then in case it was our last chance.

But being the responsible citizens we are, we drove back to the Opera House instead. On the way, I said, 'You know, if everything turns out okay tonight, and it's not too late, I thought we might go to that nice little restaurant in The Rocks.'

'The one with the candlelight?'

'That's the one.'

He nodded slowly. 'All right. If it's not too late, we'll go for a candlelit dinner.'

'Good.'

'Something to look forward to.'

We regarded each other, smiling. I felt suddenly tempted to do something wicked. I cleared my throat. 'What will you be doing during the cocktail function?'

'I'll be around. JD's cleared me with the PM's security.'

'Does the prime minister know about the threat?'

'Not exactly.'

'What *exactly* does he know?' I said.

'Nothing.'

CHAPTER 45

We parked in the Opera House car park an hour before the guests were due to arrive, and walked hand-in-hand to the concert hall. Jack gave me the car keys and said, 'If I tell you to go, you go quickly and without question. Understand?'

I nodded and dropped the keys into my bag.

Rebecca looked exquisite in a clingy dress and high, strappy heels, and I wished I'd worn the cocktail dress and Manolos. I felt sure I could run in them if I was scared enough.

Jack hovered while I worked, and Rebecca finally announced, with a toss of her ironed hair, 'Partners aren't invited.'

Jack fixed that by opening his jacket slightly so she could see his gun. 'Secret Service.' He gave her a wink. 'Don't tell anyone.' She blushed and walked away.

'Are you flirting with Rebecca?' I said.

He feigned offence. 'No!'

'Well, I think she just wet her pants.'

BIG FERTILISERS' executive team arrived ahead of the guests. I met most of them including Michael Barton, the managing director, who gave me a lingering look. I gave him one back, hoping that Jack noticed.

I knew most of the media people. I gave them information kits and pointed to the bar. That's all they really needed. I was there to schmooze and answer questions, but hoped to avoid it. Especially after one guy asked me, 'Any word on the stolen fertiliser?'

I fixed a stiff smile on my face. 'Nothing new, no.'

Rebecca and I greeted the guests and helped with name tags, and Jack stayed on the sidelines, inspecting every person who arrived. I assumed he was in touch with his guys by hidden microphone.

The premier and prime minister arrived separately and were greeted by BIG execs, rather than lowly staff like me. JD arrived, flanked discreetly by Brad and Joe, and made a beeline for the PM. JD wasn't staying long and was due to fly home straight after the function, the bombing, whatever.

Once everyone had arrived, I was able to stand back and take a breather. An old guy caught my attention and I walked over to him, glancing at his name tag.

'Can I help you, Mr Sanders?' I remembered from the guest list that Mr Sanders had VIP next to his name, and a note that his distinguished family were friends of the PM's family.

'Get me a whiskey, would you, girly?' He ogled my chest.

'Sure.' I signalled a waiter and asked him to get Mr Sanders a whiskey. 'Can I help with anything else?'

'Yes, you can.' He slipped an arm around my waist and pulled me closer, asking if I had a friend for his son. Clearly old school. The son leered, and I considered getting Rebecca for him.

Instead, I leaned into Mr Sanders and whispered into his ear, 'No, but I will get security if you touch me again.' I slipped away without waiting for his response, wondering what Jack would have done if I'd demanded security save me from a groping geriatric.

I moved to the periphery to look for someone I wanted to talk to. There was only one, and he was staring out the window with his phone pressed to his ear. I started walking toward him as he glanced at me, looking worried. Actually, not worried; more furious and horrified all rolled into one. He pulled his phone away from his ear and punched in another number, turning his back to me.

My phone rang. I answered but before I could speak, a voice said, 'You'll have to make a decision on your boyfriend's behalf. He's having a dilemma.' I kept walking toward Jack. 'I've told him that I'll trade you for all those people at the party. He needs to bring you to the car park. Right now. You've got three minutes before I blow the boat.'

I stood next to Jack. He was talking into his mobile, watching me. I looked out the window. A small boat had pulled up right under where we were standing. I assumed this wasn't what Jack was expecting.

'I'll come now,' I said to Shane McGann and hung up.

Jack finished his call, gripped my arm and marched me out of the foyer. Clearly no argument from him about my going with McGann.

He said, 'I fucked up.'

It hadn't occurred to me, not once, that Jack wouldn't save the day, that he wouldn't get all the bad guys and that everything would be fine. I found I was pulling slightly against him as he forced me through the crowd. But he didn't go to the car park. Instead, he exited the building, pushing against the flow of arriving concert goers.

'Go straight to the hotel,' he said, people bouncing off him. 'Walk fast. Stay with people. In the lobby or the bar. If you feel threatened at any time, scream.'

I stopped, wrenching my arm free. 'What are you talking about?'

He barely broke his stride as he took my wrist and forced me forward again. I trotted along behind him because I had no choice.

'Jack. Jack!' I stopped again, using all my body weight to break free and he turned to me, panic in his eyes. I said, 'I'm going with Shane McGann.'

He focused, gripped my shoulders. I sensed people giving us a wide berth. I wondered if someone would call the police.

'You'll do what I say,' he said through his teeth.

'He means it, Jack.' I pushed away. 'I need to go.'

I walked quickly toward the car park; it took a few seconds but then he was at my side.

'All right. I'll think of something.' He took my hand and we started jogging, weaving through the milling crowds. As we pushed through the car park doors I could see Shane McGann leaning against a car on the far side. The car was Jack's rented Lexus. We approached slowly, Jack glancing around, his hand gripping mine. With his other he pulled out his gun and held it by his side.

Shane McGann was talking into his mobile phone, watching us approach. We stopped about three metres away from him. He lowered the phone and smiled.

Jack said, in a low voice, 'Nothing stopping me from killing you, McGann.'

McGann held up his phone. 'Except this. They'll blow the boat if they don't hear from me.' He held out his hand, still leaning casually against the car. 'Come on, Erica. You come with me and everyone else will live. Seems fair.'

Jack released my hand and put his arm tightly around my waist, pulling me against him. 'You're not taking her.'

'Oh, but I am. Let her go.'

'Not a chance.'

McGann lifted the phone to his ear and said, 'Do it.'

There was a distant, dull explosion and I screamed. Jack yelled, '*No!*' and jerked toward McGann. But McGann now had a gun, and it was aimed at my head.

'That was the fireworks boat,' he said. 'Only two people on board. Both dead, no doubt. Probably no one else hurt. Yet.' He held a hand out to me. 'The next one will make a big hole in the Concert Hall and a lot of dead people. Right now, your party will be thinking there was a terrible tragedy with the fireworks.' He smiled.

Jack said, shakily, 'Take me, McGann. I'll do whatever you want.'

'Thanks, but no. Hand her over.'

Jack turned me to face him; he was more frightened than I was. He gripped my shoulders and shook his head slightly.

'It will be all right,' I said. I stood on tiptoes and lightly kissed his lips. 'I know it will.'

Jack let me go and I walked slowly to McGann, watching Jack over my shoulder. McGann grabbed my arm and pulled me against him, pressing his gun so hard into my cheek my teeth bit into the flesh. I cried out. Blood pooled under my tongue and trickled out the corner of my mouth.

I could see that Jack struggled to stay where he was. Every nerve in his body was pushing him to me.

McGann made another call. 'Blow the boat if you don't hear back in five.' He hung up and said, 'See, I'm a man of my word. Now, fuck off, Jones.' He pushed me toward the passenger side of the car and held out his hand. 'Who's got the keys?'

My hands shook badly as I opened my bag, pulling the car keys out of it. McGann opened the passenger door.

'Wait!' Jack held up his hands in a gesture of surrender, gun swinging off his thumb. 'I'll do anything.'

McGann yelled, 'Get on your knees!'

Jack dropped to his knees.

'Now, beg!'

'I'm begging.' Jack put his gun on the ground and held his arms out to the side, palms up. 'Let her go. Come on, Shane. Please.'

McGann sucked in a sharp breath, and I felt something change for a moment. But he shoved me into the car and, with the gun still aimed at my head, threw a set of handcuffs onto my lap. He said quietly, 'Cuff yourself to this,' indicating the grab handle above my head.

I threaded the cuffs clumsily through the handle and snapped one around my wrist, and he cuffed the other.

McGann said to Jack, 'Don't try anything, Jones, or I'll nail your girlfriend.' He laughed lightly. 'Actually, I'll nail her anyway.' He slammed my door shut and walked around to the driver's side. I could see the fear and rage in Jack's eyes as they searched for mine through the heavily tinted window.

Jack mouthed, *I'll find you*, and I believed him.

McGann got in the car, locked the doors and started the engine. Jack stood.

'I need the seatbelt,' I said.

'No seatbelt.'

Jack walked toward us. McGann dropped the gun onto his lap,

threw the car into gear and we surged forward. Jack slammed his fist into McGann's door as we screeched past. I watched Jack in the side mirror; he stood with legs apart, fist pressed into his temple, mobile phone to his other ear. I leaned forward to keep him in sight, but he vanished as we bolted up the ramp and around a bend.

We flew out of the car park and onto the street. McGann raced along, changing lanes erratically, braking late. Right then, not wearing a seat belt, I was more afraid of the windscreen than anything else. I gripped the handle.

McGann said, 'Did you see Jones begging?' He sneered and punched my leg. 'Did you?'

'Ow! Bastard.' My sense of calm had returned and I felt somehow less distressed, now that I thought Jack was safe. Safe from Shane McGann, at least. Panic subsided and reasoning returned. My eyes dropped to the gun in McGann's lap and he let it slide between his legs.

'How do you feel about your big tough boyfriend now? Hey? Answer me!' he shouted.

'He's not my boyfriend.'

'Stupid bitch. Think you're good enough for Jack Jones.'

What?

CHAPTER 46

Shane McGann drove fast through Sydney's streets and we were soon on the M4, heading for the hills. I clung to the handle and watched signs for Parramatta, Penrith, the Great Western Highway flash past, and eventually one for the Blue Mountains. I sat quietly, trying to come up with a plan. I was handcuffed to the car, and the windows were so heavily tinted there was no way someone would see me signalling in the dark. There was little chance of escape during this trip unless I could somehow con my way out. Shane McGann was human, after all, and I believed wholeheartedly that people were essentially good.

'Are you really going to blow up the Opera House?'

He grinned nastily. 'Yeah.' Maybe not everyone is good.

'Why?'

'Teach Degraves.'

'Teach him what?'

'Bastard gets everything!'

'Is this about Dega buying BIG?'

'Prick knew we wanted it.'

I said, 'So, you're teaching John Degraves a lesson on behalf of your father?'

He didn't respond, just stared through the windscreen. At least his speed now resembled something safe. Safer.

'Is your father in on this? I mean, when you're arrested, should we tell the police to pick up Martin as well?'

McGann pulled over so violently the car rocked sideways and I thought it was going to roll. I shrieked, hanging on.

He grabbed my face in one hand and squeezed; pulled me as close as my shackles would allow. He leaned in, his breath in my face. In a low, even voice he said, 'You stay the fuck away from my father.'

He pushed me away and my head hit the window. As he pulled back onto the road, wheels spinning in the gravel, he said, 'No chance for you anyway. No chance when you're dead.'

He drove. Tears rolled down my face. I didn't speak again. I wanted to ask why me, but I didn't dare. What was his thing with me? My theory that he was in love with me was well and truly out the window. Unless he had a really weird way of expressing love. Did he want to hurt JD by hurting me? Was that why he hurt the other women?

Eventually, we turned off the main highway and drove along a narrow, winding, dirt road that led to a small cabin in a clearing. Tall gum trees surrounded the clearing. Their white trunks glowed in the beam of our headlights and threw great, lurching shadows across the road. Through the trees I caught a flash of metal. A shed?

McGann hauled me out of the car, re-cuffed my wrists, and dragged me by the handcuffs along a dark gravel driveway. I stumbled behind him, biting my lip to stop from crying out. We climbed some creaky old stairs to the cabin. The only light now came from the moon, but it was full and bright. I saw no other houses, and no other signs of life anywhere apart, possibly, from hairy things in the bush. The least of my problems.

McGann opened the front door and snapped on some lights. There was a small living area that contained a sofa, a fat old armchair, a small dining setting and an open fireplace with, I noted, an iron fire poker leaning against the stone hearth. The cabin smelled smoky and was still warm from a recent fire. It should have felt cosy and lived in, but it was cold as ice.

McGann pushed me through the living room to a bedroom at the back of the cabin. He turned on more lights and shoved me onto a bare mattress on the floor. I stumbled, falling onto my face. I rolled over and sat up, looking around the room. The only other thing I could see was an old-fashioned video camera set up in the corner. I guess I knew where this was headed. I closed my eyes, willing Jack to find me. He *would* find me. I was sure of it. I just didn't know how the hell he could. I blinked back tears and fought down panic as I tried to focus on escape.

McGann fiddled with the camera. He walked over to me, pulling me to my feet, gripped my face and turned my head roughly so that I was looking at the camera. 'Say hello to lover boy.'

If Jack ever saw this video I sure as hell wasn't going to let him see me defeated and crying. I held a steady gaze, right into the lens. *Find me, Jack.*

McGann spun me around, pushed me onto the mattress on my face and lay on top of me. The weight of his body pushed the air from my lungs and the cuffs dug into my wrists and chest. I could feel his holstered gun pressing into my back.

He spoke close to my ear, but loud enough for the camera to hear. 'I'm a much better lover than Jack Jones, Erica. I bet you can't wait for a taste of me.'

I stared at the camera and drew as much breath as I could. 'Why did you kill Charlie Heiner?' It came out as a loud wheeze.

He jerked away from me, standing and storming around the room.

'The bastard left me! He was gonna tell Degraves! Stop our plans!'

'Charlie was your lover?' I ventured, sitting up.

McGann stopped and regarded me for a moment, suddenly calm, but red in the face. 'Well, if you think I'm a faggot, I'd better show you otherwise.'

He pulled me to my feet again. He kissed me roughly, his tongue darting in and out of my mouth. I gagged, but he didn't seem to notice. He uncuffed me. I glanced at the door but he said, 'Oh, no.' He reached for his gun and waved it around. 'I'll kill you before I let you go.' Another good statement for the record. 'No point thinking about escape. No one around for miles.'

'I'd rather die than let you touch me,' I said, rather bravely, I thought.

He laughed. 'Yeah, well, that's easily arranged. Yours wouldn't be the first body I've buried.' Confessions left, right and centre. 'Speaking of your body, I want to see it. Undress.'

The room was cold, but a warm bead of sweat trickled down my face. I slowly took off my jacket and dropped it onto the mattress. I stood there for a minute, staring at the floor, willing something to happen. It worked. Something did happen, but not what I was hoping for. McGann walked over to me and pulled roughly at my blouse. I staggered forward as it ripped open.

'I said undress!'

I stepped out of my shoes and unzipped my pants, letting them fall to the floor.

'Turn around, and don't forget to smile for the camera.'

I turned, but looked away from the camera. He tore the blouse right off me. From behind he put his arms around me, one hand squeezing my breast, the other holding his gun, his body pressed into my back. 'Mmm. Nice.' His breath was hot and wet in my ear. 'Now turn back to me.' I was wearing my new underwear – a black lace G-string and matching bra. I turned and he stepped back to inspect me, his eyes lighting up.

'Very sexy, Erica! Although, for future reference, I prefer black leather.'

'It's not for you,' I said, looking at the camera. 'I bought it for Jack.'

That seemed to push a button. His face turned purple, twisted into an angry snarl. 'Jack Jones! Jack Jones! I'll fucking show Jack Jones!' He threw his gun on the floor and pulled at his belt. His pants dropped and I ran from the bedroom.

McGann let out a furious yell as I dashed across the living room. I could hear him behind me, pushing through the furniture. I ran for the fireplace and snatched up the poker, turning, swinging blindly. He jerked away, arm thrown up. I threw the poker and ran for the door but he grabbed my hair, wrenching me back. He wrapped his arms around me, lifting me off the ground and squeezing me so tight I could barely breathe. He laughed.

'Feisty bitch! I like that.'

I struggled and he tightened his grip. So I stopped struggling, some distant memory of self-defence training, and McGann put me down. He pulled my hair back from my face and stuck his tongue in my ear, then sucked on my neck. I faked a small moan and relaxed my body more, leaning into him. McGann seemed to be in some kind of sexual trance, sucking and groaning and grinding his pelvis into my back. He squeezed my breast and sucked hard on my neck.

I took a small step to the side, lifting my arm and stroking his face with the back of my shaking hand, and he groaned louder. I turned slowly in his arms, keeping my hands at chest height, and his tongue tracked the movement, sliding over my neck and face to my mouth. I tolerated exactly two seconds of his wet, slimy, tongue-jabbing while grabbing two handfuls of his shirt. I stepped quickly back, pulling him sharply toward me as I brought my knee up hard between his legs. There was a sickening crunch. His face fleetingly registered shock as he collapsed to the floor with an animal roar. I raced for the door, snatched it open and flew through it.

Adrenaline pushed my body forward and I ran faster than I ever had in my life. My breathing was loud and raspy and the blood pounding in my ears was deafening. I was barely aware of the sharp stabs under my bare feet as I dashed across the gravel driveway and into the trees.

I could hear McGann yelling, 'Stop!', his voice muffled by the roar in my ears. His footsteps pounded the earth behind me. I pushed faster, harder, into the trees and branches and bushes whipped my skin. 'Eri-ca!' I tripped, falling onto my face, and he was on me, grabbing me around the middle and lifting me up. I kicked and thrashed, screaming.

'It's me!' He set me down, spinning me around and pulling me into a fierce hug.

I pushed away. 'Jack!'

He pulled off his jacket, wrapping it around me, crushing me against him again. 'I've got you.' His voice broke.

I threw my arms and legs around him, not knowing whether to laugh or cry. But I did neither. Instead, I started kissing him. No messing about with grateful cheek kisses, not me, straight for his mouth, with passion. I could feel his lips tense – surprised, no doubt – but he held me and let me kiss him anyway. Then he started to kiss me back, tentatively at first then with more urgency, until I thought we might end up having sex where we stood. Fine by me, but I suspected he was just being polite.

There were sudden gun shots. Four blasts and Jack dropped to the ground, covering my body with his. He was perfectly still for several seconds, lying on me but supporting his weight, staring toward the house while I gazed at his beautiful, moonlit face.

'Stay here,' he ordered, and leaped up, taking off for the cabin.

I sat up and watched him run, pulling his gun from its holster. I shivered, cold without Jack's warmth and the fear-of-death issue. I pushed my arms through the sleeves of his coat and wrapped it around my legs. I looked around for lurking, crawling things, and saw that flash of metal again. The light from the house caught whatever was hiding in there; a glimpse through the trees.

And then Jack was back, scooping me up and carrying me across the gravel to a waiting four-wheel drive.

He set me down and opened the back door of the car but I said, 'Hang on a minute,' walking away from him. I threw up behind a tree then staggered to the car, wiping the back of my hand across my mouth.

'All right?' he said, putting his arm around me, and I nodded, crawling across the back seat to sit in the corner with my legs drawn up, arms hugging my knees. I was very happy to see Jack and thrilled to be alive, but also a bit embarrassed. This, together the vomit breath, wasn't quite what I had in mind when I'd handed $300 to the lingerie sales lady.

Jack leaned into the car. 'I need to leave you for a minute.' He handed me a bottle of water.

I looked over my shoulder at the house. 'What's happening in there? Where's McGann?'

'Joe and Brad have him. Police are on the way.'

'What were those gun shots?'

'McGann shooting at shadows. No-one's hurt.' His eyes flicked over me and then drilled into mine. 'Are you?'

I shook my head. 'No.' I was grazed and bruised – lots of bruises – but I wasn't *really* hurt. Not in any way that mattered.

He nodded. 'Where are your clothes?'

'In there.' I glanced at the house and swigged from the bottle. 'In the room at the back.'

Jack jogged back to the cabin, and after a couple of minutes I heard shouting. Jack, yelling angry, unmentionable things and Shane McGann shouting and then I heard Joe roar, *'Jack! No!'* A couple of minutes later Jack reappeared with my clothes and sat next to me, his head turned away. I wondered if anyone apart from Shane McGann was going to jail.

I handed him the empty water bottle and pulled on my pants and shredded blouse. The blouse covered nothing, so I threw it on the floor and pulled on my jacket.

'Everything okay in there?'

He said quietly, looking out the window, 'There's a video camera. I've got the tape. The police will need it as evidence.' He glanced at me, clearly upset. I understood what was worrying him.

'Not much to see on that video.' I forced a smile. 'Except a couple of confessions you might be interested in.' Including one from me.

He turned his body toward me, fully focused, and said in a low, shaky voice, 'I want to know what he did to you.' He picked up my blouse and inspected the silken shreds. Then his eyes lifted slowly to examine me, his gaze held at chin level. Jack leaned toward me, gently cupping my chin in his hand, tilting my head back and getting a good look at my Shane McGann hickey.

His eyes narrowed. 'I'll kill him.' He turned to exit the car.

I grabbed his arm with both hands. 'No! Don't!' I was pretty sure he wasn't just coining a phrase.

Jack stepped out of the car, dragging me with him. 'Let go,' he said.

'No!' I pleaded, 'You'll make it worse. Please, Jack.'

He stood for a minute, looking down at me, and his face softened as he sat back in the car, pulling me into his arms, cradling me like a baby. 'I'm so sorry.' He buried his face in my hair.

I gave him a squeeze, as best as I could in his vice-like hug. 'He didn't hurt me, Jack. I got away. You taught me how.'

He took a deep, ragged breath, and red and blue flashing lights appeared in the distance.

CHAPTER 47

When the police arrived, Jack pulled himself together, kissed my face a dozen times and told me he'd be as quick as he could.

As he climbed out of the car, I said, 'Jack, there's something in the trees back there.' I pointed to where I'd seen the metal flashes. 'I think it's a shed.'

He nodded. 'I'll check it out.'

The police spent a bit of time in the house with Shane McGann screaming abuse and yelling that his father would sort them all out. I didn't see him again. By the time he was marched out of the house, Jack was back with me. He made me look away, saying, 'I don't want him making eye contact.'

When Brad and Joe got into the car, Brad looked at me for a second or two, which I guess was his way of showing great concern. Joe, however, reached over the seat and squeezed my hand, staring right into my eyes. 'Are you okay, Erica?'

God, all this concern from big tough guys made me feel so ... fragile. And emotional. Tears pooled in my eyes. I nodded and looked at my lap.

Jack and I sat in the back of Brad's SUV. As we made our way gently along the winding roads, I could see the city lights in the distance. Jack reached out to pull me closer and I scooted across the seat. He turned his body so I could nestle into him, and he put his arms around me. 'Put your seatbelt on,' he murmured. He then announced to us that the thing I'd seen glinting in the trees was a shed, and that it was full of BIG fertiliser. We all nodded, mumbling various positive remarks about that.

I gazed at the back of Brad's head, wondering if I could ask about Aida and her husband. And I wondered about Jack's fuck-up.

'What happened at the Opera House?' I said.

Jack stared out the window. 'We got them all.'

'How many?'

'Six including McGann.'

'Were they arrested?'

He said, quietly, 'Some were arrested.'

I assumed he meant that the some who weren't arrested were dead. I found I was hoping Brad's girlfriend's horrible husband was one of them.

'Shane McGann wanted to get at JD.' I had their attention. Joe turned his head and Brad's eyes were on me in the rear-view mirror. 'He wanted to avenge his daddy who misses out on absolutely everything because mean old JD always gets in first.'

Jack said, concerned, 'Was Martin involved?'

'I don't think so.'

'What about you?' Joe said. 'Was that to get at JD as well?'

I glanced up at Jack, who was watching me. 'No, it was to get at Jack.'

They all nodded.

Jack said, 'Payback for the charges I had against him after Iraq.'

That and the fact that he's in love with you, I didn't say.

'What about all the others?' I said, thinking about the federal cop. 'Why did they do it?'

'We assume money,' said Jack. 'McGann paid them.'

'Is that all? Like, no vengeance or political agenda or anything like that?'

'No. Just money.'

'Arseholes,' I said.

'Yeah.'

I pressed against Jack and he held me tight.

'Was anyone else killed?' I said. 'I mean, the people on the fireworks boat ...' My voice wavered as I thought about the innocent people who'd left home that night for work, and who were now dead.

'Only people involved,' he said softly. 'No other innocents.'

'Good.' I was about to ask about the prime minister, but found I didn't care quite enough. I gazed straight ahead at the lights of the approaching city. I was happy to stay in my current space for a long, long time, and I felt overwhelmingly grateful that Jack had found me.

'Oh! How did you know where I was?' I said.

'Tracking device on the Lexus.'

I nodded. 'Thank God for modern technology.'

Jack was looking out the window, frowning, possibly thinking about what might have happened without modern technology. I might have been Shane McGann's sex slave in the Blue Mountains for the rest of my life. He might have made me cook and clean the toilet, wearing black leather underwear.

I shuddered and asked, 'Where is it? The Lexus?'

'Police have it.'

We drove and after a while I felt Jack's gaze on my face, and I returned it. He lifted his hand, gently stroked my bruised cheek. He bent his head and kissed the bruise, and the corner of my mouth, and pressed his lips softly onto mine. There were no voices in my head shouting at me to stop. But I would have ignored them anyway.

The police interview was reasonably quick – I gave my statement and they were clearly happy to nail the prime suspect in the attempted Opera House bombing, who was also wanted for a number of other crimes, including Charlie Heiner's murder, and which now included abduction and attempted rape. The police seemed prepared to turn a blind eye to Jack's not-quite-legal involvement. He knew most of them, shaking hands, subdued but friendly. I wondered if they knew what he got up to in the middle of the night. Probably.

Jack disappeared for about fifteen minutes and a police woman made me a cup of tea. Then two policemen drove us back to the hotel and said we'd be needed for further interviews in Melbourne.

On the way, I whispered to Jack, 'Are you guys in any trouble for your involvement tonight?'

'No. Citizens' arrest.'

'What about your ...' I leaned close and whispered in his ear, 'guns?'

'What guns?' He gave me a small smile, eyebrows raised. Then he said, no longer smiling, 'I watched the video.'

I blushed, thinking about standing there under those bright lights in my underwear, and wondered how many others had seen it.

'You basically got a confession about Heiner's murder,' he said.

'Good. I hoped the camera would pick that up.'

'That was very clever, Erica. And very brave. Everything you did back there was brave.' He squeezed my hand, his eyes soft.

I nodded and looked out the window, thinking I'd had nothing to lose – or so I'd thought at the time – and when I glanced back at Jack he was still watching me.

'Do you think that's true?' he said. 'About McGann and Heiner?'

'That they were lovers? Yes, I think that's true.' I snorted indelicately. 'Typical that the only men to show interest in me are bisexual psychos.' I smiled at Jack, expecting him to share the joke. But one eyebrow was cocked as he regarded me. 'What?' I said.

He chuckled, shaking his head, and looked out the window.

At the hotel we walked quickly through the lobby, Jack's arm around me. We probably looked like we were rushing to our room to have sex, and I wondered if we were. But in the lift, Jack said, 'I haven't told you yet that Aida will be waiting in our room.'

'Brad's girlfriend?'

He nodded. 'Yes, he'll be here soon to get her.'

'What happened to her husband?'

'Arrested. Police suspected him anyway.'

I couldn't help feeling disappointed that he wasn't dead. I hoped God wasn't listening. I also felt nervous, like I was about to meet a celebrity. When Jack opened the door to our suite, I walked in tentatively and Aida turned from the window. She had blonde hair pulled tightly back in a ponytail. She looked sweet and gentle, like Alice in Wonderland.

Aida smiled shyly and I smiled shyly back. We crossed the room and reached for each other like long lost friends. Sisters-in-arms. We hugged tightly for a long time, until she pulled away.

'Are you all right?' she whispered.

I nodded. 'Are you?'

'Yes. You're very brave, Erica.'

'I think you're very brave, Aida.'

There was a sharp rap on the door. Jack opened it and Brad walked in, nodding briefly at Jack and me but his eyes were on Aida. They rushed to each other and Jack took my arm and led me – rather forcibly, I thought – into the bedroom, closing the doors behind us. I didn't want to go; I wanted to watch them. It was so romantic.

I whispered, 'What will they do now?'

'I've got them a room here for tonight then they've got plans they're not sharing, which is a very good idea.'

'Do you think they've had sex yet?' I tried to hear their murmured conversation.

Jack tsked. 'Not that it's any of your business, but no, I don't believe they have.'

I sighed, thinking about how special it would be. Making love for the first time without fear of retribution. True love is so ... awesome.

'Erica?'

I focused. 'Sorry, did you say something?'

'Would you like me to run a bath for you?' He leaned against the bathroom door, arms folded, watching me with amused eyes.

'Jack Jones, there's only one thing I'd rather have you do for me.'

He smiled. 'And what's that?'

I walked up to him, gripped the front of his shirt and pulled his face down to mine so that our noses were almost touching. 'Champagne, French, *now*.'

CHAPTER 48

In the bath I scrubbed myself raw. I wanted to remove every molecule of Shane McGann's touch and smell from me. I washed my hair, shaved everything, cleaned my teeth, gargled and even flossed. There was a soft knock on the door and I sank modestly beneath the mountain of bubbles with just my face poking out.

'Who is it?' I sang.

Jack opened the door a crack. 'Room service.'

'Excellent! I'll give you a tip later.'

He walked in, smiling, handed me a plate of sandwiches and a full glass of champagne. He left and returned a few seconds later with an ice bucket and bottle of Krug and put them within reach on the floor. Jack's gaze travelled over the surface of the oval tub. It was big enough for a couple of muscly mercenaries. Plus me of course.

'Hmm. Tempting.' He looked at his watch. 'I'd love to join you but I have to make some calls.'

'I didn't actually invite you to join me.'

'Sweetheart, if I decided to get in there with you, there's not a thing you could do about it.'

'Where's my gun?' I said, pretending to look for it.

He crouched by the bath. 'I got you something.'

'What did you get?'

I tried to see what he was hiding behind his back. He held it up and shook it.

'A snow globe!' I took it and held it in front of my face, watching the snow drift down over the tiny but perfect Opera House. 'That's the most beautiful thing I've ever seen.'

'Second most beautiful.'

He leaned in and kissed my forehead, then he left, and I relaxed back into the warmth. I drank half the bottle of Krug, ate the sandwiches and played with my snow globe. I got out of the bath after a while and stood in front of the mirror, watching the soapy mounds slide off my body. I frowned at the bits that wouldn't scrub or fall off. Bruises everywhere; the most annoying one, big and black on my neck.

'Well,' I said to the mirror, 'just don't look at them.'

I rifled around in the dressing room for the shopping bag from the lingerie shop. First I found the cocktail dress and Manolos, and tossed them aside. I really had no idea how to be sexy and seductive, but I smiled when I found the pretty pink bag, pulling the lacy white underwear out into the light and wondering how such tiny pieces of material could possibly be worth $300. Maybe it was the transport costs from Paris? Well, I thought they'd be perfect under my PJs. My fluffy pink socks, the icing on the cake.

When I emerged from the bedroom, nursing the ice bucket and snow globe, Jack was sitting at the desk, hanging up the phone. No sign of Brad and Aida.

'I hope you didn't want any sandwiches,' I said as I eyed an empty plate on the coffee table.

He stood, smiling. 'That's fine. I had lobster.' He poured me some more champagne and himself a whiskey and we sat on opposite sofas. I shook the snow globe and put it on the coffee table between us. I sat cross-legged, my face scrubbed clean, hair drying naturally into ringlets, and I thought I'd probably never looked sexier. Just kidding. He gazed at me though, warmth in his eyes.

'Feeling better?' he asked, smiling, checking out my socks.

'Yes. Much. How about you?'

He nodded. 'Relieved.'

'You got all the bad guys.'

'And I got you.'

'Yep. You've definitely got me.'

He relaxed into the sofa, a slightly wicked glint in his eye. 'And nothing more to do.'

'That's right.' I attempted an air of nonchalance, picking at a bit of fluff on the cushion. 'Nothing at all to do between now and getting on a plane tomorrow.' I met his warm gaze. 'I'm having the bed tonight,' I said.

'Me, too.'

'Can I trust you?'

'No.' He stretched his arms along the back of the sofa and dropped a big bare foot onto the coffee table. 'Actually, Ms Jewell,' he said in a formal voice, 'I'm thinking about tucking you into bed right now.'

Goody. I faked a yawn. 'I'm exhausted. I bet you are, too.'

He nodded slowly, smiling.

'In fact,' I said, 'I bet you're so tired you can't even undress yourself.' I stood, swallowing the last of my champagne before walking around the coffee table. Jack moved his foot, letting it drop to the floor, and I straddled his lap. 'I'll help you.' I started unbuttoning his shirt and he slugged back the rest of his whiskey. I took his glass and put it on the coffee table.

He reached behind me and squeezed my feet. 'These sexy socks are driving me crazy.'

'My secret weapon.'

'And I'm thinking about that black lace underwear.' He ran his hands along my thighs, cupping my bottom.

'I bought it for you.'

'So you said.'

'And the white lace I'm wearing now.' I batted my eyelashes.

He drew in a short, sharp breath. 'I'm looking forward to seeing it.'

'Actually,' I said, 'it cost JD a fortune. I might get a "please explain" from the accounts department.'

Jack laughed, his head thrown back. Then he looked at me again, eyes crinkled at the corners. 'Don't worry. I authorise your expenses.'

'I thought I deserved a bonus.'

'You do, and so do I.' His smile vanished. 'But ...'

I cocked my head and watched him, staying very still. 'But?'

'I can't get involved ...' he held my gaze '... with you.'

I stayed silent and still, bracing for his rejection.

'If ... if something even more terrible had happened to you tonight, it'd be hard enough to deal with. So much worse if we were involved, if we were closer, if I cared for you even more than I do now.' He looked deeply, unabashedly, into my eyes. He was offering me a chance to withdraw. To reject *him*; walk away with dignity intact.

I let out my breath as quietly as I could manage. I'd braced for much worse. The worst kind of rejection, the 'I have no feelings for you whatsoever' kind. But he cared about me. I knew that. His yearning was transparent, and Jack had no issue with serious eye contact. But he had a serious issue with relationships. I knew where that came from. He wasn't over his wife or at least, the experience of losing her.

I straightened. 'Hmm,' I said, exaggerating my consideration of that information. 'And you think *I* want to be involved with some lunatic who hangs around one of the worst kinds of evil the world has ever known?'

His expression warmed.

'And,' I said, 'do you really think I'd want to be involved with a man who every woman with half-decent eyesight wants?' He smiled. 'Think again, Jack Jones.' I waved a hand. 'Besides, you couldn't keep up with me anyway.' I resumed my focus on the shirt buttons, my heart thumping a quick, embarrassing beat.

He chuckled. 'You're too much woman for me, Erica Jewell.'

'I know.' I grinned. 'But I reckon I've earned a night in the sack with your sexy bod.' I poked his chest. 'I deserve it.'

'Now, hang on a minute. You expect *two* bonuses? Expensive lace underwear *and* a night of hot sex?'

'Yep.'

His grin was carefree, but I could sense a hidden need beneath the flippancy; one that quickened his pulse, that acknowledged the permission – the demand – I'd just given him. His voice was suddenly husky. 'And, so, do *I* deserve a night in bed with *your* sexy bod?' He slid a hand under my top and unsnapped my bra.

I sucked in a quick breath and finished unbuttoning his shirt, pushing it off his gorgeous shoulders and running my hands down his arms, staring at his chest. 'Maybe,' I said. He pulled his arms out of the shirt, leaning forward, and I tossed it on the floor. 'But I deserve it more.'

His hands found their way under my top again and he smoothed them across my back.

'Then I hope you don't fall asleep,' he said.

'Oh, I'm sure there's no chance of that.'

I started on his belt buckle, but he gently caught my wrists. 'I need a shower. And shave.'

'No, you don't.' I closed my eyes and dipped my head, drawing a deep breath, taking in his deliciously sexy smell. I wanted to stay in that heady space for a while longer but I had other, stronger needs. I pulled one hand from his gentle grip, cupping his beautifully rough jaw. 'I'm not letting you out of my sight, not for one second.' I pressed my thumb against his lips. 'Besides, you're perfect as you are.'

Jack kissed my thumb and ripped open my top. Buttons flew across the room and I gasped and shivered with pleasure, anticipation thrilling me.

But the urgency in his eyes faded quickly as he gazed *not* at my expensive silk and lace white French bra, which he'd already very smoothly undone and that now loosely covered my breasts, one strap hanging sexily off my shoulder. No, he got rid of that – tossed onto the floor with the pyjama top – and he stared at my bruises, giving each one his full attention, his face impassive.

'Just ignore them,' I said, impatiently.

But he lightly touched the marks on my upper arms and, with the backs of his fingers, delicately brushed the bruises on my breasts. He caressed the black marks around my wrists and, finally, his hand slid feather-light up my arm to my neck, and he ran his thumb over Shane McGann's stupid hickey.

'Kiss me there.' I whispered it.

He looked into my eyes, pain and tenderness in his, and I nodded slightly, encouraging him. Jack leaned into me and I tilted my head away. His lips brushed my neck, caressing it with tiny, gentle kisses. He sighed deeply, his breath hot, and he ran his hands over my back, holding me steady as his warm, soft mouth opened against my throat. He sucked gently and fire zapped through my body to the tips of my fingers, curling my toes. My fingers tangled in his hair, holding him against me as I squirmed on his lap. He pulled me closer, his hands on my hips, and kissed a warm, slow path to my chin. I turned my face to meet his delicious mouth with mine.

Jack moaned, devouring my mouth, and when all the blood in my body had rushed to one particular spot I gasped, 'I'll faint if I don't lie down.' He threw me onto my back on the sofa, dragging my pyjama pants and socks off in one fluid movement. He stood and dropped his trousers. He liked my undies, I could tell – his eyes narrowed, chest heaving – and I felt I was finally getting my money's worth. JD's money's worth.

My gaze wandered south and stopped to take in the impressive sight of his tight, sexy trunks, straining to hold him all in. Goodness.

He glanced over his shoulder to the bedroom, making a quick decision.

'Bed time,' he said hoarsely and swept me up, whisking me into our very fabulous boudoir.

LATER (ACTUALLY, not that much later), I lay on top of Jack, my body stretched out along his, our toes wrestling gently. He stroked my back lightly, his other arm tucked under his head. I lay with my cheek against his chest, listening to the strong, steady drum of his heart, my finger tracing a series of fine scars on his shoulder.

'That was too quick,' he apologised.

'I'm not complaining.' Two orgasms in as many minutes is hardly complaint worthy.

'You drove me crazy.'

I propped my chin on my crossed hands. 'It was my pink socks.'

He chuckled. 'Probably.' His eyes were warm and he said softly, 'It's been a long time for me. I'll make it up to you later.' He pushed a curl behind my ear.

I liked the sound of that, but I suspected by 'later' he meant some time during the night, not next week or for the rest of my life. I wondered about his last time. And felt immediately jealous. I turned my thoughts elsewhere. 'Jack?'

'Mmm?'

'I think JD's reinstated me to the Team.'

'Appears he has.'

'Well, I hope you're not going to fire me over this silly kidnapping thing.'

'I wouldn't dare. Look at you. You're formidable.' He smiled. 'Besides, I'm feeling quite vulnerable at the moment, with your knees positioned where they are.'

I grinned and planted a kiss on his chin. 'We forgot to go for a candlelit dinner.'

'I don't think we needed more foreplay.' He rolled me onto my back and leaned over me, his hand propping up his head.

With my usual impeccable timing, I said, 'I feel a bit sorry for Shane McGann.'

Jack's happiness vanished, of course, and he gently held my jaw, forcing me to look at him. 'Are you crazy?'

'No, it's just that he's a bit ... pathetic.'

'Well, I'm thrilled you're not traumatised and it's very nice that you feel all this compassion, but it'd be handy if you could drum up some anger for the trial. I don't want to hear you asking the judge to go easy on him.'

'Okay.' I nodded once, with conviction. 'I can do it.'

'Good girl.'

I said, 'I have a theory.'

'Let's have it.'

'Shane McGann hates women.'

'I agree.'

'And I think he's in love with you.'

Jack's mouth dropped open and he blinked at me, waiting for the punch line I guess.

'You're not joking, are you?'

I shook my head. 'I think that's why he's so bitter. He wants you but he knows he can't have you.'

Jack flopped onto his back and rubbed his hands over his face. 'Now *I'm* traumatised. Thank you.' He sat up.

'He's a pretty tragic soul.'

'Erica, don't go there. I don't want to think about it, or even consider feeling sorry for him. He's hurt and killed people, and I don't care why.' His eyes flashed. 'I'll leave that to the prison shrinks to figure out.'

Maybe I'd pushed it a bit far. Jack got out of bed and strode into the bathroom, and I listened to the shower running for a long time. Eventually he reappeared and I said, 'I'm really sorry. Are you okay?'

He climbed back into bed. 'Yes. Come here.' He pulled me into his arms, and we helped each other forget all the nasties of the night, again.

CHAPTER 49

I woke in the morning wrapped in Jack. Something I could get very used to and not something I wanted to disturb, however my squished arm was waking up and I had pins and needles. I squirmed and he rolled away.

I lay on my back and tried to gauge how I felt about things. I thought about Shane McGann and the events of the day before, wondering if I was traumatised. Nope, not yet. Maybe I was having *actual* denial. I wondered what Brad and Aida were doing. I wondered if I'd snored. I watched Jack sleeping, lying on his back with an arm curled around his head. I propped myself up and inspected his elbow for a while, feeling tempted to kiss it; my gaze slid along his arm, over the powerful bulge of his bicep, past the hair in his armpit – where I wanted to press my face – across his chest, and settled on his beautiful, full mouth. He looked peaceful and lovely. And handsome and sexy and irresistible.

I sighed, got out of bed and walked into the bathroom. I used the toilet and washed my hands, staring at the mirror, not sure exactly who I was looking at. But it was me, with hair that reminded me of Beyonce in the Austin Powers movie.

'Oh, shit!'

Jack, instantly awake, called out, 'Are you okay?'

'No! You should see my hair!'

He laughed. 'Let me see.'

'No way!' I turned on the shower and stood under it.

He came into the bathroom and I couldn't help staring at his naked body as he ambled, yawning, toward me, running a hand absently over his chest and stomach. Jack Jones was magnificent, in every respect. And watching him through the glass screen kind of reminded me of window shopping for something I couldn't afford. I felt I was welcome to try it, but any thought of taking it home was probably out of the question.

He stepped into the shower and took my face in his hands, leaning into me, causing me to go weak at the knees.

'Good morning,' he said in a husky voice and kissed me softly. He didn't even have morning breath.

'Do I know you?' I said, hanging onto him as he folded me into his arms and nuzzled my neck. Was it possible to have too much sex?

Jack stood back and looked at me seriously, cupping my head in his hands and tilting it back. 'Are you all right?' he said.

'About yesterday?'

'Of course.'

'Which part of yesterday?'

'The nasty part. And I hope I don't have to explain that in further detail.'

I smiled. 'I'm in denial.'

'Good,' he said, and kissed me again. 'But I want you to see Gail as soon as possible.'

Probably a good idea. I made a mental note to suggest that he, too, get some counselling.

AN HOUR or so later we were in the back of a car headed for the airport. Jack handed me a Qantas boarding pass and I looked at him in surprise.

'I've already got a ticket.'

'I cancelled it.'

I looked at the one he'd given me. 'This is a business class seat.'

'That's right.'

'I normally fly economy. The cheapest available, in fact.'

'Why? Business class is so much better.' He smiled and held my hand.

As we drove to the airport, I stared out the window and allowed myself a small fantasy about being married to Jack Jones. I pictured an average day in his gorgeous big house, lounging around in French underwear, buying ridiculous things I didn't need, instructing the maid. A bit boring after a while, I thought. Lots of sex, though. I'd like that. But there was the issue of kidnappings, drive-by shootings and other women trying to have sex with him. All the time. Nope. I wanted my safe, predictable, man- and vomit-free life back. I did. Definitely.

'A dollar for your thoughts?' He held up a coin.

'A million dollars wouldn't buy you my thoughts.'

'Two million?'

I lifted his hand and kissed a knuckle. 'That's what two million buys you.'

He laughed. 'I want to buy you something. Something nice. What would you like?'

'Oh, well,' I said, 'we haven't discussed my fee yet for yesterday's awesome performance.'

'Your awesome performance in bed?'

'No!' I gave him a shove, giggling, glancing at the driver.

'What kind of fee did you have in mind?'

'I was thinking something that would make a substantial hole in my mortgage.'

'I don't think you'll need to worry about your debts any more, Erica.' He reached out and ran a finger lightly down my cheek. 'And I still want to give you something.'

'Okay then, how about a first-class ticket to anywhere in the world plus all expenses paid for ... a month.'

'Done.'

'I'm joking!'

'I'm not.'

I regarded Jack's smiling face and decided he meant it. 'Well, if you reckon I no longer have to worry about debt ...'

'You don't.'

'And you're prepared to be that generous ...'

'I am.'

'Then how about, instead, you give me a couple of hours of your time.'

'My time?'

'Yes. I want your advice on buying an investment property.'

'Good girl.' He smiled. 'But holiday first. You need it.'

'All right,' I said. 'Holiday first. And then we have a meeting to discuss property investment. And our meeting has to be in a swanky bar with expensive cocktails. Fluffy ones with trees and plastic decorations like they used to do in the sixties.'

'Do they still put that stuff in cocktails?'

'Well, you'll just have to make sure they do.'

'Okay. Sounds good. I might have one too.'

'So it's settled.'

'Settled. You're easily pleased.'

'Always.'

We shook hands.

AT THE AIRPORT we went straight to the Qantas Club lounge. So much nicer than long queues and screaming kids in the food court, I thought. We found a quiet corner and Jack went to get coffee for us.

I stood at the huge expanse of window overlooking the tarmac, and watched the planes coming and going. Mostly going. I felt sad. I wished suddenly that we'd taken separate flights. I wished I was sitting in the cafeteria with screaming brats, thinking about reporting to work on Monday.

I saw Jack's reflection approach before I felt his arms around me. I leaned into him and we stood like that for a while, staring out the window, my hands resting lightly on his arms, his chin against my temple. A traitorous tear slid down my face, and I gave myself a mental kick up the butt. *Get over it, Erica*, I thought. But I'd kind of liked these past few days in Sydney – the big hotel room and shopping and being in bed with Jack Jones. Apart from being abducted, nearly raped, murdered, etc, and the Opera House nearly blowing up, it was a really romantic, lovely time.

I looked for his eyes in the window's reflection and found them already watching mine. The resolve in those steely blues spoke loud and clear. Jack gave me a squeeze and kissed my ear.

CHAPTER 50

For the next week I focused on my inner health rather than the silent telephone. I'd avoided collecting Axle from my mother's, knowing she'd demand to know what I'd done in Sydney so she could scoff and say, 'I told you so,' when I was forced to admit that yes, she was right, I wasn't really needed after all.

On Friday night I willingly rushed to drinks at the pub. I organised it, in fact. Lucy, Steve, Ben and Emma – almost ready to pop – were there when I arrived. I'd told them nothing about what had really happened in Sydney – the scary stuff, I mean – but Lucy had badgered me on the phone until I told her that Jack and I had slept together. And of course she told Steve so when I walked into the pub they were both grinning at me. But I avoided talking about it because, well, it was too painful. I was aware that my heart had a tiny tear in it and I was angry with myself for that slip-up. Okay, so it wasn't so much a slip-up as a pre-meditated act of evil – forcing myself on Jack when he could hardly refuse – but at least I'd got it out of my system. Hadn't I? I thought I'd be able to be grown-up about it, face him and resume our friendship, but there were two things I hadn't expected as a result of that one night together: one, I'd fallen a teensy bit in love with Jack, and two, I suspected I might never see him again. The first issue I could deal with and I'd already started to mend. It was only a fling, after all. My heart wasn't broken and I'd be all right. Really.

Okay, I was in full-blown love. But with or without that, point two – the very idea of it – caused me actual physical pain. So when Jack walked into the pub, his eyes searching the room, my heart flipped and I felt a smile spread across my face. I realised in that instant that I could handle him not loving me back, but I couldn't handle him not being in my life, even in the most insignificant, intermittent way.

Jack spotted me and smiled broadly, pushing his way through the crowd, leaving a trail of lustful eyes in his wake. He looked unbelievably handsome and I wondered if he'd made a special effort. Not that he needed to. He nodded to my friends, saying hello, and leaned down to me. 'I need to see you for a minute. Can we go outside?'

I stood and he took my hand, leading me through a sea of cleavages, mostly aimed at him. Even men looked at him with admiration. I could understand why Jack didn't go out too often; it was like being with a celebrity. We walked outside and moved away from a group of smokers standing near the door. He faced me and took my hands in his.

'How are you?' he asked.

'I'm good. Very good, in fact. As of today, I'm debt free and with a very healthy bank balance, thanks to you.' I smiled and he smiled.

'That's wonderful, Erica. Must be a good feeling.'

'It is. Steve's going to renovate my house and I'm going to buy a new car.'

'That's great.'

I nodded and squeezed his hands. 'I've missed you, Jack. A week is a long time for us.' I laughed lightly; a weak attempt at flippancy.

He looked concerned rather than amused, and he didn't respond.

'Great sex,' I offered with a wink, letting him off the hook.

'Yeah, it was.' He smiled warmly for a second or two, then glanced away, dropping my hands and placing his on his hips. He cleared his throat. 'I wanted to let you know I'm going away for a while.'

My heart skipped its second beat for the night. 'Away? Where to?'

He shook his head briefly.

'Somewhere dangerous?' I said.

He said, all formal, 'You won't hear from Degraves while I'm gone. He trusts you not to speak about any of it.'

'How long have you known?' I pressed. 'You didn't say anything last week.'

'The opportunity ... just came up.'

'Opportunity?' I doubted very much that some dangerous mission would be considered an *opportunity* by most people. I looked into his eyes, trying to understand what he wasn't saying.

He returned my concerned gaze. 'Erica.' He sighed. 'This is something I need to do.'

Right. Get away from me. The shackles around his heart were melting and this scared him.

'How long is a while?'

He shrugged. 'A few weeks. Couple of months maybe. And I want you to take a holiday,' he added quickly as a distraction.

'I don't want to take a holiday.'

He sighed again. 'Just humour me, would you? I'm taking Joe, but I'll get you some names of people you can call if you need ... anything.'

I nodded.

'Kate's a good contact for you. You've got her number?'

'Yes, but —'

'And Gail.'

'Okay, but —'

'Keep Steve and Lucy close.'

I reached out and squeezed his arm, searching his face. 'Are *you* going to be safe, Jack?'

He looked at me, concern in his eyes, and I caught a glimpse of something else. What was it? Uncertainty? A few moments passed. He sighed heavily, again, and pushed my hair back from my face. He gently squeezed my shoulders. 'Look after yourself.' He drew me close, kissing me softly on the forehead.

I reached up, holding his beautiful, familiar face in my hands, and he hugged me so tight I could barely breathe. I squeezed him back, my arms around his neck, and he kissed me. It was a long, deep kiss.

A wolf-whistle from the group of smokers made me pull away and glance around. Jack's gaze didn't move from my face. He kept his arms tightly around me, staring at me like he was trying to memorise my features. Maybe he was.

'You've missed me,' I whispered.

'I have.'

I pushed him gently away. 'Go on then, go fight the bad guys.'

'All right.'

'And don't forget to come home. You owe me an expensive cocktail, remember?'

'Something to look forward to.' His smile vanished in a flash and he turned, jogging down the road. Joe's four-wheel drive was there, waiting. Jack climbed in without looking back, and an arm appeared from the driver's window. I returned Joe's wave and watched them drive away.

I stood on the pavement for a few minutes, waiting for the ghost of Joe's tail lights to fade. But I knew that image was burned into my memory, at least until I saw Jack's face again. I closed my eyes and conjured up his features, remembering that last kiss and how it felt to be held by him. I would not – *not* – consider the possibility he might not make it home. I'd hone my denial skills on that particular point. Jack and Joe would come home. Until then I knew my daily life would feel somehow wrong without them in it, but I didn't mind too much because right now I felt more complete than I ever had in my life. And that was a very, very good feeling.

I allowed myself a small smile, and walked back into the pub to where my friends were waiting, probably a bit impatiently. It was, after all, my shout.

ABOUT THE AUTHOR

In 2005 Kathryn Ledson took a deep breath (whispered a prayer) and left her secure, 25+ year career as a PA in the stuffy, high-stress corporate arena which, admittedly, included a few exciting breaks to travel overseas, work on a tropical island, and tour with famous people like Peter Ustinov and rock bands Dire Straits and AC/DC.

Kathryn returned to study with relief and a great sense of home-coming, and what emerged from that professional writing and editing course was a huge surprise in the form of hapless heroine Erica Jewell, lead character in Kathryn's series of funny, romantic, action-packed novels, which so far includes *Rough Diamond*, *Monkey Business* and *Grand Slam*.

If you enjoyed this book and have a spare moment, please leave an online review. Reviews are of great help to authors.

http://kathrynledson.com/

ACKNOWLEDGMENTS

With thanks to my publishing house Pilyara Press – in particular Jennifer Scoullar, Sydney Smith and Kate Belle – without whom *Rough Diamond* would not have travelled globally.

I am still and will always be grateful to those who made the original edition of this novel possible.